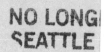
NO LONG
SEATTLE

Also by Lynnette Austin

Magnolia Brides
The Best Laid Wedding Plans
Every Bride Has Her Day
Picture Perfect Wedding

Must Love Babies
Must Love Babies
I've Got You, Babe

RECEIVED

NO LONGER PROPERTY OF
SEATTLE PUBLIC LIBRARY

SOUTHWEST BRANCH

I've got you, *babe*

LYNNETTE AUSTIN

sourcebooks
casablanca

Copyright © 2019 by Lynnette Austin
Cover and internal design © 2019 by Sourcebooks
Cover design by John Kicksee
Cover images © teksomolika/fotolia, Pavel Timofeev/fotolia

Sourcebooks and the colophon are registered trademarks of Sourcebooks.

All rights reserved. No part of this book may be reproduced in any form
or by any electronic or mechanical means including information storage
and retrieval systems—except in the case of brief quotations embodied in
critical articles or reviews—without permission in writing from its publisher,
Sourcebooks.

The characters and events portrayed in this book are fictitious or are used
fictitiously. Any similarity to real persons, living or dead, is purely coincidental
and not intended by the author.

All brand names and product names used in this book are trademarks,
registered trademarks, or trade names of their respective holders. Sourcebooks
is not associated with any product or vendor in this book.

Published by Sourcebooks Casablanca, an imprint of Sourcebooks
P.O. Box 4410, Naperville, Illinois 60567-4410
(630) 961-3900
sourcebooks.com

Printed and bound in Canada.
MBP 10 9 8 7 6 5 4 3 2 1

CHAPTER 1

A CUP OF HOT, BLACK COFFEE IN HAND AND A WELL-earned—and desperately needed—weekend fishing trip on his mind, Tucker unlocked the front door of Wylder Rides. The smell of oil and new tires welcomed him like an old friend. He liked the peace and quiet of the early morning, the solitude before his brothers arrived.

In five short days, a hot-shot Hollywood producer would fly into Savannah to pick up his '63 Corvette split-window coupe. Since the complete frame-off restoration they'd promised wasn't quite finished, Tucker took a healthy drink of coffee, then setting it aside, rolled up his sleeves.

When a breeze drifted in through the open bay door, he thanked the stars the calendar had finally flipped to October. This summer, his first in Misty Bottoms, Georgia, had been hotter than Hades. With the onslaught of autumn, though, temperatures had dipped to less humid mid-seventies.

Still, even the Georgia low-country summer had been a hell of a sight better than the sweltering heat he'd suffered during his Middle East deployment. There the July temperatures hovered above the hundred-degree mark. Add in the blistering sun, and the place could turn a man's hide to shoe leather in no time. Don't even get him started on the never-ending sand that found its way into every crack and crevice on the human body and scoured exposed skin raw.

A tough place to live. A worse place to die.

Involuntarily, his hands clenched into fists. Taking a deep breath, he relaxed them. Not today.

Eyeing the tool wall, he noticed somebody—probably Gaven—had hung several torque wrenches out of order. Impatiently, he rearranged them. With a twist of his wrist, he turned the can of brake fluid label-out.

Satisfied everything was in order, he dropped to the creeper, slid partially beneath the Vette, and got busy replacing the brake lines.

Southern rock blasted from his stereo. Over the magic of Charlie Daniels's fiddle, Tucker heard a car slow, then pull in out front. Its muffler was shot. The engine knocked, coughed, and sputtered, then shut down with a rattle.

Seconds later, a totally different sound caught his attention—high heels on the garage's concrete floor. Tucker slid a sidelong glance at the front of the bay and almost swallowed his tongue. Framed in the narrow window between the floor and the car's bumper were a pair of legs that would have any red-blooded man drooling…and they crossed slowly toward him. Laying the wrench on the floor beside him, he gave a push with his foot and slid the creeper from beneath the car.

Flat on his back, he let his gaze travel up over a body that matched the legs beat for beat, then on to a face only angels could have created. The heart-shaped face, with its sensuous lips and the biggest, bluest eyes he'd ever seen, sent a shockwave rocketing through him. Long blond hair had been caught back in a ponytail.

An illusion? Maybe he'd breathed too many gas fumes and was hallucinating?

Nope. This woman was real and, from the expression on that stunning face, in trouble.

"My car—" She waved a hand toward the front of the building.

"Could use some work," Tucker finished, slowly getting to his feet. Wiping his hands on a grease rag, he moved toward her. "Look, we're not a repair shop, but I can probably figure out what's wrong. If it's minor, I'll take care of it for you. Otherwise, you'll need to head into town to Robbie's Garage, or he can bring his tow truck and pick up you and the car. Robbie's fair, and he'll do right by you."

She swayed and reached out toward the wall.

"You okay?" As Tucker spoke, he saw those mind-blowing eyes go blank. Dark lashes fanned her cheeks.

With a muttered curse, he lunged, barely reaching her before she hit the floor. Heart racing, he held her against him and swore again. Out cold. Her skin was almost translucent. Sleeping Beauty weighed next to nothing and appeared to need a heck of a lot more help than her wreck of a car did.

"Hey, can you hear me?" He tapped her cheek but got no response. "Wake up."

Sweat broke out on his brow. Where were his brothers? They ought to be here by now. What was he supposed to do with an unconscious woman? He leaned his head close to hers, relief flooding through him when her breath whispered against his cheek.

A high-pitched wail split the air. Panicked, his head whipped up, and he glanced toward the beater parked out front. The driver's side door hung open; in the back, strapped into a child's seat, sat a little girl with her mama's blond hair—a little girl winding up for one hell of a crying jag.

And the day just got better!

He shook the limp woman gently, noticed the sheen of perspiration on her face. "Come on, sugar. For God's sake, open those baby blues."

She didn't.

Spying an old garage blanket they threw over car seats while they worked, he snagged it, one-handed, off the workbench. The baby's loud blubbering made his head ache, and, wincing, he shot a look at the car again.

First things first.

Kneeling and taking the woman down with him, he spread the blanket and laid her carefully on it, straightening the short skirt of her flower-print dress. The problem with small-town Misty Bottoms was exactly that. It was a small town, and that translated to no hospital. No ER or urgent care center, either.

With his forearm, he swiped the sweat from his brow. "Hey, wake up."

She didn't.

Okay. Time to tackle the second half of this double-feature horror show.

Edging toward the used-up Ford Escort and its young occupant in much the same way he'd approach a suspected sniper's nest, he pulled out his phone and hit 911.

The sheriff answered on the first ring. "Misty Bottoms Police Department. What can I do ya?"

"Jimmy Don, it's Tuck Wylder. I'm out at my shop." Opening the sedan's back door, he stared at the young child, at her tear-covered face and runny nose. He'd guess her to be maybe two or three years old. An opened bag of pretzels lay on the seat. Leaning in, he grabbed one and handed it to her. She raised it to her mouth and chewed, her cries dying to quiet whimpers.

Thank you, Jesus.

Not great, but better.

"Tuck? What's goin' on?" the sheriff demanded.

"A woman pulled up in front of our place and, well, she's passed out."

"Been drinkin'?"

"I don't think so, but she's hot."

"I don't care how good-lookin' she is."

"No, Jimmy Don. Not *hot* hot...*hot!* As in sweating."

"Well, why didn't you say so?"

"I did!" *Who's on first?* he thought.

"Do I hear a kid?"

Exasperated, Tucker raked fingers through his short hair, his gaze traveling over the woman. She still hadn't moved. What a friggin' mess!

"Yeah, you do. She came with the woman who's passed out on my garage floor."

"She okay?"

Tucker raised his eyes to the heavens and rubbed at his forehead. "Which one?"

"The kid."

"How would I know? Nothing wrong with her lungs, I can tell you that." The nagging start of a headache bloomed into a full-fledged whopper.

"You need an ambulance or you gonna take the gal in to see Doc Hawkins?"

"What?" Tucker pulled the cell away to stare at it. Bringing it back to his ear, he asked, "Are you serious, Jimmy Don? You want me to pick up an unconscious stranger, toss her in my car, along with a baby, and drive them into town?"

"So I guess you want me to send the ambulance out there."

"Bingo. Tell them to move it. Fast." He hung up, and the little girl started screaming again. Sticking his head inside the car, Tucker met her tear-filled eyes. "It's gonna be okay. Be a lot better, though, if you'd quit that carrying on."

The toddler threw the now-soggy pretzel and hit him square in the forehead. She let out another wail, then gagged.

Tucker withdrew quickly. "Don't you dare throw up. If you do, you'll have to clean it up, 'cause I'm not gonna." Even as the words popped out of his mouth, he realized how ridiculous he sounded. Too bad.

The kid actually went quiet for a blessed few seconds, though.

Then her lower lip trembled and she started up again.

After a quick visual, he decided that while she looked unhappy and mad as a wet cat, she seemed healthy and well-cared-for in her little pink-and-white outfit. Her mama, however, looked decidedly unhealthy, and he'd bet a dollar to a donut nobody was taking care of her. From the heft of her, he doubted she'd eaten many meals lately. Leaving the back door open to keep the kid cool, Tucker moved back inside. Reaching for the woman's fragile wrist, he laid a finger on her pulse. Strong, but way too fast.

And though her skin was damp, he'd been wrong—Mystery Lady didn't feel especially hot.

His phone rang. If that was Sheriff Jimmy Don with more questions...

"What?"

"Geez, aren't you the happy camper this morning." Gaven, the younger of his brothers, sounded chipper.

"Where the heck are you, Gav?"

"Good morning to you, too. No need to bite off my head."

"Really? I've got an unconscious woman sprawled on the bay floor and a screaming baby in the backseat of a broken-down heap, and I can only pray that knucklehead sheriff has an ambulance on the way."

"What?"

"You heard me."

"You didn't have an accident, did you?" Gaven asked.

"No. The woman pulled up out front, got out of her car, and fainted."

"Good thing you were a Marine. They're trained to handle anything, aren't they?"

Tucker hung up.

A few seconds later, the phone rang again. This time Brant was on the other end.

"What's going on?"

"You're late," Tucker snapped.

"Understood. We stopped at Dee-Ann's to pick up breakfast. To go. There's a veggie egg-white omelet in the bag for you."

"And I guess you've heard I have a woman out for the count on the floor, and a kid in the backseat of a car screaming her lungs out."

"That's pretty much what Gaven said. We're on our way."

Tucker heard sirens over the phone. "Is that what I'm hoping it is?"

"Yep. The ambulance just passed us. They're coming, pal, and so are we."

Tucker slid the phone into his pocket and wet a clean rag. He laid it on the woman's forehead, then grabbed a tissue. After a deep, fortifying breath, he walked outside and knelt beside the car door. "Honey, you need to quit that squallin'. It's not makin' anything better."

She blinked, hiccupped, then asked, "Who are you?"

"I'm Tuck."

"Tut?"

"Close enough. Who are you?"

"Daisy Elizabeth." A ragged sigh escaped her. "Where's my mommy?"

"Right in there." He pointed toward the bay. "How about I clean you up a little, Daisy Elizabeth?" He held up the tissue like a white flag of surrender.

"Can I see my mommy?"

"Yep. Soon as we're done here."

"'Kay."

Carefully, he wiped the little girl's face and nose, then fumbled with the complicated straps on the car seat. Plucking her loose, he set her on his hip and headed back inside.

"Mommy!" The tiny creature wiggled in his arms, but Tucker held on tight, relieved to see the woman sitting up.

Woozy-looking and more than slightly befuddled, she held out her hands. "Come here, sweetheart."

Tucker shook his head. "Not until the EMTs check you out."

The child's chin trembled, and she wriggled harder. "Mommy!"

"Give her to me." The woman's voice, though thin, was resolute.

"Nope. I'm not gonna risk you taking another header with this little one. I'd have both of you to catch."

Even in her present state, the woman's brows rose.

Tucker saw pride there.

"I'm truly sorry we've put you out, Mr.—"

"Wylder. Tucker Wylder."

"Elisa Danvers," she said.

Slowly, he lowered himself to the floor. Holding one of the toddler's hands, he let her climb into her mother's lap. He wrapped his other arm around the confused-looking woman to steady her.

She waved her free hand. "How did I…?"

"You went out like a light. Fortunately, I caught you in time."

She groaned. "I'm sorry…and embarrassed. I—so dizzy."

The sirens drew closer, and Tucker issued a very heartfelt prayer of thanks.

"An ambulance? For me? I can't—"

He met those incredible eyes. As troubled as they were, there was something almost magical about them that drew a man in.

Sitting on a concrete floor on a blanket that smelled of grease, leather, gasoline, and who knew what else, Elisa acknowledged she'd hit a new low. It was pure luck she hadn't fainted while driving.

She should have pulled off in Savannah and eaten a good sit-down breakfast. Instead, she'd pushed on, wanting to make it to Charleston as soon as possible. Money—or rather the lack of it—was a problem. She simply didn't have funds for another day on the road. If she watched every penny, she and Daisy could make it to her mother's empty condo with enough for groceries and gas until she found a job.

The ambulance, lights flashing, siren blaring, swung into the parking lot. Where would she find the money to cover this?

Tears welled, and she kissed the top of her daughter's head.

As the EMTs began pulling equipment from the back of the ambulance, a monster of a truck pulled in behind it. The door opened and a ball of fur scrambled out, heading straight toward them. Daisy screamed and tried to crawl up Elisa's torso.

"Shhh. It's okay, honey." As she spoke, Elisa twisted, putting herself between her daughter and the overgrown pup.

"Brant, call off your mutt!" Tucker shouted. "Go on, Lug Nut. Get out of here."

Brant whistled, and the young dog skidded to a halt, looking back over his shoulder.

"Come here. Now." Brant pointed at the ground in front of him.

Head hung low, a raggedy teddy bear in his mouth, Lug Nut trotted back to Brant, who knelt to rub his head. "Good boy. Stay." Shaking his head, he looked at Elisa. "Sorry about that. I'm working on teaching him some manners, but they're not taking as well as I'd hoped."

"It's all right. Daisy's a bit out of sorts right now."

"Guess she would be." He turned back to the yellow Lab.

"Lug Nut's about ten months old and still has a lot of puppy in him. Go find your ball, dog."

The Lab dropped his stuffed animal and tore off in an ecstatic search.

"That'll keep him busy for a bit."

"My brothers, Brant and Gaven," Tucker said by way of introduction. "And this is Elisa and Daisy Elizabeth." Brant nodded at them. "The EMTs will take good care of you."

"We'll be in here if you need anything," Gaven said. "Y'all don't need an audience."

With that, he and Brant headed for the office.

"Thank you." Elisa peeled her daughter from around her neck and set her in her lap.

The EMTs hurried into the bay, and Tucker stepped out of the way to let them do their job.

While one of them took her temperature and blood pressure, the older one asked, "Have you eaten anything today?"

"Black coffee. Guess that doesn't count, does it?"

He shook his head, then tipped his chin toward her daughter. "Has she?"

"Of course," she snapped.

"So you fed her, but not yourself."

Jaw set stubbornly, she nodded.

"Any chance you're diabetic?"

"No." Instinctively, her hand flew to her forehead. "No," she repeated, praying it was true.

"Pregnant?"

Heat raced up her face. "No."

"Heart problems?"

Alarmed, she met his eyes. "No, why?"

"Your pulse is way higher than it should be."

"Of course it is. I fainted."

He grunted.

As he asked his thousand questions, Elisa, more than a little self-conscious, kept her eyes averted from the man who'd rescued her. Thank God he'd been fast on his feet. She'd never, ever fainted. But she had today, and he'd saved her from hitting the floor, saved her from some nasty bruises at best, a broken bone or concussion at worst.

And he'd taken care of Daisy. Sort of. All things considered, this stern-looking guy had been a real blessing. With her unconscious, God only knew what would have happened if he hadn't been here, if she hadn't stopped outside his shop.

The mechanic didn't look very happy about any of it, though. In truth, he looked like a guy who'd far prefer a black hat to the white one she'd forced on him. The man was all rough-and-tumble, his chiseled face stern and covered in dark stubble. A faded black T-shirt and worn black jeans hugged a body that advertised he'd act first and ask questions later.

She could practically read his thoughts. *Of all the gin joints in all the towns in all the world...she passes out in mine.*

"We're heading to Doc Hawkins." The paramedic fastened the last strap around the stretcher to hold it in place in the ambulance. "You can follow us into town with the baby."

"Me?" Tucker pointed at his own chest, a bubble of panic forming in it. "Why not take the baby with you?"

"It would be better if you'd take her."

"I want her with me," Elisa said. "And I need my purse."

The ambulance driver nodded toward Tucker. "Can you grab the purse?"

"Get it, Gaven," Tucker bit out, seeing his younger brother peering out the office door. "Since you're snoopin', you might as well be useful."

The ambulance driver turned his attention to Elisa. "We can't take her, ma'am. Regulations would require she be strapped in, and you're on our only stretcher."

"Her car seat—"

"No way to secure it."

Brant put an arm around Tucker as he let out a wobbly sigh. "Believe me, I feel your pain. It wasn't all that long ago I hustled to Savannah after Lainey's accident. I left the hospital with our seven-month-old nephew and not a clue what to do with him."

"This is different."

"Yeah, it is. Jax is family. But there's still the responsibility. The feeling of being dumped into the deep end with no life preserver."

Tucker sucked in a deep breath. "You know, you'd do a better job with this."

"Sorry, bro. Your turn."

"Hey!" The older EMT shot an angry-father look at Tucker. "You done bellyachin'? While you stand there feelin' sorry for yourself, this young lady needs to see the doc. Now."

Elisa laid a hand on the EMT's arm. "Am I going to be okay?"

"You bet. Doc Hawkins will fix you up in no time."

"Is it something serious?" Fear skittered across her face as her gaze traveled to her daughter.

"Ma'am, I'm not a doctor. Best the doc does the diagnosing."

Tucker made the mistake of meeting Elisa's eyes. In them, he read frustration, worry, and more than a little desperation.

Holding the kid, he climbed into the ambulance and knelt beside her. "Hey, it'll be okay. Daisy and I will be right behind you, and we'll meet you at the doc's. I realize you don't know me from Adam, but these guys do. Otherwise they wouldn't trust me with your daughter. I won't let any harm come to her. Promise."

What a bunch of BS. These EMTs couldn't possibly find anyone more inept to hand this child over to.

Uncertainty lingered in her eyes, and he understood what it was to trust a stranger with something so valuable. "It's hard to believe right now, but everything's gonna be all right."

"I'd argue that point with you, but I'm so tired and I have such a headache."

She looked defeated, like she'd failed some major test, and it hurt the heart Tucker swore he no longer possessed.

As the EMT started to herd them out, Elisa whispered, "One more kiss, baby."

Tucker held Daisy Elizabeth closer to her mother. The child clung to her, crying as if positively brokenhearted.

And she probably was. Her mama was being taken away, leaving her with a stranger. Tucker hoped her mind would block this traumatic moment. He sure as heck didn't want to be the reason she had to visit a counselor later in life.

Tucker extricated Daisy and hopped out of the ambulance, the child struggling in his arms. The EMT closed and secured the door. Stepping away, trying to ignore the baby's frantic cries for her mommy, Tucker pointed a finger at his brothers. "I want you both here and working when I get back. That Vette needs to be finished before Murdoch shows up Friday."

Gaven nodded and Brant slapped Tucker on the back. "Let me help you with that car seat."

The ambulance pulled out, and Daisy Elizabeth stretched her arms out toward it. "Mommy. Mommy! Where's Mommy going?"

"Shhh." Tucker instinctively bounced her on his hip. "Your mama's okay. We're gonna take a ride and go see her. All right?"

Her big blue eyes brimmed with tears. "I want my mommy."

"Me too," Tucker said. "Honestly? I'd prefer mine, but either one would do."

"Exactly my thoughts in Savannah." Brant held the seat he'd rescued from Elisa's rattletrap car. "Let's get you on your way to this one's."

Tucker groaned as his fingers brushed over the key that dangled from his neck. The day had started so well, his head full of the planned trip to his friend's isolated cabin. Just him and nature.

Then everything had gone to hell in that proverbial handbasket. He'd never quite understood that saying, but as he pulled onto the two-lane rural road and glanced in his rearview mirror at the child slobbering on the backseat of his beloved Mustang, he swore that handbasket had hitched a ride with them.

CHAPTER 2

THE DRIVE INTO TOWN WAS THE LONGEST OF TUCKER'S life. He wanted to head back to Tansy's Sweet Dreams, grab one of her out-of-this-world cinnamon rolls, a fresh cup of coffee, and start the whole day over, because in a matter of seconds it had totally derailed.

"Do you know?" Daisy asked from the back.

No sweet roll, no coffee, no new start.

"Know what?"

"Where my mommy is?"

"At the doctor's, remember?"

"Why?"

He hesitated. If he said she was sick, the kid might spaz out again. "He's gonna give her something to help her headache." He glanced in the rearview mirror.

"Oh. I got a headache, too." The little faker squinted and put a hand to her forehead.

"Maybe Doc Hawkins can help you with that."

"Okay, but I don't want no shot."

Tucker checked his mirror again and, despite himself, grinned. The kid had it going on. "No, no shots."

"Mommy doesn't want one, either."

He remembered how frail her mama had felt when he'd held her. Daisy was right. Her mama shouldn't have any shots, either. "We'll let the doctor know."

"Okay." Then she wanted to know if he'd ever had a shot, had he cried, where *his* mommy was, and on and on until he swore his ears bled. The kid talked nonstop. All. The. Way.

Tucker prayed Doc Hawkins could fix whatever ailed Elisa Danvers—and fast.

A terrifying thought slithered through his brain. What if he couldn't? What if she was really sick? Died? He remembered those eyes, those lips.

"Are you my daddy?"

"What?" He swerved back into his own lane, his gaze flying to the mirror.

"Mommy said Daddy lived a long way away. Are you my daddy?"

"No!"

Tucker's own headache spiked to gargantuan proportions. How much farther till they reached the doctor's office? That damned handbasket was bursting at the seams.

He made the turn onto Main Street. Even with Chatty Cathy in the backseat, Misty Bottoms's charm washed over him. Lem Gilmore, the town's tightwad with a heart of gold and a deep pocket he rarely reached into, waved as he passed Dee-Ann's Diner, and Tucker waved back. Darlene Dixon walked her pair of Cairn terriers along the uneven brick sidewalk before opening her quilting shop for the day.

Fall baskets hung from the lampposts. He and his brothers had paid for a couple of them this year when the town held their *Fall Into Autumn* drive. Pumpkins and colorful leaves graced store window displays.

When he'd ducked into Tansy's bakery this morning, her shop had been redolent of apples and cinnamon. To add a little punch to the atmosphere, the weathermen were calling for an early cold front next week. He hoped they were right. He was tired of sweating.

Small-town Misty Bottoms, Georgia, had had a rebirth, thanks to three women and their dream. Molly, his middle brother's new bride, was now part of the trio's Magnolia Brides destination wedding business.

Since Brant's mother-in-law had a birthday coming up, he intended to whisk Molly away for a quick visit with her, leaving Tucker and Gaven to take Murdoch's Vette to the finish line. As much as they needed him here, Tucker couldn't blame BT. If he had a woman like Molly, he'd run off for a lot longer than a couple of days.

If. That all-important qualifier.

No wife or kids lurked in his future. He did best on his own, and the crier in the backseat sure wasn't about to change his mind.

An eternity later, they reached the doctor's. Spying an empty parking spot, he slid to the curb and watched as the EMTs wheeled Elisa through the back entrance.

When he and the kid blew through the front door, an attractive brunette met them, tucking a strand of shoulder-length hair behind one ear. "I'm Brinna Thompson, Doctor Hawkins's receptionist. You're Tucker Wylder, aren't you?"

He nodded and held out a hand.

Blushing, she shook it. "This might take a while, so make yourself comfortable. If you need anything, anything at all, you let me know."

"I'll do that, thanks." He moved to a small sofa against the far wall, aware Brinna watched him from her position behind the office counter. She caught his eye and sent him a blinding smile.

The woman was hitting on the wrong Wylder brother. Gaven might be interested; Tucker wasn't.

Fortunately, Tucker hadn't needed to visit Hawkins's until now. Ignoring the pretty little receptionist, he took a look around. The house was a marvel of past architecture. Thick crown molding edged a plaster ceiling that featured a sunburst design. Solid wood flooring shone underfoot, and a fireplace that almost begged to be lit took its place of honor against the opposite wall. The ornately carved mantel had been created by a master.

Daisy patted his knee to claim his attention. "I want my mommy."

He swallowed the groan. "I know you do."

"Where is she?"

"With the doctor."

"I wanna see her."

"Not yet."

Winding up for a temper tantrum, she stomped her foot and her lower lip jutted out in a pout. Brinna, quick on the uptake, saved the day with a coloring book and crayons. Daisy Elizabeth insisted on sharing, so to ward off the threat of more tears, Tucker dropped onto the floor cross-legged by the coffee table and gave all the princesses, with their tiaras and ballgowns, blue eyes and blond hair.

And that had nothing to do with Daisy's mama and her blue, blue eyes and sun-kissed hair.

Every couple of minutes he glanced at the door, half expecting his brothers to walk in and catch him at this.

Daisy dumped the crayons out of the box, and Tucker winced. Lining them up neatly, he sorted the reds and the blues. It took the child seconds to mess them up again. The third time, he decided it was futile and did his best to ignore the chaotic clump.

A few minutes later, Daisy crawled into his lap. He breathed deeply and took in the soft, sweet smell of baby.

Not sixty seconds later, she started squirming. "I gots to pee."

"What?"

"I gots to pee."

Brinna scooted from behind her desk. "I'll take you, sweetie." She held out a hand.

Daisy shook her head. "I want Tut to take me."

Tucker opened his mouth, then shut it. How and when had he transitioned from enemy to best pal? "Ahh, how about the three of us go? I'll wait right outside the door while you and Miss Brinna take care of things."

The little girl looked from one to another and sighed deeply. "Okay. But I don't know where the bathroom is."

"Me, either," Tucker said, "but I'll bet Miss Brinna does."

"I do."

"Okay." Taking Brinna's hand, Daisy looked up at her. "You're pretty."

"Thank you." The receptionist rewarded the little girl with a powerhouse smile, and Tucker couldn't disagree.

"I like your hair. Mommy puts mine in pigtails 'cause it gets tangled. Sometimes I cry when she brushes it." She pulled her hand away and reached up to tug at the flower-covered elastics in her hair.

"Why don't we leave those in for now?" Brinna captured her hand again. "That way Mommy won't have to fix it again."

"'Kay." She started singing her ABCs. When she hit G,

she started back at A. Apparently, G marked the end of her known alphabet.

Leaning against the wall outside the little girls' room, Tucker called his brothers. "I'm gonna be a while yet. The doctor's still in with Ms. Danvers. Work hard. We're running out of time."

The bathroom door flew open, and Daisy Elizabeth popped out. "Miss Brinna let me flush."

"Oh boy! Wasn't that special?" Into the phone he said, "Gotta go."

When Doc Hawkins came out, Tucker pounced on him. "What's wrong with her? She gonna be okay?"

"Now, you know better than to ask that, Tuck. I can't tell you much. Patient/doctor confidentiality and all that."

"But I've got her kid."

"Understood. My patient wearin' your ring?"

"Absolutely not."

"Then I can't discuss her condition with you."

He blew out an impatient breath. "Can we at least see her?"

"Certainly." He knelt in front of the little girl, his white medical coat swinging behind him. "In fact, I think this little thing is exactly what the doctor prescribed. Your mama wants to see you, Daisy."

Blue eyes solemn, Daisy stared back at him. "I wanna see her, too. Tut told me I could."

"Tut did, did he?"

Tucker shifted uneasily.

"Well, he was right." Glancing at Tucker, Doc said, "When you're with her, Ms. Danvers can share as much or as little as she wants about her condition. By the way, good catch today, son."

When they walked into the room, Daisy's little hand in his big one, Elisa was resting on an exam table, the head partially inclined. She still looked ashen, and he noticed she'd had blood drawn.

"Mommy!" Daisy flew to her.

Tucker swung her up and deposited her beside Elisa. The little girl immediately curled into her mother's side. The way they carried on, a person would have thought they'd been separated for days instead of under an hour.

As they traded kisses and hugs, he slid closer to the door, torn between stepping into the hall to give them privacy and hanging close to make sure Elisa didn't faint again and hurt both herself and Daisy. On top of everything else, Elisa's thin blue patient gown hid very little.

She picked up on his discomfort. "You're probably considering yourself the unluckiest mechanic on the planet right about now."

Mechanic. Well, that worked. "Yeah. Look, I should..." He nodded toward the door.

"Stay, please. I haven't thanked you for taking care of my baby."

"Yeah, stay, Tut!" Daisy chirped.

"Tut? As in King?"

He shrugged.

"Will your boss be mad at you for taking off like you did?"

"No."

"Are you sure?"

"Positive."

"You must have a very understanding boss."

He rubbed the toe of his work boot over a seam in the

hardwood floor. "Actually, my brothers and I own the shop. We, ah, restore vintage cars and motorcycles."

Red flushed her cheeks. "So you're not a mechanic. I apologize."

"No need to. Nothin' wrong with being a mechanic. Without them, we'd be in a world of hurt, wouldn't we?"

She nodded.

"Besides, the restorations require a lot of mechanical work, so I've done more than my share of engine overhauls. In fact, I was in the middle of a brake job when you stopped by."

"Stopped by?" She smiled. "Polite, aren't you?"

"I can be. I can also be an SOB."

Studying him, she said, "My guess is that side only comes out when it's prodded."

His eyes narrowed. "I'd like to think so, but…" He shrugged again.

"Well, speaking for Daisy and myself, I'm truly glad we met."

He jammed both hands in his pockets, uncomfortable with being thrust into the role of hero. "I'm glad I was there for you this morning, but I sure as heck hope you don't intend a repeat performance."

"None planned, believe me, and I'm sorry for the trouble I've caused…and more than a little embarrassed."

"Don't apologize." He held up a hand. "You were sick. You *are* sick. It's a damned good thing you pulled in when you did."

"Yeah, Mommy, a damned good thing."

"Daisy Elizabeth! That's a bad word."

"Tut said it first."

He grimaced. "Your mama's right. It is a bad word, and I won't say it again."

One corner of Elisa's mouth lifted. "I do believe your pants are on fire, Mr. Tut."

He laughed out loud. "I do believe you're right."

"On fire?" Daisy asked.

"Your mama's havin' fun with me."

"'Kay." She laid a hand on her mother's cheek. "I had fun with Tut, too. He colored with me."

Elisa mouthed her silent thanks.

He nodded, holding her gaze. "Back to what I was saying—before the bad word. You and your daughter must have had a guardian angel riding in that Escort with you. If you'd passed out while you were driving, well, 'nuff said, right?"

The hair on the back of his neck stood up, the memory of Brant's call the night of his sister's accident fresh in his mind. Different circumstances, but still. Elisa and Daisy could both be in the hospital and in a lot worse shape.

"You're right. I screwed up. Big time." Arm wrapped tightly around her daughter, she said, "I think we introduced ourselves before, but, well…I'm almost certain you didn't give Tut as your name."

"You were at a slight disadvantage." Holding out a hand, he took her small one in it. "I'm Tucker. One of the Wylder brothers."

"Wylder?" She tipped her head. "Is that a name or an adjective?"

He chuckled. "My younger brother would be the wilder one. For me? It's just a name."

"Military?"

He frowned.

She patted her own head. "The hair. It's a little long on top, but it still says *military*. I'm a service brat."

"Ahh. Well, that would be ex-military. I'm out. For good." He fought to keep the bitterness from his voice and hoped he'd succeeded.

"What's this, Mommy?" Daisy ran a finger over the bandage on her arm. "Does it hurt?"

"No. The doctor needed a little bit of my blood to help me."

"How'd he get it?"

"With a tiny little needle."

The child's eyes widened. "I don't need any help, Mommy."

"No, you don't, sweetie."

Daisy didn't look convinced, and Tucker tried to avert his eyes from the evidence of the needle that had drawn that blood. For all his bravado, he didn't do well with needles. They made him nauseous, but he'd admit that only under threat of death.

"Tut said I wouldn't get no shots."

Elisa kissed her daughter's forehead. "You won't." She turned to look at Tucker. "Sounds like you two have done a lot of talking."

"Oh yeah."

She almost smiled at his valiant attempt not to roll his eyes.

He reached into his shirt pocket for his phone. "Do you need to call someone? Let them know you'll be late?"

"No. There's no one to call."

That caused him to stumble. No one? Regardless of

how tough things got, his family had his back. Always had, always would.

It would suck to be totally alone.

He flashed back to Daisy asking if he was her daddy.

"Won't your husband be worried?" And yes, he was fishing, but he had to know.

A bitter expression washed over her face. "No husband."

A knock sounded at the door just before Doc Hawkins stuck his head inside. He held up a sheet of paper. "We need to talk, Elisa."

Back in the waiting room with Daisy, Tucker checked his watch. Again. Anxiety roiled in his stomach. Test results. What bad news was Doc sharing with that beautiful woman? She'd already had one hell of a morning. Was it getting worse?

The doctor had been with her for what felt like hours, but in truth had been barely fifteen minutes. Patients, though, had started to stack up in the waiting room. Sick people. Tucker started to feel more than a little antsy.

He took a second to answer Brant's text.

Kid's ok. Not sure about her mom. Still waiting.

"I wanna see Mommy again!" Daisy tossed her purple crayon on the floor.

Uh-oh. Tucker alerted like a dog on point and hit send.

"In a minute." He reached under the table, snagged the crayon, and laid it out of little fingers' reach. Every eye in the room turned to him and the child.

"I want my mommy now! Mommy!" Fat tears rolled down her cheeks.

He tried to pick her up, but Daisy wiggled and carried on till Tucker wanted to scream right along with her. Yet when Brinna stepped from behind her desk and reached for the little girl, she refused to go to her, burying her face in Tucker's shirt, her tears soaking into the cotton.

"Somebody's tired," the receptionist said.

"Yeah, I am."

Her mouth dropped opened. "I didn't mean—"

"I know. Just kidding. She needs a nap."

"No, I don't." Daisy's lip jutted out and she swiped at her tears.

He rubbed his eyes and wished himself anywhere but here.

"Why don't you take her back and sit outside Ms. Danvers's room? That might help."

"I'll try anything at this point." A plastic chair in one hand and a squirming toddler in the other, Tucker strolled down the hall. "Shhh. Listen. Can you hear Mommy?"

The child nodded.

"Let's be really quiet so we'll know when we can go in, okay?" he whispered.

"Okay." Daisy popped a thumb in her mouth and snuggled into Tucker. He looked down at her, his irritation fading. Oh yeah—it would be real easy for one of these tiny creatures to worm her way under a person's skin.

With Daisy silent, Tucker became aware of a major snag in Brinna's plan. The old house hadn't been built as a doctor's office, and the walls were thin. Too thin. He could hear Elisa and the doctor, and he was hearing way more than he should.

"I can't afford any of this, Doctor. I can't pay you for your services today, let alone any more tests. I—" Her voice broke.

Right then and there, Tucker decided that one way or

another he'd help Elisa Danvers until she could get her feet under her.

"Don't you worry about that, Ms. Danvers," Doc said. "Right now, I want you to take this glucose tablet. Then you need to get something to eat—protein. It can be as simple as a peanut butter sandwich. Come back tomorrow for that fasting test, and let's get you better."

"But—"

"No buts. Here in Misty Bottoms, we take care of our own."

"I'm not from here, sir."

"No, but you're here now, and that's all that matters."

Pride rose in Tucker for his adopted hometown. He and his brothers had definitely picked the right spot for their business expansion. Lady Luck had been with them.

She'd sure botched it with Elisa, though. What had driven her to hit the road with no money and no one to help? Where were she and Daisy headed? To what? When his mom had her stroke, the whole family pitched in and worked through it. Same thing with his sister Lainey and her alcohol problem.

Even if Elisa had no husband, there should be someone to help her. Where was her family? Her mom and dad? Siblings?

A few minutes later the door opened and Doc stepped outside, closing it quietly behind him. He studied Tucker's face. "I didn't realize you were out here."

"Daisy wanted her mom. We figured this might calm her down."

The doctor nodded and, voice lowered, asked, "How much of that did you hear?"

"Enough to know Elisa and this little one are in trouble."

Hawkins nodded. "That's putting it mildly. Here's the

deal. That young lady in there is going to be fine, but I need to run some tests. Tomorrow." He met Tucker's eyes. "You no doubt heard what she had to say about that."

"Yeah."

"I'd prefer she stay in town for a couple of days so I can keep an eye on her."

"A couple of days?"

"I'll have Brinna call around. See if she can find a room for them."

"Her and the kid." Tucker silently raised a brow and nodded toward Daisy, who'd worn herself out and had, with a child's innocence, fallen fast asleep in his arms. "I doubt you'll find anything. There's a big wedding this weekend at Magnolia Brides and most of the party were coming in today, along with some of the guests. My guess is that every room in town is filled."

"You'd know, since Molly's part of the family now, wouldn't you?"

He nodded, proud of his new sister-in-law. "All the gowns are from her boutique."

Doc jerked a finger toward the closed door. "Weddings aside, Elisa needs that test, and the sooner the better. If she had a doctor in Charleston, I'd tell her to wait."

"That's where she's headed?"

Doc nodded.

"But she doesn't have a doctor there," Tucker said.

"Nope."

"There has to be some way we can make this work."

Doc's face softened. "Beneath that stern demeanor you display to the world, Tuck, you're a good man."

"Excuse me?"

"You didn't ask what *she* could do. You said *we*."

"Semantics. You're wrong about me, Doc. But that woman in there can't take care of herself, let alone this one."

"Not your headache, is it?"

Tucker's temper bumped up from simmer to boil before he realized the doctor was baiting him. He turned down the heat. "Yeah, well—"

He didn't know what to say and couldn't decide why he felt responsible for a woman he hadn't even met till a couple of hours ago. He did know that, aside from the scarcity of rooms in town, Elisa probably couldn't afford a couple of days' hotel room charges.

"I'll take them home with me. I've got plenty of space."

The instant the words left his mouth, he could have hacked off his tongue with a rusty saw. What was he going to do with a kid and her sick mother? Throw in his night-time habits, and this spelled trouble.

"She might not like that."

Neither did he, but he'd committed, and he'd carry through. "The way I see it, she doesn't have much choice."

"Do you have any idea what you're biting off?"

"No," he answered truthfully. "And I've got a hunch I'm better off staying clueless as long as possible."

The older man tossed his glasses onto the small hall table and rubbed tired eyes. "You don't know her."

"And she doesn't know me. The way I see it, she and I are both gonna have to operate on faith."

Hawkins studied him and the little girl in his arms. "Why would you do this?"

"Let's just say I have some paying forward to do. This is as good a place as any to start."

Doc grunted. "One more thing you should know if you're determined to throw yourself into the middle of this. I've already discussed it with Ms. Danvers. Actually, we argued more than discussed, but it's nonnegotiable." His jaw set sternly. "Until I get tomorrow's test results back, I don't want her driving. There's no way she should have been on the road this morning."

"Agreed." Tucker nodded. "That shouldn't be too hard to finagle—with or without her permission. Her car's in no better shape than she is. The only reason she pulled into our shop this morning is because it started acting up. I told her I'd take a peek at it, but we've got a big project with a tight deadline." His eyes narrowed. "Don't think I'll be able to get around to it till, oh, say this weekend at the earliest. Then it'll take another day or so to fix whatever needs fixing—if we can get the parts we need in town."

Tucker looked at the doctor. "Will that give both you and her enough time?"

The doctor smiled. "That'll do it. Thanks."

"Thank you." Tucker's gut screamed at him to abort. The mission had gone south, and it was time to pull out. Instead, he asked, "What time do you need her here tomorrow?"

Hypoglycemia. Low blood sugar. Elisa chastised herself. She should have known. Doctor Hawkins believed it wasn't diabetes related. Tomorrow's test would verify that diagnosis. *Please let him be right.*

Her grandmother had had diabetes, and Elisa was all too aware the disease was genetic. But for right now, she felt better. The glucose tablet had helped. The lightheadedness and sweating were gone along with the pounding heartbeat. The headache, though, lingered.

If only she'd been able to make it to Charleston.

But she hadn't.

Although even if she'd made Charleston, she'd still have a problem and still be alone.

Tears swamped her eyes, and she angrily swiped at them. Self-pity wasn't her go-to MO. But life had dumped a lot on her lately, a veritable monsoon of disasters. At least she was the one sick this time. Her sweet little girl had been doing so much better.

She glanced at the purse someone had carelessly dropped on a chair. That worn faux-leather bag held her entire life savings, all one thousand seven hundred dollars and twenty-three cents. As a single parent, it took everything she earned to make ends meet. Daisy's situation made things even more complicated.

When funding had been cut for Bowden, Alabama's, new library, the school board had no option but to trim staff. Her. Even though she'd worked there for five years, she was the new kid on the block. The rest of the staff had been on board since shortly after Noah built his ark.

All the new initiatives, the updated technology, and the streamlined buying process she'd put in place would no doubt go down the drain right along with her job. Without her prodding, the staff would revert to what they'd always done and return to their comfort zone.

None of that was her worry anymore. However, how she would manage to stay in town for the tests she couldn't afford *was* her worry. She had no way to contact her mother, who, last she'd heard, had flown into some remote area of Mexico to unearth relics from the past, relics she cared for far more than the well-being of her daughter and grand-daughter. That's the way it had always been, the way it would always be.

She rubbed at the worry lines on her forehead with trembling fingers.

Her father? Lt. Col. Harold Eklund was unavailable, physically and emotionally. Period. End of story.

And Daisy's father? She wouldn't even go there. As far as she was concerned, love was a fairytale fed to young girls. Happy ever after? A bald-faced lie.

A knock sounded on the door.

"Yes?"

"You decent?"

Tucker Wylder. Why did the man have to be so—well, manly? So masculine, so sure of himself. His hair was thick and dark. Incredibly long lashes framed fascinating eyes that were not quite brown, not quite green. Underneath, though, she'd swear she read something in those eyes that ate at him and kept him up at night.

"Elisa?"

She sighed. "Yes, I'm decent."

"May we come in?"

"Yes. Is Daisy okay?"

The door opened, and he stuck his head inside. "She's fine." He stepped in, a sleeping Daisy cuddled against him. "Seems to me you have a problem."

"I'll handle it."

"Really? Exactly how do you intend to do that?"

She chewed on her lower lip.

Looking decidedly uncomfortable, he stepped closer, all but filling the space in the small room. "I've got you covered. You can bunk at my place till you're able to hit the road again."

Elisa's stomach sank. "What?"

"You and Daisy can go home with me. That way, you can take care of the tests Doc wants to run and do whatever else he thinks best. We'll get that car of yours healthy, too."

"You want me to move in with you?"

"Temporarily."

"I don't know you."

"I might say the same, but I'm willing to take a chance. How about you?"

Even feeling half hungover, with most of her wiring frayed, her early warning detection system activated. "I don't want to go home with you."

"Then we're on the same page. I'd be lying if I said I'm ready to do handstands at the prospect of a woman and a kid moving in. The way I see it, though, neither of us has a choice."

Her chin nudged up. "We always have a choice."

He rubbed the back of his neck. "Yeah, guess we do. I can turn around and walk out of here. You and your daughter can sleep on the street or in that broken-down heap you're driving."

She gasped at his cold-hearted callousness. A muscle ticked in his jaw, but he said nothing, simply leaned against the wall, arms around her sleeping child, and waited. She didn't think she liked him very much.

Guilt washed over her. That wasn't fair. Hadn't he disrupted his entire day to see to them?

Yeah, because he had no choice.

No, now *her* pants were on fire. He'd had choices. He could have called an ambulance and considered his job done. Most people would have done exactly that. Or he could have followed them into town, dumped Daisy here, then taken off for higher ground. Instead, he'd colored with her daughter, put up with Daisy's incessant chatter—and offered his home as a temporary sanctuary.

He switched Daisy to his left arm and dug a quarter from his pocket. Holding it out, he said, "Heads, you come home with me. Tails…" He shrugged. "You and this little one are on your own."

He made as if to flip it.

"You—wait! Before I agree to anything, I need you to understand that regardless of how it looks right now, I'm not some weak, too-stupid-to-live woman who mooches off others. Luke walked and I kept things together. Until now."

"Luke the SOB who wouldn't man up and meet his responsibilities?"

Anger flooded her. "I am not anybody's *responsibility*. I want more than that." Her chin came up a little higher. "I'm worth more."

"I won't argue that. How about I send Doc in to help you get dressed so we can bust out of this joint?"

His hooded eyes traveled slowly over the length of her.

The tiniest fragment of a long-forgotten melody played in her heart. Instead of being offended, she felt—what? Like a woman again. A desirable woman. She'd have sworn Luke had killed that forever.

CHAPTER 3

Doc Hawkins burst that bubble the second he walked in, loaded down with pamphlets on hypoglycemia and a list of the best and worst things to eat. He issued a stern admonition not to skip any meals, then handed her a box of glucose tablets, insisting they were samples.

She knew better. More charity—and how she hated that. How she'd detested admitting she had no way to pay him.

She would, though. Someday, come hell or high water, she'd pay for his help.

And now Tucker Wylder, a total stranger, was taking her and her daughter home with him. Grudgingly, but he'd stepped up to the plate all the same. In fact, he'd badgered her into it. He'd baited; she'd bitten.

This had to be the rock-bottom people talked about. She'd wondered how a person recognized when she hit it. No more, because as of today, she and rock-bottom were on a first-name basis.

As they drove through a small town that looked far more prosperous than Bowden, Tucker slowed and pulled into a parking space. "I'll run in to the diner and have Dee-Ann fix us something for lunch. We're all gonna need some fuel, and my cupboard's a tad bare."

"I'm not very hungry," she said.

He cut his eyes to her. "So despite the orders Doc just gave you, you're not gonna eat. Not gonna work on getting better."

"That's not what I said." Her words escaped, covered in frost.

"Good, then I'll get you some of Dee-Ann's soup. Chicken noodle work? That's what Mom always fed us when we were feeling off."

"You're a bully."

"And you're stubborn." His hot gaze traveled over her. "Looks like you haven't eaten much lately. Whatever you don't finish, we'll save for later. What does Daisy like?"

"Peanut butter and grape jelly sandwiches."

"Okay."

He cracked his window and slid out of the car, leaving her and her daughter in silence. When she swiveled to face the back, Daisy Elizabeth was still fast asleep. It had been a long morning for the three-year-old. Long and traumatic.

Elisa rested her head against the seat. Could she have failed more spectacularly? These past few weeks had been a disaster, and now she and Daisy found themselves beholden to an irritable and irritating stranger.

Slowly, the stillness and peace of her surroundings enveloped her, and she took her first real look at Misty Bottoms. A wide strip of green ran down the center of the street, dividing it and forming a narrow, well-manicured park. Oak and sugarberry trees mixed with groupings of flowers. A brick path meandered through them scattered with benches that invited a person to sit a while. No doubt more than a few names had been carved into them by teens in the throes of puppy love.

The town had been here a long time, and the storefronts were old but well maintained. Several appeared newly reno-vated. The brick sidewalks were uneven and added a touch of the grand old dame, a nod to days past. Dee-Ann's Diner looked like a picture postcard with its cheerful red-and-white awning.

Farther down the street, bougainvillea spilled over a brick wall, and the lonely whistle of a train filled her with a longing she didn't quite understand.

To dispel the silence that followed, she flicked on the radio. Two and a half country songs later, Tucker appeared at the diner door, talking to someone inside. With a wave, he turned and walked out.

When he reached for the door handle, Elisa put a finger to her lips. "Shhh. Daisy's still asleep."

"And we *don't* want to wake her," he said quietly.

"No, we don't." Elisa didn't fight the smile. Knowing her daughter, she had a pretty good idea what this man had put up with today.

The smells wafting from the bag promised a good meal. Her stomach growled.

"Not hungry, huh?"

She shrugged. "It's the whole Pavlov's dog thing. Stimulus, response. You can't fight it."

"Why would you even want to try?" His left eye twitched. "I say you see something you want, go for it."

Her pulse sped up, but she couldn't blame low blood sugar this time. Tucker Wylder was a force to be reckoned with. She'd have to tread carefully, because that whole Pavlov and his dog theory pertained to lots of hungers, and not all of them centered on food.

If the circumstances had been different...

He drove his immaculate Mustang easily and well, seemingly casual but always alert. It would seem cars ran in his blood. Between the long night on the road and the day's even more stressful bizarre turn, she was worn out. Sleep threatened to creep up on her, but she batted it away. Fighting to stay awake, she concentrated on the scenery. As they left town, the houses grew farther and farther apart, the spaces between thick with magnificent old trees, colorful flowers, and lush vines.

She could understand the draw of this small town. If she'd had to take a header, she'd chosen her spot well—or it had chosen her.

Tucker turned onto Firefly Creek Lane, then pulled into a curved drive. Pride shone on his face. "Home sweet home."

Silently, Elisa stared at the two-story Georgian. She wasn't exactly sure what she'd expected, but this imposing stone structure definitely wasn't it.

Tucker chuckled, apparently reading the surprise on her face. "Interesting, isn't it?"

She nodded. "It is that."

He threw an arm across the back of the seat and studied it with her. "It's not quite what I had in mind when I started house-hunting. Before moving here, I lived in a run-down, cramped apartment. I thought I'd lean toward contemporary. Then I saw this beauty. She dates back to 1860. The town's first blacksmith shop, she survived the Civil War, the Reconstruction Period, and everything else mankind threw at her. I fell in love."

"I—" She grimaced and raised a hand to her head. "Sorry. Nasty headache."

Daisy woke, whimpering, but before Elisa could do more than turn around, Tucker hopped out and unbuckled her daughter, talking to her quietly and calmly. With Daisy straddling his hip, he opened Elisa's door. "You okay to walk inside?"

"What? You'll carry me, too?"

"I could. One at a time would probably work best, though."

"No, thanks." She laughed and slid out of the car. "I'm good. I promise not to eat any more concrete."

"Where are we?" Daisy asked.

"My house," Tucker said.

"I wanna go home."

"Mommy's tired." Tucker prayed there'd be no more tears—from any of them. "How 'bout you stay here tonight?"

"Do you gots animals?"

He hesitated. "No, I don't."

Daisy raised a hand to his face and patted his cheek. "But I like animals. 'Specially doggies."

"My brother has one. You met him this morning." *And screamed.*

"He scared me."

"I know. Lug Nut ran too fast, didn't he?"

She nodded, her blond pigtails bobbing. "Can Luggie come play?"

"Not tonight."

"'Morrow night?"

He caved and gave every parent's fallback answer. "We'll see."

As he opened the front door, Elisa stopped. "I should have asked this before, but do you live alone?"

He laughed. "Oh yeah."

"And we're barging in."

"You were invited. Big difference."

"Only because you're too good a man to put a fainting woman and her child on the street."

"Huh-uh. One thing we need to get straight here—I'm not a good man."

She took a step backward.

"I won't hurt you," he said quickly. "But I'm a mess."

Elisa scanned the room as she stepped into it. "A mess? My guess is you could eat off these floors."

He shrugged, and she thought, *oh yeah.* Tucker Wylder liked to be in control, at least here at home, and that was okay because right now? She wasn't in control of anything, and it sucked. Big time.

"The place was one good gust of wind from falling in on itself when I first saw it," Tucker said, "but the potential…"

"Kind of like the vintage cars you rescue." *Along with stranded strangers.*

"Yeah." Surprise showed on his face. "Not many understand that."

"Things shouldn't be tossed away just because they're old…or not perfect. Although some people can do that. Easily." She blinked back unexpected tears and looked toward her precious daughter as Tucker set Daisy on her feet.

She angled toward him. "You're a real renaissance man, aren't you? The savior of sick women and their children. A restorer of vintage machines. And this." She waved a hand at the contemporary vibe he'd layered over the old.

"What? You expected Grandma's house? A frat house?"

"The frat house." Moving to the fireplace, she ran a hand over it. "Reclaimed wood?"

He beamed. "From an old barn."

"Very nice. I'd love to see the rest, but…"

When she trailed off, his head jerked in her direction. "You okay?" he asked.

"I'm fine."

"You sure? Because remember, I was there today when you took your nosedive."

She raised a hand to cover her eyes. "I now have an answer when someone asks, 'What was your most embarrassing moment ever?'"

He brushed away her hand and met her eyes. "Seriously, you took ten years off my life. Need a nap?"

Daisy hopped off the sofa, which she'd been using as a sitting trampoline. "I don't."

"Don't guess you do."

"I don't need a nap, either, Tucker, but I'd love to freshen up."

"Of course." He turned to her and grinned. "Sure you don't want me to carry you upstairs? This might be my one and only chance to channel Rhett Butler."

She laughed out loud, and his stomach did a crazy little flutter.

"As intriguing as that sounds, I'll walk. We'll save your back."

"Are you kidding? I could lift you with one hand."

As he started up, Elisa followed behind, Daisy holding her hand.

When they reached the top of the stairs, he made a face. "When I left this morning, I was in a bit of a hurry and hadn't exactly planned on visitors, so…"

"A little dust won't hurt any of us, Tucker."

He muttered something that sounded like "Not in my house."

Daisy squeezed between Tucker's legs.

"Whoa. In a hurry?"

"I wanna see." She flew into the room ahead of them. "Is this Mommy's room?"

"Yep."

"I like it."

"Me, too," he said.

The room was tailored and totally uncluttered, yet comfortable and serene with its soft yellow bed cover.

"My parents use this room when they visit. There's an en suite bath." He nodded toward a door and watched as Daisy disappeared inside the small room. "I'll call Brant and have him drop your suitcases on his way home."

"I can't tell you how much I appreciate this." Tears welled in Elisa's eyes.

"My guess is if the situation was reversed, you'd do the same for me."

She thought about it for ten full seconds. "No, honestly, I can't say I would. Bring a strange man into my home?"

"I should probably take exception to that. I can't deny a few quirks, but I'm not all that strange."

"A stranger, then. How about that?"

He gave her the same courtesy of considering it, then nodded. "Makes sense, especially with Daisy in the house. So if I come to your place and pass out at your feet, just walk away and leave me lying there."

She grinned and shook her head.

Daisy danced her way out of the bathroom. "I can't reach the water."

"Not necessarily a bad thing," Tucker said.

"Why?"

He met Elisa's eyes, a smile in them. "Lots of reasons."

"Where's my room?" Excited, Daisy looked up at Tucker.

He pulled at one of her pigtails. "I have a special bed for you."

"You do?" She held up her arms, and Elisa lifted her onto the bed beside her. Rolling onto her back, the little girl smiled up at him.

"I do," he said.

"She can sleep with me."

"Not necessary," Tucker said. "You need to be up early for those tests. Be nice if you got a good night's sleep. The stairs are kind of steep, but I have a gate we put across them when my nephew visits. I'll drag it out and set it up."

Her heart gave a little hiccup at his thoughtfulness. She'd worried about coming home with him. The fact that Doc Hawkins knew him had helped. More, though, the man himself had put her at ease.

Still, it was a strange situation.

Another tear welled. "Thank you."

Alarm showed in his hazel eyes. "You're not gonna cry, are you?"

"No, but it's a lot to take in." She swiped at a renegade tear. "I'll get myself pulled together, honest." A second tear streaked down her cheek.

"Oh hell."

"Oh hell," Daisy echoed.

His mouth dropped open, his head whipping to look at the smiling little girl, then back to her mother. "I'm sorry."

"I'm sorry," Daisy said.

"What are you? A parrot?" he asked Daisy.

"What's a parrot?"

He gave a quick laugh.

"A parrot's a bird, honey." Through her tears, Elisa brushed a stray strand from her daughter's face.

"A bird?" Sitting up, the tiny child turned to Tucker, hands on her hips. "I'm not a bird. I'm a girl."

"Good to know."

"Why are you crying, Mommy?"

"Because she's hungry."

Elisa squinted. "Are you a food pusher, Tuck Wylder?"

"Not usually, but Doc stressed the importance—"

She raised her hand. "Understood, but I don't want you fussing over me. We're already a bother just being here."

"No, you're not. If you weren't *here*, I'd be at the shop busting my butt, all sweaty and dirty."

Daisy slid off the bed and took hold of Tucker's big hand. "I'm hungry."

"Will the peanut butter and jelly sandwich I picked up at Dee-Ann's be enough for her?"

"Yes."

"A sammich?"

"Yep. Come on, Parrot. Let's go."

On a frustrated sigh, she said, "I'm not a parrot, 'member?"

"Oops, I forgot. You're a girl."

"Uh-huh. Can I help make lunch?"

"Sure."

"I'm gonna help Tut, Mommy."

She opened her mouth to protest, but Tucker shook his head.

"We'll be fine. Why don't you take a minute? Freshen up and get your feet under you."

"Can I see my special bed before we go downstairs, Tut?"

"Yes, ma'am."

Elisa watched her little girl and her reluctant knight-errant walk out the door together, hand in hand.

Too bad Daisy's own father hadn't been willing to step up the way this perfect stranger had.

And Tucker Wylder did, indeed, seem pretty darned perfect.

CHAPTER 4

TUCKER PLACED HIS HANDS, PALMS DOWN, ON HIS NEW quartz countertop and leaned into them. It probably wouldn't do to cry, but oh, he was tempted. His quiet, calm, organized house looked like a Cat-5 hurricane had whirled through. Grape jelly had found its way down the side of one cabinet, and a plate was covered in small pieces of crust he hadn't cut off. How was he supposed to know that's the way PB&J was served?

Now that he'd wiped half a gallon of the stuff from her face and hands, Daisy sprawled on his sofa, remote in hand, watching an animated show about some talking pig. At least she'd stopped jabbering. His ears were threatening a strike.

Elisa sat at the far end of the counter. Darned if she still didn't look pale. He grabbed a dishcloth and attacked the jelly.

"Why don't you let me do that?" she asked.

"I'm good."

"Yes, you are. Your mother must be awfully proud of you."

"She's proud of all four of us—even when we screw up."

A wistful look crossed Elisa's face, and without a word, she walked into the living room to curl up beside her daughter.

"'Member when Miss Lizzy had a party for me 'cause we were moving?"

Elisa nodded and then, no doubt the result of a stress-ful day and sleep-deprivation, drifted off in the middle of her daughter's never-ending story of her last day at preschool. Tucker put a finger over his lips and Daisy stopped talking. After he dropped an afghan over Elisa, he crooked his finger and the child followed him into the kitchen.

He fixed himself another coffee.

"I'm hungry."

"You just ate." Tucker glanced at his counter. His clean counter. The one he'd only minutes ago finished cleaning.

"I want Froot Loops."

"You like Froot Loops?"

"Uh-huh." She nodded her head, the soft blond curls, now loosed from their elastic bands, bobbing.

"What do you know? Maybe you and I have something in common after all."

"Daisy and Tut. Common." She placed her small hand in his and sent him a smile that would one day have some grown man crawling on his knees.

Where was Daisy's daddy?

"Do you have room for cereal after that sandwich?"

She nodded vehemently, stuck out her belly, and patted it. "See? Right here." She poked a spot.

"Okay, if you insist."

"'Sist, Tut. I 'sist."

Perched on a stool at the counter, he drank his coffee and devoured three of Dee-Ann's no-bake oatmeal cookies while Daisy plowed through a bowl of Froot Loops. While she ate, the little girl filled him in on everything he could possibly want to know about her and her mother—without a single mention of the missing male in the household. That left him with a bucketful of questions about

Elisa. An unwed single mom? Separated? Divorced? A military wife, the wife of a con? Possibilities swam through his head.

———————

Elisa was taking a quick shower when the doorbell rang.

"I'll get it." Daisy bounced to her feet and tore off toward the door.

"No!"

When she turned to look at him, Tucker shook his head. "Does your mommy let you open the door when you don't know who it is?"

Wide-eyed, she shook her head.

"Well, neither do I." He nodded toward the sofa. "Hop back up there. I'll see who it is."

"'Kay." With only the barest pouty-lip, she crawled back on the sofa, grabbed her blanket, and popped a thumb in her mouth.

"Aw, sh—" He'd upset her. Still, she couldn't open the door to just anybody. The bell rang again.

A dishtowel stuffed in the waistband of his jeans, he opened the door to his brother's confident, efficient wife. The cavalry had arrived.

He gave the petite brunette a heartfelt hug. "Happy to see you, Molly!"

"Me, too." The little blond head peeked around the edge of the sofa. "Tut's bein' mean."

Molly's brow rose. "Brant told me you have company."

"In a manner of speaking."

"I don't know what you're planning to feed your guests,

but I made some potato salad today and thought I'd bring you a bowl."

He took it from her. "You're a wonder, sugar. You run your own shop, you cook, you clean, and for some strange reason, you love my brother."

"I do." Her lips kicked up in a grin. Then she took a good look at the house. "This place is a disaster, Tuck."

He raked fingers through his already mussed hair. "Tell me about it."

Molly plopped down on the sofa beside Daisy and held out a hand. "I'm Molly Wylder."

Daisy put her little hand in Molly's. "My name's Daisy Elizabeth Danvers."

"That's a pretty name."

"My mommy gave it to me. Wanna know why?"

"I do."

"'Cause daisies are happy flowers."

Molly smiled. "They are, aren't they?"

Daisy bounced on the sofa. "Yep, and I'm happy, too." Then, the smile turning to a pout, she looked at Tucker. "'Cept when Tut's bein' mean to me."

"Oh, for—I wouldn't let her open the door."

Molly thought about it for a few seconds, studying the adversaries. "I think on this one, baby doll, I have to agree with Tuck. He wants to keep you safe."

Daisy sighed, as if she carried the weight of the world on her little shoulders. "'Kay."

Molly was still there when Elisa started downstairs.

"You dog." Molly elbowed Tucker.

"What?"

"I should have known," Molly whispered. "Good

Samaritan, my foot. Nobody told me your fainter was drop-dead gorgeous. Even without a trace of makeup, she's absolutely breathtaking."

"She is, isn't she?"

"You behave yourself. According to Brant, she's got a lot going on in her life. She doesn't need more."

"I'm trouble?"

"You could be."

Elisa stopped halfway down. "I'm sorry. I didn't realize you had company, Tucker. Why don't Daisy and I go for a walk? Or I can check again for a room in town—"

Molly stood. "No, please. No need. I'm Molly Wylder, Tucker's sister-in-law."

"Sister-in-law?"

Molly nodded.

"Oh."

"Tucker, why don't you and Daisy take that walk or go play in the yard."

"You tryin' to get rid of me?"

"Yes, I am. Now go." Molly made a sweeping gesture with her hand.

"Come on, Daisy. We've been banished from the kingdom."

"Huh?"

"Let's go play in the front yard."

Squealing, she slid off the sofa and threw her arms around Tucker, obviously forgiving him for his past fumbles. "Me and Tut's gonna go play, Mommy."

"Be good."

"I will."

Elisa suffered a quick jolt of panic as her daughter left

with Tucker, then forced herself to take a deep breath. He'd proven himself trustworthy today—more than once.

Molly patted the sofa beside her. "Sit. Brant explained what happened today, so I brought salad for your dinner. Tuck's a great guy, but in the kitchen?" She twisted her hand back and forth. "I thought, too, you might feel a little uneasy about all this. It's kind of scary moving into a stranger's house." She laid a hand on Elisa's arm. "Tucker's a real stand-up guy."

Elisa nodded. "I can't believe I'm in such a mess. And speaking of messes…" She grimaced at what her child had done to Tucker's room in such a short time. "Your brother-in-law has been wonderful, but it's pretty clear he's—"

"A neat-freak?"

A grin slipped out. "Yeah."

"As awful as all this is, the important thing is that you got off the road in time. And, I might add, you were incredibly lucky to stop at the Wylder brothers' shop. Their mama did a darned good job raising those boys."

"I agree—with all of that. Under normal circumstances I'd never have come home with Tucker, but my choices were pretty limited. Watching him with Daisy—well, I think I could have done a lot worse. To be honest, I don't know what I'd have done today without him."

"The Wylder boys are good men."

"I vaguely remember seeing three this morning."

"Then you've met them all. My Brant, your Tucker, and Gaven."

"Oh, but he's not my Tucker."

"In a manner of speaking. They have a younger sister, Lainey, and arguably the best parents on earth."

A hot, uncomfortable shot of envy ran through Elisa. She wasn't proud of it, but there it was. Tucker had a big, wonderful family, and she didn't. Never had, never would.

Fifteen minutes later, Tucker stuck his head in the front door. "Okay if we come in? I'd like to clean up and Daisy needs to use the facilities."

"No, I don't, Tut. I need to pee."

He chuckled and hoisted her into his arms. Depositing her by the bathroom, he sprinted upstairs.

A quick shower and a change of clothes and Tucker felt human again. Hearing chatter, he headed downstairs, but stopped in the kitchen doorway. A three-year-old giggled at the counter, the smell of baked beans emanated from his oven, and two beautiful women chatted over coffee. Both his kitchen and his living room were shipshape once again.

"I'm in awe," he said. "I failed totally, but you two have everything under control."

Molly patted his cheek. "I beg to disagree. You did good, Tucker Wylder."

"Yeah, Tut. You did good." Daisy held a green crayon and was industriously coloring a picture of a dog.

"*Tut.*" Molly grinned.

"A misunderstanding. No big deal, so I didn't correct her."

"I like it," Molly said. "King Tut, ruler of nations."

"Yeah, yeah." He jammed his hands in his jeans pockets. "So when can we eat?"

"As soon as you set the table. For three. I need to leave in a few minutes."

They worked in companionable silence, serenaded by Daisy's rendition of "Twinkle, Twinkle, Little Star."

"How are things at the shop?" Tucker asked.

"Shop?" Daisy's gaze flew to his. "I like to shop."

He chuckled. "Must be part of a female's DNA."

Molly smiled. "Tut means my store."

Daisy gaped at her. "You have a whole store?"

"I do, and it's full of gowns."

"Nightgowns?" the child asked.

Molly shook her head. "Wedding gowns."

"Like Cinderella's?"

"Just like Cinderella's." She pulled a phone from her purse. "Want to see some?"

Tucker watched as they bonded over their love of fashion. Something inside him fluttered. Outnumbered three to one by females, he found his house had taken on a new and different vibe. A pleasant one. It even smelled better...or maybe that was the beans.

His stomach growled. "Can't tell I'm hungry, can you? I finished the last of the take-out from Dee-Ann's hours ago."

Molly laughed and laid down her phone.

"Can I see more?" Daisy twirled a curl around her finger.

"You'd better eat first. Maybe you and Mommy can stop in to see my pretty dresses."

"Can I put one on?"

"Sure. I have some flower-girl dresses just your size."

Daisy squealed and clapped her hands. "I'm gonna be pretty, Tut."

"You already are, sugar."

Daisy looked like she'd won a trophy.

Elisa made a small sound. "Exactly the perfect thing to say, Tucker. Thank you." Grabbing hot pads, she turned her back and opened the oven to check on the beans.

That noise she'd made came dangerously close to more crying. Deciding the best way to head it off was to ignore it, he sniffed the air. "Smells like heaven."

"It does. Thanks for sharing your recipe, Elisa," Molly said. "I have to run now, but I assured her, Tuck, that she hasn't come home with the big bad wolf. So don't you dare make me a liar."

He caught Elisa's gaze and nodded, feeling a little like a poser because he'd had quite a few unfiltered, big-bad-wolfish thoughts flit in and out of his head earlier. Regardless, Molly was right. Elisa and Daisy were safe here.

"Think we should cover the table with a tarp?"

After dinner, he and Daisy sprawled in the living room watching the Disney channel while visions of a man cave danced through his head.

The doorbell rang.

His gaze flew to the lock, checked that it was in place as he thought of the woman upstairs making up Daisy's bed. Had someone come for her? An irate husband, despite her claims she had none? The law?

"Who's that?" Daisy came to full alert.

"Darned if I know." Tucker started toward the door.

"Darned if I know," Daisy echoed, following him.

He stopped to look at her. "Do you always repeat what someone says?"

She popped a thumb in her mouth.

Uh-oh. He'd upset her again. Dropping to one knee, he said, "How about a hug before we see who's at the door?"

She nodded and moved into his arms, carrying with her that special little-girl smell.

The doorbell rang again.

"Keep your britches on."

"Yeah," Daisy yelled. "Keep 'em on!" Then her eyes went wide. "It might be a monster!"

"No. First, monsters don't ring doorbells, and second—"

A bark sounded from outside.

"A doggy!" Monsters forgotten, Daisy flew to the door.

"Uh-uh. Remember what I said." Tucker moved her behind him, flicked the lock, and opened the door to Brant and Lug Nut.

Crouched, Daisy peeked between Tucker's legs. "Will he bite me?"

"Nope." Brant snapped his fingers and looked shocked when Lug Nut sat. "It actually works sometimes. Where's my lady?"

"She already went home."

Brant hung his head. "I missed her?"

"Yep."

"The dog and I are on our way there now and thought we'd stop by to see how things were going. Where's Elisa?"

"Upstairs getting Daisy's bed pulled together," Tucker said.

Brant moved to the bottom of the stairs. "Feeling better, Elisa?" he called up.

"I am, thanks," she answered, sounding surprised.

"Great! Okay if I feed the dog, bro? I didn't get around

to it before we left the shop." Brant dug a baggie of dog food from his pocket. "Got a paper plate?"

"Yep."

The guys started to the kitchen, Lug Nut following.

Daisy skipped behind them.

Once he'd dumped the dog food onto a plate, Brant moved into the living room with Tucker. "You doing okay?"

"I am. We're good here, but I'll be late tomorrow. Doc Hawkins wants to run a test on Elisa in the morning, and it'll take a few hours."

Brant's eyes searched his. "That'll work. We got a lot done today, so the Vette's almost wrapped up."

Tucker nodded. "Been a long eight months on this project, but worth every second. That car will be pristine when we turn her over to Murdoch."

Daisy walked into the room and tugged on Tucker's pant leg.

"What?"

"I don't feel good."

He put a hand on her head. "You're not warm."

"My tummy hurts. The doggy gave me some of his food."

Hand on the stair rail, Elisa whispered, "You let her eat dog food?"

"No!" Tucker looked at Brant.

"I didn't. Not my kid."

"She's not mine, either."

"I thought you were keeping an eye on her," Elisa said.

"I was, then Brant showed up and—"

Daisy made a gagging sound, and Tucker's head whipped around. "What?"

Blak! She tossed her cookies—along with dog food and

dinner—right in the middle of his expensive rug. Some of it splashed on him, and he gagged with her.

Lug Nut galloped into the room and headed for the mess.

"Do not let the dog eat that!" Elisa rushed the rest of the way down the stairs.

Daisy started to cry.

"My rug!"

"Your rug?" Elisa threw him a look that said *eat crap and die*.

And there was the mother bear, Tucker thought.

Brant grabbed Lug Nut's collar. "What did I tell you about sharing, dog? Don't. Ever. Got that?"

Lug Nut smiled at him.

Shaking his head, Brant herded him to the door. "See you tomorrow."

"You come in here and cause all this, then desert us?" Tucker asked.

"Damn straight," Brant said.

"Damn straight," Daisy parroted around her tears.

"Oops!" Brant winced and looked from her to Tucker to Elisa.

Tucker shook his head. "I'm telling you, the kid's antennae home right in on off-limit words."

Brant threw them a wobbly salute and headed into the night.

Scrubbing his fingers through his hair, Tucker eyed the mess on his rug. "I'll get the paper towels. Can you handle Daisy?"

"I've done this more times than you want to know. Come on, sweetheart. Let's go take a bath, okay?"

"'Kay." Then those big blues, swimming with tears, turned to Tucker. "Are you mad at me, Tut?"

"No, honey, I'm not mad." He leaned in and kissed the top of her head. "Dog food'll do that to you every time."

Tucker dropped into a chair. He'd done his best on the rug, but only time would tell.

He heard a squeal upstairs, then Elisa's voice. "Daisy Elizabeth, you get back here."

On a gleeful laugh, Daisy came ripping down the stairs as naked as the day she was born.

Tucker laughed. "Whoops, looks like somebody escaped."

Then he got a good look at Daisy, and his jaw tightened. He raised his eyes and met Elisa's.

With a quick shake of her head, she caught her daughter and slipped one of Tucker's black T-shirts over her. Swathed in the ankle-length shirt, Daisy raced across the room to him.

"You look a lot better, Miss Daisy. All ready for bed," he said hopefully.

Elisa reached for her, but Daisy drew back. "I want Tut."

"Honey—"

Tucker held up a hand. "It's okay. I'll take you up."

But by the time they got upstairs, she'd changed her mind. "I wanna sleep with my mommy."

"Not tonight."

"Are you gonna sleep with my mommy?"

He pushed away the totally inappropriate thoughts that rocketed through his brain. He'd brought Elisa—and this child—home to help them. He'd promised they'd be safe with him, but that big bad wolf Molly'd mentioned made his presence known when he remembered those legs walking toward him at the shop, when he thought about those oh so kissable lips.

Tucker swatted the wolf back into his cave.

"No." Clearing his throat, he said, "Mommy needs to sleep by herself tonight, remember? But if you need anything, we'll both hear you." They stopped just inside Daisy's bedroom.

"Will you check under my bed?"

"For what?"

Eyes wide, Daisy stood on her tiptoes and motioned for him to lean down. When he did, she whispered, "For the monsters. Mommy always does."

"But you saw the floor before I pulled down the bed."

She clapped her hands. "A mooffee bed."

"Murphy," he corrected.

"That's what I said, Tut." She wrapped her arms around his knees, those big, trusting eyes pleading with him. "Please."

"Please what?"

She let out an indignant huff. "Please look for the monsters."

Feeling more than a little silly, Tucker knelt and pulled up the edge of the bedcover. He stayed in place a few seconds to reassure her he'd taken a thorough look. "Nothing here, sweetheart."

Wordlessly, she pointed at the closet.

Resigned, shoulders slumped, Tucker tiptoed across the room and threw open the door. "Nothing except a pair of shoes and my old baseball glove and bat."

Daisy let out a breath. "Thank you, Tut."

"You're most welcome, Daisy." He smiled. Not every day a guy got to play hero.

She patted the side of her bed.

Unsure what ritual came next, Tucker crossed the room and sat gingerly on the edge. "What?"

"Down here." She knelt, folded her little hands, and bowed her head.

Tucker followed suit.

"Now I lay me on my mooffee bed...I can't 'member, Tut."

He rubbed the bridge of his nose with thumb and forefinger. "Now I lay me down to sleep..."

She repeated, and together they finished their prayer. He kissed her forehead, and she hugged him tightly. His heart pinched.

She crawled into bed, and, gently, he pulled up her covers and tucked her in. "Night, Daisy."

"Night, Tut." She threw her arms around him in another big hug, then rolled over, one hand tucked beneath her cheek. He stood where he was until, only seconds later, she fell fast asleep. He turned to leave and bumped into Elisa. His arms came out to steady them both. Those soft curves pressed into him.

"Thank you again, Tuck."

"You're most welcome." He drew in a deep breath. "You smell so good."

One side of her mouth curled in a half-smile. "It's just soap, Tucker. Your soap."

He sniffed at her neck. "Smells a whole lot better on you."

His hand rose to curl one of those long, silky strands around a finger, trying not to think of her in his shower with his soap coursing over that incredible body.

"Night, Elisa," he whispered.

"Night, Tucker." She kissed his cheek. "Thank you. For everything."

He laid a hand on her petal-soft cheek and trailed his fingers along the curve of it, then turned away.

That chaste kiss would dog him into the wee hours of the morning.

He fastened the safety gate and said his own prayer of thanks. What a crazy day.

Creeping down the stairs, he moved the fan he'd aimed at his rug, hoping it would be dry by morning. Even though it was late, he started a fresh cup of coffee. While his machine worked its magic, he rummaged in his junk drawer for the nightlight he'd bought last time his mom and dad had come to visit.

"Aha!" He raced upstairs to plug it in. Daisy might be scared of the dark—and the monsters—if she woke during the night.

Then he took his coffee into the living room. He turned off the light and sat in the darkened room. A swath of moonlight filtered in through the open blinds. His head hurt. Hell, his heart hurt. What had happened to Daisy? When she'd scampered down those stairs, he'd marveled at her innocence and pure joy.

Then he'd seen the scar on her chest. It wasn't large, but its location chilled his blood.

The third stair from the top creaked, and he glanced up. Elisa.

She stood stock-still, dressed in another of his black tees. It wasn't ankle-length on her, though. Nope. A whole lot of leg was exposed. Even in the dim light he could tell she was troubled.

She knew he'd seen the pink ridge on her daughter's chest. "Everything okay, Elisa? You doing all right?"

"I'm fine. Today was an anomaly."

He gave a curt nod. "Okay." He paused. "You want to tell me about Daisy? About the scar? The one right over her heart."

"She's had that since she was only a few weeks old. It's the reason her daddy left us."

Tucker half rose from his chair. "Tell me he didn't do that to her!"

"No. No! Sit down. Please. Daisy was born with a congenital heart defect." Elisa sat beside him on the sofa, curling those legs beneath her.

Tucker's stomach plummeted. "She seems so healthy."

"She is, but she was born with an atrial septal defect. In layman's terms, that's a hole between the upper heart chambers. The scar is from a laparoscopic peek at it."

"Your doctor fixed it?"

Elisa shook her head. "No. A lot of them close on their own, so he felt it best to wait and see. Luke, Daisy's dad, didn't wait, though. When she was two weeks old, he left. He called from San Diego to tell me he wouldn't be coming back, that he hadn't signed on for a sick kid."

He reached for her hand. "I'm no expert on love. Hell, I'd be lying if I said I even knew what love is. I'll tell you this, though. I know what love isn't, and it isn't what Daisy's dad pulled."

Interlacing their fingers, he drew her closer. "My mom and dad are pretty good examples of love that sticks. Molly and Brant? They're doing pretty well now, but Molly? She was pretty stubborn." Tucker met Elisa's gaze. "Kind of like someone else I know."

Her mouth opened to deny it, but he shook his head.

"Hey, no sense trying to pretty it up. Seems to me once you make up your mind, it's a done deal. Nothing wrong with that, I guess, as long as you're reasonable about it. I sure am sorry about Daisy, though, and about her daddy. I wonder if he has any idea what he's missing."

He kissed the top of her head. "You'd better go on up. See if you can catch some sleep. You've got another big day tomorrow."

"Thank you, Tuck, for everything. A roof over our heads, a bed to sleep in, and your understanding."

"No need to thank me, sugar. Glad I could help."

She'd already started up the stairs when he asked, "Any meds she needs to take? Any special precautions?"

"Nope. A doctor's visit once in a while to listen to her heart. That's about it."

"Okay. Good. See you in the morning."

When he heard her bedroom door close, he walked to the kitchen sink, dumped his coffee, and reached in the fridge for a beer. He'd earned one.

He'd been crazy to bring Elisa home with him. Her and those pouty lips that damn near cried to be kissed and kissed well. Those legs that went on and on. It about killed him imagining them twined around him.

While she was safe here, he darned well wasn't, because the lady touched something deep inside him that had lain dormant for a long, long time. Something that was best left hidden away.

CHAPTER 5

TUCKER SHOOK HIMSELF FREE OF THE NIGHTMARE'S grip. Sitting straight up in bed, he stared into the darkness, then turned toward the window and the single ray of moonlight. Sweaty and trembling, he breathed raggedly and ran nerveless fingers through his hair. He was a mess.

No need to check the clock. 1:33 a.m. The same time—Huh-uh, he wouldn't go there.

Tossing back the covers, he pushed himself from bed and started downstairs. With a curse, he went back to his room for a pair of sweats. With two females in the house, he couldn't run around naked.

He needed a walk or a drive. Time alone to shake off the nightmare.

That wouldn't happen. Not tonight. Until he knew darned good and well that Elisa was okay, he was stuck here. And wasn't that a heck of a way to think about her? Still, he'd seen to her problems today. Tonight he had his own to deal with.

Soundlessly, he made his way downstairs, avoiding the creaking third step, and moved into the kitchen for a glass of water. Carrying it with him, he went outside to the back porch. The temperature had dropped considerably.

His hands trembled so badly that he set the water on an upturned crate he used as a temporary table. Burying his head in his hands, he tried to think calm thoughts, tried to push away the faces of his lost friends.

They were bullheaded tonight and refused to recede to the back of his mind.

When the screen door opened, he bolted out of his seat, fists curled.

"It's me." Elisa stood in the doorway. "I'm sorry. I shouldn't have come down, but I heard you and wondered if you were all right."

Finger by finger, he unfurled them, and let his hands drop to his side. "I told you I'm a night person."

"You did. I'll go back to bed."

"That's probably a good idea. You don't want to be around me tonight."

In the moonlight, he caught the intensity of her gaze.

"I'd rather we were both in our beds fast asleep. But you're not, so I'm not, either. You helped me. Why am I not allowed to help you?"

"There's no help for me."

"I don't know what to say to that." With a frown, she turned to leave.

"Wait." He reached out and laid his hand on her arm. "Sit with me for a bit."

Without hesitation, she moved to the glider and sat beside him.

Neither spoke for a long time, but slowly, ever so slowly her hand closed the distance to his arm. He draped it around her shoulders and drew her close.

She cuddled into him, making him aware that there were still soft spots in the world. Not everything was hard and cold. At least not right here, right now.

"I don't know what's hurting you, Tucker, but I do know you can get through it. You can come out the other side."

He diverted, the way he always did. "Tell me about you, Elisa. What is it that keeps you up at night?"

She shivered, and he tugged the throw from the back of the glider and spread it over them.

"I'm not sure you want to hear my sad story."

"Okay, then, tell me what you want more than anything," he persisted.

In the dark, it was easier to share, to use the night as a shield.

"All right," she said. "All my life, I've wanted the white picket fence, the husband, and two-point-five kids. My version of a fairy tale."

"It doesn't have to be."

She snorted. "But it is, and fairy tales are make-believe. Fiction. My dad has been like some phantom being, always gone because of his career. I wonder sometimes how he and my mother were ever in the same room long enough to conceive me."

"How about your mother? What's she like?"

"She's an anthropologist, and that involves playing in the dirt—in far-flung locations. So, my poor grandmother got stuck with me. When I met Luke, I thought, here it is. My fairy tale." She grimaced. "I was wrong. The marriage didn't last long. And I returned to Gram's—with a baby."

Tucker said nothing, but her pain all but vibrated in the night air. A firefly flicked on, then off, and he realized her happiness had been every bit as fleeting.

"You'll have to forgive me if I'm a tad jaded. Apparently, I'm not meant to be a fairy-tale heroine. I lack some key element. Some crucial component."

Voice gruff, Tucker disagreed. "You lack nothing."

"If you knew me better, you wouldn't say that." She stood. "I've always been someone's burden. And now, tag, you're it. I'm so sorry."

Before he could say anything, she hurried inside and up the stairs.

Morning came way too soon.

In the hallway mirror, he caught sight of his bloodshot eyes and wild hair. If Daisy woke and saw him like this, she'd think the under-the-bed monsters had come to life. He finger-combed his hair, but there was nothing to be done about the eyes. They were what they were.

Itching to sneak out, stop by Tommy's Texaco for coffee and a ham biscuit, and finish up that Vette, he scolded himself. Not today. Elisa took precedence.

He knocked at her door and heard a muffled sound. "Time to rise and shine, Sleeping Beauty. You have an appointment in just under an hour."

"Okay."

When he didn't hear movement, he knocked again. "You up?"

Her light went on. "I am now."

"See you downstairs, but remember, nothing to eat or drink."

"Yes, Doctor Wylder."

He grinned. So she wasn't a morning person. Good to know.

"Want me to wake Daisy?" he asked.

"No, thanks. I'll take care of her." She yawned. "Sorry."

Because she couldn't have any coffee, he didn't make any for himself. It didn't seem fair to tease her with the smell.

He watched the clock uneasily. From the sounds upstairs, mother and daughter were both awake, but he hadn't had visual confirmation yet.

"Elisa? Time to leave," he called from the bottom of the stairs.

"Coming." She appeared on the landing holding her daughter's hand, her purse and Daisy's bag over one shoulder.

She looked ethereal, so delicate a good gust of wind could blow her away. All that gorgeous blond hair had been pulled back, leaving her flawless features unframed. Those sky-colored eyes met his, and he swore every molecule of oxygen had been sucked out of his house.

Careful, buddy.

He couldn't afford to get close to either the woman or the child. Things didn't go well for people he cared about.

They danced around each other awkwardly on the ride, neither quite comfortable with the vulnerability they'd revealed under the cover of darkness.

Elisa could have kicked herself for confiding so much. Why she'd opened up like that was beyond her. Maybe it was because Tucker had been hurting, too. She didn't know what ate at him, but it was clear they each fought their own demons.

She'd barely slept last night. She hated doctors and

hated needles. Today she'd face both. As much as she disliked tight spaces, she'd rather they shoot her into an MRI machine than draw blood every thirty to sixty minutes for the next five or six hours. *Oh, blubbering whalebones!*

Well, by tonight it would be over—if the tests came out okay. She prayed she hadn't inherited her grandmother's diabetes. Nondiabetic hypoglycemia? With an early diagnosis, she'd be able to manage it through her diet. Full-blown diabetes? Something altogether different. Huge strides had been made in the fight against the disease, but for the people dealing with it on a day-to-day basis, it remained a battle.

While neither she nor Tucker had much to say, Daisy had no inhibitions and chattered away a mile a minute. Maybe instead of feeling sorry for herself, she should save her sympathies for Tucker. Waking up to the energy of a three-year-old was new to him.

She glanced in the visor mirror. The cookies-and-cream Pop-Tart that apparently constituted Tucker's version of a healthy breakfast for her daughter was disappearing quickly. Elisa checked in her purse. Yep, plenty of hand wipes.

The next few hours were a blur of blood-draw after blood-draw. Doctor Hawkins finally released her after nagging her into staying in Misty Bottoms for a few more days and practically force-feeding her crackers and cheese. While Daisy sneaked a couple, Tucker had politely refused any.

Tucker. As bad as Elisa felt, Tucker looked far worse. Daisy, however, after a short nap looked as fresh as a—well, as fresh as a daisy. No doubt she was responsible for much of Tucker's fatigue.

After a quick stop at the diner for a much-needed lunch, they headed home.

"Listen," Tucker said. "You feeling okay?"

"Surprisingly, yes. You don't need to worry about me, Tuck."

"You keep saying that, but I can't quite get over yesterday. You scared me. I'm wondering, though, if it's okay to drop the two of you at the house? I really should give the guys a hand. We're fast running out of time on a big project."

"We'll be fine. And to be perfectly honest, I think you could use a break."

He smiled sheepishly. "I'd deny it, but frankly, I don't know how you do it. I have a new and deep respect for Brant. He had temporary sole custody of our nephew and actually survived it."

He pulled into the drive and helped Elisa out, then released Daisy from her seat.

"I'm gonna change my clothes before I head out. First, though, Daisy and I need to take a little hike out back."

Elisa's forehead creased in question.

"Something we need to do. It's a secret."

"Okay." She gathered Daisy's things and went inside while her daughter and Tucker walked around back.

The minute they rounded the house, Daisy jumped up and down, clapping.

"How'd you know, Tut?"

"Know what?"

"To put them here for me?" She waved her hand toward the daisies.

He hadn't really looked at the flowers closely. Now this little girl believed he'd planted them for her. Childhood was, indeed, magical.

Too bad growing up tainted that.

Feeling like an idiot, Tucker walked inside a few minutes later with Daisy—who was all but strangling the wildflowers clutched in her hand.

Seeing her mother, Daisy raced across the room, the daisies held out in front of her.

"Wow! How pretty."

"Tut has a whole bunch of them. For me."

He swore he saw stars in the child's eyes. "I—" He shook his head.

The slow grin that crossed Elisa's face said it all. She understood.

"We picked them by the water but Tut wouldn't let me get close 'cause you love me too much." She jumped onto the sofa and snuggled up to her mom.

Tucker tried not to wince at the dirty little sneakers. A smidgen of uninvited envy crept through him as he watched the mother-daughter reunion.

"I love you, Mommy." She turned those big blue eyes on Tucker. "Tut?"

"What?"

"Aren't you going to tell Mommy you love her, too?"

"I—" He opened his mouth, closed it again. "Sure."

"Tell her!"

Elisa saved him. "It's okay, honey. He's already showed

that by taking care of us, so thank you, Tuck. For everything. We'll be out of your hair as soon as I can make arrangements to rent a car."

"No, ma'am." Awkwardly, he dipped his hands in his jeans pockets. "I was there when Doc Hawkins said it would take a day or two to get your results back. He wants to see you regulated before you hit the road." Tucker thought of his long-awaited fishing trip. The one that wouldn't happen. Well, there'd be another time. "You should plan on staying at least through the weekend."

"I don't need—"

"Yes, you do. If you knew how to take care of yourself, you wouldn't be in this mess."

Her mouth dropped open, and her eyes narrowed.

"Ruffled your feathers? Good. Use that anger to get this under control. Eat right today, get on your laptop and do some research. Let's be proactive." He ran a hand over the stubble he hadn't bothered to shave. "I won't be home till late. Sure you can manage?"

"I have for quite a while now."

"Understood. Now understand this—we all need a little help once in a while, darlin'." He thought of the friends he'd left behind in the Middle East, the ones who'd returned stateside in flag-draped caskets. His heartbeat quickened and he took a steadying breath, searched for a sliver of calm. "It'll all work out."

He wasn't at all sure if the reassurance was meant for her...or for himself.

"Before I forget, Brant called. He apologized again for not bringing your suitcases last night, but he dropped them off this morning. They're in your bedroom."

And that, he thought, would be good for both of them. Tonight, she could sleep in her own nightie rather than his T-shirt. Although she sure looked good in it—a little too good for his comfort.

"He found a box, too, in your trunk."

"That would be some pictures and a few keepsakes. I left most of our things with a cousin."

"Good that he brought it, then." He gave Daisy a noisy cheek-kiss. "'Bye, sugar."

Then, just for the hell of it, he leaned in and dropped a kiss on Elisa's cheek. She blushed, Daisy giggled, and he walked out the door with a smug grin on his face.

A second later, he stuck his head back inside. "One question. Does Daisy have any allergies?"

"Allergies?"

"Molly and Brant are going to Savannah for her mom's birthday. I kind of promised to d-o-g sit."

"She loves d-o-gs," Elisa spelled back. "The one that was here last night?"

"Yes."

"Oh, you'll have your hands full."

Daisy's head swiveled back and forth at the spelling. "I wanna see your hands, Tut."

Puzzled, he held them out.

"They're not full, Mommy."

Tucker smiled. "Smart kid, there, Mom."

Elisa simply shook her head.

"Anyway," Tucker said, "I'll take him to work with me so you won't have to put up with him during the day. He's kind of our shop d-o-g, and as you've undoubtedly noticed, is still learning his manners."

"Me too." Daisy rolled her baby-blues. "Mommy tells me that a lot."

Tucker chuckled. "Mamas do that. A lot."

"Does your mommy?"

"Yes, ma'am."

"I'm not a ma'am. I'm too little."

"A little girl who's a cutie." He swung her up over his head, and she giggled. "Give me a hug. I have to go to work. For real this time."

"'Kay." Her little arms wrapped around his neck.

"'Bye, squirt."

He hesitated in the front yard. His house had gone from quiet and, yeah, kind of cold to vibrant and full of life. Thinking of Daisy, he shook his head. Were all children so wired? So curious?

Did they all come with sexy mamas with the biggest, bluest eyes?

Through the door, he heard Daisy's squeal of happiness and could only imagine what was happening inside his no longer neat and perfect home.

Craving a cup of tea, Elisa opened the pantry door. Shell-shocked, she stared at the shelves. Not wanting to snoop in his cupboards, she'd had Molly retrieve everything she'd needed for last night's beans, so this was her first peek. Every single item had been carefully placed in regimented order. Containers were lined up and labeled.

Narrowing her eyes, she closed the door and opened one cupboard after another. *Oh my gosh. Could anybody be this anal? Maintain this?* She'd dug into things and organized before—and it had lasted an entire day or two. She had a sneaking suspicion Tucker's always looked like this.

Following a hunch, she walked outside and opened the door to a small garage.

It had been turned into a woodworking shop, and, yes, everything had a place and was in it. A pegboard hung over a meticulously arranged workbench. Tucker had outlined and labeled every spot on the board. Each tool had its own space.

Holy Organizer, Batman!

On a second workbench she spotted a beautiful porch swing. It wasn't quite finished, but when she ran her hand along the slats, the wood felt smooth as silk.

How in the world could she and Daisy survive here? The bigger question: How would Tucker survive them being here? She was neat, but this went so far beyond neat she doubted even Webster had a word for it.

And yet, hadn't he plopped Daisy down at the counter and fed her a sticky PB&J sandwich? Watched as blobs of grape jelly splattered his pristine countertop?

He had—and had immediately cleaned it up.

She grinned. Actually, this might be fun—and that was mean of her. Still...

CHAPTER 6

GAVEN WAS CAREFULLY ATTACHING THE ICONIC GAS CAP cover on the spine of the '63 Vette when Tucker arrived. Shooting a meaningful glance at the clock, he growled, "You're so late I'm not sure why you even bothered coming in."

"Yeah, well, I had to take Elisa in for her tests."

"What?" Gaven stepped away from the car. "Elisa? What have you done, Tucker?"

"Brant didn't tell you?"

"He never tells me anything."

Hands dug deep into his black denim pockets, Tucker 'fessed up.

"You kept them? A woman and her kid's not quite the same as draggin' home a stray puppy or a kitten, Tuck."

"No, it isn't." He covered a yawn.

"This is the same guy who wouldn't let his own brother live with him?" Gaven asked. "The guy who made me rent a falling-down house?"

"You chose that house."

"It's cheap."

"That's so you."

"Can't argue that." Gaven slid the screwdriver back and forth between his fingers.

"Besides, they're not living with me. It's a *very* temporary arrangement. I can't put Elisa on the road until I know she's okay. Not with Daisy. And her car's a wreck. A wreck that doesn't run."

"Not our problem." Gaven pointed at the sports car. "*This* is our problem."

"And we'll have it done in time."

"Listen and listen good, big brother. You need to get that chick out of your house and fast."

"Not till we get the results back from this morning."

"She'll start nesting."

"No, she won't. She's passing through." He tugged at his right ear. "I have a favor to ask."

"No way!"

"I didn't even ask yet."

"You don't need to. Two females in your house with all their stuff? They're driving Mr. Neat Freak crazy. I'm not takin' them."

Tucker began unwrapping one of the new old-stock door handles. "I don't want you to."

"Fine. We're good, then."

"No, I still have a favor to ask."

Gaven sighed. "Shoot."

"How about you keep Lug Nut while Molly and Brant are out of town?"

"Huh-uh. No way. You agreed to do it."

"Under duress."

"Doesn't matter. He's yours," Gaven said.

"I've kind of got a houseful right now."

"One dog's not gonna make much difference."

"Says you."

Gaven grinned. "Yeah, says me."

Tucker dropped the door handle onto the tool bench. "Think I'll go finish up a few invoices."

"What?" Gaven tightened the last screw. Rubbing a

polishing cloth over it, he said, "Forget the invoices. If we're gonna have this finished by Friday, I need your help."

"Payback's hell." Tucker started to walk away.

"Remember that when Murdoch shows up and finds an unfinished car. It's not Gaven Wylder who will take the hit. It'll be Wylder Rides."

Tucker cursed, picked up the handle, and hunkered down to work.

"Hey, Bro?"

"Yeah?"

"I know how badly you needed this weekend at Nate's cabin. Have you talked to his parents lately?"

"No." Tucker stared at the fluorescent lighting overhead. "Last time I showed up at their door, his mom practically needed to be sedated. It's hard on them to see me. I'm no good for them. No good for anybody right now."

Gaven put his hand on Tucker's shoulder. "Not true, Brother. We love you." He gave his brother's head a knuckle-rub. "And if anybody asks, I'll deny that."

Tucker took a swat at him, and Gaven danced away laughing.

Finished with the second handle, Tucker gave his attention to the turn signal, which seemed a little lazy. Once he had it working right, he decided to tackle the hood orna-ment. It was nowhere in sight.

"I thought Brant ordered the hood ornament. You know where it is?"

"I don't have the foggiest idea."

"I need it."

"Understood," Gaven said.

After scouring the place and not finding it, Tucker

asked, "You willing to hop on the computer or phone and see if you can track one down in Savannah? Drive down to pick it up?"

"As great as the outside looks, the inside has to be right, too. You know that as well as me. I'm in the middle of getting ready to paint under the hood."

"I know, but I can't leave right now."

Out of patience, Gaven tossed a rubber mallet. It bounced off the counter and hit a metal can.

Tucker, not quite steady after last night's violent dreams, flung himself to the floor. On his knees, he stopped and pulled himself together, cursing furiously.

"Damn, Tuck, I'm sorry. I forget sometimes."

"Don't worry about it." Embarrassed, Tucker turned his back. "I stumbled. Period."

"Yeah." Gaven rubbed the back of his neck. "High spot in the concrete there," he lied. "We should probably grind it down."

"Yep." Tucker breathed in. His brother was willing to cover for him. Again. He felt sick to his stomach. "You gonna hop on finding that part?"

"Yeah."

After Gaven walked into the office, Tucker moved to the workbench and placed his hands flat on it, palms down. He took slow, measured breaths like the military doc had told him to do.

Gradually he felt a little calmer, but it did nothing to bring Nate and the others back.

By the time Wednesday rolled around, Tucker swore his life had jumped the rails. With Brant gone, he and Gaven were working flat-out. Gaven had finished painting the inside of the hood yesterday, so Tucker mounted the hood ornament. That crisis had been solved by Gaven who'd kept his head and called Brant, who'd admitted to leaving it on his kitchen counter.

During lunch, Tucker took a few minutes to call home. It turned out Hawkins had already phoned with the test results: nondiabetic hypoglycemia. As long as Elisa watched her diet, she'd be okay, but he'd asked her to stay in town a couple more days to be on the safe side.

All good news. The sooner Elisa got her life under control, the sooner Tucker's would return to normal—and the sooner he'd wave goodbye to Daisy and her mama. Why did that make his heart heavy? It was what he wanted. What he needed.

At seven thirty, Tucker called it quits. Bone-weary from the hours spent on the car restoration and very little sleep, he slid behind the wheel of his Mustang. Yawning, he leaned his head against the car seat and closed his eyes—for just a couple of seconds, he promised himself.

Lug Nut licked his chin.

"Argh. Get your ugly face out of mine, dog." He wiped the back of his hand across his mouth. "Aren't you supposed to ride in the back?"

The overgrown pup grinned at him but didn't budge.

"Okay, okay." He shook a finger at the dog. "But if you're going home with me, we have to set some rules. For a starter, no more kisses."

Lug Nut gave a quiet little bark, and they pulled out of the parking area.

Brant had dropped both the hood ornament and the dog off at the shop on their way out of town yesterday. Tucker had left the pup at the shop last night, but he couldn't bring himself to do that two nights in a row. Since Elisa insisted Daisy would be okay with Lug Nut, Tucker would give it a try. "You chew up one thing at the house and you're gone. Understood?"

The pup yapped in agreement.

"Okay, then."

Tucker rolled down the passenger window partway, and the pup poked his head out, ears flapping in the wind, an expression of pure ecstasy on his face.

Ashamed to admit the reason for it even to himself, Tucker stole a few minutes for a ride down by the river. He craved some alone time and knew from past experience that when he didn't get it, he could turn ugly. Rather than subject Elisa to that side of him, he'd carve out twenty minutes for himself.

Then he'd phone in an order to Dee-Ann's Diner, so everybody'd get fed tonight. He'd refused Elisa's offer to cook. Regardless of the circumstances, she was a guest.

The river was peaceful, the early autumn air soft. Not too far from the bank, a fish jumped and Tucker promised himself he'd toss his pole in the trunk for the next time.

"Okay, bud, time to go." Ruffling the dog's head, Tucker turned the Mustang around and headed home with a quick stop to pick up dinner.

When he pulled up in front of his old stone building, he studied it. He was used to coming home to darkness. Emptiness. Tonight, lights glowed in the windows, and he could almost hear Daisy's high-pitched voice and laughter, smell her mama's fresh, floral scent.

Temporary, he reminded himself. Both the good and the bad of it.

He turned off the ignition, took a deep breath, and rounded the car to pluck the paper bag holding their dinner from the trunk. He hadn't trusted Lug Nut anywhere near it.

Daisy met him at the door and leapt at him. Setting the bag down quickly, he caught her. "Hey, stinker, what have you been up to today?"

"Nothin'."

Lug Nut squeezed in between his legs.

Daisy gave a squeal, squirmed out of Tucker's arms, and wrapped herself around the pup. Lug Nut dropped on the floor, presenting his belly for a rub.

"You're shameless, dog. Brant's turned you into a sissy." Still, he said, "Daisy Elizabeth, this disaster of a dog is staying with us tonight—but no eating his food."

"I won't. It made my belly hurt."

"Yeah, I know." He eyed his rug. He should probably send it to the cleaners. "Lug Nut, say hi to Daisy."

The dog actually shocked him by rolling onto all fours and extending a paw.

Daisy giggled. "Can I keep him?"

"Afraid not, kiddo." He laid a hand on her shoulder. "We're just babysitting him for a couple of nights."

For a second, those Kewpie-doll lips drooped. Then, wrapping her arms around Tucker's legs, she asked, "Can he sleep with me?"

"We'll have to talk to your mother about that." Since Elisa stood in the kitchen doorway, he lifted his eyes to hers. "What do you say?"

"I doubt it matters what I say. I have a sneaking suspicion he'll end up in her bed regardless."

"Smart mama."

Daisy wrapped her arms around Elisa's legs. "Thanks, Mommy."

She tousled the little girl's hair. "You're very welcome."

One hand clutching Lug Nut's ear, Daisy Elizabeth turned to Tucker. When she held out her arms, Tucker picked her up. She patted his head. "Your hair isn't soft like Mommy's. It's all tickly."

"And it's dirty. Me too. I stink."

Daisy giggled. "No, you don't, Tut."

"Why don't you clean up before we eat?" Elisa nodded at the bag. "I'll set that in the kitchen. Up high," she added, catching Lug Nut's interest in it.

Daisy's arms in a stranglehold around his neck, he leaned toward Elisa and gave her a peck on the cheek. "You're an angel."

"A pretty angel." Daisy leaned to kiss her mama's cheek, too.

"You got that right." Unable to stop himself, he fixed his gaze on Elisa and went in for one more kiss. Her cheek wouldn't do this time, though. Those lips had been on his mind all day.

She didn't pull away.

Her lips were soft and sweet. His eyes closed, and the kiss lasted longer than he'd meant.

Daisy patted his cheek. "I want a kiss, too."

Breathing labored, Tucker pulled away, meeting Elisa's eyes. He said a quick prayer of thanks when he read desire in them, a desire that matched his own.

"Tut?"

"Yeah." He gave Daisy a buss on the cheek, then set her on her feet. Glancing toward the pup, he said, "See if you can keep him from eating the sofa while I'm upstairs."

"I think we can handle that. Here. Take this up with you." Elisa, looking slightly dazed, handed him a tall, cold glass of sweet tea.

"Oh yeah, an angel through and through." He fought the urge to steal another kiss, grabbed the tea, and loped upstairs to the lure of hot water and soap.

When he strolled from his bedroom, showered and changed, he felt like a new man. From downstairs, he heard voices, giggles, and Lug Nut's yapping.

Passing Elisa's open bedroom door, he stopped. The room smelled different. Sexy. Would he ever stand in this doorway again without smelling her? Without imagining her in his bed?

Without remembering the taste of those sweet lips?

He stared at the open suitcase on the bed. At the lingerie on top with its lace and soft colors—so feminine—and all worn next to her skin. His knuckles whitened on the doorframe. Dangerous thoughts.

When he hit the bottom step, Daisy and Lug Nut were hunkered on the floor together. She was telling him a story about a frog named Archie, so Tucker moved into the kitchen.

"I need to say this." Elisa's face flushed.

"If it's about that kiss—"

She laughed. "No. That?" She sighed. "Well, let me just say that you seem to do everything well. Very well." A blush traveled up and over her face. "This is about the other night. I want to say thanks. I dumped a lot of heavy stuff on you, way more than you ever bargained for."

He flashed back to her body against his, her curves beneath his T-shirt, and took a deep breath. "It was my pleasure. I mean—"

She chuckled, and he gave in to a grin. "I think we both needed an ear, Elisa. You helped me, too, so don't give it another thought."

He knew he wouldn't listen to his own advice, though. Throughout the past two days, he'd found himself thinking about Elisa and Daisy and what a raw deal they'd had. That guy she'd married had been a real loser.

She nodded at the bag. "Tomorrow night's my turn."

"Good enough."

"I hope so," she muttered.

"Why don't we eat al fresco tonight? I'll wipe off the table." He grabbed a cloth and stepped through the back door.

Outside, he stopped, eyes closed. Elisa Danvers fanned a fire in him that he'd thought long dead. Even his house held a different aura. He wasn't certain how he felt about any of it. He sure hadn't had a moment's peace since she and her daughter had wheeled into the Wylder Rides parking lot.

And work? Whew. But in a couple of days, they'd have the Vette finished and Murdoch on his knees, weeping with gratitude.

Right now, he needed to feed his girls.

Whoa. His girls? Nope. Never.

Guests. They were guests, plain and simple.

When he stepped back inside, Elisa was sitting on the sofa, Daisy Elizabeth tucked in beside her, Lug Nut at their feet. They were reading *The Princess and the Pea*. The scene was way too domestic, and he didn't dare let himself get caught up in it. Once he had her car fixed, they'd be gone and his life would settle back into its routine.

"Ready to eat?"

"I am." Elisa closed the book. "Did I tell you Tansy Elliot stopped by with her daughter, Gracie Bella, after she closed her bakery for the day?"

"No," Tucker said. "But her husband was at the shop today. He said she'd probably come visit."

"The girls got along great. So good, in fact, that Tansy's picking Daisy up Saturday afternoon for a playdate at their house."

"Gracie Bella's got kitties," Daisy said. "I like kitties."

"And I really liked Tansy," Elisa said.

"She and Beck are both great people. He runs the local lumber yard and hardware store."

"That's what she said. Your client flies in day after tomorrow for his car, doesn't he?"

"Yep."

"Is it done?"

Holding his thumb and index finger a paper-width apart, he said, "We're this close. Gav's putting in another hour or so tonight, and we'll work like dogs tomorrow. By the time Murdoch shows up, that car will be a thing of beauty and run like a charm."

"Good."

"Want to help me set the table, little one?"

"Yep." Daisy bounced to the edge of the sofa and crawled off, Lug Nut on her heels.

Following Tucker into the kitchen, she peppered him with questions. "Have you seen Gracie Bella's kitties?"

"Nope, I haven't had that pleasure."

"How come you were all dirty?"

"Because I was working."

"Mommy doesn't get dirty when she works." She scrunched her face. "Except when she works in her garden. Do you have a garden?"

"Sort of."

"Mommy wouldn't let me go outside by myself 'cause of the water. I could fall in."

"That's true."

"Did your mommy let you play outside?"

He held his hands over his head and mimicked an exploding bomb, sound effects and all.

"Why'd you do that?" she asked.

Instead of answering, he handed her paper plates.

"We're eating outside tonight."

"But not by the water." She looked at him solemnly. "'Cause I don't want to drown."

"What is with this preoccupation with the water?"

"What's *pweopation* mean?"

"It means let's get this done."

"'Kay."

He grabbed napkins, silverware, and the food and followed her and the dog outside. Elisa carried their drinks. The evening was one of those fall nights when all seemed well with the world—if you didn't count a nonstop chatterer underfoot and a barking dog who chased shadows across the lawn.

Inside five minutes, they sat around the table on his back patio, enjoying their take-out.

"This is wonderful, Tuck."

He nodded, studying her. Elisa definitely needed someone to take care of her, but he wasn't the one to do that. He was a catch-and-release guy from the get-go.

For tonight, though, they could all simply enjoy the evening. Even Lug Nut seemed to appreciate the peace. He curled up beside Daisy's chair, tail thumping loudly in the grass as crumbles of Dee-Ann's meatloaf accidentally-on- purpose rained down on him.

Tucker ignored it. For every piece that went to the pup, a bite or two went into Daisy's own mouth, and that was good enough—until Lug Nut jumped up and ran across the yard with a piece of meat in his mouth.

"Where's he going?" Daisy asked.

"I don't—Oh no!" Tucker slid back his chair.

Lug Nut was digging a hole in the yard Tucker had worked so hard to restore.

"Lug Nut! Stop!"

"Stop, Luggie."

Daisy started across the yard, but Elisa grabbed her. "Stay here."

A yipping Lug Nut followed an angry Tucker back to the table. "Stupid dog."

"He's not stupid."

Tucker hung his head. "No, he isn't, Daisy, but don't give him any more food, okay?"

"What was he doing?"

"Burying his meatloaf. For later."

"Why?"

"Because he's a dog, and that's what they do."

"Oh."

"Yeah, *oh*."

Lug Nut remained hopeful, though, and stayed close to Daisy for the rest of the meal. A couple of times Elisa shook her head, and a bite of food that had been making its way to the dog went into her daughter's mouth instead.

The stream was running after yesterday's rain. It was a happy sound, especially when combined with Daisy's delighted giggles as she and Lug Nut chased fireflies around the yard after dinner. Elisa had added a candle to the table, and the flickering light danced off her hair. He reached across the table and took her hand, kissed the palm, and smiled when she didn't pull away.

When the air turned chilly, they decided to call it a night. Elisa made coffee and plated the apple pecan cake Tansy had brought while Tucker, Daisy, and Lug Nut cleared the table out back. Their happy chatter made her almost unbearably sad.

Daisy had never known her father. Lately, with daddies coming to preschool to pick up her friends, she'd been asking about her own. Now her little girl was fast falling for this man who'd taken them in. If they stayed much longer, leaving would break her heart. Their hearts.

Luke had made so many promises. He'd claimed he'd love Elisa for eternity and beyond. Never having had love, she'd fallen hook, line, and sinker. Then, when she needed him most, he'd walked without so much as a backward glance. He'd abandoned her, just like her parents had.

She'd survived before, and she and her daughter would do fine when it came time to leave here.

When Tucker and Daisy walked into the room, she almost recanted that idea. Tucker Wylder could be featured on the cover of *People* magazine's Sexiest Man Alive cover with those high cheekbones, that narrow waist, and broad shoulders. Though he claimed to be ex-military, the man still had Marine written all over him.

A tattoo peeked out from the sleeve of his T-shirt.

"Can I be nosy?"

"Depends. What do you want to know?"

"Your tattoo. What's it say?"

An embarrassed flush reddened his neck. "Mama."

"Mama?"

"I got it on my twenty-first birthday, and I was drunk as a skunk."

"And it was your mother you thought of."

He shrugged. "Guess so." He peeled back the hem of his sleeve to show her the black and gray infinity sign with the word *Mama* incorporated into it.

Right then and there, Elisa permanently lost a tiny piece of her heart to this rugged guy who loved his mother. Lucky him to have a mother who loved him back.

"I'll confess to snooping today," she said.

His brows shot up.

"I saw the swing you're making. It's gorgeous."

"It's for her." He tapped his tattoo.

"For your mom? A lot of heart-work's gone into it, hasn't it?"

"You mean hard work?"

"No, heart-work."

He shrugged, but Elisa knew she'd hit the bull's-eye.

"This is none of my business, either, but it's probably something I should have asked before. Do you have a girlfriend, Tucker? Someone who's upset about Daisy and me staying with you? For a few days," she added quickly.

"No. The answer's that simple. There's no one." His brow arched. "Why do you ask?"

"I don't want to cause you any problems."

Those hazel eyes turned cool. "You're not. As a Marine, I had no control over where I went or when I went. What I ate or when I slept. Now I own a big house and I live alone. That's the way I like it. Nobody makes decisions for me, and there's nobody I'm accountable to."

If he were Elisa, he'd run like hell. She'd asked a simple question, and he'd pretty much shut her down. Without a word, she'd moved into the living room.

Tucker went back to the door and held it open. He whistled, and Lug Nut bounded through, headed to his water bowl. While he lapped happily, Daisy bounced into the kitchen, dragging a blanket.

She apparently hadn't gotten the memo to stay away from Oscar the Grouch.

"Can I have some cake?"

The dessert Elisa had plated sat on the counter. "Sure." Maybe he could use it to make amends. "Should we go in and keep Mommy company?"

"Uh-huh."

Elisa eyed him warily when he walked into the living room.

"I come bearing gifts and an apology. I'm sorry."

"There's nothing to be sorry for. What you do and when you do it isn't my business. You were one hundred percent right."

"Still—"

"It's okay," she said.

Her daughter threw her a cat-that-ate-the-canary smile. "Tut said I could have a piece, so I picked the biggest one."

Elisa shook her head. "That's my little conniver."

Daisy twirled on one foot, her plate wobbling.

"Sit down with that, Daisy, but not on the floor. Lug Nut can't have any."

With a sigh, she sat down on the footstool.

Tucker held out a plate to Elisa. "I brought one for you."

"Oh, I'm full. I don't think—"

"A bedtime snack."

One bite and she made a small sound of pleasure. "It's like a piece of heaven in my mouth."

"Yeah, it is." With effort, he shook off his mood. He noticed Daisy had abandoned her cake. "What have you got there, shorty?"

"My doll. But I can't get her dress on." She dropped it on his lap.

Dress her doll? A live grenade wouldn't be any scarier.

"I can do that," Elisa piped up. "Bring Cindy to me, baby."

"No," she whined. "I want Tut to do it."

"Tuck's worked all day. He's tired."

Daisy stomped her foot, the sweet little girl disappearing as bedtime drew near.

"I've got it." One deep breath, and he picked up the doll. Flicking a finger at her shorn locks, he said, "I think Cindy needs a trip to Frenchie's."

"Who's Fwenchie?" Daisy asked.

"The beauty shop."

"But Cindy's already bootiful."

"Yes, she is." He couldn't help himself. He glanced at Elisa as he said it. Big mistake. Her eyes turned misty. Sliding the dress over the doll's head, he said, "I think it's time both you ladies head up to bed."

"I'm not tired."

He turned the doll and, with fingers suddenly big and clumsy, managed to slip the tiny buttons into even tinier buttonholes. "Mommy said something about baking tomorrow. A shame you won't be able to help her."

"Yes, I can."

Tucker slowly shook his head. "Nope, I'm afraid not. In order to help you need eight hours of sleep. That's the rule."

"I can do that."

"I don't think so."

"Why?" The little girl's eyes had grown huge.

Tucker turned his wrist to check his watch. "You'd have to go to bed now, and you said you can't."

"Yes, I can, can't I, Mommy?" She grabbed her doll off his lap and scooted toward the stairs. "Help me put on my pajamas, Mommy."

Elisa and Tucker shared a moment of victory.

"Chalk one up," she said softly.

When she came back downstairs, he frowned. "What's wrong?"

"Me."

"You?"

"Yes, me. I mean, what am I going to do? I've wrestled with this till I can't see straight. I have a child I'm responsible for. But I have no job and no home. How could I have let this happen?" She buried her face in her hands, but she didn't cry. "And that sounds so pathetic." She made a frustrated sound. "Sorry. It's not your problem, Tuck. I'll figure it out."

He made the mistake of taking a good look at her and saw the tears pooling in her eyes. Her hand trembled as she swiped at them. "What? You need some juice or something? One of those glucose tablets Doc gave you?"

"No." Big fat tears rolled down her cheeks. "I try so hard, but this...this was a serious mistake. If I'd passed out at the wheel, we'd have wrecked. Daisy could have been—" Her voice broke.

Feeling as clumsy as an ox, he laid his hands on her shoulders. Women and tears about unmanned him. Then she burrowed into him, her tears wetting his shirt, and he pulled her closer, wrapping his arms around her.

"*Shhh*. It's okay. Daisy's fine. You're fine. According to Doc, all this goes with the territory. The hypoglycemia scrambles your brain and makes you confused. It's not your fault."

"But—"

"There are no buts and no blame-casting, Elisa. None of this is your fault."

Still, she cried and he held her. Finally, she straightened, knuckling her tears away.

"Time for bed. Night, Tuck."

"Good night, Elisa. Sleep well."

If she did, that would make one of them because he sure as heck wouldn't sleep tonight. He understood only too well what it was to feel responsible for someone else...and to fail.

CHAPTER 7

EVERYBODY SLEPT THROUGH THE NIGHT, INCLUDING Lug Nut. No bad dreams and no chewed-up shoes. For that, Tucker was beyond grateful. Today was a big day.

Between work and home, Thursday had disappeared in a rush. Gaven had sent a text at midnight. Things had gone well, but they still had a few ends to tie up before Murdoch came for his car—and one of them needed to meet their client at the Savannah/Hilton Head International Airport.

The dog at his heels, Tucker secured the gate across the top of the stairs, then slipped quietly out the door into the early morning. The sun hadn't yet poked its head over the horizon, but he ached for a cup of coffee. He'd stop at Tommy's Texaco station for one, though, rather than rattle around the kitchen. Elisa and Daisy were still both sound asleep, and he figured if the imp woke first, she'd crawl into bed with her mom.

Despite himself, that's exactly where his mind—and other body parts—headed. Straight into that warm, cozy bed with Elisa. After their late-night chats, he knew the shape of her body, how her curves would fit with his. His fingertips knew the texture of her skin, the swell of her hips, and the knowing only made it harder.

He rubbed his tired eyes. Elisa Danvers was strictly hands-off. Any day now, she'd be gone.

As he rounded the corner and caught sight of the Texaco sign in all its shabby glory, he felt like a man lost in the wilderness who'd somehow found his way back to civiliza-tion. Back to a world he knew and understood.

Unlocking the door of Wylder Rides, Tucker turned on the lights, fed Lug Nut, and made himself another cup of coffee on the fancy machine Brant had bought. After a couple of quick swallows, he got to work polishing the last bit of chrome. Snagging their checklist off the bul-letin board, he ran through it one last time, paying atten-tion to the tiniest details. Murdoch had spared no expense. Restoration work could be tedious, but it was totally worth it when a project turned out like this one.

By the time Gaven, who'd lost the coin toss, pulled in with Murdoch, the Vette looked better than it had when its original owner drove it off the new-car lot.

"Quite a place you have here." Murdoch ran a hand over the sleek old pumps. He snapped a few quick pictures, focusing on the flying Pegasus over the door. "It would make a great movie location."

"It's a working shop."

"Yeah, I get that. Still… I might want to change your minds one of these days."

"And maybe you can," Tucker said. "One of these days."

"Do these pumps work?" Murdoch asked.

"Nah. They were here, so we kept them. Since we work on vintage machines, they fit well."

"Yeah, they do." Murdoch took another picture. "Sorry I missed all this before. Guess I should have come to make arrangements with you myself instead of sending my assis-tant." He shook his head. "Live and learn."

Tucker nodded. "Want to see your car?"

"Do I ever!"

Gaven threw open the bay door, and Tucker drew off the cover. Speechless, Murdoch took two steps toward the car, then stopped, his gaze traveling over it. Then with a whoop of joy, he practically crawled over every inch of the Vette, laughing and talking nonstop.

He took photo after photo of the car, of himself with the car, of him with each of the Wylder brothers separately beside it, and finally of the three of them using his camera timer. Murdoch lifted the hood and peered in, poking around and grinning. The big-time Hollywood producer acted like a kid on Christmas morning.

When he finally left to drive back to Savannah, Tucker felt worn to a frazzle by his enthusiasm.

"Think he'll give it to the car hauler tonight or decide to sleep in it?" Tucker asked.

Gaven grinned. "Your bet's as good as mine. We did well, Bro." He held up a hand and shared a high-five.

"My guess is that we'll get a call from one of his buddies for another job."

"Oh yeah." Gaven rotated his shoulders. "I'm bushed. What do you say we call it a day? Go home and relax."

Tucker shot him a cool look. "You're kidding, right?"

"What? We've logged enough hours for two weeks." He glanced toward the raggedy Ford Escort. "Don't tell me you want to start on that tonight."

"No, I most assuredly do not. But while you're heading home to a cold beer and a night to yourself, I'm walking into a zoo."

"Ms. Danvers and the kid."

"Yep."

As if to remind him that wasn't all, Lug Nut galloped

over and stuck his nose in Tucker's crotch. He pushed him away. "You make me nervous when you do that, dog."

Gaven grinned. "Don't suppose you want to hear about tonight's date."

"Nope."

"Or how late I intend to sleep tomorrow."

"Definitely not."

"Or about—"

"Keep it up, Gav, and I'll sic Lug Nut on you."

"Oooh, now I'm scared." Still, Gaven snatched his keys from the counter and started toward the door. "Coming?" he called over his shoulder.

"In a minute. Got a couple of things to wrap up."

"See you Monday."

Relieved to have the Vette finished and delivered, Tucker rubbed the pup's head and watched his brother drive off in his truck. "A few minutes more, Lug, then we'll go."

He sat down at the desk in the front office, and the dog draped himself across his feet. Pulling up his laptop, Tucker typed in *hypoglycemia*. When it popped up on the screen, he scanned the information. Okay. Exactly what the doc had said. Elisa should be good to go once her car was up and running.

But since it wasn't, that meant no fishing trip and no quiet solitary time. Instead, he headed home to two females and a frisky pup who stuck his head between the bucket seats and panted in Tucker's ear.

When he opened the door, a grinning Daisy ran from the dining room to greet him. "Tut! I missed you!"

"Missed you, too, imp." He bent to swoop her up, nearly dropped her when she wrapped those tiny arms around him and gave him a big, sloppy kiss.

"You were right, Tut."

"Of course I was."

Elisa, standing in the dining room doorway, snorted. "Men. You're all alike, aren't you?"

"I don't know. Some of us are handsomer than others. Smarter than others."

"Too big for your britches, I'd say."

Daisy leaned sideways and stared at his pants. "Too big?"

"Your mommy's teasing, sweetie."

"No, I'm not." But the smile on Elisa's face gave her away.

"We made cookies. Since I went to bed like a big girl, Mommy letted me help."

"Nice." Tucker met Elisa's gaze. "What kind did you make?"

"Pumpkins. 'Cause it's 'Tober." She wiggled out of his arms and ran into the kitchen.

"Tober?" Brows raised, he looked at Elisa.

"October."

"Ahh. Sure." He watched Lug Nut make himself at home in the expensive cream-colored leather chair, burrow into the yellow afghan tossed haphazardly on it, and forced himself to let it go. Next week he'd take both the throw and his rug to the dry cleaners and have his cleaning lady in. All would be well.

In the meantime, he'd bite his tongue and do a lot of deep-breathing.

"Good job," Elisa said.

"What? Because the mutt crawled into my best chair?"

"No, because you didn't cry when he did."

Before he could answer, Daisy tore around the corner, a cookie held out in front of her. Lug Nut, smelling dessert, hopped off the chair and snagged it, wolfing it down in two bites.

Daisy stood, hand still outstretched, absolutely silent for all of three seconds. Then her lower lip trembled and she started to cry.

"It's okay, honey. We have more."

"But it was for Tut." Heartbroken, she sobbed.

Tears streamed from those big eyes, and Tucker threw in what was left of the shredded surrender towel. "Lug Nut played piggy."

"Bad doggie." She shook her finger at him. "You ate Tut's pumpkin."

Still licking his lips, the pup actually hung his head and slunk into the corner by the fireplace.

"Guess you told him." Tucker reached for her hand. "Let's go into the kitchen and see if we can find another one."

"'Kay."

Daisy skipped beside Tucker as they moved hand in hand toward the sweet smells of vanilla and pumpkin.

He stared at the sugar cookies. Each one, a work of art, had been turned into a unique jack-o'-lantern.

"Wow. These are incredible."

The little girl scampered around the kitchen island and surveyed her work with all the pride of a grand master. "Mommy rolled the dough, then I cutted them out, didn't I?" She looked at her mother for affirmation.

"You sure did. One of the best cutter-outers ever."

Daisy's smile nearly blinded him.

"It's okay to eat these?"

"It would be a shame not to. Of course, if you don't want them, that crazy dog will take care of them."

"Not if he wants to live."

"Pick!" Daisy clapped her hands.

"Oooh, this is gonna be hard." He made a big production of studying them, his hand hovering over one, then another. "How about this one?" He reached for one with a big smile and triangle eyes. "No, this is the one." He picked up an orange cookie, the jack-o'-lantern's eyes evil black and yellow. "He doesn't look like a very nice fellow. I say we take him down. How about it?"

Daisy grinned and held out her hand.

Tucker snapped the cookie cleanly down the middle, handed her half, and said, "Ready? One, two, three!"

They each bit into their half, laughing like loons. Tucker caught a loose crumb with his tongue. "As great as these look, they taste even better."

"Which one, Mommy?"

"Which one what?"

Daisy released a long, very put-upon sigh. "Which cookie do you want?"

"Let me pick one for you," Tucker said. "How about—" He considered, reconsidered. "This one." He picked up one with a surprised expression.

"It needs blue eyes," Daisy said.

"I can take care of that." Elisa took it from him, rooted around in the fridge, and came back with a disposable icing bag with pale blue frosting. She went to work and turned the big round eyes into big *blue* eyes.

"Perfect."

"It looks just like you, Mommy." She pulled the skirt of her plaid dress up to her mouth, showing off the black leggings she wore beneath.

"Put your dress down, Daisy Elizabeth. Remember?"

The child made a face, but the dress dropped back into place.

While they ate their cookies and drank ice-cold milk, Elisa asked, "Did you get the Vette finished? Did Mr. Murdoch love it?"

"We did, and he did. When he pulled onto the highway heading to Savannah, he was grinning like the Cheshire cat. That was after he gave us one heck of a bonus. Since Brant's not here, Gav and I made an executive decision to split the money three ways and actually use it as a bonus, rather than pumping it back into the business."

"That's what he'd do?"

"Without a doubt. Normally, I would, too. Thing is, I want to make an office in the attic, and this bonus will start that ball rolling. It might be selfish, but there you go."

"I don't think it's selfish. You worked hard for that money." She turned to her daughter, who was pawing through a drawer. "Daisy, get out of there. This isn't our house, and those aren't our things."

With a little pout, Daisy closed the drawer.

Tucker grabbed the child around the waist and hoisted her onto his shoulders.

She let out a little squeal, then started to giggle. "Look, Mommy. I'm tall."

"You sure are."

"How about I plop Daisy in front of the TV for five minutes while I scrub some of this dirt off me." He tipped his head. "You like pizza, imp?"

"I love pizza. But I don't like the hot things on it."

"Peppers? Or pepperoni?" He glanced at Elisa.

"Peppers. She loves pepperoni."

"I do love 'roni, Tut."

"Lots of cheese?"

"Uh-huh. Can I get a pumpkin?"

"A pumpkin?" Tucker asked. "On your pizza?"

Her blond curls flew when she shook her head. "No! To put a candle in."

"Oh, sure. After I'm cleaned up, I'll phone in an order from Mama's Pizza and Wings."

———————

Shaved, showered, and changed, he headed downstairs not more than ten minutes later.

"Tut, I've been waitin'." Daisy flew to the door. "'M'on, Tut."

"The pizza's not ready yet. I haven't even called it in."

"I know."

"Where are we rushing off to?" He dropped onto the sofa.

She sighed impatiently, hands on her hips. "To the store."

"Why?"

"For a pumpkin. Like on TV. 'Member?"

"Now?"

"You promised."

"*Promised* is a strong word. Besides, I didn't say now. I just said—" Truth? He couldn't quite remember. He went kind of brain-dead when he was in the same room as this child's mother.

The pout made an appearance.

He ignored it.

The lower lip trembled.

Springing up, he stuffed his feet into his shoes and grabbed his keys and wallet from the end table. "Elisa, want to ride into town with us? Catch some fresh air?"

"I think I would." Elisa smiled. "Yes."

Daisy bounced up and down. "Tut's buying us pumpkins."

He held up a finger. "One. One pumpkin."

When the lower lip went to work again, he manned up. "One or none. Your choice."

She dragged the side of her shoe over his beautiful, expensive hardwood floor. Inwardly, he winced, but he held his tongue.

"'Kay."

Tucker studied her. That was way too easy, which meant this was a temporary ceasefire. When they got to the store, there was a better than even chance the battle would flare up again. Well, he'd handle that if and when.

"We're gonna carve a face, Mommy, and put a candle in it. Then we'll put it on the steps."

The conniver slid her hand into his and smiled up at him. No doubt about it. She was already an expert at plying those feminine wiles.

"Outside," he said. "On the outside steps."

"Outside," she echoed.

Elisa said nothing.

"What?"

"This doesn't sound like the kind of thing you'd normally do, Tuck."

"It's not, but—"

"You can't give in to her all the time."

"Understood."

Still, he understood that without the slightest warning, he'd waded right into quicksand.

Lug Nug raised a fuss at being left behind. He howled, he whined, and in the end, he rode into town with them, keeping Daisy company in the backseat. She babbled nonstop, Lug Nut barking once in a while as though answering her. Whatever, Tucker decided. As long as the kid was happy.

When he parked, though, Tucker realized he'd have to leave the pup in the car. "Listen, dog. No chewing and no messes, you hear?"

Lug Nut gave an affirmative bark.

Tucker rubbed the back of his neck, massaging the stress-tightened muscles, then freed an excited Daisy from her seat.

"Why can't Luggie come with us?"

"Animals aren't allowed in grocery stores."

"Why?"

"Because it's the rules."

"Why?"

He closed his eyes and counted to ten.

"I'll stay here with Lug Nut and protect your car, Tucker," Elisa said.

"You're sure?"

"Absolutely. It's a beautiful night. If you don't mind braving the store alone with Daisy, I'm more than happy to sit here and enjoy a few minutes' peace and quiet."

"You're on." He turned to Daisy. "How big do you want this pumpkin to be, kid?"

She held out her arms, forming a circle. "This big."

"Okay, let's get it done."

They found the pumpkin display in the produce section, and Daisy danced around it excitedly. "Aren't they bootiful, Tut?"

"They sure are."

Someone tapped him on the shoulder and he swung around, nearly bumping noses with Brinna from Doctor Hawkins's office.

"Brinna!" Daisy Elizabeth threw her arms around the woman's knees. "I missed you."

Brinna wore a short, swingy black skirt and a bright red top. She knelt to give Daisy a hug. "Hi, sweetie. You buying a new coloring book?"

Daisy shook her head. "Tut's buying me a pumpkin. We're gonna make a face on it. Want to come home with us and help?"

Tucker nearly swallowed his tongue. Had this child really just invited Brinna to his house? For pity's sake. He opened his mouth to speak, but Brinna, standing again, held out a hand.

"Sorry, sweetie. That sounds like fun, but I can't. Not tonight." She tucked a strand of hair behind her ear.

"Why?"

"I have to go home to let my doggie out."

"We have a doggie, too, don't we, Tut?"

"For a few days. I'm dog-sitting for my brother," Tucker explained.

Brinna smiled. "Quite the do-gooder, aren't you?"

"Not really. This past week's been kind of like the perfect storm, and I ended up with a houseful of refugees."

"What's a 'fugee, Tut?"

"Ah…" He cleared his throat. "Unexpected company."

"Mommy and me and Lug Nut?"

"Exactly."

"Can we buy our pumpkin now?"

"We sure can," he said, thankful for the diversion. "See you later, Brinna."

"I'd like that."

With a silent groan, Tucker turned his attention to the bin. Daisy had hoisted herself up and was hard at work looking for her very own great pumpkin. The one he'd have to carve. He supposed he'd better pick up a candle while they were here…and maybe a carving knife.

He did not do this stuff.

Dinner went well. Daisy fed her pizza crusts to Lug Nut, who'd camped out beneath the table.

"Daisy Elizabeth, do not give that dog any more food."

"Sorry, Luggie. Mommy says no more."

Lug Nut whined and dropped to the floor, splayed out like a limp dishcloth.

"He's sad, Mommy."

"He's a pig," Tucker said.

Affronted, Daisy said, "No, he's not. He's a doggie."

Tucker laughed. "Yeah, guess you're right, but he's a moocher."

"What's that?"

"Somebody who's always trying to get something for nothing."

After dinner, they moved to the living room to watch

TV. Halfway through the third show about a Korean bunny and her best friend—some baby chick—Daisy fell fast asleep, her head in her mother's lap and her feet on Tucker's.

Elisa brushed the baby-fine hair off her daughter's forehead. "To be so young and innocent again."

Tucker's mind went straight to the things he'd seen and done in the Middle East. "Yeah. I'd give everything I have and everything I ever will have."

Her gaze moved slowly from her daughter to him. "What's wrong, Tuck?"

He gave a dismissive shake of his head. "I'm fine."

Her hard stare told him she saw right through that bit of BS.

Monday night when she'd come downstairs and found him on the back porch, he'd come close to sharing the demons that kept him awake at night. He'd blamed it on the dark, the late hour. Truth? It was Elisa. Something about the woman made it easy to share secrets.

"Would you like a quick update on your car?"

"Smooth change of subject," she mumbled.

"I thought so. I'll start on it tomorrow. Sorry we couldn't get to it sooner, but Gav and I have been up to our necks."

"I know, and we've added to your problems."

He could barely keep his eyes off Elisa. Even after the rough week she'd had, she was the most beautiful woman he'd ever seen.

And those kinds of thoughts could get a man in trouble.

"I'll pay you for—"

"For nothing."

Her back stiffened. "Labor and parts aren't cheap. I

also owe you room and board for Daisy and me. We're not moochers."

"Oh, for—I was talking about Lug Nut, not you! The damn dog's always begging for food. Totally different situation."

"Hmmm. I'm not so sure." Twin spots of color bloomed on her cheeks.

His temper flared. "Do you honestly think I'd take money from you?"

"Why not? Before this week you didn't know I existed." Her blush deepened. "Tuck—"

"Let's table it for tonight." He moved Daisy's feet slowly to the side and stood. "Time for bed. I'll carry her up."

She opened her mouth to argue, but he shook his head. "Not debatable. Neither is the money. I'm not gonna take it, so don't offend me by offering it again."

Some of the fire in her eyes dimmed, but he swore he heard wheels turning.

"Okay, how about this? I'm a librarian. Or I was until they cut our funding. I'm good, extremely good, at organizing. Since you won't take money, why don't I spend a day at your shop? I'll organize both it and your books...or your billing system."

He blinked. Mess with his system, his books? Not in this lifetime. "I have things under control."

"Oh, but—"

"Elisa, this is one of those nonnegotiables."

"Then I'll simply say thank you, and I'll put Daisy to bed. Myself." With that, she scooped up her daughter and made for the stairs.

"Not like this." Tucker took Daisy from her, then leaned

in and kissed her. She tasted like fire and ice. Still angry, she tried to hold back, but when his lips touched hers the second time, she wrapped her hand around his neck and pulled him closer.

Daisy stirred in his arms, and they each took a step back. "I'd say I'm sorry," he said, "but it would be a lie."

CHAPTER 8

DESPITE THE FACT HE'D BARELY SLEPT, THE SUN STILL rose Saturday morning. Tucker gave himself a few minutes to mourn the lost weekend before he crawled out of bed. No fishing trip, no drowned worms, and no head-time. His fingers involuntarily reached for the ever-present key. The one Nate had pressed into his hand one sweltering night when they'd lain in their bunks, sweating, eating the dust that filtered in, and ever-alert for incoming.

Nate had made Tucker promise that if anything happened to him, Tucker would keep an eye on the cabin and use it once in a while.

He'd meant to keep that promise today, but Elisa had derailed him. Well, he'd get started on her car instead. Once Doc Hawkins gave her the green light, Tucker didn't want anything holding her here.

If only she didn't look at him through those haunted eyes…or smell so good…or taste like heaven itself.

Enough.

Down the hall, he heard Daisy, then Elisa. The day had begun.

The three of them slogged through the first half hour, with Elisa finally insisting she fix breakfast while he and Daisy started a load of laundry. It wasn't long till the house smelled of roasted red pepper omelets, toast, and fabric softener.

"I'm gonna play with Gracie Bella today."

"Yes, you are." Tucker popped another bite of omelet in his mouth. "Will the kitties be there?"

"Uh-huh, and Gracie Bella said I could hold them."

"Woo-hoo."

"Tuck," Elisa warned.

He grinned. "What? I meant that. Woo-hoo. Kids and cats. What more could anyone want?"

She pointed her fork at him. "Behave."

"Yeah, Tut, behave. Otherwise Mommy will punish you."

"Oh yeah?" He threw Elisa a devilishly sexy smile. "You gonna punish me?"

"I believe I am." She pushed away her plate. "You can clean up while I get Daisy ready for her playdate."

He frowned. "Not quite what I had in mind."

"I know, but that's the best I've got."

"I seriously doubt that." He met her gaze and held it.

When her cheeks reddened, he had the audacity to laugh.

"Come on, Daisy. Let's get you dressed." Elisa stood, hand out to her daughter.

"'Kay. Can I wear my kitty sweater?"

While they headed upstairs, Tucker, stuffed to the gills, began setting the kitchen to rights.

In under half an hour, Daisy knelt on the floor by the window, watching for her ride. When Tansy finally pulled in out front, she jumped up. "They're here, Mommy. They came."

"Of course they did. They promised, sweetie."

The bell rang and Daisy bolted toward the door, then stopped and looked at Tucker.

"Can I open it, Tut?"

He swallowed his smile. "Yes, you can. We know who's there. And Daisy?"

"Yeah?"

"Thanks for asking."

She sent him that angelic smile, and his own heart smiled in return. Then he made the mistake of looking at her mama, whose pretty face wore an expression of happiness mixed with more than a little wistfulness. What was it about this woman that made him want to take care of her?

He wasn't anybody's protector.

Obviously, because he also wanted to do some naughty things with Elisa Danvers.

The door opened and the girls were all over each other, talking about the cats, their outfits, food, and everything under the sun. Daisy dragged Gracie Bella upstairs to see her *mooffee* bed.

If Beck had half as much sense as Tucker gave him credit for, he'd spend the day at his lumber yard.

"My cake's delivered for today's wedding," Tansy said, "and since they brought in their own high-end catering company to handle things, I'm free for the day. Is it okay if we keep Daisy till after dinner? We thought we'd roast some hot dogs on sticks, then stuff ourselves with s'mores. We'll make a day of it."

"You're sure?" Elisa asked.

"Positive."

After promising for the third time to call if Daisy had any problems, Tansy corralled the girls and drove off with them *and* Lug Nut. As far as Tucker was concerned, the woman was a saint.

"She'll be fine, Mama," Tucker said.

Elisa sighed. "I know. I trust Tansy."

"Good." He reached out for her hand. "I intended to head straight to the shop to start on your car, but it's a gorgeous day. What do you say we take a couple of hours, and I'll show you around?"

"Oh, but what if—"

He held up his cell phone. "Tansy has both my number and yours."

"I'd need to change."

"I'll wait."

Aware there was no Daisy to act as a buffer, Elisa walked downstairs in a cinnamon-colored dress that swirled around her legs, her long hair loose. She felt suddenly shy.

Tucker stood at the bottom, his eyes traveling over her. "Every minute of that wait was worthwhile."

"Thank you."

They stepped outside, and she decided Tucker had made a good call. Sunny and warm, with just that hint of autumn, the day couldn't have been more perfect. They rolled down the car windows and listened to soft rock on the radio.

"Thought you might like to see Magnolia House."

"Are you kidding? After Molly told me about how Jenni Beth's falling-down antebellum home morphed into *the* wedding destination, I'm dying to see it."

He laid his hand over hers. "They've got a big event this weekend—which is why there were no rooms at the inn or any of the hotels, but nobody will mind if we pull into the drive for a quick peek."

Tucker turned onto a lane bordered on both sides by Spanish-moss-draped live oaks that formed an overhead canopy. Sunlight filtered through, forming a lacy pattern of light and dark. When the house came into view, Elisa leaned forward, and he slowed. Huge magnolias flanked the stately plantation home.

"She's a real beauty, isn't she?"

"Oh, my gosh. This is where Molly's brides get married?"

"Most of them."

She sighed. "Thank you." Without thinking, she leaned toward him and kissed his cheek. Realizing what she'd done, she jerked away.

"Don't do that. Don't run from me."

"I'm not." She wet her lips. "It's—I don't know. That probably wasn't appropriate."

"Hmmm." He looked as if he was thinking it over. "I think that was okay, but this is even better." He caught her chin and leaned in, his eyes never leaving hers. His lips teased, brushing over hers lightly. Then he changed the angle, deepening the kiss.

His lips on hers felt so good, and he tasted delicious, all warm and male.

When he pulled away, she shook her head. "One more."

"Greedy."

"Yeah."

His lips curved in a slow smile as he lowered them to hers. She opened for him, and his tongue darted inside to dance with hers. He turned his head slightly and took the kiss deeper still, his hand moving from her waist up the side of her dress till his fingers brushed her breast.

Oh yeah, absolutely delicious.

This time, he blew out a breath as he raised his head. "And that would be inappropriate. Just so you know."

"Okay." She smiled shyly. "Thanks for clearing that up."

"My pleasure."

She raised a finger and wiped a smudge of lipstick from the side of his mouth. "Those lips should probably be registered as a lethal weapon, and I probably shouldn't have said that. I don't want you getting a big head."

Tucker laughed. "No need to worry about that. No big heads in our family. My brothers would slap it right out of me, and I'd repay the favor." He cleared his throat. "Speaking of brothers, how about we drive past Brant and Molly's house? I'll show you where they live. You haven't had a chance to see much since you've been here."

When they reached Brant's, Tucker slowed down and pulled to the side of the road.

Elisa sighed. "Look at that wraparound porch and all those wonderful oaks. Oh my gosh! They have a gazebo." She clapped her hands. "It's wonderful."

"Yeah, it is. It fits them."

"How about Gaven?"

"Sugar, I won't offend your eyes by showing you the heap he's living in."

A few miles down the road, he pulled onto the grassy verge by the river. "Give me a second."

He opened the trunk and snagged a blanket. Spreading it beneath a tree, he helped her down, his gaze never leaving her as she tucked her dress, the color of autumn leaves, around her legs. Their silence was easy.

Elisa couldn't remember when she'd felt so at peace.

If a person had to be stranded, Misty Bottoms, Georgia,

was one heck of a place for it. The small town oozed Southern charm and its people were beyond warm and welcoming. The man beside her? Although she wouldn't always call him warm, he ranked right up there at the top of the heat chart.

Even though she'd sworn off men, Tucker Wylder tempted her. Heck, he more than tempted—he'd whetted an appetite she hadn't known existed. But because of their situation, she sincerely doubted he'd do anything about it beyond the kisses they'd just shared.

What a pity.

A bird sang in one of the live oaks while an industrious bumblebee flitted from wildflower to wildflower. Tucker wrapped an arm around her, and she leaned into him, her eyes drifting shut.

When she woke, her head was in his lap.

Embarrassed, she laughed. "I am so sorry, Tucker. Believe me, it wasn't the company. I—"

"Shhh. It's okay."

When she started to sit up, he laid one of those beautiful, hard-working hands on her waist.

"Stay a few seconds longer." He stared at her. "I'm certain somebody, or lots of somebodies, have already told you this, but you are one beautiful lady, Elisa Danvers. I don't know what's wrong with the men in your hometown that they let you get away."

"You're so full of it, Tucker."

"No, ma'am. I'm a straight shooter." He shook his head. "I'm sorry, but I have to do this." He pulled her up and kissed her.

Her hand slipped beneath his T-shirt and she reveled in the feel of bare skin.

His lips left hers to travel the length of her neck, his fingers unbuttoning the top buttons on the front of her dress. Then his mouth followed those fingers and moved to her breasts. She moaned in pleasure.

"Elisa, I promised you'd be safe with me. I shouldn't..."

"You shouldn't stop." She pulled off his shirt and covered his chest in kisses.

They spread out on the blanket, him covering her, his desire for her more than evident.

A squirrel ran up the tree beside them, dislodging several fall leaves.

They landed on Tucker.

Breathing hard, he rolled off her. "Sorry. I forgot myself. That probably shouldn't have happened."

"Don't apologize, Tuck. I'm not sorry." Her fingers quickly adjusted her bra and did up her buttons.

Watching her, he rose on an elbow. "God, you look incredible. All mussed, your mouth swollen from our kisses." He ran a thumb over her breast and, even through the fabric, her nipple pebbled. "I think, though, that we're playin' with fire, darlin'."

He reached for his shirt. "What do you say we go get an ice cream cone from Dairy Queen?"

Elisa blinked. Talk about a segue. But Tucker was right. He'd made it very clear right from the beginning that he didn't do relationships. No long-term anything, but that was okay because she'd given up on that, too.

Right now, though, in this moment, she felt like a teenager spending a Saturday with her beau. Why not enjoy it?

And the ice cream.

"I'd love one."

Tucker pulled up in front of his house and taking her hand, helped Elisa from of the car. He didn't let go of her right away, because despite what he'd said earlier, her hand felt so right in his. Then she tipped her head up and her lips were right there. He quit thinking, simply lowered his head and kissed her. A sweet, spicy kiss that had his head swimming and his body begging for more.

Her hands came up to cup his face, those incredible eyes staring into his. On tiptoe, she touched her lips to his again. "I haven't had a day like today in forever. Thank you for a wonderful time…and the ice cream."

"You're entirely welcome. The grass out back is getting pretty high, so I'm gonna take a few minutes and mow in case Daisy wants to play out there."

When she went inside, he headed to the backyard, visions of sugarplums and angel kisses running through his head. And around the edges? A trace of regret at not making it to Nate's cabin.

After he finished the yard, Tucker drove to the shop. Being alone in the house with Elisa seemed a bit too dangerous with his lips still tasting of her kiss.

Despite his best efforts, he couldn't manage to get Elisa's Escort running, though. He called the auto store for a part he needed, and they promised it by Monday.

Hanging up, he called home and smiled when Elisa answered. "I'm on my way. How about I stop at Fat Baby's

Barbecue and pick up a couple of pulled pork sandwiches and salads?"

"I can put something together here."

"Nah. Don't bother. This will be easier."

They'd just cleared dinner dishes when Tansy pulled up and one tired little girl crawled out of her SUV.

While Daisy chatted nonstop about her day, Elisa herded her into the shower, then stuffed her into a set of Dora the Explorer pajamas.

"How much did you eat?" she asked playfully.

"A lot." Daisy flashed that incomparable smile.

"I wasn't sure you'd fit into these PJs."

"But I do."

"Yes, you do." She buttoned the top button, laughing when Daisy yawned. "Want to run down and give Tuck a good night kiss?"

She nodded and sat down on the top step, bumping her way down. Tucker waited at the bottom, where she threw her arms around him and gave him a happy kiss.

"How about if I carry you back upstairs?"

"Thanks, Tut. I'm tired."

After Daisy was tucked into bed, Elisa sank into the chair across from Tucker. "She had a wonderful time today."

He grinned. "Yeah, I heard. Your kid is a talker."

"She is that."

"I ran into Lucinda today at Fat Baby's. She has an open spot at her daycare."

"No. We won't be here that long."

He frowned. "It would be good for both of you, even if it's only a few days. Daisy's missing other kids her age. Today was good for her."

"It was, but the answer is still no."

Propping his feet on a leather ottoman, Tucker gave himself a second. "I understand wanting to protect what's yours. But you've got me wondering. Is there something else I should know? Someone who's coming after you? Wants you back? And Daisy?"

"No." She drew a ragged breath. "Nothing like that. No one wants us."

If he'd had a heart, Tucker swore it would have broken into a thousand pieces. But he didn't, so it didn't…and he'd swear to that on a stack of Bibles. Clearing his throat, he said, "I sincerely find that hard to believe."

She shrugged. "I already told you about Daisy's dad. After the requisite year of no contact and no support, I divorced him on grounds of abandonment."

"Good for you."

"I happen to agree. Daisy and I have been doing okay. I made enough at the library to support us, but not enough to put away more than a few dollars a week for a rainy day. Unfortunately, we ran smack-dab into the middle of one heck of a storm when I lost my job."

"And that's why you were on the road."

"Yes, headed to my mom's. Evonne Eklund. Maybe you've heard of her."

He shook his head. He didn't like Elisa's ex or her mother very much. Neither'd offered support when she'd needed it.

"Right now, she's somewhere in the jungles of Mexico." Elisa's yawn was every bit as big as her daughter's had been.

"Hey," he said quietly. "You're bushed. Let me help you upstairs."

She chuckled. "I can manage. I'm tired, not sick."

"Understood. Sounds like you've been doing a lot of managing on your own, though. How about for once you turn over the reins?"

Without another word, he swept her up in his arms, held her against his chest, and felt the tickle of her long hair brush across his arm.

She let out a little squeak of surprise.

"You'll drop me."

"Not in this lifetime, honey. You don't weigh much more than a two-month-old foal." As he pulled her closer and she draped an arm around his neck, he told himself to ignore the fact that she looked like one of the princesses in the storybooks his sister used to read.

He told himself to ignore that the scent of her did crazy things to his insides, that her kisses set him on fire. A few more days and she'd be gone.

He'd have his house back, and he'd be happy.

Neither his body nor his mind seemed to be listening to him tonight.

Elisa lay awake a long time after she heard Tucker come upstairs.

What made her open up to him? Share things she didn't mean to? No doubt he'd rub his hands in glee when he saw the last of her. She had to give the man his due, though. He'd done more for her these last few days than her family ever had.

It would be easier if he wasn't so darned good-looking. One sidelong glance from those dark eyes and she turned to mush. Fires long ago doused sprang to life inside her. Those shared kisses... Well, wow! And when he'd picked her up tonight? She'd almost swooned. But since she'd already done that—in the worst possible way—she'd kept her head about her. Sort of.

Turning onto her side, she willed herself to go to sleep. It didn't work. Since she'd finished the book she'd been reading, she'd look for another tomorrow. Not a romance, though. She already had too many visions of a dark-haired hero floating through her mind.

A couple hours later, she heard Tucker in the hall and tensed. The front door opened, then closed, and his car roared to life.

She moved to the window and stared out into the shadowy darkness. Where did he go at this time of night? What monsters did he battle?

CHAPTER 9

TUCKER YAWNED. TWO NIGHTS IN A ROW, DAWN'S BLUSH had filled the sky by the time he'd returned home. He'd dropped into bed and slept like the dead for a good hour and a half. Now? Time to find himself a cup of coffee and start the day.

With one hip leaning against the counter, he listened to the rumble of the coffee maker and breathed deeply as the aroma kick-started his brain. With that came memories of his chat with Elisa Saturday night. She'd no doubt confided way more than she'd meant to. Middle-of-the-night talks were like that. Something about the dark dropped a person's guard.

He admired the heck out of her. She was one brave woman. A fighter. But he couldn't keep her here much longer. His willpower was eroding as fast as the sand dunes during a haboob.

He wanted her.

He couldn't have her. Not while she lived in his house, under his protection. He'd provided a type of sanctuary for her and Daisy and couldn't break that trust. After Saturday's near fumble, they'd spent yesterday tiptoeing around each other.

Now here it was, Monday morning and a new week.

His first cup of coffee downed and a go-cup at the ready, he placed a hard-boiled egg center front on the top fridge shelf with a note that read *"Eat Me!"* Elisa wouldn't be able to miss it. Left to her own devices, she didn't think often enough about food—even after Doc Hawkins's admonishments to pay attention to her diet.

He slid his wallet in his back pocket, picked up his car keys, then sneaked out, hoping not to wake the girls.

Every single morning, regardless of what was happening in his life, he smiled when he rounded the corner and spotted the Wylder Rides shop.

Last January, when Brant had stumbled onto it, the place had been nothing more than an abandoned gas station in the middle of an overgrown, weed-filled lot. They'd left its vintage gas pumps out front and the old Mobil sign over the door—a true throwback to the fifties. It fit Wylder Rides to a T.

He loved restoring old cars and motorcycles and had joined his brothers in the business when he mustered out of the Marines. He'd loved being a Marine, too. Right up until he didn't. Right up until an arrogant commander, too proud to admit a mistake, had cost his four closest friends their lives while he'd been confined to base. Hard-Ass Harry had killed his pals as surely as if he'd pulled the trigger.

A band of stress tightened around Tucker's forehead. He massaged it and willed it away. It would creep back, though, in the wee hours of the night.

Well, he'd procrastinated long enough. Hood raised, Tucker studied Elisa's sorry excuse for a car. The dipstick was covered with sludge that took top honors as the dirtiest oil he'd witnessed in an engine still able to turn over. Before he returned the car to her, they'd have a long talk about basic car maintenance, something her father should have done. Maybe he'd make her a calendar and mark the required upkeep on it.

When she looked at that calendar, she'd be gone, living somewhere else. Why did that bother him so much?

Standing in the middle of the bay, he admitted that it had been a long time since he'd gone to bed wanting a woman. Not just any woman. Elisa. A woman who came with a lot of baggage.

He turned toward the office, then stopped. *She* came with baggage? What a joke. His own was enough to sink the Titanic without the help of an iceberg.

The two of them? A bad combination. Bonnie and Clyde bad. Romeo and Juliet bad. Anthony and Cleopatra bad.

Tucker and Elisa bad.

Time he got to work.

Since he had the shop to himself, he flipped on the radio and brought up his favorite Southern rock station.

Brant, who'd returned Sunday morning, had driven back to Savannah to pick up a few shop supplies. Gaven, who'd decided he might want to buy instead of rent, was spending the morning with Quinlyn. Tucker felt sorry for the Realtor—she'd have her hands full with his baby brother. If he could actually make a decision, Tucker would be very, very surprised.

He'd known exactly what he'd wanted from the moment he saw the old blacksmith shop. It was home.

Gaven? He'd be all over the map. The kid could never stick with anything. Well, except cars. Even his marriage had been a bust. He'd never said much about his breakup and divorce, but the ink had barely dried on the marriage certificate before he and his bride hung up their rings. They'd made it twenty-one days. Three short weeks. Whatever had happened stayed between him and Rita, and, as far as Tucker knew, Gav had never spoken a bad word about her.

What had his baby brother done to make Rita walk?

Twilight deepened as Tucker sat in his backyard and watched the flames rise into the sky from his new fire pit. At the edge of his property, the stream gurgled and a few brave fireflies flitted through the gathering darkness. A gentle breeze rustled the trees.

Soft candlelight from Daisy's jack-o'-lanterns spilled over the concrete patio. He'd already snuffed the two out front. The imp had somehow wheedled him into buying a second one for her mommy. When she'd insisted he needed his own, it was simply easier to cave. The cherry on top? They'd actually bought a fourth for the darned dog.

A dog that had gone back to Brant's. They'd had a few tears over that, but after he'd promised Daisy they'd visit Lug Nut, she'd finally settled down.

He shook his head. Life with Daisy Elizabeth was… interesting. And exhausting.

Tonight, though? As close to perfect as it came. He'd come home to find Elisa had fixed shrimp and grits for dinner. Now she was upstairs tucking Daisy in for the night.

He'd finished mowing the grass earlier and could still smell the fresh cut. The scent always took him back to summer days roughhousing with his brothers, of his mom and dad and picnics. Nothing smelled better. Well, except for a woman beneath him. The smell of that spot on her neck, right above her shoulder blade. Elisa's scent, subtle and feminine, innocent yet sexy as hell, drifted through his olfactory memory.

He blew out a big breath. Somehow, she'd crawled under his skin without even trying.

And those kisses? He couldn't risk any more.

He smelled her before he heard her, and his resolution wobbled when she dropped into an Adirondack chair across from him.

"Your car is a piece of crap."

"Why, thank you." She shot him a look that didn't match her words.

"I'm not kidding, Elisa. You shouldn't have been on the road with it."

"It's easy on gas, and it's paid for."

"That doesn't make it safe."

"I suppose not, but…" She spread her hands. "It's what I have. How much will it cost to fix it?"

"I thought we'd already discussed that." In the firelight's glow, he read the uneasy expression on her face. "I know money's a snag…"

"I'm not a charity case."

His jaw tightened. "Understood. I can get the parts at discount, and my time is free since we're between jobs right now."

"Tuck, you've already done so much for us."

"Do I look like I care?"

A bubble of laughter escaped. "Yes."

"I do not." He turned to her.

"Every time Daisy jumps on your sofa, you look apoplectic."

"That's not true."

"There are those pants on fire again."

"Elisa—"

"It's time for us to leave, Tuck."

His smile evaporated. "What?"

"I've had the tests and my blood sugar's under control. I'm all better. You've been wonderful, but our time here came with an expiration date. We've reached it."

Caught off-guard, he stared at her, rubbing his chest. It hurt and he couldn't breathe. Was he having a heart attack? It sure as heck wasn't because Elisa was leaving him.

No. She wasn't leaving *him*. It had never been about him.

And this pain sure as heck wasn't because he, well, felt anything for her. He didn't do feelings. Not anymore. He'd gone that route when he'd been twenty and dumb.

When his girlfriend told him she was pregnant, he'd seen his whole life, all his dreams, sink out of sight. But he'd loved Rachel and promised she wouldn't have to go it alone, that they'd get married that weekend.

Her father caught wind of their plans and insisted she visit their doctor to make sure everything was okay. She refused. The evening before their quickie wedding at the justice of the peace's office, Rachel came to him in tears. She'd lied. There was no baby.

It turned out she'd wanted a Mrs. degree from college more than a bachelor's.

They'd canceled the wedding, and he'd dropped out of college and enlisted in the Marines.

Rachel had played him like a Stradivarius, and he wasn't up for that a second time. Once burned, twice learned. To this day, he had nothing to do with anyone who lied to him or betrayed him.

"Tuck? Are you okay?"

"Yeah, sure." He answered too quickly. "I, ah... Want some coffee?"

"No." She sent him a searching look.

"It's none of my business, but why are you so dead-set on Charleston?"

Surprise reflected on her face. "I told you. My mom's house is there."

"That's it?" His fingers ran down the side of her arm of their own volition.

"Look, I'm not proud of this, but I'm basically home-less." Nervously, she played with her hair, scooping it into a tail, then letting it drop around her shoulders. "My grand-mother left her house to me, and I lost it."

"How?"

"Do you really care?"

"Yeah, I do. Humor me."

"Okay. Here's the abridged version of my sad, sad tale." Rather than meet his eyes, she stared into the darkness beyond the tree line. "When the divorce was final, Daisy and I were no longer covered under Luke's insurance. Her medical bills piled up, and no matter how hard I tried, I couldn't stay on top of them."

"But you were working. Didn't you have insurance?"

"Yes, but it only covered a small part of her care." She shook her head. "On top of that, Luke... Fudge berries!"

"Fudge berries? That's the best you've got?"

She blushed.

"Where do you get these—" He circled his finger. "These substitutes for swear words."

"When you have a little one around, you learn to be

creative. You saw how fast she picked up on your 'damned good thing' at the doctor's."

"Yeah, well, fudge berries works, I guess." He squinted at her. "What is it you don't want to tell me?"

"Like I said, Grandma Nita left her house to me, free and clear, so that no matter what happened, Daisy and I would always have a home."

"Where was home?"

"Bowden, Alabama. It's a tiny little town near Enterprise, dubbed Southeast Alabama's most beautiful little city and the home of the Boll Weevil Monument." A sliver of a smile crossed her lips.

"Ah, the almighty boll weevil."

She nodded. "I screwed up. When Luke took off, I was dealing with so much. It never crossed my mind to cancel our joint credit cards. He ran up some hefty charges, in addition to opening a couple of personal loans, forging my signature. Then he dropped off the map, leaving me to deal with everything. Because the interest charges were killing me, I took out a pretty large equity line mortgage on my grandmother's house to pay them off—before the board cut the library funds."

Tucker made an innately male sound of disapproval. "You lost your job, then the house."

She worried a cuticle on her thumb. "Yes. The house went into foreclosure."

"Does Luke know?"

"A better question might be does Luke care. Honestly, I have no way to get in touch with him. He literally disappeared. I'm sure his family knows where he is, but they won't tell me."

"Not all men are bastards, Elisa."

"I do know that." She turned to him. "You've already done more for me than he ever did. And how sad is that?"

"I'm sorry."

"I don't need or want your pity."

"Good, because you don't have it. Believe me, what I'm feeling for you is a long, long way from pity. Anger at the situation you're in? Yeah. Disgust for the miserable bum you married? You bet. Pity for the self-sufficient, brave woman you are? Never."

She blinked back unwelcome tears.

"You had no safety net? Your parents refused to help?"

"I refused to ask."

He stared at her, disbelief etched in that strong face. "Why?"

"That would be another long, sad tale."

"I've got time."

"Maybe later. Bottom line, I can stay at Mom's in Charleston until I find a job and get back on my feet…or until she comes home."

"You don't know anyone there?"

"No."

"Stay here," he offered.

"I—"

Before she could say more, he leaned in, drew her to him, and kissed her. For one brief second, she hesitated, then opened to him, embracing the feel of him.

"I've wanted to taste you again so badly I hurt."

It was probably a mistake, but she fisted her hand in his T-shirt, pulled him to her, and kissed him again. And again.

His arms slid around her, one hand moving to the back of her head to draw her closer still.

She wasn't too disoriented to register the testosterone level—or the fact he was fighting it. What must it be like when he unleashed all that passion? Let it run free?

She shivered, and he instantly pulled away. "Lissie, I—forgive me."

"Forgive you? I was right here, Tuck, and what just happened was mutual."

He shook his head, a strand of dark hair falling across his forehead.

"I think it's time for me to say good night, Tuck."

"Elisa?"

"Yeah?"

"Stay another couple of days. What will it hurt?"

Let me count the ways, she thought.

Tucker woke feeling grumpy.

Elisa wouldn't take sex lightly. There'd be no one-nighters for her. She'd want and expect a commitment. The idea of that made him sweat...and take one step back, then another.

He didn't do long-term; he didn't make commitments.

That didn't stop his heart from nearly leaping out of his chest when she walked into the kitchen dressed in black leggings and a long, lightweight cotton sweater the color of ripe peaches. Daisy trailed behind her, wearing a pair of hurt-your-eyes-pink pajamas.

To keep his hands from doing anything stupid, he busied them pouring coffee. He handed a cup to her. "Morning, ladies."

"Good morning, Tuck."

"Morning, Tut. I slept all night." Daisy wrapped the arm not holding her raggedy blanket around her mother's leg. "Mommy's proud of me."

"I'll bet she is." He gave her a thumbs-up and moved back to the counter. "Scrambled eggs and toast okay?" He looked over his shoulder to Elisa, sitting with Daisy in her lap.

"Absolutely. How about I make the toast?"

"Have at it." He nodded toward the toaster. "Butter's on the counter."

Elisa set down her coffee and settled Daisy on her chair.

"Where you goin', Mommy?"

"I'm making toast for you."

"I like toast 'cause I'm a big girl."

"Yes, you are," Tucker said. He nabbed the coffee cup from the table, emptied the remains in the sink, and placed it in the dishwasher.

"What are you doing?" Elisa stood, one hand holding a butter knife, the other on her hip.

"Fixing breakfast."

"What did you do with my cup?"

"Your cup? I put it in the dishwasher," he said.

"I wasn't finished with it."

"You set it down."

"I did, and I planned on a second cup. Oh boy, you are so fussy."

Tucker frowned. "I am not. I like things tidy. Efficient. That's all."

"Right. Keep telling yourself that, Mr. Neat-Freak."

"The eggs are done."

And so was the conversation.

CHAPTER 10

TUCKER WIPED THE WORST OF THE GREASE FROM HIS hands, then dropped the hood. "That's as good as it gets. Elisa's chomping at the bit to head to Charleston, so I need to get this to her."

He chucked the rag into the hamper.

"But?" Gaven asked.

"But nothing. Doesn't matter to me one way or the other."

"You're really gonna stand there and hand me that bald-faced lie?"

"You calling me a liar?"

"Yeah, I think I am." Gaven resettled the ball cap backwards on his head. "I see the way you look at her, at that little girl. You care about them, Tuck."

"Her life isn't here."

"Understood. That doesn't mean you won't be sorry to see her taillights."

Tucker ignored his brother. "I'd intended to drive her car home tonight. Have you follow me, then bring me back for mine. Instead, I think I'll pile them in mine tonight and take a ride, then pick hers up on the way home."

"Good idea. It'll do you all good. It's cooled off, so you can put the windows down and enjoy the nice evening."

"Yep. Blow the dust off the kid and let her run around out here. My house is taking a beating."

Gaven pointed a finger at him. "You'd better face facts,

though, Tuck. Like it or not, you've invested a lot of yourself in Elisa and the kid. When I stopped by and saw you
and Daisy eating cereal in your living room, I wondered if I
shouldn't send for Doc—for you."

"She was hungry."

"In the living room?"

"The stools in the kitchen are kind of high. Sometimes
she's okay with them, other times they scare her."

Gaven hooted. "Like when she wants to eat Froot Loops
in front of the TV. Oh boy, that little girl's got you wrapped
right around this digit." He held up his pinky.

Tucker stuck up a different finger.

"You'll need a cleaning crew to come in while you're on
your fishing trip." Smile gone, his brother asked, "You are
still goin', aren't you?"

Tucker's amusement died. "Yeah, eventually. I'd planned
that trip BD—Before Daisy. I'm not sure when I'll be able
to get away now."

"Sorry." Gaven draped an arm around his brother's
shoulders. "I know what that trip means to you."

"I'll survive. I always do."

———————

"Tut's here, Mommy," Daisy cried out from where she stood
by the living room window.

Like an old faithful dog, she'd taken to watching for
Tucker when it was time for him to come home. Elisa worried about that. Her daughter had fallen head over heels for
their knight in his dented and rusty armor. Sir Tut, on the
other hand—and despite his protests otherwise—wanted

nothing more than to scoot them out the door. The sooner, the better. Tucker Wylder wanted his tidy life back, and she couldn't blame him.

His soft leather sofa was buried beneath doll-babies, and no matter how many times she'd been told not to, Daisy had thrown the expensive toss pillows on the floor. Tucker's cashmere afghan had been pressed into service as a blanket for her dolls.

Joining Daisy at the window, she watched as Tucker gave Daisy a happy little toot. Sliding out of his Mustang, he waved, then sauntered up the walk. He'd obviously put in a hard day's work, but oh, it looked good on him. His hair was mussed, his black shirt and pants covered in heaven-only-knew, the scuffed work boots untied, and the lower half of his face dark with stubble.

The key he wore 24/7 hung outside his T-shirt and piqued her curiosity. What secret did it hold?

Just before he reached the door, her little girl hurried to it and threw it wide. She burst through the opening and launched herself at him from the top step.

Elisa's heart dropped to the floor but settled back in place when he caught her to him with a big grin.

"I missed you, Tut!"

Lifting her up, he put her on his shoulders, stooping to get through the door.

"I missed you, too, Daisy." He set her on her feet and did a quick scan of the room. She registered the wince he couldn't quite hide, but he said nothing. Instead, he held out a set of keys. "Look what I have for your mommy."

"My car's done?" Elisa asked.

"It is, and it's waiting for you at the shop."

"Thank you, Tuck."

Daisy twined her arms around his legs, then stood on his boots. "I'm tall."

"Yes, you are. Do you think we could talk Mommy into taking a ride? I thought we'd stop at the Dairy Queen for dinner—"

"Dairy Queen?" Daisy clapped her hands. "I like Dairy Queen!"

"I know you do, and after you eat your dinner we'll run out to the shop and pick up the car." He turned to Elisa, his eyes once again taking in the ruins of his living room. "The kid can run off a little excess energy there. If you'd rather not, Gav can follow me home tomorrow with it."

"No, it'll do Daisy and me both good to get out."

"I desperately need to wash up." He ran a hand over his chin. "And shave."

Daisy reached toward his face. "Are you scratchy?"

He leaned to brush his cheek against her hand and she giggled. "Give me ten minutes. Will that work?"

"We'll be ready, won't we, baby?"

"Uh-huh." Daisy sent Tucker a sweet smile. "Can I sit up front with you?"

He grinned at her. "Oh, you're good, but no can do. Gotta go with the law, sugar. I don't want Deputy Sam or Sheriff Jimmy Don pulling me over and giving me a ticket." He held out his hands, palms up. "Then I wouldn't have enough money for ice cream."

Her eyes popped wide. "Ice cream? We're gettin' ice cream, Mommy! Tut's buying us some."

A hand to his head, he sent Elisa a sheepish grin. "I should have asked you if that was okay."

"Probably." She watched the little girl dance around the room. "All things considered, I'll simply say thank you. You've made somebody extremely happy."

"Can Lug Nut come, too?"

The dog, hearing his name, skittered around the kitchen corner. Tucker groaned. He'd forgotten about the darned dog, the one he'd had Brant drop off this morning because Daisy missed him. Lug Nut had come for a sleepover, but tomorrow morning he'd go back to Molly and Brant. In the meantime, though, here he was.

"Absolutely. I'm not leaving that mutt alone in my house."

"We're going for ice cream, Luggie." Daisy skipped across the room toward him.

Elisa grimaced. "Don't kiss that dog, Daisy. I've already told you that a thousand times today."

"'Kay, Mommy."

The second Elisa turned her back, she heard Daisy giggle.

Tucker laughed.

"She kissed him, didn't she?" Elisa asked.

"Yep."

"And he licked her face."

"Yep."

When she sighed in resignation, Tucker sent her a jaunty salute and raced up the stairs.

"Get your shoes, sweetie. We need to be ready when Tuck is."

As she held her squirmy little girl and tied pink sequined tennis shoes, Elisa tried very, very hard not to think about Tucker upstairs, naked and wet, in his shower.

She lost the battle. Totally.

On their way to dinner, the back window rolled half-way down and Lug Nut's head sticking out, ears flapping, Tucker suggested they take a ride down Main Street.

"It's idyllic. I love the brick streets and the park in the center," Elisa said. "Dee-Ann's red-and-white diner is pure nostalgia."

"Wait till you see the town now. Over the weekend, it got decked out for fall," he said.

She smiled. "My favorite season."

"Really? Tell you what. How about we take a short walk through the median park? This time of night, the place is all but deserted. A person could roll a bowling ball down the street and not hit a thing." He pulled up to the curb. "I'll get Daisy." He turned to Elisa, who sat quietly looking out the window. "You okay?"

She sent him a smile. "I'm more than fine."

"You can say that again," he mumbled.

"I'm sorry. I didn't hear you."

"I said that's great."

She looked up and down the street, taking in Darlene's Quilty Pleasure shop, Henderson's Drug Store, and the little gift shop. "This might be one of the prettiest small towns in America."

"It gets my vote. Brant outdid himself when he found the spot for our shop here in Misty Bottoms. Even better than the pretty, though, is the people. Best anywhere."

"I'll miss it," she said.

"Let's not talk about that right now." He tipped his head toward the little girl he was unbuckling, then snapped a leash on the pup's collar.

"You're right."

With Daisy riding piggyback and a firm grip on Lug Nut's leash, he opened Elisa's door for her.

"Thanks. I'll take Lug Nut." Elisa reached for the leash. "You're a good boy, aren't you?" She knelt and scratched the dog's head, sending him into waves of wriggling joy.

Tucker couldn't help himself. One hand behind his back to hold Daisy securely, he reached for her mother's free hand with his other.

When she laced her fingers with his, his world felt better than it had in a long, long time. They crossed into the park, and Tucker crouched down so Daisy could crawl off.

Hand in hand, the three of them—four, if you counted the Lug—wandered along the path lined with vivid chrysanthemums and late roses, crunching their way through the fallen leaves. Daisy skipped and sang, Elisa smiled more than he'd seen before, and he found himself actually feeling like some damned hero. He half expected Julie Andrews to pop out from behind one of the trees singing "The Sound of Music" or "My Favorite Things."

Even Lug Nut seemed to appreciate the evening stroll, stopping several times to leave his mark.

When they came to a display featuring a ratty scarecrow, a pile of pumpkins, and a cool wooden wagon, he said, "Hey, kiddo, why don't you hop in that wagon and I'll take your picture?" He whipped out his phone. "Kind of a souvenir of your time in Misty Bottoms."

"'Kay!" More than game, she ran to it and scrambled in. "Come on, Mommy. You have to be in Tut's soupaneer, too."

"Honey, he doesn't want—"

"Yeah, he does," Tucker said, his voice gravelly. "He'd like that. Very much."

"Tuck—"

"Elisa—"

Her laugh was sexy as all get out, and Tucker's belly did a little flip.

Elisa shook her head. "You're as bad as Daisy when it comes to wheedling your way into what you want."

"I can be pretty persuasive when I want to be."

"I don't doubt that for one second."

Still smiling, she moved to stand behind Daisy, who grinned up at her. Lug Nut licked Daisy's cheek and Tucker captured the moment.

"I wasn't ready," Elisa cried out.

"Me, either," Daisy said.

Tucker laughed. "Say when." He snapped again, but he knew it was the first shot he'd have printed for himself.

His gaze traveled beyond where they stood to the town's memorial to their lost soldiers. The newest addition was a granite marker commemorating two of the area's young people who'd given their all in the Middle East. He touched the key at his neck. Nate, Angie, Jorge, and LeBron—his friends had given their all, too. They'd never walk through another park with the smell of autumn in the air, an arm wrapped around a special lady, or in Angie's case, the good-looking guy she'd been engaged to. They wouldn't play with their kids, their friends' kids, nieces and nephews.

His chest grew tight. He forced himself to breathe, deeply, slowly. Not tonight. He couldn't think about it tonight. Not here. Not now.

"You okay?" Elisa laid a hand on his arm.

"Sure." He sighed. "Why do you ask?"

"You looked, I don't know, sad. Lost for a minute there."

The woman was too sharp, too perceptive. "I'm good. You ladies ready to go?"

"We are. This was nice."

"It was, but I'm starving. Time for dinner."

"Dairy Queen." Daisy danced around them, then knelt to hug the dog. Jiggling the keys in his pocket, torn between the past and present, Tucker walked them back to the car.

At the end of Main Street, Tucker turned left.

"I thought the Dairy Queen was in the other direction." Elisa pointed behind them.

"It is. As long as we're out, though, I want to show you one more thing."

"I'm hungry, Tut," Daisy whined.

Lug Nut barked in agreement.

"This will only take a couple of minutes, imp."

"'Kay." Daisy patted the young dog's head. "Just a minute, Luggie."

The dog whimpered and dropped onto the seat, his head lowered to his paws. Tucker shook his head. The peanut gallery was obviously not happy with him.

They'd get over it.

As they neared the house at the end of the street, Elisa gasped. "Oh my gosh, that's incredible."

"It is, isn't it?" He slowed to a stop. "Tansy's aunt lives here."

"Did she paint the mural?"

"She did."

"Mommy, look at all the pretty dresses."

"I see them, honey. They're all brides."

"Magnolia brides," Tucker said. "They've all been married at Magnolia House."

She sighed.

"The story behind the mural is even more amazing." He opened his door. "Why don't we get out?"

"She won't mind?"

He laughed. "She thrives on visitors."

The front door opened and Coralee, dressed in one of her go-to Lucille Ball shirtwaist dresses, crinolines and all, stepped onto the porch. The clash between the pink dress splashed with purple polka dots and Coralee's bright red hair was nearly blinding. The green cowboy boots? He wasn't even going there.

"Well, if it isn't Tucker Wylder. Who are these pretty ladies?"

"Coralee, I'd like you to meet Elisa and Daisy Elizabeth Danvers."

She held out a hand to Elisa. "You must be the one Jimmy Don sent the ambulance out for last week."

Elisa blushed. "Yes, ma'am."

"Feelin' better?"

"Much."

Coralee threaded her arm through Tucker's. "He's a good boy, isn't he?"

"He's a man any mother would be proud to call *son*."

Tucker swore his heart actually stopped for a beat or two. "Thank you, Lissie."

Coralee's head swiveled from one to the other, and a sly grin appeared. "Uh-huh. So, what brings you by this evening?"

"I wanted to show off your artistry, Coralee. I thought

Elisa should hear the story behind it." His gaze fell on Daisy, who'd trotted right up to the mural that covered the length of the house. Lug Nut sat beside her.

When he looked back at Coralee, he knew she'd understood his unspoken message.

"Why don't we let Tuck keep an eye on that darling girl of yours while you and I have a little chat on the porch?"

"Okay." The word, drawn out, carried a basketful of hesitancy.

Tucker walked across the lawn to Daisy.

————————

"Daisy's, what?" Coralee asked. "Two and a half? Three?"

"Three and a half."

"I've got an idea Tuck brought you here for a reason."

"I'm not sure I understand."

"The grooms of these Magnolia beauties paid to have them included in my mural. Their donations help children with congenital heart defects."

Goosebumps raced along Elisa's arms. "Seriously?"

"If you don't mind my asking, what have the doctors told you about Daisy?"

Elisa started to cry, and oh God, she hated that.

Coralee dug into a pocket and handed her a tissue. "You go ahead, honey. Get it out. Tucker and that dog have all of your daughter's attention. Tell me what's wrong with that sweet child."

Around her tears, Elisa found herself pouring out her heart, sharing the anguish of facing Daisy's condition alone. The stark fear during the exploratory surgery when she'd been so tiny. The anxiety every time she had to leave Daisy for work because she still worried something would go wrong.

From another pocket, Coralee pulled out a business card and a pen. "I'm jotting down a website for you to check out. It's manned by parents of children like your Daisy. On it you can find everything from information on your daughter's condition to support groups to tips to help make doctor and hospital visits less traumatic—for both of you."

"I don't know how to thank you, Coralee."

"No need. I'm happy to be able to help. If you ever need anything, you call me. My number's on the other side of the card."

"Mommy," Daisy called, "come look at the pretty pictures."

Elisa sniffled and swiped at her eyes. "Be right there, honey."

The four of them meandered the length of the mural, pointing out detail after detail.

When they reached the end of it, Daisy tugged on Tucker's pant leg. "I'm hungry, Tut. You said we could have ice cream." Her bottom lip stuck out.

"After dinner."

She held out her hands, palms up. "But we don't gots no dinner."

"We'd better take care of that, then." He scooped her up and set her on his hip. "Coralee, thanks for putting up with us."

"Any time a good-looker like you wants to stop by, who am I to say no?" She fluffed her fiery hair.

Elisa smiled and gave her a hug. "Thank you so much," she whispered.

Coralee patted her arm. "You're more than welcome." She turned to Tuck. "Take care of these two, you hear?"

"I'm tryin'." He slapped his leg. "Come on, dog, or I'll leave you behind."

"No, you won't," the feisty redhead said. "Tempus Fugit wouldn't stand for that."

"Who's Tems Git?" Daisy asked, trying to wrap her tongue around the unfamiliar words.

"Tempus Fugit's right there." Coralee pointed at the front room window. "Her name means *time flies*."

A stately Siamese sat on the windowsill, looking for all the world like royalty.

"A kitty! Can *she* fly?"

Coralee laughed and shook her head.

"Oh." Daisy thought about that. "Can I pet her?"

"Not today," Coralee said. "She'll smell Lug Nut on you and have a regular hissy fit."

Daisy blinked. "What's a hissy fit?"

Coralee opened her mouth to explain, but Tucker shook his head.

"Another day. Right now, it's time *we* fly." Tucker sent Coralee a wave and, with Lug Nut and Elisa following, headed to his car.

Once they were settled, Elisa laid a hand on his leg. "Thank you. I can't tell you what that meant to me."

He curled his fingers over hers.

———————

They ordered at the DQ window, then moved to a small outside table. Tucker tied Lug Nut's leash to one of the legs, and the dog dropped down, nearly all his weight on Tucker's foot.

He moved a little and so did the dog. Tucker gave him *the look*; Lug Nut doggy-grinned.

A quiet smile on her face, Elisa watched. "He loves you. You make him feel comfortable and safe. You're a good uncle."

"Lucky me." He scowled at the dog, which smiled back at him, tongue hanging out.

Elisa could have disagreed, could have insisted she and Daisy—along with the dog—were the lucky ones but decided to keep it light. She pulled a hat out of her bag and slid it over her daughter's blond curls, then buttoned the top button on her jacket.

"Too cold?" Tucker asked. "Should we move inside?"

Elisa looked down at the dog. "I don't think—"

"I could put Lug Nut in the car."

She heard the dread in his voice and almost laughed. She had a pretty good idea the kind of grief even the thought of an animal alone in his beloved Mustang caused him. And yet he hadn't hesitated to include the dog in their evening when Daisy asked him to.

Yep, they were definitely the lucky ones. He might be brusque and a total neatnik, but inside lived a warm and caring man. A small smile played over her lips.

"What?"

"Nothing."

He grunted.

"We're good out here," Elisa said.

"Hey, Tuck." A young girl, eighteen at the most, walked over to their table with a large tray of food.

"Hey right back at you, Gabbie. Archie came out the other day to see about getting his car painted."

The girl grinned ear to ear. "Isn't he the cutest thing?"

Tucker made a face. "Not exactly my type."

"Guess not, but he sure is mine." She flashed him a smile, then turned her attention to the others at the table.

"Gabbie, this is Elisa and her daughter, Daisy. They're, ah, they're—"

"We're on our way to Charleston," Elisa supplied. "We stopped to visit for a few days."

"Nice! We've got a good town here."

"You certainly do."

"Who gets what?" She nodded at the food on the tray.

Elisa smiled at her. "I have the grilled chicken salad."

"Figured that. Guess that's why you look like you do." Gabbie shrugged her shoulders. "I like cheeseburgers and fries, but Archie says it just gives him more to—" Blushing, she broke off. "Anyway, I'll bet the chicken-strip basket is yours, sweetie." She set it down in front of Daisy.

"Uh-huh. I think Lug Nut wants one." She picked one up, but Elisa stopped her before she fed it to the energetically tail-wagging dog.

"Toss him one of your fries. Just one," Tucker said. "No chicken. You need to eat that so I can buy you an ice cream."

"But he wants one."

"That dog wants anything he can fit in his mouth." He tipped his head at the tray Gabbie still held. "You gonna give me my burger?"

"Whoops." She blushed again. "Sorry." The teen slid it in front of him. "Anything else?"

"Nope, not right now." Looking directly at Daisy, he added, "But if everybody finishes dinner, we'll head back to the window for dessert."

"I don't want dessert," Daisy whined. "I want ice cream."

After everyone, including Lug Nut, finished their ice cream, they piled back into the Mustang and headed to Wylder Rides.

"This is the part of the trip I made in the back of the ambulance." Elisa watched the passing scenery.

"Yeah, with me and Daisy following. I swear I aged ten years in those first few minutes you went down."

"I didn't plan it."

"Yeah, Tut, she didn't plan it."

The adults laughed and Daisy, not understanding why, joined in.

When they reached the shop, Elisa gaped at the building. "Tuck, this is wonderful. I didn't pay much attention the first time I was here."

"Gosh, I wonder why," Tucker said dryly.

She rolled her eyes. "It's like something out of a movie set. I'd swear I just stepped into the fifties."

"It is pretty cool, isn't it? Brant spotted it, and we snapped it up. Inside, it's modern, with all the latest technology. Out here? We figured what better place to restore vintage cars and motorcycles than in a vintage building."

An old terra-cotta-colored metal canopy sheltered antiquated pumps. Weathered metal signs covered the front of the building. But the big red Mobil flying horse over the door was the shining star.

"Pegasus."

"Yeah. Pretty cool, huh?" Tucker jammed his hands in his jeans pockets to keep them from stroking the sides of her face. He wanted to touch her, and that would be a huge mistake. He blamed it on those stolen kisses, the stolen touches. He'd been a fool to think that would be enough.

Instead, he craved more.

The second go-round had only made the hunger worse.

He reminded himself that Elisa was vulnerable right now with her future so uncertain.

And she had a child.

Good reasons for putting this hunger for her on the back burner. Heck, for locking it away forever.

Sometimes logic simply didn't work, though. The bottom line was that he ached for another kiss, another touch, and he doubted that was gonna change. The sooner she left, the better off they'd both be. He understood that.

But the knowing didn't make him want her gone, nor would it stop him from trying to talk her into postponing her departure.

"It's like a museum or something you'd see at Disneyworld." Elisa's musings broke into his thoughts.

"Yeah. The thing I love most about it, other than the feel of the place, is the land. We've got room to spread out and expand."

Lug Nut barked, so Tucker opened the car door for him. When the overgrown pup hopped out, Tucker groaned. Dog hair blanketed his custom backseat.

Elisa patted his arm. "It'll vacuum up."

"I suppose it will."

He showed them around inside, then took her and Daisy out to the downdraft paint booth they'd built in the back. "This is where Gaven does his magic. We all have a hand in the restorations from top to bottom, but only my little brother touches the paint."

They wandered outside. While Daisy and Lug Nut played in the backyard, Tucker brought out a couple of chairs for him and Elisa. Turning on the coffee machine, he made a cup for each of them.

"Here you go."

She took a sip. "Mmm. Thank you. And thanks again for introducing me to Coralee."

"She's a little different, but she's a good woman. If you ever need help, Lissie, she'll be there for you. No matter where you are."

"Yes, I believe she would be."

Tucker kicked back in the chair, legs outstretched and feet crossed at the ankles. Every once in a while, a breeze carried Elisa's delicate, feminine scent to him. Daisy's happy laughter and childish giggles mixed with Lug Nut's ecstatic barking.

Not a bad way to spend an early fall evening.

"Why do you call me Lissie?"

He went blank and shrugged.

She nudged him with her elbow. "Come on. Why?"

"I don't know. Elisa…it's a beautiful name, but kind of formal. Lissie is…softer. It fits you." He shot her a sideways glance. "What do your friends call you?"

"Elisa."

"Your ex? Your grandmother?"

"Elisa. Nobody has ever given me a nickname."

"Until now." His voice dropped a notch.

"Yes." A slow smile crept over her face and lit those pretty eyes of hers. "Until now."

CHAPTER 11

MUSIC DRIFTED UP FROM DOWNSTAIRS. OLD MUSIC. Romantic music, rather than the edgier stuff Tucker listened to during daylight hours. Slipping from bed, Elisa grabbed her robe and crept into the hallway, leaving her door ajar. Partway down, the step creaked.

Tucker lifted his head, his gaze colliding with hers. He sprawled the length of the sofa, barefoot like her, but fully clothed in his black jeans and T-shirt. "You okay?"

"That's what I meant to ask you."

He sat up, finger-combing his hair. "I'm having trouble sleeping tonight. You should go back to bed."

She continued down the stairs. He looked tired. Sad. "I'm a bit of an insomniac, too. Sometimes the mind won't shut off."

He grunted. "I didn't wake Daisy, did I? I can turn off the music."

She shook her head. "Daisy's fine."

"Lissie, do both of us a favor. Turn around and go back upstairs."

"No." She saw his start of surprise, and her eyes narrowed. "I don't know what's wrong, but something's bothering you. Is it Daisy and me?"

"No. Absolutely not."

In an almost-whisper, she asked, "What's hurting you?"

"I'm not—"

Saying not a word, she shot him her best mother look, the one that wouldn't let a person fudge the truth.

He caved. "I'm not sick, and I'm not hurt. Not physically. I told you right from the beginning that I live alone because I need to. Things rattle around in my brain at night when the rest of the world shuts down, but it's nothing I can't handle. Trust me on that." His voice grew quieter, more intimate. "You need to go to bed, Elisa, where you're safe."

She rubbed her hands together, suddenly cold. The coward in her wanted to flee, to take those stairs at a run. The woman who'd been hurt and understood what it could do to a person wouldn't let her.

"Tony Bennett. 'The Way You Look Tonight.' Not your usual music."

"What can I say?" He shrugged. "I have eclectic taste."

The music changed. John Mellencamp's "Ain't Even Done with the Night" played.

"I love that song. Dance with me, Tuck." Drawing on every ounce of courage she possessed, Elisa extended her hand. "It's been a long time since a man's held me. That music, that song makes me want to dance."

"I'm a soldier, not a dancer, Lissie."

"You'll do fine."

And he did. He started very formally, holding her away from him. Then, with a groan, he drew her in and made her feel sheltered and desired. He made her feel like a woman again. She closed her eyes and breathed in the scent of him. Pure middle-of-the-night male.

"Maybe it's the dark, the feeling of the two of us alone in the world, but I want to bury my face in all this gorgeous hair." He brought one hand to her head, ran his fingers through the strands, and pressed his cheek against her face.

The other hand lay low on her hip, his heat seeping through the thin cotton of her nightgown and robe.

She slid her hands into his back pockets, felt his muscled body, his smoldering heat. Tucker kicked up longings she thought she'd set aside forever.

His mouth close to her ear, he whispered, "I want to lose myself in you, and that should scare the hell out of you."

"It doesn't."

A slow burn started deep within her. His thumbs brushed the undersides of her breasts, and the burn erupted into a raging blaze.

He cursed, and she felt his body tense.

"Don't, Tuck. Please don't step away from me."

"Lissie, I want too much. I can't kiss you, then send you up to bed. If we start this, we need to carry it through to the end."

"Yes." She laid her hand on his cheek. "We do. It's been over three years since—since I've been with anyone."

"Are you sure? This…sex. It'll change everything."

Nodding, she rose to her tiptoes. As she kissed him, she felt the barriers fall away.

Swooping her up, he carried her to the sofa. His hands, so strong and confident, shook as he untied her robe and thumbed it open. "You're wearin' too much, darlin'."

He eased up the hem of her nightgown, kissing behind her knees, up the inside of her thighs. When he uncovered her belly button, he flicked his tongue inside, and she arched up.

"Tucker."

He raised his head. "You okay?"

"More than." She slid her hands under his T-shirt and

pulled it up and over his head, then nipped at his collar-bone. A shaft of moonlight gilded his skin.

Tucker slid her nightgown over her head. "Oh, honey, you are magnificent."

Elisa reached for Tucker's waistband, but her hands trembled. "Help me, Tuck."

He did, and in minutes they were skin to skin, tasting and touching, free to enjoy one another.

Elisa felt like it was her first time. She'd never been with anyone so giving, so careful to please her. Tucker took his time. He didn't neglect a single inch of her body, and she felt both loose and as tight as a drum.

When they finally came, he groaned her name even as she called his. His body slumped over hers. "I'll move in a minute, but I don't think I'm capable of it right now."

She grinned and kissed his neck. "Thank you, Tuck."

He raised his head to look at her, then dropped a kiss on the end of her nose. Rolling to the side, he covered her with her robe.

They lay there, cuddled into each other, the night sounds of the house surrounding them and the music playing softly. No matter what happened, Elisa knew she'd never forget tonight, this moment. Every time a John Mellencamp song came on the radio, she'd think of Tucker.

"You'd better head up to bed." He kissed the top of her head. "If we fall asleep and Daisy wakes up before us—"

She nodded and scooped up her nightgown. "Night, Tuck."

"Night, Lissie." Halfway up the stairs, his deep voice reached her. "Elisa?"

"Yes?"

"I think you were right. It is time for you and Daisy to leave."

Wordlessly, she climbed the stairs.

She closed her bedroom door quietly and leaned against it as the tears fell. What had just happened?

By the time her daughter crawled into bed with her the next morning, the sun had inched above the trees. Elisa had barely slept a wink.

Daisy's little-girl scent was balm for her shattered soul. "Are you hungry, sweet girl? Want some breakfast?"

"Tut gived me a Pop-Tart."

"What?" She sat up. "When?"

"When I got up. He carried me downstairs, and we had breakfast. He said, 'Shhh. Don't wake Mommy. She's tired.'" Daisy raised her little hand to Elisa's face. "Why are you tired, Mommy? Are you gonna fall down again and go to the doctor?"

Elisa shook her head. "No, sweetie, I'm not." She did, though, now own another black mark. First, she'd made a clumsy attempt to help Tucker last night, an attempt that had morphed into a wish to satisfy a need of her own, and she'd ended up making a fool of herself. Now she'd slept through Daisy's waking, and Tucker had fed her breakfast.

A swift lick of doubt swept through her. How did Tucker feel this morning? Did he regret their late-night lovemaking…or his final words? Nipping at the heels of that came a sensation of warmth. For the first time since her grandmother had passed, someone was thinking of her. Taking care of her and making sure she got enough sleep.

Tucker might act all tough and gruff, but that façade hid a compassionate man. A man with *Mama* tattooed on his arm couldn't be all bad, and Tucker had proven that quite a few times this past week—even if he wouldn't admit it under threat of torture, or worse, under threat of damage to his prized Mustang.

But he wanted them to leave. Hadn't she been the first to bring it up, though?

She looked down to see her daughter still watching her. "I'm okay, baby. Honest. I'm not going to, ah, fall down again." Tossing back the covers, she said, "I should go downstairs and see if Tuck needs anything."

"He doesn't." Her darling little girl, eyes solemn, said, "He told me to come upstairs 'cause he had to go earn his daily bread. I told him you'd buy some for him, but he just laughed."

Elisa couldn't hide the smile.

"You would, wouldn't you, Mommy?"

"I certainly would."

"I almost forgotted."

With that, Daisy raced downstairs.

"Slow down, Daisy Elizabeth."

"'Kay." When she returned, she danced back into the room holding a paper bag. "Here, Mommy."

"What's this?" Red and yellow crayon flowers covered the bag.

"It's pretty. Tut helped me. See?" She pointed to one of the red flowers. "He colored this one."

Elisa swore her heart pinched. Opening the bag, she pulled out a note.

You know you want me.
　　　　Doctor Wylder and Nurse Daisy

Laughing, she pulled out a protein bar and a plastic container holding a hard-boiled egg.

If he was truly sorry they'd made love last night, if he really regretted it, would he send her an egg in a bag with a red flower?

"You're 'posed to eat them, Mommy."

"I will. Afterward, why don't we get dressed and take a ride?"

"A ride? Oh boy!" She jumped up and down, clapping her hands. "I love rides." Her smile disappeared. "But not long ones."

"No long rides today." Even as she said it, her heart hurt. Soon, they'd have to take the rest of that ride to Charleston, away from Misty Bottoms and Tucker Wylder. Despite what he'd said, last night hadn't changed anything.

Brant leaned in the office doorway, a hubcap in his hand and a scowl on his face. "What crawled up your butt, brother?"

"Not a thing." Tucker slammed the filing cabinet drawer closed with his foot.

"Then where'd the wrecking crew go? There's enough slamming and banging out here for ten guys with sledgehammers."

Tucker dropped into the chair and tossed a file holding the month's invoices onto the desk. "I'm fine. Why don't you find something to do?"

"Huh-uh. That's not how this works. You're not in the desert anymore, and thank God for that. You're here now, with your family. That means you're safe, but it also means you're not an island. Family shares—both good and bad."

Tucker sent his brother a glare when he realized he didn't intend to back off. "Okay, you want it? Here it is. The good and the bad all rolled into one. They're driving me nuts."

Brant frowned. "Not following you."

"Good. Then that makes two Wylders who are confused." He rubbed the back of his neck. "It's Elisa. The woman's enough to make a grown man cry. To make him get down on his knees and beg."

One side of Brant's mouth kicked up in a lopsided grin. "She's beautiful, all right."

"She's more than that, Brant, and last night—"

Brant straightened. "You didn't hurt her, did you?"

"Physically? Nah. I wouldn't—I couldn't do that. But there are other ways to hurt someone. I was cold. I, well…" He couldn't share everything that had happened, not even with his brother. "Let's just say I froze her out."

"You've gotten pretty good at that."

"Guess I have, but Lissie doesn't deserve it."

"Lissie?"

"Elisa," Tucker growled. "She mentioned it might be time for her and Daisy to go." He raised his eyes, stared into his brother's, and knew his own hurt showed. "I told her I agreed."

"Ouch."

"Yeah." He closed his eyes, then opened them again. Hell. "That was after…well, after."

"What?"

Tucker held up a hand. "The first time we almost went there was my fault. But before you chew my butt about it, last night was hers."

"Of course it was. I've seen how aggressive that woman is."

"Cute, Brant, real cute. I understand sarcasm when I hear it."

"I sure hope so. Tell me, what did this wanton woman do that had you lusting after her?"

"I couldn't sleep last night. Nothing new there, except that I'm not alone anymore. I thought my music was low enough not to wake her or the kid, but I should have known better. Elisa's a light sleeper, and I guess that comes from listening for Daisy at night."

"And?"

"She asked me to dance with her."

He saw the grin his brother fought back.

"That's practically a criminal offense, isn't it?" Brant asked. "Let me go ask Gav. He'd know."

"You say a word about this and you're a dead man. I'll tell Mama you had an accident."

"She won't believe you. Then you'd lose your status as favorite son."

Tucker snorted. "Fat chance of that, since I only held it for one year. Once you came along, she barely looked at me."

Brant hooted. "Boy, you're playing the sympathy cards today, aren't you?"

Tucker shrugged. "Why not? Besides, you *are* the favorite son—but only because of Molly. You showed up on our parents' doorstep with her, and Gav and I might as well not exist. You've given Mama a second daughter."

"I did, didn't I?" Brant tossed him a smug smile. "My bride is one in a million."

"She is that."

"Elisa's not chopped liver. I think Mom and Dad—"

"Don't even go there." His hand came up, brushed the ever-present key. "I'm not fit for anybody. Now get back to work. If we're gonna keep the doors open another month, I have to send out these bills."

CHAPTER 12

EVEN AFTER LAST NIGHT, ELISA COULDN'T WIPE THE grin from her face. It felt so good to go where she wanted, when she wanted. Fantabulous!

The overhead bell tinkled when she and Daisy stepped inside That Little White Dress. A sigh escaped her. Oh yes. Molly Wylder's wedding boutique epitomized every female's dream come true. The large front window was a nod to autumn and its brides, while the inside of the shop exuded femininity and whispered *classy*. The pale blues and whites wrapped themselves around her. In the corner, a wonderful papier-mâché tree dripped with wisteria and twinkling white lights. Lacy-looking birdcages hung from its branches.

"Look, Mommy. Birdies."

"I see."

"Will they fly away?"

"Not these ones, honey. They're pretend, but aren't they wonderful?" When her gaze moved to the collection of incredible, once-in-a-lifetime dresses, she sighed again. She'd married Luke in a simple white cotton dress. No splash, no frills, no magic—except the love she'd imagined they'd had for each other, a love that had proved to be one-sided and had died under the harsh demands of reality.

Yet the dream still tugged at her.

"Hey, Elisa." Molly, dressed for work and looking like a million bucks, stepped out from the backroom, several honeymoon-worthy nighties draped over her arm.

"Molly, your shop is every bit as mind-blowing as Tansy said, and then some."

"Thanks. There are still mornings I walk in and think I must be dreaming." Molly hung the nightgowns, then crossed the room, dropping to one knee to kiss Daisy. Running a hand over the ruffled sleeve of the little girl's dress, she said, "Pretty!"

"I picked it out."

"Good job."

"Mommy taked me to see the river."

"Did she?"

"Uh-huh." She dug the toe of her shoe into the carpet and did a little pirouette. "And I saw some duckies. They was hungry so we gave them some bread, but only little pieces so they didn't choke."

"Yellow rubber duckies?" Molly teased.

Daisy frowned and looked at her mother. "Were they, Mommy?"

"No, that's the kind that swims in your bathtub. What color were the ones we saw? Think hard."

Daisy closed her eyes. "Black." Her baby-blues popped open, and she looked at her mother for confirmation.

"You're right, pumpkin. They were black."

"Tut gived me a Pop-Tart."

"Did he?"

Elisa saw the look of speculation in the other woman's eyes. "They were both up before me this morning."

"That doesn't surprise me. The man rarely sleeps." Molly's smile faded. "I'm so glad you stopped in. You look a world better than the last time I saw you. How are you feeling?"

"I feel great. I think that was a one-time deal."

"How are things going in general?"

She stared up at the ceiling. "It's time for me to move on, Molly."

"Why?"

"Why?" Daisy stood at the window, watching cars pass.

Dropping her voice, Elisa said, "I'm a single woman living with a single man. We're not related, and I'm not his housekeeper or nanny. People are bound to start talking—if they haven't already."

"Jeez!" Molly settled onto one of the soft blue chairs and waved at Elisa to do the same. "I hadn't given much thought to that."

"Well, I have, and I'm pretty certain I'm not the only one who has." Elisa perched on the edge of a chair. "Every time I've mentioned leaving, Tucker's had an argument for why I should stay a few more days. Last night he didn't. My car's running again, so it's time I finish my trip to Charleston. As much as I hate moving into my mother's, and as much as I love Misty Bottoms, I think that's best."

Across the shop, a woman stepped from the dressing room and cleared her throat.

"Ohhh. I didn't realize you had a customer. I'm so sorry." Elisa turned from Molly and met the woman's eyes. "I truly am. I—" She spread her hands.

"Don't you worry, honey. Sounds to me like you've found yourself a barrelful of trouble."

"Unfortunately, yes, but—"

She wagged a finger. "'Spose you think you need to handle it alone. You don't. I think I can help you shovel some of that trouble right out of the way. Maybe lighten that barrel some."

Like Molly, her customer was dressed in black. However, that was where any and all similarity ended. While Molly's simple long-sleeved black dress was decorum itself, the other woman wore a peasant-style long-sleeved blouse adorned with bright blue Western embroidery. Her full skirt was calf-length and covered the tops of cowboy boots. A black Stetson rested on her head, and a chunky turquoise squash-blossom necklace nestled in her ample cleavage.

It was totally over the top and, surprisingly, totally appropriate for this buxom, outgoing, larger-than-life woman. A silk nightgown and robe in rich scarlet were slung over her arm.

Before Elisa could gather her wits, Molly's customer crossed the room, her ring-bedecked hand extended.

"Desdemona Rosebud Hamilton. I've been away, so I missed greeting you when you came to town. Been living in Colorado the last couple of years with husband number three." She gave her head a disconsolate shake. "I was very, very fond of that man. The good Lord took him home this past spring. After rattling around in that monstrosity of a house for a while, I decided it was time to come home. So now I'm banging around in a ridiculously enormous house here." She laughed, loud and uninhibited.

A slightly intimidated Daisy crawled into her mother's lap, eyes huge as she studied this new person.

"Mind if I take a load off?" Desdemona asked Molly.

"No, please." Molly waved to the unoccupied chair to Elisa's left. "Would you like coffee? Tea?"

"Tea with lemon would be just the thing. By the way, Molly, I'm taking these. They're perfect." She laid the sensuous garments on the arm of her chair and studied Elisa. "Maybe a cup for my new friend, too, with lots of calorie-laden honey in it. I swear if a good wind comes along, we're likely to find her hell and gone to Atlanta."

"One minute." Molly hopped up and headed to the back-room where an older woman stood in the doorway, making absolutely no attempt to look busy.

Desdemona spotted her. "Well, Lettie Dowmeyer, how the heck are you?"

"I'm keepin' out of trouble."

"Heard your hubby finally sold his business."

"He did, and that's why I'm here. Molly needed a seam-stress, and I needed an excuse to get out of the house a couple days a week now that he's retired. I love the man, but darned if I can be cooped up with him day after day."

"Men!" Desdemona chuckled and slapped her hand on her knee. "Gotta love 'em, but you're right. Can't take too much of a good thing."

"Frank sold the station to the Wylder brothers. Brant, the middle one, married our Molly here. The man's a real looker. So are Tucker and Gaven. Those boys have turned Frank's place into a shop to fix old cars and motorcycles."

Molly, carrying a tray with fancy little teacups, *tsk*ed. "They restore vintage cars and motorcycles, Lettie."

"Ain't that what I said?"

Elisa wondered if she'd fallen down Alice's rabbit hole.

Lettie, bless her heart, changed the subject. "I was real sorry to hear about your Mr. Hamilton, Desdemona Rosebud."

"I appreciate that, Lettie. I had a real soft spot for Reginald. He had a wicked sense of humor and a lust for life. The old coot lived a good life and a full one. He turned ninety-four August before last." Then she jerked a thumb sporting a turquoise ring surrounded by diamonds big enough to count as solitaires in Elisa's direction, talking as if she were no longer in the room or didn't have ears. "What are we gonna do about this one?" Desdemona took a sip of tea and rolled her eyes. "Mmmm. Good. Mint?"

Molly nodded.

Desdemona's gaze slid back to Elisa. "My guess is, at the base of all your difficulties, we'll find a man that's done you wrong. You and this baby."

"I—I had a problem when I first got to town," Elisa said. "Tucker took us in while I dealt with it. He's a good man."

"I have no doubt about that. Been hearin' nothin' but good about those handsome Wylder brothers. Haven't been lucky enough to more than eyeball any of them yet, though." She grinned at Molly, then nodded toward Daisy. "My guess is this little one's daddy didn't treat you quite as well."

Elisa froze. Grandma Nita had frowned on publicly airing dirty laundry and taught her that a person kept her worries to herself. With Daisy sitting here all ears, this conversation wasn't going to happen.

Before she could decide what to say, Molly came to her rescue.

"Mrs. Hamilton, why don't you have a cookie?" Molly held out the tray.

"Don't mind if I do." Desdemona, at five-six and running right around a hundred-seventy or so pounds, helped herself to one. "But I have to warn you. This won't keep me from pryin'. And the name's Desdemona Rosebud, not Mrs. Hamilton. Never did stand on formality." She licked a crumb from her lip. "Delicious. You should sell these, Molly. You'd make a fortune."

"Actually, I bought them this morning from Tansy over at her Sweet Dreams bakery."

"Heard she'd opened a new shop and that Kitty finally retired. End of one era and the beginning of another." She shook her head. "I'll have to stop by there on my way home. She bakes like this, she'll do fine." Desdemona Rosebud concentrated on the cookie for a few seconds. "Didn't mean to eavesdrop earlier." Her nose wrinkled. "Oh hell, yes I did. I'm guessin' you saw the doc."

"The doc?"

"Yancy Hawkins."

"Actually, I was delivered, quite literally, to his doorstep by ambulance."

Desdemona's plucked and penciled brows arched. "Really?"

"The woman passed out at Tuck's feet in Frank's old place." Lettie delivered the news in her dry manner. "Had the boy flustered."

Elisa blushed. "He was wonderful. The doctor, I mean. Well, Tuck was pretty great, too, but Doctor Hawkins wouldn't even let me pay him."

"Yancy's one of the good guys."

Desdemona's eyes turned just dreamy enough that Elisa wondered if he and this woman had some history. Maybe a few embers still glowed from whatever fire once existed between them.

Then Desdemona turned serious. "Your mama plannin' on helpin' you once you get to Charleston?"

"She won't be there." Elisa hesitated, then decided *what the heck*. Trying to hold back against this steamroller was useless. "And *because* she won't be home, I *can* go there."

"I see." Desdemona popped the last bite of cookie into her mouth, then slowly sipped her tea.

Elisa could practically smell the smoke as the other woman's mind revved into high gear. She liked Desdemona, but the woman had something up her sleeve and it was making Elisa nervous.

"I'd like to show you something. You have a little time?"

She grimaced. "I have nothing but time."

"Finish your tea and have a cookie while you're at it." She shoved one at Elisa and handed one to Daisy. "You, too, sweetheart."

"Thank you." Daisy beamed a smile at her.

"Good manners. I like that. Yes, I do."

Said the spider to the fly, Elisa thought.

As though she didn't have a care in the world, Desdemona Rosebud sauntered down Main Street beside Elisa. Daisy danced beside them, twirling and singing "Itsy Bitsy Spider". Elisa found it more than a little ironic, considering her earlier thought.

"We're only walking to the corner. Well, not quite that far." Elisa frowned.

"Have you noticed the bower there?" Desdemona asked.

"How could anyone miss it? It looks like the entrance to a fairy land."

Desdemona smiled. "I like to think so, too, but I'm afraid I've neglected it. It needs sprucing up. I'll get Teddy or someone to do that. Maybe Cole can help."

"With the bower?"

"No, Teddy, my handyman, will take care of that. I'll need Cole's help with the building, though. He's married to Jenni Beth, the owner of Magnolia Brides, and runs the most amazing architectural salvage business in Savannah. The man can find anything." Desdemona glanced at Elisa and noticed her furrowed forehead. "Ahh, you haven't noticed the small building at the end of the path."

"I haven't, no, but then, I've not exactly been out and around. My car was sick."

"The Wylders get it runnin' for you?"

"Yes, they did."

"The building's pretty well hidden right now." They stopped at the overgrown bower, and Desdemona pushed aside the leafy vines. "Go ahead. It's okay. I own the place."

"You own this?"

"Look, Mommy. A pretty house." Daisy ran toward the porch.

"Wait, sweetie." Puzzled, Elisa stared at the magical little building. With elaborate Victorian gingerbread trim along the gables and over the doors and windows, it looked like a dollhouse. She turned to her new friend. "What is it?"

"It's not so much what it is as what it could be. What I'd like it to be. I'm hoping to turn it into a bookstore. A cozy, get-away-from-reality bookstore. Misty Bottoms could use one."

"A bookstore." Elisa sighed. "I wanted to be a writer, wanted to create stories that would wrap around people and take them away from their own worries, even if only for a little while. I especially wanted to write romances with their happily-ever-afters." She shook her head. "I tried, but the truth? I suck at it. I also sucked at creating my own happily-ever-after. My strength lies in enjoying stories others create—and sharing them. The librarian job I had in my hometown fit me to a T."

Desdemona wrapped an arm around Elisa's waist. "It does take two for that fairy-tale ending, you know."

"You're right. It does. However, the heroine needs to pick the right hero. I fell down on the job when it came to that."

"Maybe you just needed some practice." Desdemona chuckled. "Myself? I've been busy practicing, although I've loved every man I've been with. I think Reginald was my last trip down the aisle, though. How about you? You love this guy you were married to?"

Elisa stumbled, blamed it on the uneven sidewalk. "*Do* I love Luke or *did* I love Luke?"

"Either. Your choice." Desdemona Rosebud shrugged carelessly, but Elisa read an intensity in the woman's gaze that belied her nonchalance.

Casting a sidelong glance at her daughter, Elisa said, "I'm not sure this is a good time—"

"You're absolutely right, and I'm a nosy old busybody."

"An *old* busybody? Oh, you're so far from that!"

"I notice you didn't denounce the nosy part." Desdemona's eyes sparkled good-naturedly.

"No, I didn't." Elisa grinned. "Like good old George, I cannot tell a lie."

When they laughed, Daisy skipped back to them and caught her mother's hand. "What's funny, Mommy?"

Elisa chucked her under the chin. "We're talking about people and what makes them fun to be with."

"Like Tut?"

"Yes," Elisa answered. "Like Tut."

"Tut?" Desdemona Rosebud's elegant brows arched.

"That's Daisy's take on Tucker." Elisa stopped in the middle of the winding brick walk and took in the little building. The place needed some work, but it had incredible bones. At a quick guesstimate, she figured there'd be eight- or nine-hundred square feet inside to devote to the magic of books.

Oh, the possibilities. "Can't you picture a couple of colorful Adirondack chairs on the upstairs deck? Flowers spilling over the railings from wooden planters. Maybe some ferns and an old-fashioned rosebush street-level." She placed a hand on her cheek. "And wind chimes. Hummingbird feeders. The landscaping and the front porch would welcome customers and draw them in."

Desdemona smiled. "You, dear, are exactly what the doctor ordered."

Elisa made a noncommittal sound.

"If you could choose any color for this building, what would it be?"

"I don't even need to think about that. I'd paint it pale, pale pink with white trim. A light green door. But—" Elisa held up a finger. "If you want a bookstore that guys will be willing to step into, I'd lean toward the deep green or garnet red of an Irish pub, again with white trim."

"Hmmm." Desdemona tipped her head and studied the building. "Either would be a winner, but I'm trusting Southern men are sure enough of their masculinity that a pink building won't stop them from running in to pick up the newest CJ Box or Robert Crais book."

"The pink would be delicate and so beautiful." Elisa nodded. "The building is practically crying for it."

"Have time to run to Beck's hardware store to pick out the right shade?"

"Me?"

"The two of us. Actually, the three of us." She tipped her head toward Daisy, who was now clambering up the steps and onto the small porch. "I think we'll be able to agree on one. There's a snag, though."

"What's that?"

"I need someone to help me set it up, to do the ordering, to run the business for me. Know anyone who needs a job and might be willing to take it on?"

Elisa felt herself pale. Stress and delight battled inside her. Had Desdemona Rosebud just offered her a chance to stay in Misty Bottoms? To stand on her own rather than be indebted to her mother?

"Mommy, Mommy, come look." Daisy pressed her nose against the big front window.

"One minute, honey." She turned to Desdemona. "I want to be sure I'm understanding you. Are you asking me to help with the store?"

"No. I'm asking you to run it. I'd like you to manage it for me."

"But you don't know me."

"You're wrong. When you walked into Molly's, I knew everything I needed to know about you within minutes. I like you." She enfolded Elisa in a big hug, the scent of her woodsy fragrance wrapping itself around them. "And I know both what it is to need a hand up and what it's like to be alone." She pulled back and wiped at a tear. "Damn Reginald for dying on me. I miss the old fart."

"I'm sorry, and I know how inadequate those words are."

"Not when they're heartfelt." The older woman took a steadying breath. "Want to go inside and take a quick peek?"

"Just try to keep me out." Elisa grinned.

The inside was every bit as wonderful as the outside. Nearly the entire front wall was taken up by the door and one very large, multipaned window which brought the outside in and streaked the hardwood floors with sunlight.

Desdemona swiped a cowboy-booted foot over the dark cherry. "The floor needs cleaned and polished, but it's in good shape under all the dust. Shame on me for letting this place sit empty so long. When I left for Colorado, it wasn't a top priority."

Elisa wandered to an old stone fireplace. "Does this work?"

"Sure does. I'll have a sweeper come clean it out, though, and make sure some little birdie hasn't built herself a nest in it."

"A birdie?" Daisy's eyes grew wide and she crouched to look up inside it.

"See anything?" Elisa asked.

Daisy shook her head.

"Good." Desdemona nodded, setting her massive turquoise chandelier earrings swinging. "I thought we could line this back wall and the left wall with bookshelves, fit a couple of smaller ones beside the fireplace."

"Maybe a pair of chairs here in front of the window," Elisa added. "Give customers a place to relax. A side table with a cute lamp, a vase of flowers, and the newest bestsellers on it. Make it feel like a well-loved sitting room. Again, welcome those guests in and hold them hostage."

"Mm-hmm. Exactly what I want." Desdemona's eyes took on a sharper look. "What about you?"

"Me?"

"I want you, too."

CHAPTER 13

Fifteen minutes later, Elisa neared the parking lot outside Elliot's Lumber Yard in her old Ford Escort. Ahead of her, Desdemona drove a snazzy new Land Rover.

Elisa used the short drive to settle her nerves and decide what portion of the flutters in her stomach were caused by excitement and what percentage were the result of anxiety bordering on terror.

When she'd woken this morning, who'd have guessed that before lunch rolled around an opportunity like this would practically fall into her lap? Still, she hesitated. The offer didn't come without consequences—good and bad. It was a huge decision, one that affected not only her but her daughter.

Her mind was a jumble. She loved, loved, loved books of all kinds, and Desdemona was offering her the opportunity to be a matchmaker of sorts, giving her a chance to pair people with books they'd love.

The biggest bonus? She could be independent again. She wouldn't have to depend on her mother—or Tucker. When he'd told her last night it was time for her to leave, she'd been devastated. But he was right. It *was* time. She'd said so herself earlier.

And now that they'd crossed that line, it would only be harder to stay—and harder to leave.

Desdemona had offered her a graceful exit, a way to provide for herself and Daisy by doing what she loved. Try as she might, she couldn't remember any of the cons, and literally pinched herself to make sure she wasn't dreaming.

Daisy talked nonstop the entire way. Thankfully, she hadn't needed more than a few *mm-hmms* and head nods which gave Elisa thinking time. When they reached the lumberyard, she lifted her still-jabbering daughter out of the car and waved to her new friend. Her future employer?

Halfway across the lot, Desdemona asked, "Made up your mind yet?" She followed the question with a horse-laugh. "Sorry. I promised you time to decide, but you've probably guessed by now that patience isn't my strong suit."

Elisa squirmed. "My mind is racing with the possibilities of your offer. I'd be lying if I said it wasn't a dream come true."

Daisy stooped and picked up a handful of gravel.

"Put that down, baby. It's dirty."

"Okay." Daisy slowly opened her hand and let the pebbles trickle through her unclenched fist.

"I'm dying to do this, Desdemona, but there's a lot to consider."

"Such as?"

"I don't know anyone here."

"Sure you do." She started ticking off names on her fingers. "You know Molly and the three Wylder boys. Doc Hawkins and his receptionist. Tansy and Gracie Bella, and you'll meet Beck, Tansy's good-looking guy, when we go inside. Oh, and me. That's a darned good start. Misty Bottomers are friendly. Within a couple of weeks, you'll feel like you were born here."

Surprisingly, Elisa didn't doubt that for a second. "I'll give you that point. A bigger hurdle is a place to live. I'll be brutally honest. I lost my job back home because of budget cuts, and it came with no warning. One morning I went to work as usual, and an hour later I didn't have a job."

Desdemona made to say something, but Elisa raised a hand. "Wait. As a single mother, I haven't been able to save much." She tipped her hand back and forth. "There are a few complications that made it even tougher, things I don't want to go into right now. I'm not feeling sorry for myself, just telling it like it is." She paused. "There's something about you that makes me so comfortable."

"I'm glad, because I feel the same way. That's one of the reasons I might be able to help."

"By offering me a job. I understand and appreciate that. I'm not sure, though, as much as I want it, that I can afford to take the job." She shook her head. "And how sad is that?"

"Move in with me."

"Excuse me?"

"Move in with me. I've got a big old house with way more room than I need. It's totally over the top for one person, but it's been mine forever. I was born there, and I've kept it through all three husbands. The house gives me a sense of security, knowing I have a place to come home to. You and Daisy would have an upstairs suite to yourself, so you'd be able to get away when I drive you crazy."

"I can't do that," Elisa said.

"Why not?"

"Why can't I impose on you?"

Desdemona frowned. "Impose? Correct me if I'm wrong, but unless I've taken a turn into la-la land, this was my idea. Believe me, I wouldn't have made the offer if I didn't want you. As for that little one? It would be a true joy to have a young child in the house. Bring some life to it."

"Oh, she'd do that, believe me."

"Tell you what. I still see doubt in your eyes. How about, for now, we go pick out that paint? Exterior and interior. I'll have Beck set me up with someone to do the actual painting."

Elisa started to argue that she wasn't the one who should choose the color.

"The place needs tending to, regardless of who I hire to run it. You can at least get me on the right road by helping with the color scheme, can't you?" Pulling a lace-edged, perfumed hanky from her purse, she dabbed at her face, then fanned herself. "Let's head inside. The calendar might say October and the town might be crazy with pumpkins, but I've been in Colorado's mountains too long. I've got to reset my internal thermostat to match the Low Country's climate. I'm starting to sparkle."

Elisa smiled to herself. Sparkle, yes. Women like Desdemona Rosebud Hamilton never, ever perspired or sweated. They did, indeed, glitter and sparkle.

They weren't inside the hardware store thirty seconds when a Dierks Bentley lookalike strolled up to them. Elisa found herself wishing she had one of Desdemona's hankies, the man was that good-looking.

He wrapped Desdemona in a bear hug. "Heard you were home." He cocked his head. "Sure took you long enough to come see me."

"I wasn't sure my heart could handle all this pretty." Playfully, she pinched his cheek.

Dimples flashing, he growled, "Handsome, Desi. Guys are handsome, not pretty." Swinging his attention to Elisa, he said, "You must be the beauty who threw herself at Tucker's feet."

She groaned. "I'm never going to live that down, am I?"

"Probably not." Grinning, he held out a hand. "Beck Elliot, Tansy's husband. Nice to finally meet you, Elisa."

She smiled. She liked Beck Elliot. He sealed the deal by crouching in front of her daughter.

"And hello again, Daisy Elizabeth." He looked up at Elisa. "Did she tell you how many marshmallows she managed to put away?"

"No, she didn't."

Daisy spun in a little circle, then held up four fingers. "I eated this many."

"Wow!" Elisa said. "Pretty impressive."

"A girl after my own heart," Desdemona said. "I ran into your new bride yesterday morning. I'd say she's a lucky woman, but damned if I don't think you're the luckier one."

"You'd have that right." He reached into his back pocket and drew out his phone. Bringing up a photo, he held it out to her. "Gracie Bella's first day of kindergarten."

Elisa's heart stuttered. Oh yeah. She'd say all three of them had lucked out in that relationship. Beck, Tansy, and Gracie Bella, who now shared Beck's name. Tucker told her Beck had adopted the child within days of the wedding. Another mark in his favor.

"You come in just to see my handsome face?" Beck baited.

"Not that I wouldn't, but I've come to buy paint and to hire a painter," Desdemona said.

He frowned. "Didn't we paint that house of yours top to bottom and inside out last year when you and Reginald stopped by for a couple of weeks?"

"You did, and thank you very much for that. I'm happy

with my house exactly the way it is. For now, anyway." She grinned cheekily. "You know my building on Main?"

"I do."

"It's about to become Misty Bottoms' new bookstore."

"About damn time." He glanced at Daisy and winced. "Sorry about that. With Gracie Bella around, I should know to be more careful."

"It's okay." Elisa held her daughter's hand while she twirled in circles. "Makes you dizzy to watch, doesn't it?"

He nodded. "What color are you thinking, Desi?"

"Pink."

"Pink? Are you kidding me?"

Desdemona set a hand on her hip. "Don't tell me there's not enough testosterone in that gorgeous body to walk it into a pink building for Michael Connelly's latest Harry Bosch book or one of Nora's books for Tansy's birthday."

"When you put it that way—" he admitted.

"Seems to me I just did. So? Would you?"

"Yes, I would." He grimaced. "It isn't going to be all frou-frou inside, is it?"

"That'll be up to Elisa here," Desdemona said.

"Oh!" Elisa raised a hand to her throat. "I—We—"

Desdemona threw back her head and let out another of her guffaws. "Despite the evidence otherwise, the girl is actually able to string a sentence together. I wouldn't trust her with my business otherwise."

Beck sent Elisa a look of pure understanding. "She's rail-roading you, isn't she?"

"Well, I—" Elisa wet her lips.

"There's my answer." He turned to Desdemona. "How much pressure are you squeezing her with?"

"Everything I've got," Desdemona admitted without blinking. "Otherwise she and this little one intend to leave us. We need them right here in Misty Bottoms, where we can look out for them."

Beck simply shook his head. "Let's check out some paint chips."

Elisa would have sworn there couldn't possibly be so many colors or shades…and they'd considered every single one in the last half hour. But they kept coming back to pink. Not the soft pink they'd originally decided on, though— instead they went for a piggy-bank-pink. If they were going pink, then by darned they'd go pink. They'd paint the trim deep purple. This building would make a statement, and nobody would walk past without noticing it.

Beck shook his head. "Gotta give it to you. Despite my initial misgivings, I think these colors will be perfect for that building. When Tansy insisted on a light lavender and green for her bakery, I gave her all kinds of grief. I was wrong. When do you want the Winkler twins to start prep and painting?"

"Why don't you give either Davie or Denny a call and see what they have open? I'm good to go, so the sooner, the better."

"But—" Elisa held up a finger.

"Honey, I plan to do this with or without you. I'd much rather it be with you, but Beck's right. That needs to be your decision." Turning her attention back to Beck, she said, "The inside needs a fresh coat of paint, too. We'll think about that a bit more. And I'll want bookshelves. Can the twins build those or should I hire somebody else for that?"

"They're good with just about anything, Desi," Beck said. "They'll be able to handle whatever you need."

"Great." Eyes narrowed, Desdemona asked, "You going home, Elisa?"

"Home? As in Bowden, Alabama, or Charleston? Or Tuck's house?"

"I had Tuck's house in mind."

"I love Tut," Daisy said around the thumb she'd planted in her mouth.

"Me, too, sweetie, and I haven't even met the man." Desdemona patted the little girl's cheek. "He's been real good to you and your mom."

"Uh-huh." She nodded vigorously. "He smells good, too, but he's not my daddy."

Elisa's eyes went wide. "Daisy!"

"What?"

"Why would you even say that?"

"'Cause I asked him."

With a small whimper, Elisa tipped her head to stare at the ceiling. Heat flooded through her. Rather than meet Beck's or Desdemona's eyes, she rubbed a hand over her own.

When she heard Beck's snort, her hand dropped and her gaze flew to his. "You think that's funny?"

"I do."

Her mouth dropped open.

Around a grin, Desdemona said, "I do, too."

"Listen, Elisa," Beck said. "I went through all this not long ago myself. It's trial by fire. When a kid's involved, everything's fair game. No question is unaskable." He laughed again. "I'd have loved to see the look on Tuck's face when he fielded that one."

"Is Misty Bottoms really on the map, or have I dropped into some third dimension?"

"Oh, we're real, all right," he said. Then he tossed a glance toward Desdemona. "Most of us, anyway."

The older woman pulled herself up to all of her five-foot-six height. "I believe I'll take that as a compliment, Mr. Elliot."

With a mischievous smile on his face, he answered, "As you should."

"Mommy?" Daisy patted her mother's leg to get her attention.

"What, sweetie?"

"You said Daddy lived a long way away. We're a long, long way away, so why isn't Tut my daddy?"

She opened her mouth, then closed it, not having a clue how to answer her daughter's question, one that for a three-and-a-half-year-old made a lot of sense.

"Daddy lives far away somewhere else," Desdemona said.

"Oh." She yawned. "Can we go there someday?"

Before Elisa could come up with a reply, Beck said, "You look tired, sweet pea."

"I'm not. I don't need a nap, 'cause I'm a big girl. Huh, Mommy?"

"Yes, you are." Elisa rolled her eyes. "But even big girls take naps sometimes."

Daisy shook her head hard enough to send her blond curls flying. "Not me. Not now." She spoiled it with another big yawn.

"Want to take a peek at my house before you make a decision, Elisa? See if it will suit?"

Elisa stole a sidelong glance at Daisy, whose head drooped to one side. "As much as I'd love to, I think Daisy could use that n-a-p."

"You're right. Give me a call when it'll fit into your schedule."

A laugh spurted out of Elisa before she could stop it. "My schedule? I think we decided earlier that would be nonexistent right now. It's like I've dropped into some great big sinkhole. If I was a car, I'd be stuck in neutral."

"Well, let's get you jump-started then. You willing to give the bookstore a shot?"

"Thought you were gonna give her some time," Beck said.

Wearing an expression of feigned innocence, Desdemona simply shrugged.

"Willing?" Elisa couldn't fight it anymore. "I can't wait to get started."

"Yes!" Desdemona's arm shot into the air in triumph. "First step? Let's get that child home for her n-a-p."

Elisa fretted the entire way back to Tucker's house. What had she done? This was a huge step, and she needed to think. Yet she'd already said yes to Desdemona.

Wasn't this exactly what she'd been praying for, though? A real job, a place where she and Daisy could sink roots, make friends, and start new traditions.

The downside? Same as the upside. Tucker Wylder lived here. She'd see him every day, would run into him and watch him settle into his own life, a life that wouldn't include her. She understood that. He'd taken her in because, in addition to being the handsomest, sexiest man she'd ever met, he was a truly nice person. A little uptight and self-contained, but wonderful.

If she expected him to change his entire lifestyle for her or because of what happened last night, she was living in fantasy land. All it took was a single look around his house, at the precision in every item and every corner, and there could be no doubt he was a bachelor from the top of that barely grown-out military cut to the tip of those steel-toed work boots he wore.

Once she came to terms with that, she'd be happy living here and running Desdemona's bookstore. Wonder what she'd name it? One thing for sure, it would be cozy and welcoming. There'd always be a pot of coffee and hot water for tea. Maybe a cat curled up on an overstuffed armchair.

Books and people. She loved both. Working in the library had suited her. Yes, there'd been days when things hadn't gone well and she'd arrived home tired and frustrated. But watching a child's face light up during story time, teaching fifty-seven-year-old Mr. Stimple to read, or tucking away a new gardening book for Rita Mae had been worth every night she'd crawled into bed exhausted.

That life had been snatched away. Now? She had an opportunity to spend her days doing all that again, thanks to a chance stop at Molly's bridal boutique and Desdemona Rosebud Hamilton. It would be a safe bet that some thought the woman was a little out there. Okay, a lot out there.

Elisa thought her extraordinary and more than a little magical.

Since Daisy had fallen asleep the second the tires started turning, Elisa decided to take a drive out to Wylder Rides. She didn't like the way she and Tucker had ended things last night. On the way there, she'd need to come up with an excuse for showing up in the middle of the day.

Spotting Sweet Dreams, she pulled in. Why not take the guys a treat? Besides, she was beyond curious about Tansy's bakery. Since she'd just met Beck at the hardware store, why not stop by for a visit with his wife? If she planned to live here…

She let out a shaky breath. No, she wouldn't think about that. At least not right now.

Daisy wouldn't wake if she carried her inside. She could grab some coffee and her growing-up-too-fast daughter could get the nap she needed. The world would be a far better place without a cranky child, which was exactly what her sweet little girl turned into when tired.

Last night, though, Tucker had crowned himself King of the Crank-Buckets.

In a heated argument with his brothers about whether or not to take on a second project for a hard-to-please client, Tucker's ears tuned in to the sound of a car out front.

Elisa's rattletrap. It might be in far better shape than when she'd first driven into town, but the woman needed a new car. His knees went a tad wobbly at the memory of her dropping at his feet, and even more so when he thought of holding her, of dancing with her last night, of kissing her and then making her his. But he hadn't really, had he?

He tossed down the air hose and hustled outside—there she stood. Uneasy, he tried to gauge her expression. Surprisingly, she didn't look angry.

"Hi, Tuck. I wasn't sure you'd be here."

"Yep. Full workday, but the boys and I are having a disagreement. Good you stopped by. We needed a time-out."

"Tut!" Daisy, invigorated by her short nap, threw herself at him the second Elisa freed her from her seat. A megawatt smile lit up her face.

He caught her close, gave her a big noisy smooch on the cheek, and tossed her in the air. "You and your mom out causing trouble?"

"No. We've been good, haven't we, Mommy?"

"Yes, we have." She held up the carrier Tansy had given her. "And…we come bearing gifts." Reaching inside the car, she pulled out a bag and handed it to Daisy. "That's for Tuck."

The little girl, still nestled in his arms, held it out to him. "Here, Tut. Brownies. They're really good."

"Did you snitch one?"

She smiled. "Noooo."

"Then how did those crumbs get on the corner of your mouth?"

"Mommy snitched two. One for her and one for me."

Elisa snorted a chuckle. "Ungrateful child."

"What's that mean?" Daisy asked.

"Never mind." To Tucker, she said, "Daisy and I ate our own. There're still plenty in that bag to share with your brothers."

"Good." Gaven sauntered out through the bay door and grabbed the bag from Tucker.

"Hey! Hand that over or you get none of Tansy's coffee."

"You brought coffee, too?" Gaven, looking for all the world like a kid on the first day of summer vacation, practically danced back outside. Swinging the bag, he said, "I'll trade a brownie for a drink."

"You'll trade more than one," Tucker growled. Setting

Daisy on her feet, he took the cup carrier from Elisa. "Give the bag to Elisa. Then we'll negotiate."

Wiping his hands on a garage rag, Brant stepped outside into the fall day. "I swear, Elisa, if I didn't have Molly, I'd ask you out on the town." He shrugged toward Tucker. "Don't suppose this oaf has?"

"I will!" Gaven volunteered. "Tuck, you won't mind babysitting while Elisa and I sneak away to play, will you?"

After last night's foot-in-mouth moment, Tucker glanced at Elisa, at the uncertainty on her face. Was it because she wasn't sure Gaven was kidding? Didn't know how to tell him no? Or because she wanted to say yes?

Before it went any further, he blurted, "Forget it, Gav. We're working late tonight, but Elisa, Daisy, and I already have big plans for tomorrow night."

"Oh yeah?" Brant raised a brow.

"What's up?" Gaven asked. "Where are you going?"

"I don't believe that's any of your business." Tucker was afraid to look at Elisa, certain she'd call him out for the fibber he was. He nodded toward their back room. "Why don't you run the numbers on that project again? I'll be with you in a few."

Gaven started to answer, but Brant grabbed his arm and a coffee. "Come on, Bro. I don't think they need us here."

Tucker gave him a thumbs-up. "Brant, you've just moved into my-favorite-brother spot."

CHAPTER 14

ELISA TUCKED A SWEET-SMELLING, SLEEPING DAISY INTO
bed. What a day. A trip out for some fresh air had resulted in
a new, rather eccentric friend, a job offer, a possible temporary home, and, if he'd been serious, a date tomorrow night
with Tucker—one that included her daughter. Maybe he
didn't want her to leave any more than she wanted to—but
then again, maybe he'd just been poking at Gaven. Tucker
could be hard to read.

She hadn't shared her big news with him. It wasn't an
intentional secret, but it hadn't felt right spilling it in front
of Brant and Gaven. Then after they'd gone inside, she'd
hesitated and missed her chance.

Tonight would have been a good time to tell him, but
Tucker had, after a nice visit with her and Daisy, worked
late. He'd called at six to say he'd be a few hours still, so she
and Daisy ate their favorite dinner—pancakes and bacon.
After half an hour in the tub and three bedtime stories,
Daisy had finally given in to sleep.

Moonlight sifted through the curtains and tossed shadows across the room. Elisa turned restlessly in bed. She'd
heard Tucker come home well past ten, but she doubted he
was asleep, either. Sitting up, she listened. Absolute quiet
but for the ticking of the clock on her dresser.

1:47 a.m.

As long as she was awake, she might as well check on
Daisy.

Standing in the hallway, she noticed Tucker's door stood open. Strange. He kept it closed; it was his sanctuary. Tiptoeing down the hall, she realized neither the room nor the bed had been used. Her heart hurt for him. He appeared to be so in control of himself and every situation, yet something ate at him, something that, even with his strength, he couldn't control.

Heading to the other end of the hall, she peered inside her daughter's room. Curled up on her side, Daisy slept the sleep of the innocent. Elisa blew her a kiss, then belted her robe and slipped downstairs to check on Tucker.

Wouldn't that fry his butt to think someone felt the need to do that?

Expecting to see him sacked out on the couch, she was surprised to find it empty. So were the rest of the rooms. She moved to the window and stared out. No Mustang.

Where had he gone under the cover of the night's darkness?

Telling herself it was none of her business, she headed back upstairs. Halfway there, she stopped. Hadn't he caught her when she fell? Didn't she owe him the same? She didn't imagine for an instant he'd thank her for it. Still…

Dressed, she carried a sleeping Daisy to the car and strapped her in. The child never stirred.

As she drove away from the house, her little voice chastised her for this fool's errand, one that would, no doubt, have Tucker kicking her and Daisy out. If that happened, if he hated her for interfering, she couldn't stay in Misty Bottoms.

Regardless, she couldn't turn her back on his pain.

Driving aimlessly, she thought back on the day at the park and remembered how his gaze had strayed to the war memorial. Her mind caught on that ever-present key around his neck and his time as a Marine. All parts of the puzzle that made up Tucker Wylder, that kept him up at night.

When she turned onto Main, she spotted his Mustang. In the dim light, she made out Tucker's silhouetted figure. He sat in the grass, one hand on the granite marker.

Suddenly, she was every kind of sorry she'd come. She had no business snooping on his private moments, and this was definitely one of those. She had to leave, had to go home without him seeing her.

Heart beating rapidly, she searched for a side street to turn onto.

Too late.

His head came up and he stared at her headlights, at her car. He'd know it was her, that she'd headed into territory he'd warned her against.

Slowly, he rose to his feet.

Resigned, she pulled in behind his car and cut her lights. Rolling both her window and the passenger side one partway down, she quietly opened her door and slid out. Tucker stood ramrod-straight, his hands at his sides, clenched in fists.

For one second, she felt the slightest frisson of fear. She didn't really know this man, didn't know his history or what he might be capable of. She'd thought she'd known Luke, only to find out she'd fallen in love with a façade.

"Tucker?"

"What in the hell are you doing here, Elisa?" His voice was deep and gravelly, each word clipped. "Where's Daisy?"

And that told her everything she needed to know. She didn't need to fear Tucker. Despite whatever was going on inside him, his first concern lay with her daughter.

"She's asleep in the car." Elisa cursed the tremor in her voice. "I left the windows partially open, so I'll hear her if she wakes."

"Why are you here?"

"That's what I'm wondering." She took several steps closer. Even in the filtered light, she saw the despair etched on his face. "Why are *you* here, Tuck? Why aren't you home in bed?"

He raked unsteady fingers through his hair. "We've been through this. Sleeping's not one of my talents."

"Why?" Her question was whispered.

"Why?" His laugh wasn't one of humor, but of self-degradation, of self-loathing. "How much time do you have?"

"All night." Taking his hand, she pulled him back to the grass.

"How'd you find me?"

She shrugged. "Does it matter?"

"Guess not." He plucked several blades of grass and let the breeze carry them away. "Look, this doesn't concern you. It's my problem."

She shivered.

"You're cold." He took off his jacket and draped it over her shoulders.

His heat warmed her and made her that much more determined to help him.

"Go home. Go to bed, Lissie. If it'll make you feel better, I'll follow you."

"No."

"No?"

She read the disbelief on his face. "You didn't walk away from me when I needed help."

"I don't need—"

"Stop." The single word snapped in the night air. "Don't you dare lie to me. Don't you dare feed me some line. Not here. Not now. Do you have any idea how hard it was for me to accept help from a total stranger? To become your charity case?"

"I *never* thought of you that way," he bit back angrily.

"Good. I'm glad to hear it." Satisfied she'd sparked anger over self-pity, she went on. "You're not a charity case, either. But I'll tell you one thing, Mr. Tucker Wylder, that's as clear as that aristocratic nose planted in the middle of your face." She jabbed a finger into his chest. "You need saving every bit as badly as I did. And by damned, you'll let me do it."

He dropped onto his back and stared up at the stars. "Okay, the lady has a temper."

"You'd better believe it. People look at me and see soft. Far from it. I've gone through too much to be soft. Naive, maybe. Innocent? Not so much. I won't be walked on, and I won't be belittled."

"I wouldn't do that."

"You are—by assuming I can't help you."

He sighed deeply. "Look, you're right, okay? I've got a problem. But—" He held up a hand. "I can solve it. Myself. It's time to roll up my sleeves and tackle it head-on. That's why I'm here tonight."

"It's something that happened in the Middle East." It wasn't a question.

"Yeah. I lost four of the best friends a guy could ever have because a pompous, arrogant lieutenant colonel decided to throw his weight around. He refused to listen to anybody. Hard-Ass Harry always knew best. Since he wasn't the one out there getting blown to bits, what did a few grunts matter?"

"Hard-Ass Harry?" Elisa's throat constricted.

"Yeah. My LC. A total prick. I hope to hell he gets what's coming to him." He rolled to his side, studying her. "Hey, you okay? You're white as a sheet."

"It's the moonlight."

"Like hell. It's you. You shouldn't be out here in the night air. You're gonna get sick."

"No. I'm not." She shook her head. "I'm not some hot-house orchid." But her stomach pitched, and she thought she might lose those pancakes she'd eaten. Lt. Col. Hard-Ass Harry. Oh God! "Tell me. Tell me everything. I need to know."

"I haven't told anybody everything."

"Then it'll do you good. If you want, I'll lie beside you in the grass. You won't need to see me, and I can't see you."

"Like a confessional?"

"If that works."

"You know, if Sheriff Jimmy Don or Sam decides to do a drive-by, they'll haul our sorry asses off to jail."

"I'm willing to risk it."

"There's a whole other side to you, isn't there, Lissie? You can be pretty pushy."

"Darned right, so don't you forget that."

They lay side by side in the grass, hips touching. The dark enveloped them and provided a blanket of anonymity. He eased into it, and she let him.

"I'm gonna start by saying that anyone who's gone to war has things that eat at him or her. I'm not alone in this, and I'm not feelin' sorry for myself."

"Understood."

She felt more than saw the unwilling smile touch his lips.

"You're something else, you know that?"

"Yeah. Too bad nobody can figure out what that something else is."

"I think I have a pretty good idea," he said.

"And *I* think you're procrastinating."

"All right." He took a cleansing breath, then let it out slowly. "Here goes. When I joined the Marines, I'd intended to be a lifer. That didn't work out so well. I did my tour, signed up for a second, then left the minute I was free to go. Things happened that I can't get out of my head. During the day, I can pretty much manage to keep them at bay. At night? They come crawling out."

"Is that why you won't share a house with Gaven?"

"Partially. I need a lair, a place of my own. Truth is, though, even before I became a Leatherneck, I tended to be somewhat of a recluse. I love my brothers, but I need head time. Maybe it came from Brant and I being born so close together. There was never a time when it was just me. And doesn't that sound selfish and petty?"

"No, it doesn't."

"When Gaven came along, the twin beds became a twin and bunks...and a snotty-nosed little brother. Mom finally got tired of my whining and turned our small den into a room for me. But nine months later, my sister, Lainey, showed up and that room became a nursery, so I went back to bunking with Brant and Gaven."

"I grew up alone, wanting brothers and sisters," Elisa said. "Guess we're never happy, are we?"

He turned to her. "You said your mom was always off digging up relics. What about your dad? Where was he?"

Oh, zigzagging dragonflies. How did she answer that? "He, um, was rarely home, then he and my mom divorced."

"I'm sorry." He reached for her hand. Heart aching, she tightened her fingers around his and prayed she was wrong. If he found out—

She shrugged. "It is what it is."

"Not to throw your own words back at you, but don't feed me a line."

"You're right." She squeezed his fingers. "I hated not having my parents around. I hated being different from everyone else at school. I hated that my grandmother had to take care of me and that I'd created a problem for her."

"You didn't create any of it. You were the victim."

"My grandmother was, too."

"You know, I doubt very much she thought of herself as a victim or you as a headache. My guess is she figured herself blessed to have you."

"That's what she said," Elisa whispered.

"Then you should believe it."

She was silent for a few heartbeats. "We've strayed way off-track. What happened, Tuck?"

"You are nothing if not persistent."

"That's right. So spill it. You'll feel better."

"I sincerely doubt that." He fingered the key at his neck. "First off, the names on this stone?" He nodded at the slab of granite. "My name should be on one like it somewhere."

"But it's not."

"No, it's not. You know why? Because while my friends walked into a trap and died, I stayed behind, safe at base."

"My guess is that wasn't your choice."

"Not directly. I disagreed with Hard-Ass Harry's orders to carry out a plan that had zero chance of success."

"Hard-Ass Harry." The words came out in a whisper, her heart working to block them, barely allowing the sound to escape. She swore her heart would implode. Did she dare ask his lieutenant colonel's last name?

"Yeah." Bitterness oozed from him. "The egotistical jackass was dead wrong, but he wouldn't even consider he might have misread the situation. Because I dared to insinuate I knew better than him, I had to be taught a lesson."

"Tuck."

She didn't think he even heard her, his mind reliving that night. She didn't know if she could bear hearing the rest.

"My punishment?" His voice broke. "I was confined to base. Because of that, I lived. The others all died." His fingers tightened on the key. "Angie, Nate, Jorge, and LeBron. They're gone. Forever. If I'd been there, I might have been able to stop it."

Her heart broke. There was nothing to say, no words to heal this kind of hurt.

"Because of a bad decision made by an arrogant prick—excuse my language—but because of him, some very good people lost their lives. Their futures."

She had to leave, and the sooner the better. He'd never forgive her if he found out. It had to remain her secret. She'd hoped...but no. Not meant to be.

"Go on home," he whispered. "I'll be there in a few."

"Tuck—"

He leaned on one elbow, touching a finger to her lips. "Shhh. It's okay. I'll get through this."

"Do you have to do it alone?"

"I do. Can you handle Daisy by yourself? Get her inside to bed?"

She smiled sadly. "I've been doing it for three and a half years. I think I can manage it tonight."

"And you're doing it alone," he said.

"Point made." She rose to her knees. "Your friends. They wouldn't want this, Tuck. They wouldn't blame you, and they certainly wouldn't have expected you to be able to fix everything or to change the outcome. Maybe you're giving yourself too much credit."

His mouth dropped open in surprise.

"Superman only exists in comic books."

Even in the muted light, she saw the heat on his cheeks. She assumed it was anger and was sorry, but she wouldn't take it back. Unlike Atlas, Tucker couldn't carry the weight of the entire world on his shoulders. She knew, though, he'd continue giving it one heck of a try.

"Promise you'll come home soon."

"Home." He sighed. "I will. If I can ever truly find it."

CHAPTER 15

TUCKER WAS GONE WHEN ELISA STUMBLED DOWNSTAIRS the next morning. A note lay on the counter beside his coffee machine, the handwriting, bold and black, splashed across plain white paper.

> *Tons to do. Left early. Be sure you eat—carbs and protein. Thanks for sharing the night. Hope you got back to sleep.*
>
> *Tuck*

Not a wasted word. Very Tuck. A sigh bubbled up from her toes. *Thanks for sharing the night.* Words to make her heart stutter. If only they'd shared it differently. Just thinking about Tucker made all her girlie parts want to sing. Remembering the night they had come together made those parts stand up and belt out the "Hallelujah Chorus"—until she replayed the ending.

The man was so off-limits he wasn't even on the map.

Maybe.

Did she dare risk another night with him in his bed, in his arms?

He'd told Gaven they had a date tonight. After the shared nocturnal confidences, would he keep it—or had it simply been bluster for his brothers? And for heaven's sake, what was with all these questions, the mental debate? Her head felt ready to burst.

She hit the brew button, hoping to sneak a first cup before Daisy scooted down the stairs. While she waited, she scooped her hair up and off her neck and secured it into a long tail.

If things hadn't already been complicated enough, Hard-Ass Harry had now been thrown into the mix. The omnipotent Lt. Col. Harold Eklund, leader of men and abandoner of family. She'd barely slept a wink last night. After demanding that Tucker share all, could she do anything less?

If she'd ever hoped, down in the deepest pocket of her soul, that there was the slightest chance for her and Tucker, last night had extinguished it.

Good old Dad had finally shown up. What perfect timing.

Tucker ran the final calculations and entered them into the computer-generated estimate sheet. After a lot of back and forth, he and his brothers had decided to restore the second car for their pain-in-the-butt customer, the one they'd been arguing about when Elisa paid her surprise visit.

She seemed to make a habit of popping up unexpectedly. She'd sure caught him off guard at the park last night, insisting he'd feel better if he got it off his chest. He hadn't. If anything, he'd felt rawer. In telling it, he'd relived that day, that night—every minute of it. Maybe in time it would settle. Right now, he wondered how he'd ever face her again.

Nothing to do about that now, so he hit PRINT. He'd file a hard copy of the estimate, then send one off to their client.

He heard Gaven drive up. Brant had located a few

hard-to-find parts for the project they were working on, and Gaven had made the Savannah run to collect them. The bell over the door jingled as he swung through. Two steps inside, his younger brother stopped. "Whoa. You look like hell. Bad night?"

"You could say that."

"Did you get any sleep?"

"A couple of hours."

Gaven, usually cavalier, set the can of paint he'd tucked under one arm on the counter. "Why don't you go home and grab a couple of hours of shut-eye? There's nothing pressing here. Leave whatever you're doing, and Brant can either finish it up when he gets back with lunch or you can do it tomorrow."

"I'm okay."

"You're not." Arms folded over his chest, Gaven leaned against a bookshelf that held their manuals and parts lists. "It's time we all quit pretending you are. Everybody's been pussy-footing around this, but you're not all right, Tuck. You're different. Whatever happened to the Marine over there changed you, the person. Why won't you share what's going on in that hard head?"

"I'm telling you, I'm good."

"Not buying it." He pinned Tucker with a hard stare, the easygoing younger brother having disappeared. "Do you need to see someone? Maybe visit a doc down in Savannah? Nobody here would need to know."

Tucker blew out a ragged breath. "Look, I know you worry about me. Don't. This will pass."

Time to see Doc Hawkins. Elisa had meant to do it yesterday, but Desdemona had kind of derailed her plans.

"Where are we going, Mommy?" Daisy's question snapped Elisa out of her reverie.

"To see Doctor Hawkins. Remember him?"

"Uh-huh. He was nice. He didn't give me no shots."

"No, he didn't."

"The lady was nice, too."

"Brinna."

Daisy nodded.

While she chattered away, Elisa drove into town. When she thought about her time here, tears pooled in her eyes. Misty Bottoms had proved to be a miracle. Tucker? A gift from heaven. He'd done so much for her and her daughter. More, though, he'd reminded her of what life was supposed to be and that she was a woman. A young woman.

She'd all but lost herself and had forgotten what it was to be desirable. To desire. To dream.

Now that part of her was awake, and she hadn't a clue what to do about it. Especially after last night. Since sleep had remained elusive, she'd crawled into bed with her laptop. A little research proved that Hard-Ass Harry, the man who'd led Tucker's friends to the slaughter, was the same man who'd fathered her.

She couldn't keep it from him. That kind of secret festered and grew if it wasn't lanced. Every day that passed would make the telling harder and Tucker angrier when he found out.

For the life of her, though, she couldn't think of a way to do it. What could she say? "Hey, Tuck. The funniest thing. You know that jerk behind your friends' deaths? He's my dad." Or maybe something a bit less in-your-face. "I don't think I ever told you my maiden name, did I? It's Eklund. Same as my father's. Harold Eklund. Lt. Col. Harold Eklund."

She parked, and together she and her daughter headed inside.

She'd worry about Tucker and her dad later.

Brinna smiled when they walked through the door. "Boy, you look a lot better than the last time I saw you!"

"I feel better, too. Daisy and I have appointments."

"Yes, you do. Doc has a patient with him, but he shouldn't be long." Brinna turned to Daisy. "Do you want some crayons and a coloring book, sweetie?"

"Uh-huh." She looked up at her mother and quickly added, "Please."

Elisa took a seat and Daisy knelt by the coffee table, ready to color.

When Brinna returned, she dropped to the floor beside the little girl, tucking her crimson skirt beneath her. "I think you were coloring a princess last time."

Daisy nodded. "I—"

"Well, if it isn't Daisy Danvers." Doc Hawkins stood in the hallway, a blue-haired older woman beside him.

Daisy jumped up and scooted into her mother's lap.

"Brinna, would you make an appointment for Ethel in six months?" He turned to his patient. "Remember what I said about that ice cream. It's fine to have some once in a while, but not every night."

"Spoilsport," the woman complained. "Does he watch your diet like a hawk, Brinna?"

"I don't let him see my lunch." The receptionist grinned.

"You're a smart one, but then, so's your mama."

When she left, Doc Hawkins turned to Elisa. "Ethel Lawton taught everybody in town. Fourth grade. The woman forgets nothing. When I chewed her out today about the ice cream, she reminded me I used to eat paste." He rolled his eyes. "So how are you feelin'?"

He led her and Daisy back to one of the exam rooms.

"I'm good."

"Keepin' an eye on your diet?"

"I am. So's Tucker."

He chuckled. "He's a good man."

"He is." She licked dry lips. "It, ah, is possible we might be staying in town, so there's something else I'd like to talk to you about."

"You're movin' in with Desdemona, from what I hear."

She stared at him. "How do you know that?"

He laughed. "Small town and wagging tongues. Couple of the town gossips saw you and Desdemona together at Molly's boutique. Somebody else said the two of you went into Desi's building, and Andy Gibson caught you at Beck's discussin' paint colors." He spread his hands, palms up. "And there you have it. Putting two and two together, I'm guessing she's considering a new business and that you're involved in it, since another of my patients heard Desi mention you moving in with her."

"Seriously?"

"My informants have no qualms about eavesdropping." When she opened her mouth to speak, he said, "Don't hold it against them. They mean well."

"Hmm. No secrets," she said.

"Not many."

She thought of the one she hid from Tucker and the one she'd share with the doctor today. "I'd prefer what I tell you now remain private."

"Anything you tell me stays right here."

"Of course it does. Sorry." She picked at a thread on her dress.

"No need to be sorry. Something's worrying you."

"No. Yes." Her gaze shifted to her child who was playing with a model of an ear. "Do you think Brinna would keep an eye on Daisy for a few minutes? I know that's asking a lot, but—"

"Not at all. She loves kids." He moved to the door. "Brinna, Daisy's coming out to visit with you for a few minutes."

"All right!" Brinna rushed to the door and held out a hand. Daisy left with her, smiling and waving goodbye to her mother.

Doc Hawkins closed the door. "Now. What's bothering you? You still not feeling well?"

"I'm good. Honest. It's Daisy." She explained her daughter's heart problem and handed him a thumb drive. "Her medical records are on that. Right now, everything seems fine, but I'd feel better if someone monitored her."

"I agree. I'll do a quick check today." He went into the waiting room and chatted with Daisy. He made playtime out of his checkup, and Elisa loved him for it.

Afterward, they moved back into the exam room. "The hole hasn't closed."

"No."

"My guess is that it won't at this point. But it might not ever give her any trouble, either. I'm kind of surprised they didn't fix it as long as they were already in there. But that's second-guessing, and I'm just a small-town general practitioner, not a heart specialist." He rubbed his chin. "You know what to watch for, Ms. Danvers?"

"Elisa, please, and yes, I do."

"Everybody calls me Doc. You headed over to Desdemona Rosebud's?"

"That's our next stop."

"It's Hamilton now, but it was Collins when I took her to the prom. Prettiest girl there."

"You took Desdemona to the prom?"

"My lucky night. Phillip Durst, the team's quarterback and the senior-class heartthrob, broke her heart earlier that week. I picked up a few of the pieces and let her save face."

A smile spread across his kind face. "Figure I'll learn a little more about what you're up to when I see her tonight. I called her just before Ethel came in. Seems Desdemona Rosebud and I are having dinner."

Elisa managed to restrain herself. No whoops, no air pumps, no I-knew-its. But oh yeah—the doc and the widow definitely had some spark between them.

Speaking of the widow, it was time Elisa firmed up Desdemona's offer. She'd be crazy not to. The job was perfect, and they could make the house work until she found something else for her and Daisy. Before she pulled away from the doctor's, she took Desdemona's card from her wallet and punched in the number.

After the second ring, the phone was answered. "Desdemona Rosebud Hamilton. What can I do for you today?"

"Well, I thought maybe you could give us the nickel tour of your home. Unless you've changed your mind about taking us on."

A hearty laugh rolled over the airwaves. "Honey, I've been thinkin' about you and that child and hopin' you'd give me a call. Where are you, and how soon can you be here?"

"Desdemona, it's gorgeous." Elisa's head swiveled back and forth. "And that's such an understatement, I'm ashamed of myself. But, honestly." She turned a full circle, taking in the two-story brick wall, the curved staircase, the crystal lamps and artwork. Some of the knickknacks had to be worth more than her annual library salary. Despite all that, the place felt like home. It was cozy—albeit a very upscale cozy. "You can't possibly want a child here."

"Oh, darlin', you have no idea how badly I want a little one's laughter in this house. Not having one of my own is the biggest sorrow of my life. Share Daisy with me—for a little while, at least." Desdemona, dressed in winter-white silk pants and a candy-apple-red tunic, raised a hand. "Let me show you around."

The dining table could seat at least a dozen without bumping elbows. And oh, the chandelier!

"How did you ever leave this house, Desdemona?"

"It was hard, but when you love someone, you want to be with him. I enjoyed my time away, but no matter where I went, home waited for me right here. It never judged me, simply accepted me back."

Elisa saw beneath the flamboyance to a very vulnerable

woman…and liked her so much more for it. Here was a woman who had known great joy and, if she wasn't mistaken, great sadness. But she hadn't let the bad make her afraid to reach for the good.

"I think we could be very, very good friends, Desdemona."

"I think we already are."

They hugged. Daisy, wanting in on the action, wrapped one arm around her mom's neck and one around Desdemona's. Elisa swore she saw tears in the other woman's eyes.

Desdemona cleared her throat and walked into the kitchen.

"Oh, now this is seriously mind-blowing."

"It's pretty, Mommy."

"Yeah." Pretty didn't begin to describe it. Straight out of *Better Homes and Gardens* or *HGTV* magazine, the room was functional, cozy, and phenomenal. "Do you use it?"

Desdemona laughed. "Look at me. I'm a very happy plus-size, which I maintain through my love of food. Heck yeah, I use the kitchen. I love to cook." She took inventory of Elisa. "And you need somebody to cook for you. Let me."

Elisa's heart fluttered at the simple, honest request.

"Let's head upstairs. I'll show you your suite."

Like a steamroller, Desdemona kept moving.

When they passed a very masculine bedroom, Elisa's brows rose.

"Not everybody shares my love of glitter and glam," Desdemona explained.

Elisa smiled.

"You'll have two bedrooms, a small sitting area, and a bath. Hope you don't mind, but I did a little fussing to kind of sweeten the pot in case you came by."

Elisa stepped into a room that smelled of sunshine and

lemon oil. Fresh flowers in fall colors shared a vase with vibrant autumn leaves on a short white dresser. The mirror behind them doubled their impact.

Daisy threw herself at the massive bed covered in a soft-pink duvet. A snowfall of toss pillows mounded near the headboard.

"Up, Mommy." She raised her arms and held them out to Elisa.

"I'll sit you on the edge, but you can't climb on the bed. You have your shoes on."

"'Kay." She sent a big smile toward Desdemona. "I like your house. Tut has a nice house, too, doesn't he, Mommy?"

"Yes, he does, baby."

Desdemona gave Elisa a look only another woman would understand, a look that said yep, as young as she was, even this little girl appreciated Tucker.

This house, Elisa thought, with its crystal, brocade, and fripperies, was the polar opposite of Tucker's clean lines and no-clutter house.

Both fit their owners to a T.

The small sitting area with its comfy white sofa and chairs would make the perfect curling-up spot at the end of a long day. But the best feature? A set of French doors that led to a small balcony and looked out over that to-die-for backyard. She imagined morning coffee there or an evening cup of tea as the sun set.

Gratitude and happiness had her heart nearly bursting from her chest. Elisa wanted so badly to say yes.

Still, she held back.

"Mommy, you look funny. Does your tummy hurt?"

Her tummy didn't hurt, but oh, it was turning

somersaults. "No, honey. My tummy's okay. I'm just thinking."

Desdemona came up beside her as she stared out the window. "I'm asking a lot, aren't I?"

"No. You're *offering* a lot." Her voice broke. "Do you have any idea what this would mean to Daisy and me?"

"I think I do, yes. I've been on my own, and I didn't like it." She nodded her head toward Daisy. "And that was without a child who depended on me." Desdemona cleared her throat. "If you decide to move in, I expect you to treat it like your home. No walking on eggshells or worrying about making a mess. I expect that. I want that."

"Oh, Desdemona Rosebud Hamilton, be careful what you wish for."

Desdemona winked at her. "The bathroom's in there. I'm afraid you'll have to share."

"We always have."

Daisy ran on ahead of her. "A swimming pool, Mommy!" She jumped up and down, clapping her hands.

"Not quite." Desdemona ruffled her hair. "Almost as big, though, I guess, to someone your size."

Elisa had to agree. Desdemona didn't do anything by half measures. The whirlpool tub could have fit an entire Brownie troop with room left over.

They wandered into the smaller bedroom. Soft cotton curtains hung at the window and colorful throw rugs were strewn across gleaming hardwood floors. An upholstered chair and hassock sat in a corner. A single bed hugged the far wall.

"Look, Mommy, look!"

A dollhouse, a replica of the one they stood in, sat on a small table, the windows in its Victorian gables gleaming.

"My father commissioned it for me one year at Christmas. It's been hidden away in the attic, so I brought it down yesterday and gave it a good dusting."

When Daisy peeked inside it, Desdemona said, "You can touch, sweetheart. It's meant to be enjoyed and played with."

Daisy picked up the crib from the bedroom. "Just like mine. When I was a baby," she added quickly.

"Right. You sleep in a big-girl bed now, don't you?"

"Uh-huh."

"While she plays with that, come help me pick out a dress. I have a date tonight."

"So I heard."

"You saw Doc today?"

Elisa nodded.

Desdemona disappeared inside her closet. "Let me show you what I'm thinking."

Doctor Hawkins wouldn't know what hit him, Elisa thought. Desdemona had finally decided on black slacks and a black top that showed off her assets to perfection, an understated outfit for her until she added the killer heels and a purple-and-green sequined sweater.

With a last wave, Elisa started down the sidewalk, Daisy in tow.

"I'm hungry, Mommy."

"Me, too, sweetie. Let's eat."

"Can we get some ice cream?"

"No ice cream."

"I want ice cream." The little girl's lower lip slid out in a pout.

"Well, then, we'll go home and eat there."

"I'm sorry, Mommy. Picnic, please."

"That's better." She nodded, feeling totally overwhelmed. She'd driven into Misty Bottoms about as low as a person could get. Now she had options and opportunities, and it was pretty darned wonderful.

Not everything was perfect, though. She thought about Tucker.

The sins of the father…

CHAPTER 16

CRUISING DOWN DUFFY MILL ROAD IN THE SWANKIER section of town, Tucker downshifted and slowed to a crawl. Dressed in a pair of black leggings and a long-sleeved pink sweater, Elisa stood in front of a house that could easily serve as a boutique hotel. Daisy twirled her way along the path, the skirt of her dress swirling as she circled again and again and again. Tucker felt dizzy watching her.

He pulled up to the curb.

Daisy spotted him first and let out a happy squeal. "Tut!"

He got out of the car and sauntered up the walk.

When she ran to him, he leaned in and tickled her belly. "Hey, baby girl, what are you and Mommy up to?"

"A picnic!"

"And you didn't invite me?" He slid a sidelong glance at Elisa.

"You can come," Daisy said. "Huh, Mommy?"

"Can I, Mommy?" Tucker grinned at Elisa. "You willing to put up with me as well as the rug rat here?"

"I'm not a rug rat. I'm a girl."

"And a pretty one. So's your mother."

He leveled a look at Elisa, and his grin slid away. "I owe you an apology. Several of them, actually."

"No, you don't."

"I do. I screwed up night before last, then dropped a lot of heavy sh—stuff on you last night. Stuff you didn't need to hear. My guess is you didn't get much sleep."

She didn't blink, didn't back off. "No, I didn't. Still I'm glad you shared with me." Elisa touched his arm. "It might not seem like it now, but I honestly think verbalizing something like what you went through is the first step to healing…or at least learning to live with a bad situation you can't change."

He said nothing.

"And Daisy and I would love to have you join us for lunch."

With a nod toward the blue cooler on the backseat of her car, he asked, "What are we having?"

"Peanut butter and grape jelly sandwiches, Granny Smith apple slices, and milk," Elisa rattled off.

"Yum! All my favorite foods."

"Mine, too," Daisy chirped. She wrapped her arms around his legs. "Mommy peeled my apples, though, 'cause I don't like the stuff on the outside. I frowed up when I ate it, didn't I, Mommy?"

Elisa grimaced. "Yes, you certainly did."

"I don't like to frow up. It hurts."

Tucker wrinkled his nose. "It does."

"Lug Nut made me frow up, too."

"Yeah, I remember that well." Tucker's attention moved from his abused rug back to Elisa. "Where are we having our picnic?"

"I thought we'd go down by the river."

"Good idea. Why don't you ride with me?"

"You sure?"

"Absolutely. Your car will be fine here." He glanced toward the house and saw a curtain twitch. Someone watched them. With a shoulder jerk toward the big house, he said, "Nice place. Who's it belong to?"

"Desdemona Rosebud Hamilton."

"This is her house?"

"Yep."

"I'm hungry, Mommy."

Elisa hoisted the child to her hip. "After her third hus-band passed away, Desdemona decided to come back here from Colorado."

Tucker plucked the squiggly Daisy from her and hoisted the child to his shoulders.

Daisy giggled. "Look at me, Mommy."

"I see you, sweetie."

"Did you say third husband?"

Elisa nodded. "She's a former Miss Georgia. And that's enough gossip here in her yard." She sighed. "Speaking of yards, look at this one. I could weep at the idea of Daisy having a place like this to play."

"She has a pretty darned good yard at my place."

Elisa laid a hand on the side of his face. "She does, Tuck. Thing is, that's temporary."

He flinched. Yeah. Temporary. Wasn't everything? The sun drifted behind a cloud, and the world became a little less sunny.

———————————

On the way to their picnic, Tucker passed a house that was all but falling in on itself. An overgrown, weed-infested yard erupted around it. Toward the back of the lot, nearly obscured by tall grass, sat a rusted-out pickup.

He whistled, hit the brakes, and put the car into reverse.

"What's wrong?" Elisa asked.

"Not a thing. In fact, I think Christmas has come early."

"Christmas?" Daisy piped up. "Santa Claus?"

Elisa slid her sunglasses down her nose. "Now you've done it."

He thumped a fist against his forehead. "I didn't mean it literally, sweetie."

"Huh?"

"A three-and-a-half-year-old doesn't understand the difference." Elisa decided to let Tucker field this one.

"Okay." He pulled to the side of the road and turned to face Daisy. "Santa's not coming for a couple of months yet, but I saw something I'd like to put in my Dear Santa letter."

"I like Santa."

"Me, too. I'm gonna go look at it, okay?"

"'Kay, Tut. Can Mommy and I come, too?"

"Sure." He opened his door and whistled. "Oh, baby. I want this truck."

"Why don't you ask Santa for one? A red one like a fire truck."

"Call me crazy, Daisy, but I like the old ones."

"Mommy's car is old."

"Yeah, it is," he agreed.

Elisa groaned. Then she asked, "Are there snakes in that high grass?"

"For this beauty, I'll risk it. Besides, I came dressed for it." He patted his jeans and lifted a foot to show his sturdy work boots.

"Well, Daisy and I didn't." She lifted her daughter from the car and went as far as the sidewalk. When Daisy wiggled to get down, Elisa let her. "We'll wait right here."

"But, Mommy, I wanna see what Santa's bringing Tut."

Just then, the door to the house opened and a man dressed in bib overalls shambled out. "Howdy. What can I do ya?"

Daisy plastered herself to her mother's leg.

"Somebody lives here?" Elisa whispered to Tucker as she wound a protective arm around her daughter.

"Guess so." He stepped forward, hand out. "Name's Tucker Wylder."

"I know who you are, boy. Seen you on TV with your brothers. Watched y'all turn old heaps into beauties. Whatcha doin' here?" He spit a stream of tobacco juice into the weeds.

"What's he doing, Mommy?"

"Nothing, sweetie." She hefted Daisy onto her hip.

"Howdy, ma'am." He tipped his stained ball cap, smiling at Daisy. "How are you today, little one?"

"Good," Daisy answered before she hid her face against Elisa.

"She shy?"

"Sometimes," Elisa said.

"I'm Finch Spivey. My guess is you spotted Beulah out back."

"Beulah?" Elisa echoed.

"My daddy bought her a few years after he came back from World War II."

"A '49, right?" Tucker asked. "Mind if I look at it?"

"Not at all. Help yourself."

Tucker waded through the tall grass and weeds, with Finch right behind him talking a mile a minute about his old Studebaker.

"Interested in selling it?" Tucker asked.

"Might could be."

From her perch in her mother's arms, Daisy watched the men. "What are they talking about, Mommy?"

"Tuck's looking at Mr. Spivey's old car, kind of the way you look at toys in the store."

"Will he ask you to buy it for him?"

Elisa laughed. "I seriously doubt that, but he might buy it for himself."

"Why?"

"That is a very good question."

When Daisy started to fidget and whine, Tucker promised Finch he'd call later.

At the park, Elisa spread a blanket and set out their food. Tucker's eyes followed her every move and made her feel clumsy.

"Tuck, why don't you put half a sandwich on Daisy's plate, then take one for yourself?"

"You have enough?"

"I always pack extra. Never know when you'll run into some hungry, good-lookin' guy."

"You think I'm good-lookin', huh? Handsome, virile, able to move mountains."

"Yeah, yeah, yeah, but don't break that arm patting yourself on the back."

He leaned in unexpectedly and dropped a quick, hot kiss on her lips.

She closed her eyes and simply enjoyed the moment, deciding to make the most of this shared picnic lunch with an extraordinarily sexy man.

"You need to smile more." Tucker's voice took on a lower timbre.

Daisy patted his knee. "Kiss me, too, Tut."

"Thought you'd never ask." One quick, noisy smooch later, he glanced at Elisa. "How about the apple slices?"

"What?"

He held up the plastic container. "How many slices will Daisy eat?"

Just like that, she dropped back into the real world. "Give her two. There're a couple of bottles of water in there that should still be cold."

She watched as both child and man plowed through their portions and realized they'd been truly hungry. So had she, for the first time in a long time. Could be the mountain-moving guy across from her was responsible for that.

And yet a shadow hovered, a shadow she couldn't tackle today, not here and not in front of Daisy. Her secret would keep.

There was something she could tell him now, though, and should. She took a deep breath. "We need to talk, Tucker."

He glanced at her, frowning. "What's wrong?"

"Nothing. It's good news." Fighting not to wring her hands, she folded them in her lap.

"Good news puts a look like that on your face?" He set down his unfinished sandwich. "I'm not gonna like it, am I?"

"Actually, I think you will. From what you said earlier, I assume you don't know Desdemona."

"Nope, but I ran into her at the grocery store. She reminded me of Delta Burke. That same overblown personality. The clothes."

"From *Designing Women*?"

"Yep. Suzanne Sugarbaker."

"She is a lot like her, now that I think about it." Elisa

studied him. "That show's been off the air practically forever. How do you know about it?"

"Through osmosis."

She swatted him.

"Hey!" He rubbed his arm.

She made a face. "Want me to kiss it and make it better?"

His eyes darkened and took on a smoldering heat. "Yeah, I'd like that."

"So not going to happen."

"More's the pity." Daisy crawled into his lap. Without a word, he wrapped an arm around her and snuggled her in. "Anyway, *Designing Women* isn't defunct in my parents' house, not on the rerun channels. My mother has watched every episode at least ten times."

Elisa smiled. "What was Desdemona wearing when you met her?"

"We didn't actually introduce ourselves over the salami and Virginia ham, so I'm making an assumption it was her." He rubbed his chin. "She had on a long-sleeved red silk dress, red shoes with—I swear—eight-inch heels, and a double-strand pearl necklace. Sparkly earrings and a ring on every finger. You know. Your typical grocery-shopping outfit."

"Pretty observant."

"Details. A big part of my job."

There was her opening. "Speaking of jobs, Desdemona offered me one."

"What?"

"And a home." Stretched out on the blanket, her daughter now asleep in Tucker's arms, Elisa told him about the bookstore and the possibility of her and Daisy moving in with Desdemona.

Tucker said nothing, and the silence stretched into uncomfortable.

"Stay with me." His hazel eyes held an intensity she'd never seen there.

She twisted the small gold ring on her pinky. "It doesn't look good, Tuck. It was one thing when my car quit, I was less than a hundred percent, and we had nowhere to go. I'm forever in your debt—"

"I don't want you in my debt. I want you in my—" He broke off and blew out a breath.

"This situation has trouble written all over it, Tuck. I know it, and you know it. Besides, you said it yourself. It's time for Daisy and me to leave."

"I didn't mean it."

"Yeah, you did."

"Not for the reason you think," he growled. "Truth? I'm not sure you're safe with me."

Elisa rose on one elbow. "Funny, but I've never felt safer."

"What do you say we table this discussion for now?"

"Deal." She held out a hand. Instead of shaking it, he drew it to his lips and dropped a kiss in her palm. "Oh, Tuck. What am I going to do with you?"

"You don't want to hear my answer to that question, darlin'."

Tucker realized he owed Gaven big. This break had done him far more good than a month of Sundays on some therapist's couch. Now that he had his head straight, though, he needed to get back to work. "As much as I've enjoyed this, sugar, I'd best see what my brothers are up to at the shop."

When he stood, Daisy shifted and woke, yawning.

"Thanks for coming with us, Tuck," Elisa said. "This was nice."

Daisy smiled up at him sleepily. "Yeah, Tut. Nice."

He tugged one of her braids. "I agree, short stuff."

"I'm not short stuff. I'm Daisy Elizabeth."

Tucker smacked the flat of his hand against his forehead. "Of course you are. How could I forget?"

Daisy extended her arms out to her sides. "I don't know."

Laughing, he carried her to the car and opened her door. "Hop in, Miss Daisy, and I'll drive you and your mama back to your car."

He stowed the blanket and picnic basket in the backseat beside her.

Eyeing Elisa over the top of the car, he said, "We're not done with our conversation."

"I didn't think we were."

When they reached Desdemona's, Daisy had fallen back asleep. Tucker pulled to the curb behind Elisa's old four-door sedan.

"You need a new car."

She shook her head. "You keep saying that, but this one's paid for."

"Understood. But it's worn out."

"It's what I can afford."

"Let me look around, see what I can find."

"No. Absolutely not. This works for me."

With a disgruntled mutter, he got out, only half closing the door, and rounded the hood to help Elisa out.

Rather than dropping her hand once she stood beside him, he pulled her close and, unable to stop himself, gave her a light kiss. Since she didn't pull away, he kissed her again, taking it deeper till her blood churned and she forgot they stood in the middle of someone else's sidewalk.

When he stepped back, he threw her a wink. "Don't forget about our date tonight."

The corner of her mouth kicked up in a small smile. He hadn't forgotten.

Daisy stirred, and Elisa gathered her up, as well as her seat. Her body tingled and she raised fingers to touch her lips, his taste still on them. What did he have planned for tonight?

CHAPTER 17

WHEN TUCKER LEFT WORK, HIS MIND SHIFTED TO THE mechanics of setting things up for tonight's movie under the stars. He'd switched vehicles with Gaven, since he needed the truck to haul stuff. After a few quick stops and a coffee from Tommy's Texaco, he headed home. Daisy and Elisa had called to tell him they were visiting Tansy, Gracie Bella, and the cats, so he'd told them to stay away a little longer.

He'd managed to round up six bales of hay. As Tucker lifted them from the truck and arranged them, he whistled Lynyrd Skynyrd's "Sweet Home Alabama" and thought about Elisa. Alabama sure did raise them pretty—and stubborn as all get-out.

He used four bales to form a base, then stacked two more as a back to lean against—a sofa made of hay. Prickly hay. Running inside, he unearthed some old flannel sheets to drape over them. Given the cooler weather they'd been having lately, he'd make Elisa and Daisy wear long pants and sleeves. They'd need jackets, too.

Cursing and wishing he'd asked Gaven to lend a hand, he fought with the canvas tarp, finally managing to hang it on the side of the old shed. He pulled it tight to remove as many wrinkles as possible and nailed it in place. Darlene at Quilty Pleasures had cajoled Effie, the town's librarian, into lending him the library's DVD projector. Tucker swore Darlene could lay her hands on anything a body wanted.

Cleaned up and changed with five minutes to spare,

he was in the kitchen throwing the food together when he heard the crunch of Elisa's tires on the gravel out front. He tossed the bag of rolls on the counter and stepped outside.

"Hey, pretty ladies. You're just in time."

Tucker grilled hot dogs over the big fire pit while Daisy raced around the yard hunting wildflowers and pretty stones.

Elisa kept a close eye on her. "Slow down, Daisy."

"As long as she doesn't get too close to the water—"

"It's not that." She tapped a fingertip over her heart.

"She's such a force, I almost forget sometimes. Want me to find something else for her to do?"

"No, I know I worry too much."

"I didn't say that. You're doing a great job with her, Lissie, and you're entitled to a get-out-of-jail-free card on the worry thing."

She laid a hand on his arm. "Tucker, I have to say this. I don't know what fluke of nature or cosmic woo-woo decided you should be the one to catch me when I fell, but I've thanked my lucky stars every day since that it was you."

Before he could find the right words, she asked, "Dogs about done?"

He cleared his throat. "Yep. We're good to go."

"Tut says the hot dogs are ready, Daisy. Come eat."

"'Kay, Mommy."

The woman cut him off at the knees. She was gorgeous, but it was the things a man didn't see at first glance that he loved most. *Loved*? No. Admired.

And her daughter. Daisy had wrapped herself around his heart.

When she plopped down in the grass, Tuck took a good hard look at her. She was ashen and her breathing was rapid and shallow. "Lissie—"

"She'll be okay. Once she's quiet for a bit, she'll even out."

"You're sure?"

She nodded.

"Okay." He took a big bite of his hot dog. "Mmm. I need to do this more often."

"Yeah, Tut. More often," Daisy repeated.

She kept them entertained with stories about Gracie Bella and the kittens while they finished eating. Then, after peanut butter cup s'mores, Tucker settled her and her mama on the hay bales and arranged a soft plaid throw over them.

He added a couple more logs to the fire. "Warm enough?"

"Oh yeah." Elisa pulled her daughter in to her side.

"C'mon, Tut." Daisy patted the spot beside her. "You sit, too."

He laughed. "I will. As soon as I get the movie started."

"I didn't ask what we're watching. Is it okay for Daisy?"

He arched a brow. "You think I'd show her *Fifty Shades* or something? Give me some credit, Ms. Danvers."

She held up a hand. "Sorry."

"You're forgiven." Hearing her quick laugh of surprise, he smiled, then reached for the thermos he'd prepared earlier.

"What's that?" Daisy leaned closer to smell it.

"It's warm apple cider."

"Do I like that, Mommy?"

Elisa chuckled. "Yes, you do. It's like apple juice, only better."

"Yay!" Daisy clapped her hands.

"By the way," Tuck said, "I went back to Finch Spivey's this afternoon."

"And?"

A grin split his face. "Beulah, his daddy's old Studebaker, is now mine."

"You bought it!"

"Yep."

"I knew you would. You wanted it the second you saw it."

He lifted a brow. "Some things you know right off are meant to be."

She raised a hand to her throat. "Tucker—"

"Ready for that movie?"

"Yes!" Daisy started to clap. "Start it, Tut."

The hay proved comfortable with its flannel sheet covering. A blanket of stars spread overhead in the inky sky, and he had the two most wonderful females on the planet beside him.

When he hit play, Daisy squealed in delight as Disney's *Tangled* filled the canvas screen.

"I love *Tangled*!" Daisy put her hand in his.

The luckiest man alive, Tucker thought. It simply didn't get any better.

He didn't want them to move out. Him and his big mouth.

Well before the end of the movie, Daisy fell asleep, her head on her mother's lap. Tucker took advantage to move a little closer and draped his arm over Elisa's shoulders, brushing a kiss over her hair, behind her ear.

She lifted her head. "Tuck."

His mouth closed over hers. When she parted her lips, his tongue slid inside to dance with hers. Hot, so damn hot. He wanted her so bad he hurt.

Because of that, he pulled back. There, in the dark of the night, he leaned his forehead against her hair. "I probably shouldn't have—"

"This has been one of the best nights I can remember," Elisa whispered. "And yes, you should have. But I think it's time for bed."

He swallowed hard. Best he let that one alone. Instead, he asked, "You don't want to see how it turns out for old Flynn and Rapunzel?"

"I think I've got a pretty good idea."

"Since Daisy sang along with all the songs, I'm gonna guess you've seen this a few times."

"And I'm sure we'll watch it a few more. Don't you love Maximus?"

"That horse stole the show." Tucker took Daisy from Elisa. "I'll carry her upstairs. You're sure she's okay? Want to run her in to see Doc Hawkins tomorrow?"

"No. We were actually there today. There's nothing he can do."

Elisa tucked her daughter in and dropped a kiss on her cheek. When she turned around, Tucker was gone. She couldn't fix her daughter; she couldn't fix Tucker. Why did life have to be so difficult at times, so unfair?

She moved into her room and got ready for bed, but sleep eluded her. When it did come, it was light and fitful.

When a small noise woke her, a glance at the bedside clock showed it was only twenty after one. The front door creaked open and she heard Gaven's borrowed truck spring to life. Despite the wonderful evening she and Tucker had shared, he was out prowling again. It was almost worse now because she knew where he went…and why.

He'd told her he needed space because he didn't sleep well. That was an understatement—and one of the reasons she needed to leave.

———————————

Tucker let himself back into the house, doing his darnedest to miss the squeaky stair.

"Is that you, Tucker?" Elisa whispered.

"Yeah." He stuck his head in her bedroom door. "You should be sleeping."

"So should you."

"That's—different."

"I don't think so," she argued.

He stepped inside her room and inhaled the scent of woman. "I need to go to my room, sugar."

"Why?"

He swallowed hard. "You have to ask? It's the middle of the night and—"

"And we're both wide awake," she finished.

Taking a deep breath, he said, "I want you, Lissie, more than I've ever wanted anything or anyone."

"Then why are you standing way over there?" She rose to her knees, holding out her arms to him. The sheet slid down, revealing her thin cotton nightgown.

"If I so much as touch you, I won't be able to leave."

"Good. Come touch me," she whispered. "Please."

He closed the door with his foot and moved to her, drawing her into his arms. His lips devoured hers. One hand slid up to cup her head while the other traveled down her back, then up again, brushing the underside of her breast.

Sweet little sounds escaped her, driving him even crazier.

"Tuck." Breathless, she pulled back and slid from the bed. Her gaze met his.

She hadn't pulled the drapes and in the moonlight he saw in her big blue eyes the same desire that galloped through him.

Her forehead against his, she whispered, "I want to be with you tonight."

"I can't promise anything, Lissie."

"I don't want promises. They're too easy to break. Tonight. That's all I want."

"You—"

She touched a fingertip to his lips. "Don't treat me like a porcelain doll, Tucker. I'm a flesh and blood woman, and I need you."

"You're sure?" A part of his brain screamed at him to be quiet and take what she offered. But he had to be certain. This was Lissie.

"Positive. But—" She chewed her bottom lip.

"If you have any reservations, this is the time to speak up. You wait much longer, and it's gonna be hard..." He trailed off. "Bad choice of words there." His brows rose. "What's wrong?"

"You probably noticed the other night that I'm, ah, not very good at this."

He frowned. "At what?"

"At—you know. This. Luke said—"

"Time to get that man gone, sugar. If you were any better at this, I'd be a dead man."

She grabbed the neck of his T-shirt and pulled him to her, kissed him long and deep, their tongues mating.

"Oh yeah," he breathed. "You and I are gonna make new memories, sweetheart. Let me tell you what I'm gonna do to you and that hot little body." He leaned close and whispered into her ear.

Another taste and he backed her up against the wall, forgot she might break.

When he caught his breath, he scooped her up and carried her to his room. "I want you in my bed tonight."

She was everything he could ever have imagined. Soft, sensual, giving and taking. Their bodies fit perfectly, and Tucker lost himself in her.

His fingertip traced the small tattoo on her right hip. "What is this?"

"A phoenix rising. I got it right after my divorce was final. I felt I'd been reborn."

"Thank God." Tucker kissed the tattoo reverently, then made to pull her beneath him.

"Uh-uh. Suit up first."

He fished in the back pocket of the jeans he'd tossed to the side of the bed and withdrew a foil packet. "Got it covered."

Elisa sent him an arch look. "Not yet, you don't."

He chuckled. Then, his voice deepening, he asked, "Why don't you do the honors?" When her hands touched him, he made a low sound in the back of his throat. "You're killin' me."

Raising her hands above her head, he laced their fingers

together. Watching her, he entered slowly. Her eyes widened and a soft, sexy-as-hell smile played over her swollen lips—just before he covered them with his.

Heat consumed him as she surrendered totally to him. He couldn't get enough of her, touching, tasting her, and when they came, they came together.

Once he could move again, he drew her to him and closed his eyes. She smelled so good—a mix of spicy and floral. Female. He ran a finger down her spine and smiled when she shivered. His fingertips glided over smooth, soft skin and he dropped a kiss on her shoulder, felt her smile. Gently, he lifted a silky strand of blond hair and rubbed it between his fingertips. He wouldn't, couldn't keep her forever, but for now he had her right here in his arms. In his bed.

She curled into him, her finger tracing over his hip. "Tuck, I need to go back to my room."

"Why?"

"If Daisy wakes before me…"

He sighed. "You're right."

He slipped out of bed and stood looking down at her.

"You're naked," she said.

"I am." In one fluid motion, he scooped her up. "So are you."

She squealed. "What are you doing?"

"I think we both need a shower." He grabbed a foil packet from the nightstand.

The water was still cold when he followed her in, but it didn't bother either of them. Picking up the soap, he lathered every inch of her body, giving extra attention to spots that drew him, rinsing then kissing her now-warm skin.

She grabbed the soap from him and played and teased till his body couldn't take it anymore.

Backing her against the wall, water streaming over them, he suited up. This time he entered her quickly, felt her gasp, her body opening for him.

Her orgasm came hard and fast, and he was right there with her.

Oh, this lady wasn't just good. She excelled.

It was the SOB she'd been married to who was lacking.

They took their time drying each other.

After she went back to her room, Tucker pulled her pillow close. Inhaling her scent, he fell asleep.

No dreams haunted him.

Neither of them mentioned their late-night encounter in the morning. If it weren't for the permanent blush that travelled over Elisa's face and chest every time she caught his gaze, Tucker might have thought he'd dreamed it.

He hadn't.

He'd been so sure being with her one more time would take away the want. The need. Instead, it had made him hungrier.

How would he ever keep his hands to himself now that they'd held her again?

Tucker growled at anybody who even looked at him. After he and Brant had words about the way the tools had been put away the day before, Tuck decided to bury himself in supply ordering.

He was in the middle of double-checking one of the vendor's sheets when Gaven stepped into the office. "The Charger we're doing. What was the paint number on that?"

"I don't know," Tucker snapped. "Look it up. You can work a computer, can't you?"

"What the hell is wrong with you this morning?"

"Nothing."

"Really?"

"Don't you have something to do?"

"Yeah, I do, but I need that paint number. I'll head to the back room and dig it out of my laptop—far away from your black cloud. Don't think I want to get caught in the storm when it breaks."

"Good. I have work to do."

"We've already had this talk, Tuck. Work's not the problem. You have a fight with Elisa?"

"What? No!"

Gaven shook his head. "Can't say I blame her for moving in with Desdemona if you're like this around her."

Tucker's head snapped up. "How do you know about that?"

"What?"

"That she's moving into the widow's. I just found out yesterday afternoon."

"Small town, Bro. After work, I stopped by Duffy's Pub for a cold brewski and one of his roast beef sandwiches. Word is Dee-Ann saw Desdemona and Elisa talking in front of the bookstore, then Sheriff Jimmy Don spotted them at her house. Somebody else was picking up a potted plant at Cricket's flower shop and overheard Desdemona say she'd bought a few things for Daisy's room and how excited she was to have a child moving into the house. One and one and one adds up to a new residence for the Danvers ladies."

"Damn it all to hell."

"No secrets in this town, Tuck, but you need to chill. You're not at war anymore, so get a handle on that temper. Remember how to interact with people. Think about it." With that, Gaven headed to his laptop.

Jaw tight, Tucker tossed the file onto his desk.

He'd made a real mess of things. It wasn't his fault that Elisa had picked their shop to faint in. It *was* his fault, though, that he'd let her and her little girl crawl right into his…life. Not heart. Still, their predicament had become very personal.

What must she be thinking today?

What had *he* been thinking? His mother would snatch him bald if she found out—and rightly so. Penny and Neal Wylder had raised their boys better.

Still, they'd been two consenting adults, both of whom had been without sex for a long time. He'd have liked to salve his conscience by saying they'd both scratched an itch and that was that, but it didn't wash.

The worst of it? He couldn't undo it and he couldn't fix it. He had nothing to offer her and no promises to make. His well was dry. It had gone dry the day his friends died—while he sat on his thumbs because he'd questioned an order.

He'd never been so sorry to be right.

CHAPTER 18

THE NEXT TWO DAYS PRACTICALLY FLEW BY, WHILE the nights dragged endlessly.

Tucker avoided both Elisa and Daisy, leaving for work before they woke and not coming home till they were in bed. It broke Elisa's heart to see her little girl sit by the window, watching for him, disappointed when he didn't show.

The fault was hers. She'd pushed the boundary between them—even after he'd said it wasn't a good idea. He'd seemed a more than willing participant, but maybe he'd only slept with her again because he felt sorry for her. She felt the blush creep up her neck. Could anything be worse?

Or maybe she'd disappointed him. She'd warned him she was no good at sex. Afterwards, he'd insisted she'd been wonderful, but if that was true, why was he keeping his distance?

She'd considered staying up and pressing the issue, but she couldn't bear to hear him say the words. Couldn't listen while he told her she hadn't lived up to expectations. All her life, she'd heard that—from her mother, her father, and Luke. Now Tucker.

She'd missed the mark. Again.

"Time for you to go home." Gaven dried his hands, checking again to make sure he'd removed all the day's grunge from beneath his nails. "What did you do to make her mad?"

"Who's mad?"

"Elisa. Why else would you be hanging around here?" He shot him a hard look. "Tell me you didn't."

"Didn't what?" Tucker's voice took on a hostile edge.

"You slept with her, didn't you?"

Tucker scowled at him. "That would be filed under *none of your business*."

"Why'd you do that? She's sick."

"No, she's not. Her blood sugar's under control. You think I'd mess around with her if she was sick?"

"I don't know."

"Now you're making *me* mad, Gaven. You don't understand."

"Yeah, I do." Gaven cocked an arm on his hip. "I've been married, remember?"

"Oh, yeah, that's right. For, what? Twenty-four hours?"

Gaven tipped his head and studied his brother. "You didn't used to be mean, Tuck. No matter what, you didn't hurt people."

Contrite, Tucker scrubbed his hands over his face. "I'm sorry. Damn. Elisa's got me tied up in knots. I don't want her at the house because—" He blew out a huge breath. "Too many reasons to list. But more than that? I don't want her to leave. But she is. Tonight."

"So what are you gonna do about it?"

"What can I do? I'm no good for her or anybody else. I have nothing to offer."

"You're selling yourself short, Bro." He flipped off the lights.

"Hey!" Tucker shouted.

"Shop's closed." Gaven held the door open. "After you."

When Tucker stepped inside his house, the first thing he spotted was Elisa's luggage in the hallway. It seemed he'd made it home in time to load her car. Maybe he'd tag along and see her settled at Desdemona's.

"Tut?" Daisy shot out of the kitchen and straight into his arms. "Tut!"

Her mama leaned against the wall, looking feminine and desirable as hell in a soft floral dress. A rosy-pink cardigan added a blush of color to her cheeks.

When he came home tomorrow, the house would be empty. Dread filled him. Did Elisa understand this move was killing him? Did she realize how important she and Daisy had become to him?

"Mommy says we gotta go. That we can't stay here anymore." Daisy played with his hair, pulling on it, then tapping it flat again. "I'm gonna miss you, Tut." She buried her face in his shirt.

A lump formed in his throat. He held Daisy close and looked over her head to her mama, reminding himself that grown men didn't cry.

"We were just ready to leave, Tuck."

"I'd like to tag along, Lissie. I'd like to meet Desdemona."

"But you said—"

"That I'd run into her at the store," he said. "Not the same as meeting her or talking with her."

"Fine."

At least she and Daisy would still be in Misty Bottoms. That might be both a blessing and a curse.

"No sense you fighting with your luggage. I'll stow it in your car, then unload it at your new place."

"I can manage, Tuck."

"Gonna make this hard, aren't you?"

"No."

He raised a brow. "Good. I know you can handle the luggage, make breakfast while standing on one foot, and undoubtedly shoot an apple from a tree." He ignored her look of indignation. "You're an independent, competent woman. Understood. Here's the thing. My mama raised all three of her boys to be gentlemen. If I don't do this for you, I'll have let her down. You seriously gonna make me lose face with my mama?"

She chuckled. "Oh, you're slick."

"I can be. When forced." He jammed a hand in his jeans pocket and hoped like heck she wouldn't make him beg for a little more time with her and Daisy. And he did want to meet Desdemona and see where his girls were going. He needed to make sure they'd be safe.

"Far be it from me to ruin your relationship with your mother."

"Good." He put on his best game-face and followed them into town.

When she parked, he sauntered over to her car.

"Hi, Tut," Daisy greeted him from the backseat. From the excitement on her face, a person would have thought they hadn't seen each other for weeks instead of the ten minutes the drive had taken.

But he knew how she felt. Their time together was fast running out.

He lifted her from her seat. "I sure do like those shoes, Daisy. Are they new?"

"Mommy bought them for me before we came here." She lifted a foot to admire the red patent leather Mary Janes.

Daisy on his hip, Tuck rounded the car to where Elisa struggled to lift the suitcase from the trunk. "I thought we'd had this conversation." He handed Daisy to her. "You take the kid, and let me get this. Please."

She folded her arms over her chest and nailed him with her I-can-do-this look.

"Yeah, yeah," he said. "Like I said earlier, you're capable of handling any and every situation by yourself, Wonder Woman. Let me pretend, just for a few minutes, that I can do something to help."

"You can. You do," she argued, reaching for her daughter.

"Good. Then I've got this." He pulled her battered luggage from the trunk, slammed it shut, then started along the walk with Elisa and Daisy following.

The ornate front door swung open and Elisa's new landlady stepped out. One good look at Desdemona and Tuck understood why men flocked to her, vying to be her next husband. The woman oozed warmth and sex appeal. Everything about her exuded confidence. Here was a lady who not only knew who she was but liked that person. Elisa's new housemate was no shrinking violet.

She wore black slacks with a sequined red silk blouse... and killer heels. Her dark hair was piled high and a mountain of jewelry clung to her. All in all, it was quite a look for a woman relaxing at home.

He held out a callused hand. "Tucker Wylder. I don't think we've formally met."

"No, we haven't, Tucker, but I remember you from our little encounter at the deli. It's pretty impossible to forget a face like yours. Your mama and daddy made themselves some good-lookin' kids." She took his hand in hers and held on. "Desdemona Rosebud Hamilton. I've heard a lot about you and your brothers."

"Not sure whether that's a good or a bad thing."

"Good. All good." She gave his hand one last squeeze, patting it with her other. "Thank you for watching out for these sweeties."

A questioning smile formed. "You're welcome. It's been…a new experience for me."

"Why don't you bring that load in here? A big boy like you won't have any trouble toting it upstairs."

"Don't guess I will."

She swung the door wider.

As he drew nearer, he caught a whiff of her perfume. Something very feminine and very expensive. Yet it didn't hold a candle to Lissie's scent when she wore nothing at all.

He paused. "Can I ask you something?"

"Sure. I'm an open book." The quick grin belied her words.

"Not that it's any of my business, but you know what they say about curiosity and that cat. Both times I've run into you, you've been done up to the nines. Do you ever dress down? Own anything casual? Jeans, sweats, T-shirts?"

"I do. I own all those things. Of course, they're covered in bling, and I wear them with heels and tons of jewelry. Nothing's more fun than a sweatshirt and pearls…or diamonds."

A smile on his face, he nodded. "Good to know. I like you, Desdemona Rosebud Hamilton."

She lifted a brow. "I can see why Elisa swooned when she met you."

Behind him, Elisa snorted indignantly.

He laughed and then, barely inside, stopped and gave a whistle. The outside was magnificent. But inside? "Wow. Lissie said your place was incredible. Seems that was an understatement."

Like the old blacksmith shop, this structure had stood the test of time. But while his had been built for function, then abandoned, Desdemona's house had been designed to impress, and impress it did.

If he didn't know better, he'd swear it had been constructed with Desdemona in mind. The place suited her larger-than-life personality perfectly.

"Haul those bags upstairs," she said. "Then I'll give you a tour."

She turned to the little girl who stood quietly in the hallway, nervously sucking her thumb.

Desdemona knelt by her. "Do you remember which room is yours, sweetie?"

Daisy nodded.

"Can you show Tuck how to get there?"

Daisy nodded again. Taking Tuck's free hand, she tugged at him. "Come on, Tut. I'll help you."

Her little duffel bag slung over her shoulder, she pulled him in her wake.

Elisa and Desdemona followed.

When they reached Daisy's room, the little girl squealed and Elisa's mouth dropped open. The room had been freshly painted sunshine yellow, and embroidered daisies covered both the bedspread and throw rug. A vase of fresh daisies sat on the dresser. Dolls and stuffed animals were strewn throughout the room and over the bed, and the dollhouse they'd seen before sat in its place of honor. A small mirrored vanity rested in one corner with a Daisy-sized stool in front of it.

"Desdemona?"

"Now, I know what you're gonna say. Don't." She held up a hand, bracelets tinkling together at her wrist. "I wanted to surprise Daisy, and I can afford it. Let me have some fun."

Elisa simply stared. "But this is too much."

"Isn't it great?" Desdemona grinned. "Do you like your new room, sweetie?"

Daisy nodded. After bouncing on her bed a few times, she slid to the floor and ran toward a three-foot stuffed frog by the window. "Mine?"

"If your mommy says so."

"Oh, aren't you crafty." Elisa narrowed her eyes. "If I say yes, you get your way. I say no, and I'm the baddie."

Desdemona smiled and shrugged her shoulders.

When Elisa turned to him, Tucker held up his hands. "I'm Switzerland."

Walking into his dark house an hour later was like stumbling across the Rub' al-Khali—the *Empty Quarter* in the Arabian Desert. He and a few of his fellow Marines had had the displeasure of flirting with the edge of its inhospitable dunes. That's how his house felt tonight. Inhospitable and barren. Totally lifeless.

He switched on a table lamp, then turned it off when it only served to highlight the emptiness. He'd been happy before Elisa had burst on the scene with her little one, and he'd be happy again. It would just take some time.

Besides, they hadn't left the country. Any time he wanted, he could hop in the car and visit. It wouldn't be the same, though. He and Daisy wouldn't sneak Pop-Tarts for breakfast while Elisa grabbed a few more minutes of sleep. When he came home from work, Daisy wouldn't be standing at the front window waving to him and blowing kisses.

Maybe he should get a dog.

Okay, now he was thinking crazy. No shedding, slobbering dog in his house.

Tucker headed for the kitchen and a cold beer. He'd settle in and watch an uninterrupted replay of Sunday's game as loud as he wanted—and stay up as late as he needed. It would be good.

Right.

CHAPTER 19

THE NEXT COUPLE OF WEEKS BECAME A FLURRY OF workmen and book orders, paperwork and decisions as the bookstore came to life. Elisa loved every single minute. It turned out she did, indeed, have a fairy godmother, and her name was Desdemona Rosebud Hamilton.

Despite all the busyness, though, Elisa managed to sneak away a few times for dinner at Tuck's while Desdemona and Daisy enjoyed a girls' night in. The first time he'd called and invited her to his place, she'd been like a high school girl invited to the prom. Heck, she still was. Every time her phone rang, she prayed it was him. She'd been so afraid that night they'd moved to Desdemona's would be the last she saw of him. Thankfully, she'd been wrong.

Their evenings always ended up in that huge bed of his. Her body came alive remembering his touch and the unbelievable care he took with her. The man was fast becoming a habit.

Luke had been so wrong. He'd been the one who wasn't very good at lovemaking. Then again, for him maybe it had just been sex. If he'd loved her, he wouldn't have walked away.

Since she was a working mother again, she'd followed Tucker's earlier advice and enrolled Daisy in Lucinda's day care. It was a good move for them all. Daisy was blossoming there.

Her phone rang, and she checked the ID. "Good morning, Fairy Godmother. How are you on this beautiful day?"

"Sweatin' bullets," Desdemona said. "The shop's almost ready to open, and we still don't have a name for it."

"True." With the phone tucked between her ear and chin, Elisa cut open another box of books, then leaned into it, taking a deep breath. New books had a smell all their own, one that was totally addictive. One she'd never take for granted.

Over the phone, Elisa heard the beep of a car horn. "What's that?"

"Yancy. The old fool won't come to the door for me. Instead he sits out there and honks."

"Come to the door for you?"

"Yes, ma'am. We're driving to Savannah for lunch."

A silly grin played over Elisa's lips. "Well, you children have fun."

"Ha!" She dropped her voice. "If I'm not home when bedtime rolls around, be sure you lock up. I'll have my key." Then, with barely a hitch in her stride, Desdemona asked, "What do we do about the name?"

Elisa swallowed her groan. They'd spent a lot of time brainstorming this.

Desdemona plowed on. "I'm still leaning toward *Rosebud's Reading Paradise.* We can use a rosebud design on our business cards, on the rugs, chairs, lamps—anything and everything."

"It's your store, so if that's what you want…"

"But you don't like it."

"That's not true. It's a great name—if you've changed your mind about our clientele."

"What do you mean?"

"We went way outside the box with the pink exterior. Now you want to splash rosebuds everywhere. In my opinion, that's likely to cost you the entire male citizenry of Misty Bottoms."

"Well, horse feathers! You're right." Her deep sigh carried over the line. "Got any other ideas?"

"I do. At two o'clock this morning it woke me up."

"Honey, at two in the morning, you should have had that handsome Wylder brother in your bed and been too preoccupied to think about business."

Even though she was alone in the store, heat crept up Elisa's neck and face.

"You still there?" Desdemona asked. "Or are you daydreaming about that handsome man at work out on Old Coffee Road?"

"I'm here. I thought maybe we could call it *Just Books*. On the window beneath that, add *...and a little more*."

A few seconds of silence followed. "*Just Books...and a little more*. I love it!"

"Good." Elisa chuckled. "Because I already told Jenni Beth's husband Cole to stop looking for rosebuds and start scrounging the countryside for anything with books on it. Lamps, rugs, knickknacks, whatever. It sure is handy to know an architectural salvager."

"Well, shut my mouth! You and me, Elisa? We make a great team."

Yancy laid on his horn again.

"Guess I've kept my beau cooling his heels long enough. The name feels right, Elisa. Let's run with it."

She'd barely hung up when the phone rang again.

Her head still on her conversation with Desdemona, Elisa decided to take the new name out for a spin. "Good morning, *Just Books...and a little more*."

"It's the *little more* I'm interested in."

Her knees turned to jelly. "Tucker."

"I know you're busy, but I've been thinking. Now that you're not living with me, is it okay if we—I don't know—date? Openly?"

A smile the size of Texas on her face, she did a fist pump.

"Lissie, you still there?"

"Yes. Yes, I am. And yes, I think that would be totally appropriate."

"Appropriate, heck. Not a single thing I have in mind comes close to appropriate, sugar, but we'll start there."

They talked a few more minutes, then he said, "Got to go. Brant's after me about some order he can't find. Call you later."

She sank onto one of the little chairs she'd placed by the window. She had a bona fide date with Tucker Wylder and felt absolutely giddy. Shades of high school!

Hauling another box of merchandise from the storage room, Elisa unpacked it, her mind ricocheting between Tucker and decorating ideas for the store. She wanted the shop to be comfy and cozy. Peaceful. A place where a person could sit and read or visit with friends. The trick would be maximizing the small space. Admiring the newly sanded and refinished floors, she heard a knock at the door.

Cole stuck his head inside. "Got a couple of things for you in my truck. Be right back."

When he returned, he carried the drop-leaf table of her dreams. A second trip to his truck netted the perfect lamp to set on it, a lamp *not* covered in rosebuds. Instead, the base looked like a pile of slightly askew books. She loved it. *Just Books…and a little more.*

"That the new electric fireplace box?"

"Yes." She picked up a remote, pushed a button, and the fire sprang to life. "Nice, isn't it? And safer. After a lot of back and forth, Desdemona and I decided an honest-to-goodness fire in an old building full of books probably wasn't the best idea."

Before he left, she handed him a book. "Take this to Jenni Beth. It's a new one on outdoor weddings. If she likes it, it's hers. If not, she can bring it back and I'll put it on the shelf in the wedding section."

"The wedding section?"

"With Magnolia Brides such a huge part of Misty Bottoms' economy, you'd better believe I'm playing it up."

"That makes sense."

"I'm including a section for car and motorcycle enthusiasts, too. Since the Wylder brothers have their shop here, Misty Bottoms gets a lot of car lovers along with the brides. Again, we might as well capitalize on it."

"And to think Bowden let you go. They lost a treasure." He gave her ponytail a small tug. "You'll do well." His wife's book tucked under one arm, he gave her a wave and headed out.

The newly painted front door might as well have been a revolving one. While she loved meeting and talking to all the Misty Bottomers, it slowed her work—but it would pay off in business later.

Stealing a few minutes, she hunted up the chalkboard she'd stashed in the back room. In a pretty flourish, she wrote, *All y'all are welcome to come in, sip a glass of sweet tea, and take a peek at Misty Bottoms' newest business—Just Books...and a little more.*

Then she carried it outside and hung it on the door.

She'd take advantage of the curiosity and, at the same time, lock down the name. Now that she'd put it out there, Desdemona couldn't change her mind. Again.

That Wednesday evening, Desdemona had been more than happy to keep an eye on Daisy while Tucker and Elisa drove into Savannah for dinner. The night had been heavenly, but Elisa's work-night bedtime had long since come and gone when they drove past the Misty Bottoms city limits sign. Since it was too late to detour to Tuck's house, they'd done some pretty heavy necking parked in front of Desdemona's. The result? A lot of pent-up needs and more than a little frustration.

Right now, though, that seemed years ago.

It was Friday night, the end of a long week, and Elisa was dog-tired. She wanted a glass of wine, a good book, and a long soak in her big tub. None of that was going to happen, since it was Halloween, with trick-or-treating bumped up to first place on the to-do list.

When she pulled into the day care's parking lot, she realized that, even as tired as she was, she hadn't been this happy, this satisfied in years.

Yet as she opened the car door, a dark cloud drifted overhead, both literally and figuratively. The figurative one had a name. Hard-Ass Harry.

She should have told Tuck already. Every day, every night they spent together made the secret a bigger betrayal. She knew that, knew she was living on borrowed time. He deserved the truth, and she had to be the one to give it to him. If he found out—no, *when* he found out, because he would.

Daisy loved Tucker, and she'd be caught in the crossfire.

Harry would hurt them all—Daisy, Tucker, and herself.

As wonderful as all this had been, she had to stop imagining a future with Tucker in it. It was time to sandbag her heart. Time to protect herself and her daughter.

But was she strong enough to take that step?

She honestly didn't know. A huge part of her wanted to play the ostrich and squeeze out every last second.

The instant she stepped through the day-care door, Daisy Elizabeth ran to her. "Mommy, Mommy, look what I made." She held up a pumpkin-shaped paper. "I colored it myself."

Elisa grinned. "I see that."

"Can we put it on Miss Desdi's refrigerator?"

"Desdemona's," Elisa corrected slowly and carefully.

"That's what I said, Mommy." Those innocent blue eyes lifted to her mother's.

"I think she'd like that."

"We had pumpkin pancakes for lunch today. Teacher didn't put no syrup on them. She said it was 'cause we didn't need no more sugar."

Over the sea of small heads, Elisa met Lucinda's gaze. "Thank you."

"My pleasure. Good luck tonight, and stay safe."

Taking Daisy's hand, the little girl still clutching her pumpkin picture, they stepped outside.

"The weather's perfect, baby girl. Why don't we put down our windows and take a drive along Main Street so you can see all the Halloween displays?"

"'Kay, but I won't be scared 'cause the monsters and ghosts aren't real."

"That's right."

A touch of cool tinted the breeze. That little nip in the air cried out for trick-or-treaters, apple cider, and a blazing fireplace.

Turning onto Main Street, Elisa nodded. Once again, Misty Bottoms had done it up right. The shop windows showcased vibrant red, orange, and yellow fall leaves, carved pumpkins, and gold and bronze mums, along with ghosts and goblins. Even the lampposts wore autumn garlands.

When they reached the street's end, Elisa pulled to the curb in front of Tansy's Sweet Dreams Bakery.

"Pretty, Mommy."

Elisa glanced in the rearview mirror at her daughter's face pressed to the window. Everything became new and fresh when viewed through a child's eyes.

Tansy had transformed the front porch of her Victorian from summer to fall with jack-o'-lanterns, pots of autumn flowers, and an orange and black wreath on the front door. A scarecrow stood to the right of the porch stairs, and an old wagon loaded with pumpkins, a small ghost, and fall leaves held place of honor on the left.

"Gracie Bella's mommy owns this pretty house."

"Uh-huh. Can we get out, Mommy?"

"For a couple of seconds, then we have to go home. We have lots to do tonight."

Daisy clapped her hands. "Twick-or-tweeting."

Laughing, Elisa freed her daughter. "I'm sure there will be plenty of tweeting tonight—of a different kind."

The house's front door opened, and Tansy and Gracie Bella stepped out in costume.

Daisy ran to Gracie Bella, waving her paper pumpkin. "I made it."

The girls plopped down on the steps, studying the badly colored jack-o'-lantern and trying to decide which of the ones that lined the steps matched it best.

"Wonder Woman and Batgirl. Nice. Did you make your costumes?" Elisa asked.

"I did, with a whole lot of inappropriate language. I can bake. I cannot sew." Tansy patted her tummy. "I made my cape a little bigger to hide my baby bump."

Elisa sighed. "I loved being pregnant and feeling that new life inside me. I'd hoped to have a couple more, but... plans change."

Tansy plucked a dead leaf from a plant. "Don't rule it out. I never in a million years expected Beck to be back in my life and another baby on the way."

"I'm happy for you, Tansy, I really am, but we don't all get fairy-tale endings." She shook her head. "And listen to me. Debbie Downer's done, I promise. Daisy and I are morphing into Cruella de Vil and one of the Dalmatian pups."

"That'll be fun. Who are you going with?"

"Just the two of us. I thought we'd stop at a couple of houses, enough to give Daisy a taste of tradition."

"Why don't you come with Beck, Gracie, and me?"

Reluctant to play the third wheel, Elisa shook her head.

"Oh, come on. The girls will have more fun together."

"We're not intruding?"

"Not at all. We'll pick you up."

A very fast forty-five minutes later, peanut butter sandwiches practically inhaled, Elisa finished transforming herself and Daisy into Disney characters. Beck's truck pulled up out front while she was drawing the last spot on her daughter's face.

Daisy, getting into character, barked as she crawled on all fours to the door. Before they left, Desdemona insisted on being the first to put treats in the girls' bags, then took enough pictures to fill an album.

When they finally slid into the backseat of the truck, Elisa sniffed. "What do I smell?"

"Warm apple cider. I have cups for everyone." Tansy reached for her thermos.

"Tut gave us cider, too. And we watched *Tangled*."

"Oh yeah?" Beck grinned. "Got the big bad Marine watching chick flicks, huh? Interesting."

Tansy elbowed him. "*Tangled* isn't a chick flick. It's a kid's movie."

They stopped at Beck's parents' first. Orange pumpkin lights had been strung along the front porch and votives lined the sidewalk. His mom and dad stepped out, cameras and candy in hand. Daisy turned shy, so Elisa picked her up. The little girl buried her head in her mom's shoulder—until a candy bar dropped into her bag.

Cautiously, she peeked at Mrs. Elliot, then into her bag. "Mommy, Mommy! I got candy."

"That's what tonight's all about."

"Will other people give me candy?"

"If you remember to thank them."

"Thank you," Daisy said quickly.

"You're quite welcome," Mr. Elliot boomed. "You kids have time for a fast picture?"

"More pictures?" Beck protested.

His father ignored him and herded the group into a cozy,

well-lived-in family room. The five of them stood in front of a huge stone fireplace and smiled for the camera. After, Elisa played cameraman and took a picture of Beck's parents with the others.

Then they bundled back into the truck and headed down the driveway.

"Darlene's place is on the way to your mom's, Tansy. How about we stop there next?" Beck asked.

"Perfect." Wonder Woman gave Green Lantern a quick smooch.

Darlene, who owned the quilting shop in town, had festooned her house with jack-o'-lanterns and a life-size witch on the front door.

Daisy walked beside her mother this time. "Will she give me candy, too?"

Elisa nodded.

The instant the door opened, Daisy stepped right up, the treat bag wide open.

Beck laughed. "She catches on fast."

"Yes, she does." Elisa nudged Daisy. "What do you say to Miss Darlene?"

"Thanks, Miss Darlene."

"You're welcome." Just then, Moonshine and Mint Julep, Darlene's Cairn terriers, came sliding around the corner.

Daisy let out a happy squeal. "Doggies!"

"They don't bite?" Elisa asked.

Darlene shook her head, but it was unnecessary, as both Batgirl and the Dalmatian pup were already rolling around the floor with the dogs, who wore Halloween sweaters.

Tansy gave them a few minutes, then said, "Okay, girls. Tell Miss Darlene good night."

With more than one glance over their shoulders, the girls allowed themselves to be led back to the truck.

Beck, who was a reluctant Green Lantern, lifted both girls into his pickup, belted them in, then headed out of town.

"I still have those green tights, Beck, if you change your mind," Tansy teased. "They'd go well with your green shirt."

He glanced at his wife who sat in the shotgun seat. "I wouldn't be caught dead in them. This man doesn't wear leotards. Ever."

After a stop at Tansy's mom's, Daisy piped up. "I want to go to Tut's."

"Oh, honey, he won't have candy." Elisa didn't want to visit Tuck tonight. She didn't know what to do about him. Her emotions were in turmoil.

"Sounds like a great idea." Beck turned toward Firefly Creek Lane.

"You don't have to drive clear out there," Elisa argued.

"No big deal."

But it *was*. For Cruella, anyway. Her secret was eating her up. Why hadn't she told him about her dad the instant she'd suspected? It would be done with. *They'd* be done with.

Oh, snickerdoodles.

When they pulled into Tucker's driveway, Cruella's palms grew damp and she fought flight's siren song. No decorations here, but he had turned on his porch light. It cut through the darkness as though he expected someone, but Elisa was dead-certain he wouldn't guess that someone would be her and Daisy. Maybe. Then again, maybe he'd hoped to see them.

Well, it didn't make any difference what she thought. Since Beck was driving, it was out of her hands.

She needn't have worried.

Tucker opened the door, a big goofy smile on his face. He hadn't shaved and looked so gorgeous Cruella nearly drowned in her own drool.

Tucker leaned down to Batgirl and gave her a big smooch. "Does Batman know you've left Gotham City?"

Gracie Bella giggled. "It's me, Tuck."

"No! Gracie? I didn't recognize you. Why are you out with Wonder Woman and Green Lantern?"

She giggled again. "'Cause it's the night everybody gives us candy!"

Daisy ran across the yard and tugged at Tucker's jeans. "Hi, Tut."

"Do I know you?" Tuck asked. "I'm not sure I've ever met a talking Dalmatian. I know a poodle and a couple of terriers, but a Dalmatian? I don't recognize these spots."

Bending her head, Daisy studied the spots on her outfit. Then she tipped her chin to meet Tucker's gaze. "They're not real spots. They're 'tend, huh, Mommy?"

"Pretend," Elisa corrected. "And yes, they are."

"I don't know." Tucker rubbed his chin.

Daisy patted his knee. "It's me, Tut. Daisy Elizabeth Danvers."

"Daisy? No! I think you're trying to trick me. My Daisy is a sweet little girl, not a puppy dog."

"We're just 'tending."

"Tell you what. Give me a kiss. Right here." He tapped his cheek. "I'll know my Daisy's kiss."

He bent down and she kissed him.

He grinned. "Darned if you're not right. You look cute, Daisy."

"Thanks." Shy again, she studied her feet.

"Am I right in assuming you and Batgirl want some candy?"

"Yes," both girls cried.

He disappeared into the house and came back with a fistful for each.

"Look, Mommy. Look what Tut gived me!"

"I see." She glanced at the mound of candy, then pinned Tucker with a hard stare. "Do you think you gave them enough?"

"Hey, you came to me." He held up his hands, palms out. "Just sayin'. Besides, I figure Beck can help Tansy ride herd on a sugared-up little girl tonight." He waggled his brows. "Speaking for myself, I'd be more than happy to go home with you—you know, to help out."

"You're incorrigible."

"What's that mean, Mommy?"

"It means he's...stubborn."

"Oh. So can he come home with us tonight?"

When Tucker chuckled, Beck joined him.

Tansy and Elisa shared a look that said there was no use fighting it. Boys would be boys.

"Give me a couple minutes to throw together a costume."

"Tansy has a pair of green tights in the truck," Beck offered.

Tucker stopped half in, half out of the door. "Are you serious?"

"Wanna borrow them?" Beck asked.

"Not in this lifetime."

"See?" Beck rounded on Tansy. "Told you. Real men don't wear tights."

Elisa, Tansy, and Beck chatted on Tucker's porch while they waited. The girls, candy abandoned for the time being, chased each other around the yard.

Not five minutes later, Tuck stepped through the door in his camos. He looked so big, so bad, so male that he stole Elisa's breath.

"I swore I'd never wear these again, but this was pretty short notice to come up with a costume." He whistled for the girls, who came running. He knelt in the grass. "What do you think, ladies? How'd I do?"

"You're a soldier." Daisy crawled onto his knee and gave him a big hug. "I love it, Tut."

"Me, too," Gracie Bella chimed in.

He dumped the rest of his candy in a basket and set it on the top step.

"Honor system?" Beck asked.

"You bet. It won't matter because nobody will come clear out here for a candy bar."

"We did," Elisa said.

"Yeah, but only because you know what kind of goodies I have."

She turned pink, and he laughed.

"Cut it out, Dumbo." She elbowed him in the stomach.

"Nobody but you picked up on that double entendre."

"I wouldn't be too sure about that." She tossed a sideways glance at Tansy and Beck who were both doing an excellent job of looking innocent. "They know."

"Considering they're practically newlyweds, yeah, they probably do." He had the audacity to wink at her. "Since there's six of us, we should take two vehicles."

The girls didn't want to split up. Since Daisy's car seat

was already in Beck's truck, she went with them. Elisa and Tucker followed.

Alone in the car with Tucker, Elisa again became all too aware of his maleness, and the man smelled so good. She chewed her bottom lip.

Tucker laid his hand over hers. "Don't worry. I won't bite. I'm a soldier, not a vampire."

She sighed. "I know."

"I miss you and Daisy at the house."

She snorted. "You do not. I'll bet you turned cartwheels when you got us moved into Desdemona's."

He shot her a sideways glance. "No, I didn't. I'll admit to a small bit of unease when you first moved in." He caught her expression. "Okay, a lot of unease, but you kind of grow on a fellow. I was hoping to see you tonight."

"Even though Daisy wants you to, you can't stay tonight," Elisa warned.

"Understood." At the next stop sign, he leaned toward her, wrapped a hand behind her neck, and pulled her in for a whopper of a kiss that curled her toes. "Guess that'll have to do, huh?"

Heart racing, she simply nodded.

The tension broken, they chatted nonstop on the drive into town.

Their last stop would be Tansy's aunt's house. Before they'd left Cricket and Sam's, Tansy said, "Be warned. Aunt Coralee not only colors outside the lines, she's erased them."

"Actually, we've met her," Tuck said. "She's one heck of an artist."

"Did she tell you she nearly landed in jail over the mural?"

Elisa had smiled. "No, she left that part out. She did tell

us what she does with the money, though, and I think it's wonderful."

Tucker took her hand, his thumb tracing over the back.

He wouldn't betray her confidence. Neither would Coralee or Doc Hawkins. Elisa wanted to keep Daisy's heart issue quiet as long as possible because once people knew about it, they tended to treat her differently.

When they reached Tansy's aunt's house, the vehicles were barely unloaded before the front door opened and a very eccentric-looking witch stepped out.

Gracie Bella ran to her, but Daisy tried to crawl up her mother's leg. Elisa lifted her.

"What a group we have," Coralee cackled. "I see someone is afraid of me." She swooped Gracie Bella into her arms. "Tell your pretty little friend I'm okay, Gracie. She's been here before, but I wasn't a witch the day she visited."

"Auntie is nice, Daisy," Gracie said.

"And I have lollipops," Coralee added.

"Lollipops?" Daisy wiggled to get down, and Elisa lowered her to the sidewalk.

Daisy held out her bag and followed Witch Coralee to the porch for goodies.

When Tansy's aunt suggested they move inside for some cocoa, Tucker bowed out.

"Afraid I've got an early morning appointment. If I let Gaven meet with the client alone, he'll give away the shop. The kid's great with cars, but he's clueless when it comes to the business end of things."

"Would you mind dropping Daisy and me at the house first?" Elisa asked. "My little Dalmatian is dragging butt."

Cocooned in Tucker's Mustang as he drove her home,

Elisa said, "Next Halloween I'll pass out candy at the bookstore, and the decorations will have everybody stopping by, young and old."

"You're loving this, aren't you?"

"I am." She twisted slightly in her seat. "It's like a dream. I lost my job, my home, my hope. The entire bottom fell out of my world. Then I pulled off the road at your shop and, well, as awful as all that was, it turned my life around. I wake up every morning reminding myself how lucky I am."

Tucker parked in front of Desdemona's and glanced in his rearview mirror. "You were right. Daisy was worn out."

Elisa nodded. "The pup hit the wall." Folding her hands in her lap, she said, "Thanks for coming with us tonight."

"I enjoyed it. Is Desdemona home?"

"No. Robin Hood and Maid Marion are at a costume party."

He threw her a sexy grin. "The chaperone's away?"

She nodded toward the dashboard clock. "It's late."

"I lied about the early morning appointment."

"Why?"

"You looked a little upset. I figured you wanted to get the kid home."

And there it was. Tucker understood her better than people she'd known a lifetime. Certainly better than the man she'd married ever had.

"Why don't you at least let me carry Daisy inside?"

"I'd appreciate that."

Once she had Daisy tucked in, no doubt dreaming about her bag of Halloween loot, Elisa tiptoed down the elegant staircase to find Tucker waiting. Sprawled on the velvet loveseat in his worn camos, he looked perfectly at home.

Tucker Wylder was comfortable wherever he found himself. She envied him that.

Tucker watched Elisa come down the stairs toward him. What was he going to do about her? He'd thought that once she left his house, she'd also move out of his thoughts. How wrong he'd been. If anything, he craved her more. He craved seeing her, hearing her, smelling her. He craved touching her and sharing morning coffee with her.

He missed Daisy's laughter, her oh-so-innocent wonder at the world around her. It was fascinating to watch her, to see how her mind wrapped around ideas. She changed every day—and he was missing out on it.

He'd wanted to be alone. Now? He'd never realized how empty and cold a house could be. The nights Elisa came over? The best and the worst.

He unfolded himself from the loveseat and met Elisa at the bottom of the stairs. Wrapping her in his arms, he kissed her as though his life depended on it. And right then, he wasn't sure it didn't.

When she ran her hands up his back, slid them beneath the camo shirt to touch his skin, a sound of pure male pleasure escaped him. His lips never leaving hers, he lifted her off her feet and carried her to one of the fancy little loveseats Desdemona liked. The kiss deepened and his hand moved up that elegant neck and touched, not her silky hair, but the black-and-white wig.

"Can we lose Cruella?" he mumbled as his lips traced her collar bone.

"Whoops, I forgot."

"Let me." Tucker removed the wig and pulled on the band that bundled all that gorgeous blond hair. As it tumbled around her shoulders, he ran his fingers through it. "You're so beautiful, Lissie."

"Kiss me, Tuck."

He did.

Her fingers worked the buttons on his shirt, while his undid the zipper of her slinky Cruella dress.

Skin to skin, his heart fairly galloped. "I need you, sugar."

"I—"

A car's headlights shone through the open curtains.

"Oh, blithering bandits. Desdemona." Elisa slid her dress up over her shoulders. "Zip me. Quick."

Tuck's fingers trembled. "Sorry. My hands…so clumsy."

When he finally got the job done, he grabbed his shirt and shot his arms into the sleeves. "I'll, ah, slip into the bathroom and make myself a little more presentable."

"Good idea." Frantically, she began to finger-comb her hair.

Their eyes met, and they broke out laughing.

"I feel like I'm fifteen again and just got caught by the parents," Tuck said.

"Same here, but it would have been Grandma."

The doorknob turned and so did Tuck. He headed for the powder room—leaving Elisa to face the music alone. He acknowledged that made him a dog.

When he had himself under control, Tucker braced for the male version of the walk of shame.

Yancy had tossed an arm over the back of the loveseat he shared with Desdemona while Elisa, looking sexily disheveled, curled up in a chair across from them.

"Doesn't our girl look great, Tuck?" Desdemona boomed. "Yancy and I came in to find her bloomin' like a rose."

He met Elisa's gaze and saw both amusement and embarrassment in them. "Yeah. Seems she's stumbled onto something good."

"Or someone," Desdemona said. "I don't think she's alone in that."

Doc Hawkins picked up her hand and kissed the back of it. "It ought to be Valentine's Day instead of Halloween. Lots of love floatin' in the air tonight."

Love? Tucker's stomach quivered. Nah. Doc Hawkins had it wrong. It was hormones, that's all.

Love had a way of sucker-punching you, then abandoning you while you were down for the count. He didn't do love.

CHAPTER 20

EVERY MORNING, ELISA OPENED THE BOOKSTORE'S door, took one step inside, and closed her eyes. Breathing deeply, she inhaled the scent of books and candles, and smiled.

She'd never have believed anyplace could be better to work at than the library in Bowden, yet this was. She could still share stories and recommend books, but no one had to be shushed. She chatted with her customers and shared an occasional cup of coffee with them. Guilt sometimes nipped at her because Desdemona was actually paying her to do this—while providing her and her child a wonderful place to live.

Her new happiness came with a dent in it, though. Tucker had inexplicably pulled back. He rarely dropped by, and when he did, there were no innuendoes, no flirting. He came as a friend.

She'd made lots of friends in Misty Bottoms. That's not what she needed or wanted from him.

Halloween, she and Tucker had done quite a lot of treating and she'd hoped for...what? She wasn't sure. But something she couldn't put her finger on had scared Tuck away.

Before him, it had been so long since she'd touched, since she'd kissed. *Been* touched and kissed. She'd almost convinced herself she didn't need or want it. Tucker had set off a deep longing in her, though, one she was afraid only he could satisfy. But he, obviously, didn't feel the same way.

Maybe. The man was hard to figure out.

If she was more like Desdemona, she'd know what to do—and have the guts to do it.

While her mind raced, she started a pot of cinnamon-flavored coffee, then moved around the shop to give the shelves a quick dusting and to light pine-scented candles. Now that the calendar had flipped to November, the holiday season barreled toward them.

She couldn't wait to decorate a small tree and start playing Christmas carols in the shop. She hoped the sights, sounds, and smells of the season would have people buying early for Christmas. Thanks to Desdemona, she'd have a little extra money this year to help Santa. Last year things had been pretty tight.

As far as Desdemona went, even if she could overcome her reluctance to ask her help in the romance department, her friend was rarely home in the evenings. She'd fed Elisa a line about helping Doctor Hawkins reorganize his office. Since she'd seen first-hand what a tight ship Brinna ran, Elisa doubted that ship needed any patching. Besides, Yancy and Desdemona could have set to rights every business in town in the amount of time they spent together.

Her feminine intuition told her there was more monkey business going on than actual business.

Doc almost always picked Desdemona up. When he dropped her off, a considerable amount of time passed between when Doc's Caddy pulled into the driveway and when the front door opened. Add in his comment about love on Halloween and Elisa figured things were getting interesting. Desdemona Rosebud Hamilton didn't like living alone, and maybe she wouldn't have to for long.

Selfishly, Elisa realized that meant she and Daisy would need to find somewhere else to live. Somewhere in Misty Bottoms.

Somewhere she could run into Tucker occasionally.

She missed him and knew that when the truth came out about Harry, his role in Tucker's sorrow would put an end to even their friendship.

Maybe it was best she was weaned off him slowly.

Tucker dragged his butt up the walk. His back ached and his knees hurt from kneeling on the bay's concrete floor. Yet as tired as he was, he'd stayed at the shop way past quitting time. Again. A new habit he'd developed, a bad one. Brant had gone home a couple of hours earlier to a wife and dinner. Gaven had plans to meet friends at Duffy's Pub for a meal and an evening of darts. Tucker'd been invited; he'd declined.

Instead, he was coming home late and alone. He unlocked the door and let himself into the quiet, dark house, carrying with him even darker thoughts. It had been a while, though, since he'd felt compelled to leave the house in the wee hours of the morning to drive around or visit the war memorial.

A heavy sadness dragged at him.

He hit the light switch and studied his immaculate house. Nothing out of place and no pictures askew. No sugary, dried cereal stuck to his expensive quartz countertop, no laughter or whispers or a little girl's high-pitched voice singing "Twinkle, Twinkle, Little Star." Breathing deeply, he smelled no girlie-girl lotion or hair products.

No Daisy and no Elisa.

At least he hadn't driven past Desdemona's tonight. The last time he'd done that, Daisy'd been playing in the yard. She'd recognized his car and waved. Busted by a three-and-a-half-year-old. When her mama came to the door, he'd sped away, ashamed of himself.

He should have stopped and asked how things were going. Instead, he'd run like a coward. Would he have done that the day his friends died?

No. He'd have faced that enemy and, no doubt, died alongside his friends. What would that have done to his mother? To his father and brothers? His sister?

If he'd been there, could he have changed the outcome? Or was that, as Elisa had said, giving himself too much credit, thinking he alone could have saved them all?

He'd gone 'round and 'round with these questions—especially in the middle of the night. Bottom line? He had no answer. He had no way of knowing if Hard-Ass Harry had saved his life that day or, by ordering him to stay back, sealed his friends' death warrants.

Heading to the kitchen for an icy beer, his thoughts returned to Elisa. To compare what was happening with her to his time overseas? It didn't work.

First, she sure as hell wasn't the enemy. Second, she scared the socks right off him, and yet he found her irresistible. That woman touched places in his heart he hadn't even known existed, and that was downright frightening.

He'd had a taste of her. Heck, he'd had a lot more than a taste, and he wanted more. Every time he looked at her, every time they were in the same room, the air practically vibrated. Sleeping with her had been a huge mistake—but it was one he couldn't regret.

Opening his beer, he took a long swallow.

He toed off his boots, emptied the contents of his pockets into the little bowl on the counter, then dropped his pants, covered in dirt and grease, right there in the kitchen. His shirt came off next and he added it to the pile by the refrigerator. Going to the sink, he scrubbed his hands again.

The temperature had dropped, inside and out, and he shivered.

Moving into the living room, he flopped onto the couch in T-shirt and boxers. He wedged a throw pillow under his head and closed his eyes. How many times in the past couple of weeks had he stopped at Dee-Ann's and ordered takeout?

It wasn't because he actually wanted it. His appetite had moved out right along with Elisa and Daisy. The food was a ruse. While he waited, he took a walk—a walk that carried him past Elisa's bookstore.

Between Desdemona's money and Elisa's eye for design, the place had transformed from a rundown, tucked-away building to a magical place. The windows glistened after a good cleaning, and the paint, even though it was what he called fairy-princess pink, had been the perfect touch.

Despite himself, he'd stepped more than once onto the winding brick sidewalk to peek inside. With his salvage contacts, Cole had been tapped to find the furnishings and lighting and, from what Tucker could see through the window, he'd done one heck of a job.

Books were artfully arranged on shelves and in the display window. A bench outside welcomed customers to sit. Flowers hung from the small porch and others flourished in planters, adding a splash of late fall color.

They'd opened without any fanfare, yet the whole town knew about *Just Books*. He'd actually stopped by a couple of times and gone in, but only when other customers were there. A nod of his head was the only acknowledgment he'd given Elisa.

And again, shame on him.

When he rolled over on the sofa, his fingers touched something beneath the cushion. Rising on an elbow, he pulled out a little blue bow. Daisy Elizabeth's. He ran a fingertip over the silky ribbon, a ribbon the same shade as her eyes, as her mama's eyes.

He swore.

Jumping up, he headed to the shower.

The hot pounding water didn't help. Tucker was clean, but he still ached to see Elisa, to talk to her. Hell, to kiss her. Striding to his closet, he pulled out a clean shirt and jeans. It seemed he'd take that ride to Desdemona's after all.

The house was dark when he pulled up out front.

He should go home.

He couldn't.

Quietly getting out of the car, he stood in the middle of the street and stared at the huge house. The temperature had dipped lower still and his hair was wet. If he had any sense at all he'd get back in his car, turn up the heater, and go home. Instead, he hustled through the yard toward the back. That's where his girls slept.

What did Elisa sleep in? He'd seen her in her flowery

nightgowns and his shirts. He liked her best in nothing at all...and that didn't speak well for him, he supposed.

Heck, on second thought, there was nothing wrong with that. It made him a red-blooded male, that's all. Elisa was a beautiful, sexy woman. Nothing wrong whatsoever with him wanting her.

Coming here in the middle of the night? That might be a different matter.

He stopped beneath what he was pretty sure was Elisa's room. If he screwed up and popped into Desdemona's, all hell would break loose. He didn't doubt for a second the woman slept with a pearl-handled pistol beneath her pillow.

Maybe he should reconsider.

Nah. He'd come this far, he might as well put it all on the table. A large oak grew directly outside Elisa's balcony. It had been a long time since he'd climbed a tree to get to a girl. He grinned. Guess he'd find out if he still had it in him. A flying leap gave him the height to grab a bottom limb. If it held, he was golden.

He swung himself up, wrapping his legs around the sturdy branch. Once he got himself righted, the climb was easy. Transferring to her balcony proved a little more difficult. When he glanced down, the ground sure seemed a long way away. This might not have been his best idea ever.

But the doorbell would have woken the entire household and kind of ruined his plans. He didn't want to make small talk with Desdemona or deal with a cranky little girl. He wanted to spend some time with her mama, maybe do a little necking if Mama was so inclined.

Carefully, he hoisted himself over the railing and onto her balcony. She'd left her drapes open, and moonlight spilled into the room, highlighting her face. She slept on her side, one hand tucked beneath her cheek. His chest grew tight.

Okay now, this was wrong. He couldn't stand out here watching her. That felt way too much like a Peeping Tom and wasn't the reason he'd come. Raising a hand, he knuckle-rapped on the door's glass.

Her eyes popped open.

"It's me, Lissie."

"Tucker?"

"I'm cold. Let me in."

"Are you crazy?" She sat up, clutching the bed covers to her chest. "You can't come in."

"Why not? I risked life and limb to get up here."

"Well, risk it again and go back down." She tossed aside the bedcovers and moved to the door.

"Lissie. Come on, babe. Open the door."

She was stunning. Her long blond hair was mussed, reminding him of the way it looked after he'd run his hands through it when they made love. Those incredible eyes were all sleepy and dreamy, and her voice was sleep-husky.

No flannel nightgown for Elisa tonight. The strap of the silky slip of a thing she wore slid off one shoulder, baring it. Tuck fantasized about dropping a kiss right beneath her collarbone, then nuzzling his way up her neck.

"Why did you stay away so long?"

"Because you…I…the two of us… It scares me."

The lock *snick*ed and the door opened.

She shivered.

"You cold, too?" he asked.

"I am now." Reaching out, she snagged the front of his shirt and pulled him inside.

She kissed him, her lips hot on his chilled ones. Her skin beneath his cold hands felt smoother than any silk.

When she started to pull away, he dropped his forehead to hers. "One more minute. Let me hold you one more minute."

She did. Another kiss followed, then another, until both were breathing hard.

"Why are you here?"

"I miss you."

"You've totally ignored me."

"And it's about killed me."

"Really?" Her voice softened. "I'm mad at you."

"I'm mad at me, too, and I'm very, very sorry." He dropped that kiss beneath her collarbone. "Forgive me?"

She sighed. "Don't ever pull that again."

"I won't." After another kiss, he said, "I want to take a look at your bathroom. Desdemona's tour didn't include your suite."

"I wonder why."

He winked. "Daisy's told me about your tub, though." He sneaked past her and flicked on a small lamp, his eye catching on a display of the photos she'd brought with her from Alabama, one of a grinning Daisy at what looked to be her first birthday party.

Then he took in the rest of the room. "Holy Hannah! This place is—"

"Yeah, it is."

He turned to her, put his hands on her arms. "I could never give you this."

"I don't need this. I never expected it."

Kicking himself, he loosened his hold and moved across

the room, scrubbing a hand down his face. Why in the hell had he said that? He could never give her this? That implied a future. A permanent arrangement. Not what he was looking for. But then, didn't you sometimes find what you wanted, needed, when you weren't looking?

Put that thought away, he warned himself. *There's danger there. Take care of tonight.*

He snaked an arm around her waist. "Want to fill that tub with bubbles?"

"Oh, fudge berries!"

He grinned. "I'll take that as a yes."

CHAPTER 21

THANKSGIVING WAS LESS THAN TWO WEEKS AWAY. ELISA couldn't quite figure how that had happened. Already, Desdemona was stewing over the menu for the big dinner she planned. A couple dozen of her favorite people would share it with them.

Tucker wouldn't be one of those. Elisa sighed at the tenderness he hid behind the sometimes brusque exterior he wore. The night he'd come to her room she'd felt like Rapunzel, her hero scaling the wall for her. Heat rushed to her cheeks as she remembered their shared bath. She couldn't even look at that tub without going all tingly.

Desdemona had invited him and his brothers for the day, but they'd declined. Their mom, dad, and sister were driving in from Tennessee to spend time before the holiday with them, then the boys and Molly would drive to Lake Delores for Thanksgiving. Since their mother was still recovering from a bad stroke, they felt she might be more comfortable with only the family this year. As much as Elisa would miss Tucker, she understood. The Wylder men were doing the right thing. Family came at the very top of the priority list—if you were lucky enough to have one.

Her grandmother had loved the holidays, but she was gone. Elisa hadn't heard from her mother, so she assumed she'd spend Thanksgiving in Mexico. Her father could be anywhere on the planet, and since they'd never shared a turkey wishbone, it didn't much matter. She and Daisy would make their own traditions, and this year it would include dinner with Desdemona.

Then would come that mad runaway slide into the Christmas season.

She rubbed her hands together from both the anticipation and the chill. The cold front the weatherman predicted had arrived early and had her digging through her closet for something warm to wear.

Unearthing the remote control from beneath a pile of books, she turned on the electric fireplace. The shop would be nice and toasty in no time.

The door flew open and Tucker blew in. Elisa's heart gave a happy little lurch.

Quickly, he shut the door behind him. "Brrrr. It's nippy out there." Tuck perused Elisa. "You look good."

She screwed up her face. "I look like the stereotypical uptight librarian with my hair in a bun and wearing tortoise-shell glasses."

He leaned in and whispered, "So is this where I toss your glasses onto the nightstand? Tear the pins from your hair and run my fingers through it?"

Her gaze moved to the large front window. "Afraid not."

"You're no fun."

She threw him a suggestive smile. "I can be."

"That I have first-hand knowledge of." He ran a finger down her cheek and kissed her forehead. "Actually, I came because I heard you need some help. Beck said you were closed today. Apparently, you've changed your mind about some of the colors and have a bit of painting to do." He opened a bag. "I came prepared with a brush, a roller, and a strong back."

Despite that big window, she hooked a finger in the front of his sweatshirt and pulled him in for a kiss that warmed them both up.

For the next couple of hours, they laughed, talked, and painted.

When they'd finished and cleaned up, she said, "Today calls for soup, homemade bread dripping in butter, and hot chocolate with marshmallows."

"In a perfect world."

"It so happens I brought all that with me today. Want to share lunch?"

"You're kidding."

"Nope. I made both the soup and the bread last night. The chill in the air seemed to call for it."

"Elisa, you're almost too good to be true."

Pain shot through her, and she closed her eyes.

"You okay?"

She shook her head.

"How about we head into the back room?" He moved toward her.

"Wait." Heart pounding, she laid a hand on his chest. "There's something I have to tell you. Something you need to know." Tears filled her eyes.

"Whatever it is, it's okay, baby."

"No," she whispered. "It's not."

"We're both adults, sweetheart. We've done things and said things we're not proud of. I don't need a confession."

Her tongue darted out to wet Sahara-dry lips. "But—"

Desdemona chose that moment to walk in, a chattering Daisy beside her. "That soft French blue is fantastic." She glanced toward Elisa and stopped dead. "Uh-oh. Bad timing?" Then she took another longer look. "You're not planning to faint again, are you? Did you eat?"

Before Elisa could come up with an answer, Daisy moved to Tuck. "Look, Tut. I got a new baby-doll. Desdi bought her for me."

"Does she have a name?"

"Uh-huh. Annie."

"Annie, huh? I like that." He knelt down. "She's one of the prettiest dolls I've ever seen." He stood and took Daisy's hand in his. "It's time to eat. Why don't you join us, Desdemona? You, Daisy, and Annie."

"Do you have enough?"

"Oh, yeah," Elisa said.

What she didn't have was courage. Maybe her Halloween costume should have been the Cowardly Lion.

CHAPTER 22

ON THE DRIVE INTO TOWN THE NEXT DAY, TUCKER waffled. Maybe he should have let Elisa get whatever was bothering her off her chest. She'd picked at her lunch, and even Daisy'd had trouble keeping her attention.

He didn't need to know any more about her past, though. She'd had a hard time before coming to Misty Bottoms, and now things were looking up. Wasn't it best to let bygones be bygones?

And wasn't he a good one to talk about that!

A song came on the radio about lost love, and Tucker switched stations.

Elisa and Daisy mattered to him. He was slowly beginning to realize that if his life was ever going to get back on track and have any meaning, any worth, he needed them in it, and that scared the bejesus right out of him.

Parking in front of Molly's bridal boutique, he hurried inside, out of the wind.

He peeked around the shop's door. "Anybody here?"

"Just Lettie and me."

"Good. I need your help."

"Hmm. Let me think." Closing her eyes, she placed a finger to her temple. Then she laughed and met his gaze. "Since your family's coming for a visit and you're in charge of dinner, my guess is you'd like help with the food."

"Hey, you got the easy part," he said. "They're sleeping at your place. How hard can that be?"

"You're right. Lettie, will you keep an eye on the front?"

"Sure. You ought to call in an order from Fat Baby's Barbecue and be done with it," Lettie suggested. "That's simple enough."

Tucker glanced toward Molly. "Should I?"

"Not if you want to win any points."

He hung his head. "I don't actually need help fixing the food, just figuring out something I can make that won't kill us all."

"That makes me feel much better!"

He spread his hands.

In no time, Molly laid out a menu for him, all stuff he could handle. She glanced up from the grocery list. "I suppose you've heard about Doc and Desdemona."

"Doc Hawkins?"

"Yeah. Know another in town?"

"Not right off hand. You gonna tell me, or do I have to guess?" When she hesitated, a mischievous grin on her face, he said, "I'll bet you a burger at Dee-Ann's Diner it has something to do with those feelings they've been dancing around."

Her mouth opened, but no sound escaped.

Tuck laughed. "You didn't pick up on that? Those two give off heat when they're within fifty feet of each other."

"Why, Tucker Wylder. Since when did you come to be so astute?"

"Always have been. I simply keep all that astuteness to myself."

Tucker drove from Molly's shop straight to the bookstore. When he walked in, he wanted to kick himself clear across the country and back. Elisa looked like she hadn't slept last night. What deep, dark secret could she be harboring that bothered her so much?

None. Not Elisa.

But then, she tended to fret about every little thing. She needed to get over that.

A couple of customers browsed the shelves. Annabelle, who ran the B&B, stood with her back to him, but he'd recognize that fifties-style orange-and-blue housedress and those sloppy-big purple Converse tennis shoes anywhere. With her here, anything he said would be public knowledge within seconds of her leaving the store.

He couldn't let that stop him. "I've come to apologize."

Annabelle turned, sliding the glasses she wore on a chain into place. The better to see him, he supposed.

Elisa's forehead creased in puzzlement. "For what?"

"For putting you off yesterday."

"We should take this conversation into the backroom."

"Do you want to share now?"

"No!" She shook her head. "No. Not now. Not here."

"You sure?"

"Maybe you should give her a kiss," Annabelle said. "That might help."

He cocked a brow at Elisa. "Would it?"

"It wouldn't hurt."

When he moved toward her, she held out a hand. "But again, not now. I'm working."

"Ah. I thought maybe since we, ah…" He looked toward their audience. "Ah, you know, things might have changed. That a little PDA wouldn't be out of line."

She blushed. "Wrong!"

He kissed her anyway.

"'Bout time," Annabelle said. "Come on, Beatrice. Let's have a piece of Dee-Ann's pie at the diner. We can come back afterwards for our books."

The bell over the door tinkled as they left.

"You know that little scene will be all over town."

"I don't care," he said. "Lissie, I—I—You're important to me. I know everything about you I need to know." He didn't see the expected relief in her eyes, so he decided to back off. "How's Daisy?"

"She misses breakfast—and Pop-Tarts—with her Tut."

He grinned. "On that note, I have a favor to ask. A pretty big one and one that includes Daisy. My parents are coming day after tomorrow for a preholiday visit."

She nodded.

"They're staying with Brant and Molly, but everyone's coming to my place for dinner. I'd like to have you and Daisy there." He wiped the palms of his hands on his jeans. "I want Mom and Dad to meet you."

"Tucker—"

"I know. A big ask." His eyes met her clear blue ones. "Say yes. Please."

"Yes."

Meatloaf, mashed potatoes, and corn casserole. Tucker, feeling pretty darned good about the meal he'd prepared, slid the rolls into the oven. There, he'd cheated—with Molly's blessing. They'd come from the freezer section of the grocery store.

The doorbell rang, and Daisy and her mama stood on the stoop.

"Come on in." He swung the door wide, then leaned down to catch Daisy up in a hug.

"Tut! We're gonna eat with you!"

"Yes, you are. You been good for your mama?"

"Uh-huh. Haven't I, Mommy?"

"You have."

"Lissie, you look great."

"You think?" She ran a hand over the skirt of her soft-orange print dress. "I wasn't sure what to wear. I mean, your parents are coming, so—Are they here?" Her gaze skittered past him, into the living room.

"Not yet." He laid a hand on her shoulder. "Relax. They'll love you."

She grimaced. "I don't know." She nodded toward Daisy. "Do they know this one will be here?"

"They can't wait to meet her. My sister, Lainey, will have her little guy, too. Jax is, gosh, I don't know, about a year-and-a-half now."

"Have you put your valuables up high?"

"Nope. My most valued just walked through my door." He frowned at her expression. "What's wrong, sugar?"

She flashed him a too-bright smile. "Not a thing… And we come bearing gifts. Or *a* gift." She held out a pecan pie. "Freshly made this morning. Daisy helped."

He gave Daisy a quick cheek-kiss, then took a little longer thanking her mama.

———

It wasn't long before his fairly large house nearly burst at the seams. Eight adults, two kids, and Lug Nut.

"Why'd you bring the dog, Brant?"

"He wanted to come."

"Oh, give me a break," Tucker said.

Molly, Elisa, and Lainey finally shooed the men out of the kitchen, including Tucker.

"Take Jax with you," Lainey said.

Brant slung the toddler under his arm. "Hey, Jax, looks like it's you and me again, pal."

Jax gave him a slobbery grin.

"Take the dog, too," his mother said.

While Penny, Tucker's mother, sat on a stool supervising, the girls did the final prep and got the food on the table.

"How about we walk into the dining room together?" Elisa helped Tucker's mother from the stool.

Penny patted her hand. "When Brant brought Molly home, I cried tears of joy. My middle son chose well." She smiled. "It seems the oldest of my boys has good taste, too. I'm so glad you're here today, Elisa. You and darling Daisy."

Elisa opened her mouth to clarify the situation, but Tucker, standing in the doorway, caught her gaze and shook his head. He was right. Now wasn't the time.

The food was excellent and the conversation flowed smoothly. Jax entertained everyone with his jabbering, and Daisy fell in love with him, hovering over him like a mother hen.

Tucker leaned into Elisa. "She's found herself a real live doll."

"I think you're right. I hope she doesn't cry to take him home."

Brant broke into the conversations by tapping a spoon gently against his glass.

Everyone grew quiet.

"What's up?" Gaven asked.

"Molly and I have an announcement to make." He took his wife's hand and kissed the back of it. "Come next summer, Jax will have a new cousin. Molly and I are pregnant."

"Yeah, *we're* pregnant. I get to handle all the morning sickness, and he gets all the bragging rights," Molly added.

Tucker's mouth had dropped open.

Molly laughed. "So Tuck, where's all that astuteness you claimed to have?"

"Apparently I used it all up on Doc. I swear I didn't have a clue." He hugged her. "You're gonna be a mama. Way to go, Brant!" He high-fived his brother.

Penny shook her head. "You're right, Molly. The men take all the credit, don't they?"

More high fives and congratulations followed. Elisa listened to the family's happiness and was glad she'd come.

Beside her, Daisy let out a squeal. "No, Lug Nut!"

"What's he doing?"

"He taked my roll."

"Lug Nut." Brant pointed toward the living room. "In there. Now."

The dog—who'd spent the entire dinner begging for food, then slinking away after each scolding only to appear under the table again—slunk off once more, tail between his legs.

"He'll come back. Bad pennies always do."

Dessert finished, Tucker set a stack of dirty dishes on the counter, mentally patting himself on the back. He'd done it, managed a meal for the entire family. He'd had some help, but still…

His dad came up behind him. "How about you and I step outside for a minute? I want to take a look at that stream of yours."

"Sure." Since his dad had already been here a few times and had definitely seen his stream, Tucker wondered what was up.

The screen door slapped shut behind them.

"Is Mama okay?"

"She is. How about you, Son? You okay?"

"I am, Dad. In fact, I'm in a better place than I've been for quite a while."

His father nodded. "It's none of my business, but— Hell with that. It is my business. You're my son, and I love you." He pulled him in for a man-hug. "Your mama and I worry about you. It's pretty obvious to the whole family that something went very wrong during your last tour."

"It did, and I lost four good friends." A muscle in his jaw worked, but he kept talking. It was time. Elisa had been right about that. "The mission was doomed from the get-go. My commander made a bad decision and sent them to their deaths as surely as if he'd stood them in front of a firing squad."

"You discussed it with him?"

"I did, and that's the only reason I'm here. My LC got pissed and restricted me to base. I should have been with my team."

"Got some survivor's guilt, I'd guess."

Tucker swiped a foot through the grass. "Yeah, I do."

"Look at me, Son." His father stared straight into Tucker's eyes. "Selfish or not, I'll be forever thankful you weren't with them." He lifted a hand. "You can't fault me for that."

"I don't." His voice broke. "But it's a hell of a thing to live with, Dad."

"I reckon it is."

Tuck nodded. "Let's move on to something happier. I see you brought the truck like I asked."

"Sure did."

"Let's go inside and get Mama. I want to show her something."

His mother was doing so darned well after her stroke, but because the ground was a little bumpy, Tucker wrapped an arm around her and walked her out to his shed. His dad followed them.

He opened the door and extended a hand toward the swing, which he'd finished up two nights ago. "I noticed yours was looking a little worse for wear last time I was home."

Penny's jaw dropped. "You made this?"

"I did."

"Oh, honey." She rubbed a hand over the smooth finish. "It's beautiful."

Behind her, his dad cleared his throat. "Son, this is damned fine work."

"I learned from the best." Tuck slung an arm around his father's shoulders. "The boys and I will load it into your truck. When you get home, call Shorty and he and a couple of his guys will come unload it and hang it for you."

Tears rolled down his mother's face.

"Hey." Tucker wiped them away with his thumb. "This was supposed to be a good thing. It was supposed to make you happy."

"It does. These are good tears." Penny laid a hand on her oldest son's cheek and kissed him. Then she ran trembling fingers over the arm of the swing again. "I'll treasure this, Tucker. Every day when I sit on it to drink my first cup of coffee, it'll be like getting a good-morning hug from you."

He made excuses to keep Elisa around until everyone else had gone.

"Stay with me tonight, Lissie."

"I can't."

"Why not? Give me one good reason." He raised a brow. "And don't use Daisy. She's sound asleep in her Murphy bed, and we both know it would take more than a sonic boom to wake her."

Elisa laughed. "True."

He leaned in and kissed her, long and deep. "My parents loved you, and Daisy was quite the hit. She and Jax sure got along well." Pulling Elisa closer, he ran his hands up her back, into all that beautiful hair. "You do things to me, sugar."

"Kiss me again."

He did.

"I need a promise, Tucker."

He stiffened. "I'm not good at makin' promises."

"I understand that, and if you can't, I need to know that, too."

"Fair enough."

"Promise me you'll never disappear from my life again like you did after Halloween. If something's wrong or something's bothering you, tell me. Talk to me about it. Don't leave me in limbo."

"Understood."

"No, I don't think you do. That's exactly what Luke did. He left without a word. He abandoned me."

"I talked to you."

"Not in the same way. You went from lover to distant friend with no warning and no explanation."

He rubbed the back of his neck. "I was confused. I screwed up majorly, didn't I?"

"You did, but I'll give you a mulligan. This time. Understand, though, if it happens again, there are no more do-overs. No second second chances. I can't."

"Message received loud and clear. You have my promise." He took her hand and led her upstairs to his bed.

———————————

Much later, she stood under the warm shower water, enjoying the feel of it as it beat down on her, reliving the last hour. Tucker's kisses, his hands on her body. His heat mixed with hers.

The shower door opened and he stepped inside, wrapping his arms around her from the back, dropping kisses on her smooth, wet skin.

She leaned against him, placing her hands over his. "I could get used to this."

Without a word, he took the soap from its niche and

lathered her up. Then he shampooed her hair, ran his fingers through its length, and massaged her head and neck. She'd never experienced anything as sensuous.

The water ran cold by the time they sagged against the tiles, spent and holding each other up.

Elisa smiled and whispered against his neck. "You're a great host. I've never enjoyed dinner more."

"It's late. Why don't you sleep here tonight?"

"I can't."

He narrowed his eyes. "You can, but you won't."

"That's semantics."

"No," he growled. "That's me sleeping in a lonely bed."

"Tuck—"

He shook his head, then pulled her in for another kiss.

An hour later, a barefooted Tucker buckled a sleeping Daisy into her car seat. "I still don't understand why you won't stay."

"How many reasons do you want, Tuck? When Daisy wakes, she'll be confused. I can't explain why Mommy decided on a sleepover, and she'll expect to do it again. Second, Desdemona will know."

"She won't care. Do you honestly believe she doesn't know that you and I—"

Elisa held up her hand. "Don't go there. Third, I have to open the bookstore in—" She glanced at her watch. "A few hours, and I'd prefer to do it in a different outfit than the one I wore today." She arched a brow. "Need more?"

He leaned in and kissed her soundly. "Oh yeah. I need so much more."

On a sigh, she wrapped herself around him and kissed him back.

Finally, she pulled away. "Goodnight, handsome."
"Night, babe."

Desdemona wasn't home. A soft light burned in the kitchen beside a note. It looked like she and the good doctor would be gone for a couple of days. Interesting.

Morning came quickly, and the day was long. She and Daisy ate a light dinner and watched the Disney channel. It seemed strange to have the entire house to themselves.

When Daisy fell asleep halfway through a movie, Elisa decided a long bubble bath was in order, although thoughts of that tub brought memories of the night she'd shared it with Tuck. Then memories of last night's—or, more correctly, this early morning's—shower. Whew.

She slid into the warm water and read a few chapters of the new romance book that had come in today. Then she laid it on the floor beside the tub and thought about her plan to repay Doc.

She'd taken the first step today. She'd posted the flier.

CHAPTER 23

"HEY, GAV, I'M GONNA BE A COUPLE MINUTES LATE," Tucker said when his brother answered the phone.

"What are you up to?"

"I just turned onto Desdemona's street. I need to talk to Elisa."

"Got it bad, don't you?"

"Maybe, baby brother, maybe."

"Better you than me," Gaven said. "You should take her coffee if you're stopping by this early."

"Already taken care of." Tucker glanced at the Sweet Dreams mugs in his cup holder. "Later."

When had the irritation at having his life disrupted by this woman and her child turned to something else? Something he wanted—something that should scare him but didn't. Elisa and Daisy had become a vital part of his life, one he'd nearly let slip through his fingers.

A trip to Savannah had taken longer than he'd expected yesterday, so he hadn't had a chance to so much as see Elisa. They'd talked on the phone, but it wasn't the same. He figured he'd bring her morning coffee and maybe earn himself a kiss. He'd brought along one of Daisy's Pop-Tarts, too. Breakfast with his girls—almost like it used to be.

He slid from the car, grabbed the coffee, and jogged up the sidewalk to the front door, amazed all over again by Desdemona's home. Why one woman would own a house this big, this…everything, he couldn't imagine. But then, logic didn't always come into play.

Nobody answered the bell. A check of his watch showed not quite seven thirty. Hmmm. Maybe Elisa was still asleep. He knocked. Once, twice, three times.

Glancing at the wall mailbox mounted by the front door, he noticed a large manila envelope that had been rolled and placed in it. Elisa must have forgotten to take in the mail last night.

Well, he'd deliver it along with her coffee.

When he pulled it out, he wished he hadn't. It was addressed to Mrs. Lucas Danvers. The return address? None other than *Mr.* Lucas Danvers. Husband or ex-husband? He was suddenly sorry he'd come.

The door opened and Elisa stood there, dressed but looking awfully tired.

"Tuck. I didn't expect you this morning."

"Were you expecting this?" Stiffly, he handed her the envelope.

She stared at it. "I filled out a form asking the post office to send my mail here. This was forwarded from Bowden."

"I see that." He jerked his head toward the piece of mail. Voice cold, he asked, "Is this the deep, dark secret you haven't been able to share with me, Lissie? The one that's tying you in knots?" He felt as though he was suffocating, but he had to know. "Are you still married?"

"No." Her eyes didn't meet his, though.

"I don't sleep with other men's wives."

"I'm no one's wife, Tuck."

"Why's he writing you and addressing it to Mrs. Lucas Danvers?"

Daisy, hearing his voice, stuck her head around the corner. "Tut! You comed to see us!"

"Yeah, but I can't stay, sweetheart."

"Why?"

He drew in a ragged breath. "I have to go to work. First, though, this is for you." He reached into his pocket and pulled out her Pop-Tart.

"Look, Mommy. Look what Tut brought." She gave him a grin, then started tearing the wrapping from it.

He slid a finger beneath Elisa's chin, forcing her to look at him. "Something's wrong, and it's destroying you. You're not sleeping, and you're losing weight again. It's all about trust, Lissie. Not just me trusting you, but you trusting me to accept whatever secret you're holding on to. Until you do—" He shook his head. "Unless you *can*, it's probably best we don't see each other."

"I'm not married."

"Good to hear. Really good to hear." He studied her face. "But you are hiding something. Like I told you before, the one thing I can't abide is people who aren't truthful."

He nodded toward the envelope. "I'll leave you to deal with that in private. Let me know if we need to talk. The ball's in your court."

He held up the coffee. "Room service, Ms. Danvers."

Setting the cardboard tray on a small table, he turned on his heel, closing the door quietly behind him. Had she told him the truth and her ex was up to something, or had he been duped by a pair of big blue eyes?

———————

Elisa stared at the envelope as the sound of Tucker's Mustang faded into the distance.

"I'm hungry, Mommy."

"Well, then, let's eat."

"I want to eat Tut's Pop-Tart."

"Okay." Elisa felt numb...and cold deep inside.

Once Daisy was settled at the kitchen table, Elisa opened the envelope and scanned the letter. Luke's parents had told him she'd left town, and he assumed she'd sold the house. He actually had the nerve to ask for his half of the profits from the sale.

She choked back a sobbing laugh. As if. Without his bills, she would still have a house to live in. What had she ever seen in Luke? Had she really been that innocent, that naive? The man was a user.

And now Tucker, who had every right to doubt her, had walked away. How many times had she tried to tell him about her dad and failed? He'd accused her of keeping a secret. He was right.

She could prove she was no longer married to Luke. To take care of the other, though, she'd have to come clean and tell Tucker who her father was. Either way, they would be finished—and she couldn't blame him.

It was a lose-lose situation.

CHAPTER 24

THE NEXT MORNING, ELISA WAS STILL FIGHTING WITH herself about Tucker. She could clear up the Luke mess easily enough, but that still left her secret, the one Tucker knew existed. If she told him the truth, it would hurt him. It would also hurt her and Daisy, because he couldn't possibly want anything to do with Hard-Ass Harry's family. If she didn't tell him, it would remain a barrier to any kind of relationship between them, and if he was smart, he'd walk.

Trust, he'd said. Oh, it came hard.

However she chose to deal with it, though, she accepted that the next move was indeed hers.

Desdemona had returned late yesterday but intended to head to Savannah that afternoon for a spa visit. Elisa poured herself a cup of coffee and sat down across from her friend.

"Good morning, Desdemona."

"Is it? You tell me."

Elisa frowned. "What's wrong?"

Desdemona snorted. "What's wrong? This place is like a tomb. Doesn't take a clairvoyant to see what needs doing. Go pay Tucker a visit. Talk to him. Set him straight...and trust him."

Elisa nodded. She'd told her friend about Luke's letter and Tucker's ultimatum. "I will. First, though, I need to drop Daisy at day care, and it's my turn to take the snacks."

Desdemona made a shushing noise. "You don't trust me to take care of that?"

"Of course I do, but—"

"Uh, uh, uh. Stop right there. Go. I've got this." She gave Elisa a critical scrutiny. "Before you rush off, run back upstairs and make yourself a little more...a little more. You're a beautiful woman. Play it up."

Elisa frowned.

Desdemona shooed her again. "Go. Time's not standing still, and you've got a bookshop to open sometime today."

"Thank you. For everything—including the letter your lawyer sent to Luke."

"That should put to bed that piece of nonsense. It's up to you to straighten things out with that man of yours, though."

"Oh, but he's not—"

"He is, and it's about time the two of you accept that. Now go."

She went, taking the stairs quickly.

A few minutes later, Daisy wandered into her room. Scrambling onto the bed, she asked, "What ya doin', Mommy?"

"I'm getting ready for work, honey. I have a couple errands to run first, so Desdemona will take you to school today."

"'Kay."

"Don't let her forget the snacks for your class. They're on the counter."

"I won't."

"Good girl." She dropped a kiss in Daisy's sweet-smelling hair, then spent more time on her makeup than usual.

"You look pretty, Mommy. Can I have some lipstick, too?" She pursed her little lips.

"In another twenty years or so." Daisy's lip jutted out, and Elisa laughed. "Maybe a little sooner."

"'Kay."

Hands on her hips, Elisa studied her closet. Not wanting to look too obvious, she slid into gray jeans, a white long-sleeved T-shirt, and simple white sneakers. Because the temperature had slid south, she pulled on a soft, oversized gray sweater and added a warm, darker-gray scarf.

Straightening her shoulders, she grabbed a pair of large sunglasses and her purse. Time to do it.

She found him under a car at Wylder Rides, swearing a blue streak. That wasn't a good omen, but there was no putting this off.

"Tuck?"

The swearing stopped.

"Can we talk?"

Gaven and Brant, at the far end of the bay, looked at each other.

"Hey, Elisa," Brant said. "Want a cup of coffee?"

"No, thanks."

Gaven nodded a greeting before the two brothers made a beeline to the office.

Chickens, she thought. At least, though, she'd have privacy to swallow whatever amount of crow this called for.

Slowly, Tucker emerged on the creeper. A smudge of grease coated his left cheek, his hair was disheveled, and his jeans had definitely seen better days. Despite the cool day, he wore a shirt with the sleeves torn off, his tattoo showcased. She'd never seen a man who looked more wonderful. Sexier. Angrier.

He sat up but didn't bother to stand.

Heat raced up her neck and across her face, but she stood her ground. "First of all, I want you to know that I'm not married. I have my divorce papers in my purse if you need to see them." She met his gaze.

"I don't need to see them."

"Are you sure?"

"Positive. Does Luke want you back?"

A derisive smile on her face, she shook her head. "He wants half the profits from the house sale."

"Profits? I thought it went into foreclosure," Tucker said.

"It did. Apparently his parents missed that memo."

"I'm sorry to say this because he's Daisy's father, but he's slime, Elisa."

"Yes, he is, and that makes me a terrible judge of character."

"Not necessarily. We all make mistakes." He sighed heavily. "I sure did."

"With me?" She wanted to cry.

"Definitely not with you," Tucker insisted. "It was years ago."

"And it's left you wary."

"That and a few other things that have happened, yes."

She waited a beat. "Just so you know, I haven't slept with anyone but you since Luke walked out on me."

A tic played in Tuck's left eye, and his nostrils flared as he breathed deeply. "What do you want me to say to that?"

"That's up to you."

In a flash, he was on his feet. He pulled her in and kissed her till she didn't know which end was up.

His arms still around her, he asked, "You gonna answer his letter?"

"I've had a lawyer contact him."

"That's not what I asked. Are you going to answer him?"

Her breath was deep and shaky. "No."

"Anything else you want to tell me?"

Heaven help her, she couldn't. This wasn't the time or the place. But then, it didn't ever seem to be. "No."

"You should probably leave, then. I've got a lot to do and a lot to think about."

Wordlessly, she nodded and walked back to her car, carrying her secret with her. Her own personal albatross. A single tear dripped off her chin, and she swiped at it as she drove back to town to open the bookstore.

He wouldn't forgive her.

She'd lost him.

Daisy had lost him.

Chris Young's song "It Takes a Man" came on, the lyrics arrowing straight to her heart. Chris was right. Just because a man could make a baby, it sure didn't mean he'd be a good daddy. Luke had made Daisy, but he hadn't cherished her, hadn't laughed or cried with her, and he never would. Elisa couldn't, under any circumstance, imagine Tucker running away from a child of his. He'd be a father, a daddy that stuck. No matter what.

And it made her unbearably sad that Daisy would never know that kind of love.

It was beginning to feel like Christmas. All the stores and street lights were decorated, and people seemed just that little bit friendlier. Elisa stood in the doorway of *Just Books... and a little more*. Outside, she'd strung lights and hung an evergreen wreath on the door. Inside, colored lights glowed in the window, and Christmas music played quietly in the background. The fresh fir she'd decorated shimmered, and the scent of warm mulled cider added to the atmosphere.

The Christmas books on the table display were selling like hotcakes. Picking up the newest, she studied its cover. A romance. She sighed. It was hard to get in the holiday mood with Tucker absent. A single envelope had sure messed things up.

But then, it wasn't the envelope—it was the baggage stuffed inside.

The bell over the door rang, and Desdemona walked in with Daisy.

"Hi, Mommy!" Daisy skipped over to her.

"Before you say anything," Desdemona said quickly, "we dropped off the snacks. Daisy and I decided it might be fun to play hooky today."

"You did, did you?"

"Yep." Daisy sent her a big grin.

"It's a day made for Christmas shopping. Maybe we'll bake some cookies."

"Desdemona, you don't need to do that. She's okay at school."

"I agree. She is fine at school. But I love having a little one around, seeing the magic of the season through her eyes. Is it okay?"

"Of course, but I don't want you to feel obligated."

"*Blessed* is the word I'd use."

"Don't you have a reservation at the spa?" Elisa asked.

"I'll go tomorrow. Did you talk to Tuck?"

"Sort of, but it didn't go well."

The door opened and Elisa startled.

Under her breath, Desdemona said, "Calm down, sweetie. You're making me nervous."

An older man walked in. "I'm looking for a book my wife wants. You have this?" He handed Elisa a slip of paper with the title and author.

While she located it for him, a pair of women wandered in. Friends of Desdemona, the three started chatting. Before long, the little store was bustling. Apparently, Elisa's boss wasn't the only one with holiday shopping on the brain.

No stranger to work, Desdemona rolled up the sleeves of her Armani sweater and pitched in, suggesting books, filling cups with mulled cider or coffee, and ringing up purchases. Daisy curled up in a corner with *If You Gave a Mouse a Cookie*, one of her favorite books.

Desdemona sidled up to her. "Good marketing, Elisa."

"What?"

"I've heard you tell more than one customer that by giving a book, they'd be giving a gift that could be opened again and again."

"It's true. Look at Daisy. I've read that book to her so many times, she knows every single word. Still, she loves it."

They ate peanut butter and honey sandwiches in the back room for lunch. Considering the rocky start, the day turned out to be fun, and Elisa was thankful Daisy and Desdemona had joined her.

"I hear you've started a new book club," Desdemona commented.

"I have. It's for diabetics and people with hypoglycemia." Elisa shrugged. "I'm certainly no expert, but we're reading books on the subject and talking about them. Besides the nonfiction, there are an amazing number of fiction books where one or the other plays a big role. It's good not to feel alone when you're dealing with something like this."

"Kind of a support group under the guise of a social setting?" Desdemona asked.

"Exactly."

"I heard you're serving snacks and desserts."

Elisa walked over to a shelf and pulled down several cookbooks. "I'm taking the recipes from these. We're learning that you don't have to do without. It's simply taking control."

"You're a good person, Elisa."

"Doc Hawkins is the good person. He saved my butt and wouldn't take a penny. I swore I'd find a way to pay him back. Through this group, maybe, just maybe, I can help some of his patients. I'm simply repaying a kindness shown to me."

"Like I said, you're a good person. I don't suppose you have any more of those cookies Eleanor said you served the group yesterday?"

"I do, and I think you'll be surprised at how good they are."

Later that afternoon, the door opened to Tansy and Gracie Bella.

"All of my customers are talking about *Just Books*," Tansy said. "Since I'm closed for the day, Gracie and I thought we'd stop by and see what you've added." She rubbed her growing baby bump and turned to take in the shop. "It looks and smells like Christmas. I love it."

"Sit, and let me fix you some tea," Elisa said.

When the door opened again, the ladies were in the middle of a nice chat, the girls coloring in front of the fireplace.

"Cozy," Tucker said.

Elisa's nerves went on full alert and, confused, she made to stand. She'd left him at his shop grumpier than a grizzly bear. Now he strolled in like nothing had happened?

"Nope, stay put," he said. "I'm gonna check out the new car magazines. I'll let you know if I need help."

"You sure?"

"Oh yeah." He met her eyes. "I'm good."

Elisa kept a close eye on Tucker. Why had he come? The whole magazine thing was a fabricated excuse. Every time she glanced at him, he was watching her with an intensity that unnerved her.

Had he come to talk? Had the "I'm good" been his way of saying he'd cooled off, that he was willing to offer her a mulligan of her own?

Gracie Bella and Daisy joined the women and climbed onto the loveseat beside Tansy.

"Do you have a baby brother?" Gracie asked Daisy.

"No." Daisy pulled a loose thread on her sleeve.

"I'm gonna have one, huh, Mama?"

"Yes, Gracie, you are."

The girl patted her mother's belly. "She's keeping him in here right now, but pretty soon he'll come out so we can play."

Daisy studied Tansy's belly solemnly, then put a hand on Elisa's. "Do you have one, too?"

Feeling Tucker's eyes on her, Elisa blushed. "No, sweetie, I don't."

Daisy's face fell. "Why not? I want one."

Tansy grimaced. "Sorry. Gracie's—" She threw up an exasperated hand.

Elisa smiled. "It's okay."

"How do you get the baby out?" Daisy asked.

Behind her, Elisa heard Tucker's half cough, half choke.

"Ah, you don't have the magazine I wanted," he said. "I'm gonna run."

Elisa glared at him. "Coward."

"You got that right, sweet cheeks. But you and me? We need to talk."

With that, he was out the door.

Sweet cheeks. Elisa almost sighed.

"Why did Tut leave?"

Desdemona guffawed. "Because he's a man."

CHAPTER 25

A HORN TOOTED OUTSIDE THE HOUSE THE NEXT MORN-
ing.

"There's my ride." Desdemona checked her lipstick in
the hallway mirror.

"Doc Hawkins is takin' you?"

"You bet your silk stockings. The man's crazy about me.
Things have never worked out quite right for us before.
Now? Well, we'll see."

Elisa's brows rose.

"I requested a king bed in my spa suite." She grinned.
"That big of a bed can get lonely."

"Any bed can get lonely."

"Ain't that the truth, darlin'. I left my keys on a hook in
the laundry room. The cars are in the garage if you need
either of them. Both were filled yesterday, so you'll have
plenty of gas."

Elisa rolled her eyes. Like she'd use that expensive Land
Rover or the sleek little Mercedes. She'd stick with her
Ford Escort, thank you. Since Tucker and his brothers had
worked on it, the thing ran like new.

She'd miss Desdemona the next few days. The woman
had more life in her little finger than most had in their
entire bodies. And she never, ever hesitated to say what she
thought. Life in the Hamilton house was a whole lot quieter
when Desdemona Rosebud wasn't in residence.

After Tuck's visit to the store, she'd hoped he'd stop by
last night. He hadn't, and she honestly couldn't blame him.

Desdemona wrapped Daisy in a hug and covered her in kisses. "Be good for your mommy, sweetheart."

"I will."

Then she pulled Elisa close.

"Have a wonderful time, Desdemona!"

"Next time, you'll go with me."

"Yeah, sure. You need to get going. There's a handsome guy out front waiting for you. And me? I have to go, too. I don't dare open the store late. My boss—well..." Elisa leaned in and whispered, "Ever see *The Devil Wears Prada*?"

Her boss threw back her head and laughed. Leaving a trail of sultry French perfume in her wake, Desdemona Rosebud Hamilton sailed through the door.

At the end of the day, Elisa stood in the doorway of the day care and listened to the happy sounds of children at play.

Lucinda looked up from the table where she and some of the children were finger painting. "I hear your new bookstore is the bomb."

"Thanks. It's Desdemona's, though," Elisa said.

"Isn't she a hoot? She might own the place, but you've put your stamp on it. Everybody says walking inside is like stepping into a friend's house."

"Really?" Elisa put a hand to her heart. "That's exactly what I was hoping for. A place you can find a good book, have a coffee, and chat with friends. *Just Books...and a little more*." Then she took a closer look at Lucinda. "Is everything okay?"

Lucinda stood. "Daisy was kind of listless today. I can't

put my finger on anything concrete, but she's usually a ball of energy."

"Desdemona's gone for a few days. Maybe that's bothering her more than I realized. I'll keep an eye on her, though. Thanks for the heads-up, Lucinda."

Just then, Daisy came around the corner from the other room.

"Mommy."

Lucinda was right. Something was wrong. Her daughter's eyes didn't shine. Instead of running and throwing herself in Elisa's arms, she trudged slowly to her.

Elisa knelt and raised a hand to her child's forehead, brushing back her hair. No fever. Standing, she scooped her daughter into her arms.

"Are these your papers from today?"

Daisy nodded.

"Anything else?" Daisy shook her head, and Elisa met Lucinda's gaze. "Thanks again."

"You bet. See you tomorrow, Daisy."

"'Kay, Miss Lucinda."

By six o'clock, Daisy had turned whiny.

"Aren't you hungry?"

"No."

Even after Elisa cut off the crust, Daisy barely ate any of the grilled cheese sandwich she'd wanted. Instead, she tore it into small pieces and pushed them around on her plate.

Recognizing defeat, Elisa asked, "How about a bubble bath in my big tub?"

"I'm tired, Mommy."

"It's pretty early for bed, honey." Her heart did a little stutter. Her baby looked very wan and very, very tired.

Elisa slipped Daisy into pajamas, brushed her hair, and tucked her into bed. She'd let her sleep with her tonight so she could keep an eye on her. Even though it was only eight o'clock and there was a lot she could and should do, Elisa got ready for bed herself.

When she settled into bed with a new novel by one of her favorite authors, Daisy curled into her. Elisa gently brushed the fine, wispy hair from her little girl's forehead and gave her a kiss. "Sleep well, Daisy Elizabeth."

"I will, Mommy."

But she didn't.

As fifteen minutes turned into half an hour, Daisy's breathing quickened and became shallow. Elisa fumbled for her phone. What to do? Doc Hawkins wasn't in town. He had, indeed, stayed in Savannah with Desdemona.

No doctor, no hospital.

She hit 911. Frannie, the emergency operator, answered immediately.

"I need an ambulance, Frannie. My daughter has a heart problem…and oh, please hurry!"

"Help's on its way, honey. You still at Desdemona's?"

"Yes, yes, I am."

"You want to stay on the line?"

"No." Elisa's panic increased with every breath Daisy struggled for. "I have another call I need to make."

"Go downstairs first and turn on the porch light and unlock your door," Frannie advised.

"Oh! Yes, of course. I'm doing that now." Elisa leaned over and kissed Daisy. "Mommy will be right back."

"Don't go, Mommy." Tears welled in her eyes.

"I have to, baby, so the people who will help us can get in."

"'Kay." Her dark lashes fluttered against ashen skin.

Praying as she sped down the stairs, Elisa unlatched the door and flipped on the light, then hurried back to her room. She stuffed pillows behind Daisy to prop her up. "Better?"

Her answer was several tears that streaked down her daughter's face.

"Please, please hurry," she prayed, straining to hear sirens.

Silence.

She tossed on jeans and a sweatshirt, then got back into bed. Snuggling her daughter against her, Elisa told Daisy a story about a princess who went for a ride in an ambulance with lights and sirens because she was so important and all the people in the kingdom loved her.

"Like me, Mommy?"

"Exactly like you, sweetie. I need to make one more phone call, okay?"

Daisy nodded.

Before she could talk herself out of it, she called Tuck.

He answered before the first ring ended. "Elisa?"

She started to cry.

"What's wrong?"

She walked to the window, then turned to keep an eye on her daughter. "It's Daisy," she whispered. "Her heart. The ambulance is almost here. I have to go, but I needed to tell you. I needed to hear your voice."

"You riding in the ambulance with her?"

"Yes."

"I'll follow," he said.

"But—"

"They'll need to stabilize her. I'll be there in time."

Tucker didn't bother knocking. "You upstairs?"

"Yes. Come on up, Tucker."

He took the stairs two at a time. His knees nearly buckled when he saw Daisy. They hadn't put her on the stretcher yet, and the large bed practically swallowed her. Her skin held a bluish tint and fear danced in those baby-blue eyes. Even as young as she was, she knew she was in trouble.

"I don't feel good, Tut." She reached for him.

"Okay if I'm on this side?" he asked the pair of EMTs working on her. "I'll stay out of your way."

They nodded.

He crawled into the far side of the bed and lay down beside her, holding her soft little hand as they started an IV in the tiny vein.

"It hurts, Tut." Her lips trembled.

"I know, honey, but they'll put medicine in it to make you feel better."

"'Kay."

He felt more than heard Elisa's sob. Patting the bed beside him, he reached for her. She curled into him and held on to his free hand for dear life.

"Mommy and I are right here, sweetheart." He turned his head to look at her mama. She was every bit as pale as her daughter. "Everything will be all right, Lissie, and I'll be right here with you. I'm not leavin'."

Tuck followed the flashing red lights of the ambulance through the otherwise dark night. "Come on, Daisy. We're nearly there. Hold on a little longer, sugar, and the doctors will make you all better."

His fingers itched to hit Elisa's cell number, to talk to her, to reassure Daisy.

He was half crazy with worry and could only imagine Elisa's anguish. Her daughter was her world. If anything happened— No. He wouldn't let himself even go there.

The EMTs had called ahead and a medical team met them at Savannah's pediatric hospital. An artificial Christmas tree had been shoehorned into one corner of the waiting room and looked as forlorn as the parents and children who huddled there.

After a quick stop for a consult, some blood work, and X-rays, they wheeled Daisy to surgery with Elisa on one side of the stretcher and Tucker on the other. The anesthesiologist had already given Daisy a mild sedative, so she was woozy but calm.

"Time to give your daughter a quick kiss before surgery, Mom and Dad. You'll have plenty of time afterwards for lots more."

Tucker didn't refute the doctor's words. Instead, he leaned down and bussed Daisy's cheek. "You be good in there, short stuff."

"I will, Tut."

Elisa bent down and kissed her daughter. "I love you, sweetie."

"Love you, too, Mommy."

Elisa's lower lip trembled. Once Daisy was inside those blue double doors she could let go, but not until then.

She made the mistake of glancing at Tucker and wished with all her heart this man was Daisy's daddy. His face was strained, his jaw tight. He, too, was fighting back tears. This good man had become an important part of their lives…and she'd botched it.

With one last, tiny wave, Daisy disappeared through the operating theater doors. Elisa took several steps backwards, bumping up against the wall. Without a word, she simply slid down it until she sat on the floor, her forehead on her knees.

Tucker pulled her to her feet and wrapped her in his arms. "Bring it in, sweetheart, bring it in." They stood in the middle of the hallway with him holding her, swaying and murmuring absolute nonsense while she sobbed.

Footsteps sounded in the hallway as Doc Hawkins practically ran to them. "Elisa! We just heard. Desdemona's parking the car. She'll be here in a minute." He nodded toward Tucker. "Thanks for coming. She needs you."

"I wouldn't be anywhere else."

Yancy slapped him on the back. "I'm goin' in to scrub up. This isn't my specialty, but I'll keep an eye on things."

"Thank you." Elisa could barely speak through her tight throat.

The good doctor disappeared, and Elisa felt her legs give way.

"Oh no you don't." Tucker grabbed her and forced her onto a hard vinyl chair, pushing her head between her knees. "Breathe, baby, breathe deep and slow. That's my girl. Come on."

"Oh, Tucker, what if Daisy—" She sobbed. "What if she—"

When she began crying inconsolably, he put an arm beneath her knees and around her shoulders, picking her up. With her clinging to him, her face turned into his chest, he made his way to the surgical ward waiting room. Settling on one of the miserably uncomfortable loveseats, he cradled her.

Neither spoke, and every sweep of the clock's hand felt like an hour.

"I'm sorry, Lissie." He buried his face in her hair. "I'm so damned sorry."

"Why hasn't anyone come out?" Even to herself, her voice sounded rough and ragged.

"Because they're busy fixing her. That no one's had to speak to us is a good sign, a sign that everything's proceeding the way it should." He thumbed the tears from her cheeks.

Dark circles rimmed her tear-reddened eyes, and yet, even now, she was the most beautiful woman he'd ever seen.

The door opened and Desdemona flew into the room like a force of nature. One look at Elisa and Tuck and she started to cry. "Oh damn!" She dabbed at her eyes. "I came to help, and look at me. Blubbering like a baby."

Elisa hugged her friend. "Yancy's with her."

"He'll take good care of her."

"How did you know?"

"Any time one of the ambulances goes out, he's notified. We didn't get the message right away or we'd have been here sooner."

When Elisa slipped into the restroom, Desdemona swung around to Tucker. "How's Daisy really doing?"

"I don't know. God, she looked so tiny, so scared." Tears spilled over and ran down his cheeks. "Sorry. I—"

"You're staying strong for Elisa, and it's taking a hell of a toll. Come here." She held him, patting his back, and rocking back and forth.

When the door opened, she handed him a handkerchief and he turned his back for a moment.

"Have you heard anything?" Elisa asked, looking from Desdemona to Tucker.

"Not yet," Tucker said, his voice husky.

Elisa's phone rang and she jumped. Forgetting it was on speaker, she answered it. "Hello?"

"Annabelle from the inn, here. I've got a scanner and heard you had some trouble. You got anybody there with you?"

"Tucker's here."

"Now, there's a good man. All those Wylder boys are."

Tears flowing, she nodded wordlessly. "Desdemona and Doc Hawkins are here, too."

Tucker took her phone and, turning off the speaker, spoke quietly to Annabelle.

"'Bout time for Gaven to come draggin' a baby home, isn't it?" the innkeeper asked.

"Gaven?"

"For all your yammering and belly-achin' about it, you Wylder boys seem to be baby magnets. First Brant with that darling little Jax, now you with Daisy. Seems to me it's Gaven's turn."

He had no answer for her.

"Take care of that baby and her mama," she said.

"I'll get back to you when we know more. Thanks for calling, Annabelle."

The door flew open again, and Tansy's aunt Coralee hurried in, wearing another of her I-love-Lucy dresses with a pair of yellow cowboy boots. Her red hair curled wildly around her head as though she hadn't taken time to comb it.

Elisa stared at her. "What are you doing here?"

"I got a call from Tansy, who got a call from Annabelle." Coralee sat down beside Elisa and reached for her hand. "I made a few calls of my own on the way here. The only thing you need to be concerned about, honey, is your child. The finances are taken care of. Consider the hospital and doctor bills paid in full. All that's off your plate."

Elisa's eyes went round. "What?"

"This right here is the reason I painted that mural on the side of my house."

"Your charity?"

Coralee nodded. "The one I help support. They take care of children like Daisy."

Elisa couldn't stop the tears. A seemingly endless supply of them spilled down her cheeks. "How can I ever thank you?"

"By bringing that baby of yours to visit me once in a while. I've got a yard that's crying out for kids to play in it. Gracie Bella loves it, and I'm sure she'd enjoy some company." A tear streaked down Coralee's weathered cheek and splattered on her hand. She didn't bother to wipe it away.

"I'm overwhelmed. For so long, it's been just Daisy and me. No help and no support. Now you all are here for us." Her lower lip trembled again.

Tucker put an arm around her.

"That you all came here tonight..." Elisa continued.

Desdemona scooted her chair closer. "Why do you think I keep coming home to Misty Bottoms? There's no better place in the world."

Blinking back more of the unrelenting tears, Elisa dropped her eyes. Her mouth fell open. "Desdemona?"

"Yes, sweetie?"

"Is that what I think it is?" She caught Desdemona's hand to look at it more closely. "Did you and Yancy—"

"We did. That's why we didn't get your call right away. I'm sorry."

"Don't be sorry! I'm so happy for you!" Elisa threw her arms around her friend.

"What's goin' on? What am I missin'?" Coralee stared at them, then looked toward Tucker, who shrugged.

"Show her." Elisa nudged Desdemona.

"This isn't the time—" she protested.

"Sure it is. Good news is exactly what we need," Elisa insisted.

Desdemona held up her left hand and wiggled her ring finger. A shiny new gold band, embellished with a row of diamonds, encircled it.

"You and Yancy?" Coralee asked.

Desdemona nodded.

"'Bout damned time," Coralee said.

"I couldn't agree more," Desdemona said.

Tucker gave her a squeeze. "Congratulations."

"Thank you. And," Desdemona added in a whisper, "thank you for taking care of my girls."

Silence settled in again.

"I'll go rustle up some coffee." Desdemona got to her feet. "Why don't you come with me, Coralee?"

"Think I'll stay here if you don't mind."

"I do mind. I need you to help me carry."

Elisa caught the little head jerk toward Tucker and her.

"Oh! Oh sure, that's a good idea." Coralee practically sprang from her chair, and the pair disappeared down the hall, chatting a mile a minute.

"You okay?" Tucker asked quietly when they left.

"No. It shouldn't take this long, should it?"

"They want to get it right, Lissie. One and done. When they bring Daisy back to you, you can quit worrying about her. She'll be able to run and play like all the other kids without growing breathless." He rubbed her back. "Why don't you close your eyes? The minute the doctor even casts a shadow on that door, I'll wake you."

"I can't sleep. I'm afraid if I close my eyes, I'll lose her."

His hands moved to grip her shoulders, to turn her to face him fully. His voice hard and no-nonsense, he said, "Listen to me, Elisa Danvers. We are not going to lose Daisy. I won't allow it, understood?"

His voice broke, and he dragged her roughly to him. His tears wet her hair; hers stained the front of his shirt.

"We're a mess, aren't we?" Tucker asked.

Silently, she nodded.

When Desdemona and Coralee came down the hall with steaming cups of coffee, both swiped at their eyes. Tucker gave Elisa a quick, hard kiss, then took the cups from the women.

The second hand made its slow, grueling trip, minute after minute after minute.

Finally, the waiting room door opened, and Doc Hawkins stepped in. Even though he looked exhausted, a big grin lit his face.

All four leapt from their seats, talking at once.

Yancy held up a hand. "Hush, now. Daisy is out of

surgery." He reached for Elisa's hand. "She did better than fine, Mama. That little girl is a fighter."

"She's had to be from the second she was born."

"Well, it's paid off. She's in recovery. The surgeon will be out in a few minutes to fill you in, but things went perfectly. Your little girl won't even have another scar. They did what's called a cardiac catheterization and inserted a device into the opening in Daisy's heart to plug it. Doctor Menendez is a genius."

"One and done," Tucker said. "What did I tell you?"

Elisa broke free of Yancy and threw herself, laughing and crying, into Tucker's arms.

"Now if y'all will excuse us, Desdemona and I have a honeymoon to get back to."

The room buzzed with congratulations.

"Goes to show what pigheadedness will do. I finally won the heart of the prettiest girl at the prom," Yancy said.

"The shop—" Elisa began.

"Will be there when you get back," Desdemona said. "People in town will understand if we're closed for a few days. I'd run back and put a sign on the door, but that won't be necessary. Come noon tomorrow, everyone will have heard."

Elisa nodded.

Tucker shook hands with Yancy and thanked him again, while Elisa hugged and kissed Coralee, Desdemona, and the doctor.

Yancy held out a hand to his new wife, extending his other toward Coralee. "Why don't you walk out with us? These two will be busy in a bit visiting one brave little girl."

Daisy's eyes fluttered open. "Hi, Mommy."

Elisa blinked back happy tears. "Hi, sweetie."

"Tut!"

He moved to the bed. "Hey, sugar. You sure did sleep a long time."

"I was tired." She yawned.

"I know."

"I'm in the hospital. I 'member. Did the doctors make me all better?"

Elisa's chin quivered. "They did."

"Can I go home now? I wanna play with Lug Nut."

"Ah, the miracle of modern-day pain killers," Tuck mumbled. "You're gonna have to stay here a couple of days so they can keep an eye on you, but Mama's gonna stay with you. She has a bed right here by yours."

"We can have a pajama party," Elisa said.

"With ice cream?"

"You bet!" she said.

"Can I have somethin' else?"

"If it's at all possible, honey," Elisa said.

Her little fingers reached out to touch Tucker's. "I want Tut to be my daddy."

"Oh, sweetheart—"

"It's okay, Lissie." He crouched beside her bed so he and the child were face-to-face. "How about I be your honorary daddy?"

"Honor one?"

"Close enough. 'Cause I'll tell you what, sugar, it would be an honor of the highest level to be your daddy." He heard a sniffle behind him and turned to Elisa. "Of course, if that's okay with your mama."

"Is it okay, Mommy?"

"It's totally okay. You're sure you're up for this, Tuck?"

"Yes, ma'am."

The nurse stuck her head in the door. "It's time for her meds and a bandage check where they inserted the heart catheter. If you don't mind stepping out for a few minutes?"

The nurse adjusted the IV drip, and Daisy's eyes drooped.

"I gave her a little extra so she doesn't feel anything," the nurse explained. "We'll keep her comfortable. No need for this sweet thing to hurt."

"No, ma'am," Tuck answered. "There sure isn't."

Alone, Elisa and Tucker stood in the middle of the waiting room.

Hands jammed in his jeans pockets, Tucker broke the silence. "Marry me, Elisa. Let me help."

Shock ricocheted through her. "What?"

He wetted his lips. "I said—"

"I heard you." *Marry me.* Words that should have been magical, should have made her heart soar. Instead, regret nearly drowned her. She stared at him, realizing she'd waited too late to tell him the truth. Then it hit her. "You're offering because of Daisy?"

She registered the slight hesitation and loved him all the more for it.

"I know the worst is over, but you shouldn't have to handle all this alone."

She laid a hand on his cheek and felt the stubble that had shadowed the lower half of his face over the long night. "Tuck, that's the most wonderful, the most perfect offer anyone has ever made me. Thank you."

"Then you'll marry me?"

Heart breaking, knowing the secret she carried would destroy any feelings he had for her, she said, "No, Tuck, I can't."

His eyes darkened and he frowned. Hurt and confusion raced across his handsome face. "I was an ass. I know that, and I'm sorrier than I can say."

"You had every right. Neither of us handled that very well. But it's not that."

"Then I don't understand."

"I know," she said softly. "And that's why I can't marry you." Rising to her tiptoes, she kissed him gently. "I need to get back to Daisy."

"Tell her I love her."

"I will."

She left him standing there, felt his gaze on her and refused to look back.

She didn't think she was strong enough to walk away twice.

CHAPTER 26

SHE'D TURNED HIM DOWN. FOR THE FIRST TIME IN HIS life, Tucker had offered marriage willingly and been shot down.

Carrying a cup of coffee and his phone to the back patio, he slumped into a chair and rested his feet on the hassock. After thinking it through, he realized it was totally his fault. If he'd deliberately set out to sabotage himself, he couldn't have done a better job of it. What woman would have said yes to that proposal?

He'd asked Elisa to marry him...and had somehow managed to make it sound like he was doing her a favor. For the love of Mike! A fish jumped in the little stream at the edge of his property and Tucker wondered idly who the heck Mike was and why everyone wanted him to love them.

Argh. *Keep your head in the game, Wylder.*

Had he told Elisa he loved her?

No.

That he wanted to spend his life with her?

No.

Instead, he'd appealed to the mother in her rather than the woman. But that was only in his approach, because while he'd held her, the scent of her, the silkiness of her hair, the warmth of her had all touched him and made him weak with desire. For her.

He loved Daisy and wanted to make her his daughter. He wanted to watch her grow and flourish. He needed to put the fear of God in her future dates, and when she managed to fall in love despite that, he wanted to walk her down the aisle.

But Elisa touched a part of him he'd lost. A part he'd put away and thought never to take back out. He wanted her. More, he needed her in his life—forever.

He'd bungled things badly almost from the beginning. He generally thought things out, devised a plan, and stayed the course. With Elisa? He'd been Ricochet Rabbit.

She might have been the one on the floor, literally, the first time they'd met, but she'd had him off-center from the word go. When he'd peeked from beneath that Vette and watched those legs walking toward him, his pulse had kicked into fourth gear—and it hadn't slowed down since.

He'd laughed with her and cried with her. He'd cuddled her after they'd made crazy love and hugged her while she cried for her sick child.

He'd had the nerve to ask her to trust him after he'd gone alpha male on her and all but accused her of lying about being divorced. Why Elisa hadn't simply told him to get lost was beyond him. Unless she loved him, too. Time would tell, because he refused to give up. Doc thought he was pigheaded. Hah, that's because he hadn't seen a Wylder dead-set on something.

Once Tucker had himself together, he'd strike again— and he'd do better this time. He'd prove to Elisa that he wanted more than to offer help. That he needed her and Daisy in his life. That he wouldn't be whole again until they were a family—not out of obligation or a sense of duty, but because he loved them.

The sun sat low in the sky when he finally woke from a nap.

He needed food and his brothers.

On his way to the Wylder Rides shop, he took care of the first at the Dairy Queen, where he fielded questions about Daisy from what seemed like half the town.

When he walked into the shop, Gaven looked up from the computer, surprised. "I didn't expect you today. We thought you'd still be in Savannah."

"No, I've got a couple of things to take care of, then I'll drive down again tomorrow."

"I sure am glad Daisy's doing well."

"Me, too. That was a nightmare."

He considered a chat with Gaven about all the stuff banging around in his brain, then thought better of it. Since Gaven's marriage had fallen apart almost before it began, he might not be the best advisor.

"You got plans for tonight, Gav?"

"I'm having dinner with Quinlyn."

"You two are spending a lot of time together," Tucker said.

"The woman's beautiful, isn't she?"

Tucker nodded and rubbed his red eyes.

Gaven pushed away from the computer. "The thing is, she feels like my sister or my best friend. It's sad. I had such high hopes."

Tucker actually laughed at his brother's disappointed expression.

"I like her. I really like her," Gaven admitted. "So it's probably better this way. We won't have to break up and quit talking to each other. We can stay friends."

"Most of your exes stay friendly."

"True. It's my magnetic personality."

Tuck snorted. "Magnetic personality, my eye! It's the line of BS you feed them."

"That, too." Gaven grinned.

Tucker pulled up a stool in the bay where Brant worked on the front end of a '68 Charger, the *Dukes of Hazzard* lookalike they were restoring.

"You doing okay?" Brant asked.

Tucker nodded. "Question for you."

"Okay."

"How'd you know, Brant? How'd you know Molly was the one?"

"I couldn't imagine my life without her."

"That simple?"

"That simple."

The next morning, Tucker awoke thinking about Elisa and Daisy. Grabbing his cell phone, he hit Brant's number.

"Can you get along without me today?"

"Sure. We assumed you'd be heading to Savannah."

"Yeah."

"Look, none of my business, I suppose, but we didn't expect to see you yesterday."

Tucker grunted in response.

There were a few seconds of silence, then Brant said, "I've been thinking about yesterday's conversation. When you get back, why don't we grab a beer and talk?"

"Think I'll take you up on that."

On the drive to Savannah, he prepared himself for the fact that Elisa might not want to see him. They'd deal with it, because one way or another, he had to see his girls today. He couldn't imagine life without them. Brant was right. It really was as simple as that.

When he walked into Daisy's room, Elisa was sitting beside the bed. The smudges that rimmed the undersides of her eyes were darker.

"Did you sleep at all?"

"I caught a few minutes here and there. They're keeping her longer because she's so young. An adult would already have been sent home."

"That makes sense. It's hard to keep a kid down. Have you eaten anything?"

She nodded. "Yes, they brought me a tray when they brought Daisy's so I wouldn't have to leave her."

"That's good. When Daisy gets home, she'll need you to be healthy. Did you have some protein?"

"I did."

He pulled a chair up to the child's bed so he could see for himself that Daisy was really and truly okay.

"*Pssst.*" He grinned when her eyes opened. "How are you doin', short stuff?"

"Tut, you came." She sounded sleepy.

"Of course I did." Very carefully, he leaned in for a kiss.

"I had ice cream. For lunch."

"Whoa. Lucky you." He tapped a finger to the end of her pert nose, trying to ignore the IV that still invaded her tiny body.

After a few minutes, Daisy's eyes drooped and she fell back asleep.

"Think the Sandman's shown up."

"It's the drugs. They need to keep her as still as possible till the catheter incision closes." Elisa turned from the window. "Tuck, we need to talk. About yesterday. About—before."

"Okay." The rigid way she held herself warned him he wouldn't like this conversation. "Is it something I've done?"

She shook her head. "No." Taking another long look at her daughter, she asked, "You think she'll be all right for a few minutes?"

He nodded.

"Is there somewhere we can talk? Somewhere we can be alone?"

"Sure." That sealed the deal. He definitely wasn't going to like whatever it was she needed to get off her chest. "You're not leaving Misty Bottoms, are you?"

She stared up at the ceiling, her eyes misty. "That will depend on what you want."

His heart beat a little faster. Maybe this was gonna be okay. "You change your mind? You'll marry me?"

Sadness veiled her face.

"*Bzzz*. Guess not," he said. "Grab your sweater. There are some tables outside the cafeteria. It'll be chilly, but we'll be able to nab some privacy."

Stopping at the nurse's desk, Elisa told them where she'd be if they needed her.

As they walked down the hall, a nurse rumbled by with a cart full of meds. A cartoon with a dancing pig played on the TV in one of the rooms they passed, while *Sesame Street* filled the next one.

"Is this gonna be as bad as the expression on your face suggests?"

She nodded, but refused to look at him.

Oh boy. A trickle of sweat rolled down his spine.

When they reached the cafeteria, he asked, "You want some coffee? Tea?"

She shook her head. "No, but if you want something, I'll wait."

"Darlin', you've got me so nervous, I don't think I could swallow a single drop."

"I'm sorry, Tucker. It's—"

"Lissie, it's okay. Whatever it is, we'll deal with it together." He rubbed damp palms on his jeans. Taking her ice-cold hand in his, he led them outside and around the corner. The chair scratched over the concrete when he pulled it out for her. Once she was seated, he leaned down and buttoned her sweater.

Tears swam in her blue eyes. "Tuck, you're making this so much harder." She laid a hand on his cheek. "You're the best man I've ever known."

He dropped into the chair across from her. "Why do I hear a 'but' in there?"

She took a deep breath. "There's something I have to tell you."

"Wait." Real fear reared its ugly head, and he held up a hand. "You're not sick, are you?"

"No."

"Daisy's still doing okay?"

"She's doing wonderfully."

"Okay. Good. We can deal with anything else."

"We," she repeated. "Oh God. I have to do this fast, or I'll lose my nerve." Opening her purse, she withdrew a photo and handed it to him with trembling fingers.

His heart stuttered as he stared at the gawky teenager in front of a Charlie Brown Christmas tree and the man beside her. "I don't understand. Where'd you get this?"

"A friend took it the one and only Christmas my father spent with me."

"Your father?"

She nodded.

"Hard-Ass Harry is your dad?" The words came out in a ragged whisper.

"Yes."

And there was that sucker-punch he'd been waiting for. Expecting.

Yet it caught him completely off guard. The chain around his neck seemed to tighten, and he tugged at the key as if it was strangling him.

"How long have you known?" he asked.

"I suspected it that night in the park."

Everything inside him turned cold.

She wetted her lips nervously. "I tried to tell you more than once. But Desdemona and Daisy interrupted us one time."

"At the book store."

"Yes. Other times, I started but couldn't make myself finish. You were right. I didn't trust you." She blinked back tears, then pulled a tissue from her pocket and dabbed at her nose. "Every time you look at me, you'll think of your friends."

A muscle worked in his jaw. "You lied to me." He didn't say it with malice, simply a statement of fact.

"Not at first."

"But you did lie."

She nodded, unable to speak.

He felt empty. Slumped back in his chair, he studied her. Minutes ticked by.

Finally, he said, "I'm not sure what to say, but thanks for trusting me with this, Elisa. I know it was hard." He pinched the bridge of his nose. "I think it's probably best I leave now. I need some time to digest this, to come to terms with it. You've really thrown me for a loop."

"I'm sorry, Tuck. I'm so, so sorry."

"Me, too, Lissie. Me, too." He leaned down and kissed her cheek. "Give Daisy my love, will you? Tell her—tell her I had to leave."

He'd fallen in love with Hard-Ass Harry's daughter and granddaughter. Fate must be laughing her ass off right now.

Rather than go to Duffy's Pub where they'd have eavesdroppers, Tucker made plans to have Brant pick him up at his house.

"I tossed a cooler in the back. One beer for me and two for you since I'm driving," Brant said.

He drove to the river and pulled off beneath a grove of live-oak trees. Brant opened the trunk and handed Tucker the camp chairs. "Take these. I'll get the beer."

For the first five or ten minutes, they watched in silence as birds landed, fed, and took off again. Once Tucker started to talk, it all spilled out. He told Brant about his lieutenant colonel and the role he'd played in his friends' deaths. He explained why he'd been restricted to camp and the guilt he felt.

"You should have shared that with us sooner, Tuck, so we could have helped you."

"Yeah, you're right. I shared a little with Dad last time they were here. Other than him, I've only told one other person."

"Elisa?"

Tucker gave a wry chuckle. "Yeah. I asked her to marry me yesterday after Daisy was out of surgery and we knew she'd be okay."

"So why the long face?" Brant's forehead wrinkled in confusion.

"She said no."

His beer halfway to his mouth, Brant stared at Tuck. "No way."

"I might not have handled the proposal quite as well as I could have."

"You told her you loved her, right?"

Tucker shook his head.

"What am I going to do with you, Tuck? You didn't make it about the kid, did you?" One look at his brother's face and Brant rolled his eyes. "You did."

"Guilty. But as clumsy as I was, something else has been going on. Elisa's had something bothering her for quite a while now, something she wouldn't share. Today she showed me a picture of her and her father during their one and only shared Christmas. Hard-Ass Harry is her dad." Tucker took a long drink of his beer. "What am I gonna do?"

"So, basically, Elisa grew up with a stranger for a father?"

"Guess so."

"He barely acknowledged her as his kid," Brant said.

"Yeah."

"Has he ever met Daisy?"

Tucker went quiet for a minute. "I honestly don't know, but I doubt it."

"Remember the time Dad took us all out on the lake and told us how proud he was that we were his sons?"

Tucker grimaced. "I do. As I recall, that was just before he dumped us out and told us that as his sons, we were strong enough to swim to shore."

"Yep. He didn't boat away and leave us, though."

"Nope," Tuck said. "He followed close behind. We all knew he expected us to make it on our own, but he was there to help if we needed it."

"Exactly. My take on Elisa's situation is that old Harry never did anything like that for her. Instead, he hopped in that boat and shot off like a rocket, leaving her to sink or swim."

"Damn you, Brant."

"Makes it a little harder to hate her for her father's misdeeds, doesn't it? Sometimes, brother of mine, you've got to take that swing and hope for the best."

"I don't hate her." Tucker picked up a second beer and popped the top. "You're driving me home, right?"

"I am, because I've got your back, too."

CHAPTER 27

TUCKER SPENT THE NEXT FEW HOURS NURSING HIS hurt. Midnight came and went and found him wide awake. Wandering into the kitchen, he put a pod in his Keurig and hit start. As the scent of coffee filled the room, his gaze caught on the scrap of blue he'd tossed on the counter. Reaching for it, he ran Daisy's hair ribbon through his fingers. He collapsed onto a stool and rested his head in his hands. Life could be so damned unfair. What had that baby done to deserve such pain?

Her mother hung on by a thread, and his reaction to the picture she'd shown him? He'd left her sitting there, broken-hearted. It shamed him.

He'd like to believe that given another chance, he'd do better. He was honest enough to admit, though, that if he had a *dozen* do-overs, he wouldn't handle it any differently. Hard-Ass Harry was Elisa's father. How in the hell was he supposed to react to that news?

Right now, he couldn't do a thing about it. He carried his coffee to the window and stared into the darkness. Time for a come-to-Jesus meeting—with himself.

Vulnerable and hurting, he'd go to ground like any wounded animal. The key around his neck jangled. Nate's fish camp would provide a safe harbor.

Grabbing his duffel from the closet, he tossed a few essentials inside. He'd call Brant or Gaven after he figured they were awake, but right now he had to get out of

Dodge. It was time to wrestle the monsters in his head to the ground, then send them out to pasture.

Tucker made the drive on autopilot and black coffee.

The night sky was still pitch-black when he reached the turnoff to the cabin. Nobody'd been here in a good long while, and the rutted road jarred his teeth.

When he rounded the final bend, his headlights swept over the rustic building. It looked neglected and more than a little down on its luck. Perfect. He parked the car so its lights aimed at the door, then removing the key from around his neck, he trudged through the tall grass and weeds to climb onto the small porch. After unlocking the door, he nudged it open with the toe of his boot. Stale, musty air rushed at him, but when he flicked the switch, the overhead light came on. Nate's dad was still paying the electric bill.

Tuck dropped his duffel.

Walking to a battered dresser, he picked up a photo of Nate and his fiancée taken right here in this room. He cursed and threw on his jacket, grabbed the six-pack he'd picked up at an all-night convenience store, and made his way to the lake.

Frogs croaked, and a fish jumped close to the bank. Other than that, the night was silent and dark. When the moon slid from behind a cloud and lit up the inky night sky, he barely resisted throwing back his head and howling.

Elisa's photo had unlocked the dark within him. It spilled out, overwhelming him. Sprawled in the tall grass, the moon shining down on him, he gave in to the anguish and despair. Sobs wracked his body. Until now, he'd screamed, he'd raged, and he'd tried to ignore. But he hadn't shed a single tear for his friends—not when he'd been informed of their deaths and not when he'd stood with their parents at the funerals.

He had a lot stored up.

When his tears finally dried up, he popped the tab on a beer and stared into the sky. There in the middle of nowhere, he asked Nate, Angie, Jorge, and LeBron the big question. "Why did I live and you all die? Was it fate? A fluke? Some Big Guy up there pulling the strings?"

He waited for an answer, but none came.

When the sun broke, it found him still at the lake's edge.

Time to go to bed.

He picked up the empty beer cans and decided no more alcohol. He didn't want to mask his feelings. It was past time to acknowledge them. He owed his friends that much.

Back at the cabin, he dropped fully clothed onto one of the bunks and fell asleep almost instantly. For the first time in ages, he slept dreamlessly. When he woke, he took a walk, stopping by the lake to fish and allowing his mind to remember his friends—the good times as well as the bad.

Then he called Elisa to check on Daisy and explain where he was and why.

"I'll be home in a couple of days."

"Take whatever time you need, Tucker. You should have done this a long time ago." She hesitated. "We messed up your earlier plans to go, didn't we?"

"Truth? You and Daisy are the bright spot in all this. Showing up like you did has made me face life and deal with things." His head ached, and he was dead tired. "I know the timing sucks with Daisy and all."

"It's okay. I have plenty of help—more than I've ever had."

They chatted a few more minutes, then Tucker said, "I have to go, Lissie. Talk to you tomorrow." He hung up and placed a call to the hospital's gift shop.

The volunteer who answered promised to deliver the bouquet of daisies as soon as possible—with lots of balloons. From Tut.

The day moved along, his mind in turn accepting, rejecting, then accepting again his loss. He fought to come to terms with this new twist, the arrival of Hard-Ass Harry's daughter and granddaughter in his life.

He couldn't quite wrap his mind around the why, though. Why he'd bid farewell to the Middle East in one piece, his heart still beating, while his friends left in flag-draped coffins.

Maybe there was no answer.

Exhausted, he fell into bed again and was sound asleep almost before his head hit the pillow.

The sound of a pickup making its way along the pretense of a drive woke him. From the height of the sun, he figured it must be nearly noon, an unheard-of time for him to wake. Despite all the emotions and unanswered questions, he'd had his best sleep since he'd slapped his buddies on the back and saw them off on their ill-fated mission.

He grabbed a pair of jeans from the chair where he'd tossed them and stepped into them. Pulling a sweatshirt over his head, he stepped onto the porch in time to see his brothers climb out of Gaven's truck. He should probably be pissed. Instead, he choked up. As always, they did indeed have his back.

"What brought your sorry butts up here?"

"Thought you might want some company about now," Brant said.

"Hmph."

"Hope you've got some food," Gaven said. "I'm starved."

"Hey, you invited yourself. You wanted to eat, you should have brought some grub with you." At Gaven's chagrined expression, Tucker relented. "I've got eggs and bread. I figured I'd catch a couple of nice trout to round it out."

The three dug up some poles Nate had kept at the camp and headed to the lake.

"What's going on in that head of yours?" Gaven asked. "You gonna let us in?"

"Ask Brant. I already told him."

"He said it wasn't his story to share."

Brant shrugged. "I don't kiss and tell."

Tucker shook his head. "I did not kiss this lout's ugly mug, Gaven."

While they dropped their lines in the water, Tucker wove his story once again, careful not to gloss over the hard parts.

"None of that was your fault." Gaven reeled in his line and cast again. "You did what you had to do. Sounds to me like your LC was a total jerk."

Tucker nodded his head in agreement. "Moving to the present. Enter Elisa and Daisy Danvers."

Gaven frowned. "Don't they fall on the plus side?"

"You'd think so, wouldn't you?" Tucker asked. "Instead, they've kind of muddied the water."

"I don't understand." Pole in hand, Gaven studied his brother.

Tucker gave a wry laugh and rubbed a hand down his face, heavy with stubble. He hadn't shaved since yesterday morning. "Here's where things hit the fan. Honestly? I'll preface this by saying that if it wasn't happening to me, I might not believe it."

He put fresh bait on his line.

"But?" Gaven made a *come on, finish your story* motion.

"Turns out Hard-Ass Harry is Elisa's father and Daisy's grandfather."

"What?" Gaven bobbled his pole. "You're making that up."

"Nope. I don't have enough imagination to come up with that. I mean, first of all, what's the chance of a stupefyingly beautiful blond literally dropping at my feet? Then for her to be the daughter of my nemesis? I'm telling you, Fate's got me in her sights, and she's not shooting blanks."

"You're sure?" Gaven asked.

"Yeah. Elisa told me—after she turned down my marriage proposal."

"Your marriage proposal?" Gaven looked shell-shocked. "When did that happen?"

"After Daisy's surgery."

Gaven turned to Brant. "You knew about that, too?"

Brant nodded.

"Don't pout," Tucker said.

"I'm not pouting. Did Elisa know about your pals?"

"Yeah, Gav, she knew."

"He told her before us." Brant's words held the slightest hint of censure.

"Yeah, I did. I thought—I felt—ah, hell, Elisa and me had something special."

"Had. Past tense?" Brant eyed him.

"Has to be. She said no."

"Plus, she's got a sorry excuse for a father, huh?" Gaven said. "She should probably have that tattooed across her forehead."

Tucker frowned at Gaven, but guilt nipped at him. He'd been angry she hadn't told him sooner, but would he have had the nerve to confess that if the tables were reversed? Ever?

At some point, his anger had morphed into sadness that Elisa'd had to spend any time at all with the jerk and compassion that her mother ran off on archeological digs and left her only child with an aging grandmother. In his books, that put Mom only one slim notch up from Harry.

"Well, at least you won't have to spend any time with your father-in-law," Gaven said.

Tucker held up a hand. "Whoa. Lt. Colonel's not my father-in-law."

"Not yet," Gaven said.

Tucker shook his head. "Not gonna happen. The lady doesn't want to marry me."

"I disagree." Gaven wasn't about to give up. "In my opinion? She thinks you can't want her now that you know, and she's trying to make it easy on you."

"As much as it hurts to agree with the kid, I think he's right," Brant said. "Time you head home, Tuck. You've got some work to do."

"And I've got a bite." Gaven pulled a beauty from the water, looking for all the world like a kid on Christmas morning.

"Good." Brant nodded. "Another couple of those, and we can eat."

The brothers fished, talked, napped, ate, and then napped some more. It had been a long time since they'd spent an entire day together unrelated to work.

The cabin no longer felt gloomy.

Tucker stole a few minutes to text a good-night message to Elisa and Daisy. He missed them.

The three of them stayed up late playing cards, then talked long after lights-out. Early the next morning, Brant and Gaven headed back to civilization, leaving Tucker alone again.

He needed one more day at the cabin. He had things to do.

After the dust of his brothers' departure settled, he took a long walk, then headed to the lake with coffee, paper, and pen.

He spent the rest of the morning and the better part of the afternoon writing letters. He wrote to Angie, Jorge, Nate, and LeBron. He wrote to Hard-Ass Harry. Although every word all but ripped out his guts, the process was cathartic. When he returned to the cabin, he fixed himself a can of only slightly out-of-date soup from the cupboard. He and his friends had eaten a heck of a lot worse when they'd been on recon missions.

After he washed the few dishes he and his brothers had dirtied, he wandered onto the porch, letters in hand. Leaning against the railing, one hand wrapped around Nate's key, he knew what he needed to do.

Folding the letters, he stuck them in his back pocket while he gathered wood and stacked it in the fire pit, feeding it until he had a roaring bonfire. Bright red, blue, and orange flames shot high and lit up the night sky. One by one, Tucker laid his letters to his buddies on the flames. As they burned, he said his farewell to each.

He snapped the chain at his neck and pocketed the key. "Thanks for the loan, Nate. It did the trick. I won't need it anymore."

When he pulled the last letter from his pocket, he tapped it on his palm. Hard-Ass Harry's letter didn't deserve to be in the same funeral pyre as his friends'. They wouldn't want him there. He found a sandy patch by the lake. Using a lighter he'd unearthed in the cabin, he lit the edge of the paper and watched as the flames licked at it, the edges curling and turning black. When it was reduced to ashes, he crushed those with the heel of his boot. So long, Harry.

His heart still throbbed like the worst toothache ever, but he was drained. He needed some sleep. As he flopped onto the old bed and closed his eyes, he realized his load had lightened…and he had a plan.

CHAPTER 28

DAISY HAD BEEN HOME FROM THE HOSPITAL FOR ALMOST two weeks and was back at day care for half days. Tucker was running out of reasons to stop by every evening to see her and her mama.

The first visit had been the hardest, but Elisa had been gracious when he'd called, and again when he'd shown up at her door. She'd listened while he filled her in on his trip to Nate's cabin and about the soul-searching he'd done there. He even told her about the letters he'd written to his pals and to her father.

"Where's Nate's key?" she'd asked.

"Gone. It did what he meant it to do." Tucker had picked up Elisa's hand and held it in his own. "I'll never forget my friends, never forget what happened, but it's time for me to move on."

He'd raised her hand and kissed the back of it.

She hadn't kicked him out on that visit or any of the following ones, but he wanted more now, and it was up to him to make it happen. He tied his sneakers and went for an early morning jog.

Forty minutes later, sweaty and out of breath, inspiration hit. It would require a lot to pull it off, though. "Lady Luck, you owe me one. It's time you paid off, 'cause I'm going to Vegas."

He'd show them all. Oh yeah. Stick-in-the-mud Tucker Kennedy Wylder could color outside the box when he wanted to, and boy, did he want to. Pulling a notebook from his back pocket, he jotted down his to-do list.

Making a U-turn and heading back to the house, he called Brant. "Got a favor to ask."

"How come you sound so out of breath?"

"I'm out for a run. Listen, I need a couple more days. Think you can slog along without me?"

"Gonna take the leap?" Brant asked.

"Yes, sir. It'll take a lot of pieces coming together, though, to make my plan work."

Gaven piped in. "Just bend that knee and ask her."

"You on the speaker, Brant?"

"Yeah, sorry."

"That's okay. I already tried that, Gav. Well, minus the knee. It didn't work."

"You're sure you want to do this?" Gaven asked. "It's not always what you think it'll be, and I'm speaking with the voice of experience."

"More often it *is* as great as you imagine. Better than," Brant added. "I say go for it."

Tucker hung up, his mind ticking off boxes. He'd call in some favors and beg for a few more. Reaching his house, he toed off his shoes and headed to the kitchen for water.

Since Desdemona was the glue that would keep everything from falling apart, he called her next. "I have a huge favor to ask, but it's for a great cause. Actually, I'm gonna ask for two favors." He explained his plan, and before he'd even hit the halfway mark, big-hearted Desdemona was in tears.

"Here's the thing. You'd have to handle both Daisy and the bookstore for a couple of days. Can you do it?" he asked her.

"Wearing my spiffiest cowboy boots and with one hand tied behind my back."

"I love you, Desdemona Rosebud Hawkins."

"Love you, too. Gonna take me a while to get used to my new name." She giggled like a schoolgirl. "I am just bursting with happiness, sweetie."

"As long as you don't burst in front of anyone. This needs to stay our secret."

"Believe it or not, even with this big mouth of mine, I can keep a secret with the best of them when I want to." She hesitated. "Yancy hasn't sold his house yet, so he's not here all the time. With everything Daisy's been through, Elisa might kick up a fuss about leaving her. You might tell her that a certain doctor will be joining Daisy and me for our pajama party. If he stays the night, Elisa will rest a sight easier."

"And yet another of your stellar qualities is that self-sacrificing soul."

Her hearty laugh threatened to burst his eardrum.

"We're good, then?" Tucker asked.

"You bet. We'll do fine. You take care of our Elisa."

"Thanks, Desdemona. I'm hopin' to do that for the rest of my life."

He hung up and checked another item off his list.

The next call had him fidgeting. Fingers crossed that his new sister-in-law would be willing to play the role of fairy godmother, he took a deep breath when she answered. "Hey, Molly. Busy?"

"Not right now. Caylee Davenport and her mother danced out my door a few minutes ago. I'm not sure either's feet touched the pavement."

"Wedding gown shopping?"

"Better. Wedding gown purchased!" Molly said.

"How about we make that two sales today?"

"What?"

"I need a wedding gown. One that's fun, but still fairytale-ish," Tucker said.

Silence followed.

Finally, Molly said, "I don't understand."

"You sell wedding gowns."

"I do."

"I need one."

"Why?"

He exhaled loudly and concentrated on a fluffy cloud drifting outside his kitchen window.

"Okay, Tuck, I get it. You don't want to tell me. I'll need to know the size, though."

"To fit my Lissie."

"Your—"

He held the phone away when Molly erupted in a loud squeal.

"You asked her to marry you? She said yes?"

"Yes and no," Tucker said.

"What does that mean?"

"It means I fumbled the ball first time out."

"You screwed up?" Molly asked.

"Royally. Brant didn't tell you?"

"No, and he'll pay for that. If she said no…"

"I know what I did wrong, Molly, and I hope she'll give me another chance." He filled her in on his hare-brained scheme.

"Oh, Tuck." She let out a long sigh. "That's so romantic. So not like you."

"Hey, I can be romantic."

"I guess you can." Then she said, "Other than the wedding gown, she won't have any clothes besides the ones she leaves in."

"She won't need any." He swore. "Sorry, that was crude and uncalled for."

"Um, Tuck?"

"Yeah?"

"Are you forgetting I'm a new bride?"

He chuckled. "Okay. Still—"

"Is money a concern?"

"Nope."

He could practically hear her rubbing her hands together in anticipation.

"How long will you be gone?" she asked.

"Tonight and tomorrow. We'll be back tomorrow night. Desdemona and Doc are willing to babysit Daisy, but I doubt I'll be able to keep Elisa away from her any longer than that."

"Good call. I'll let you have the gown, Brother-in-Law— and I know exactly the one—for my cost. Shoes, too. Oh, and undergarments."

Tucker powered up his internal calculator. Well, he did tell her to ignore the price tag.

"Don't worry, Tuck. When you see her, both in and out of that gown in those little scraps of silk and lace, you'll get down on your knees and thank me."

He imagined her devilish grin. "I'm already there, Molly, and Lissie's worth every penny of the money you intend to spend for me."

She chuckled. "You Wylder guys. How can Elisa say anything but yes?"

"She managed it fairly easily before."

"Well, she won't this time around," Molly assured him.

"From your lips to God's ears."

"I'll run down to Sue Ellen's dress shop and pick out a couple of outfits for tomorrow. A girl needs a choice, after all. Everything else, I'll pull from my stock. I've got suitcases stored upstairs in my old apartment that you can use."

"I owe you, Mol."

"You do. But if you talk Elisa into marrying you and add her and that adorable little girl to our family, you can consider the debt paid."

"I'm gonna do my best."

"Everything will be ready inside an hour. Lettie will be here in ten minutes or so, and she can watch the store."

When he hung up, he rested his head against the back of the kitchen chair. Doubts crept in. What if she said no again?

She wouldn't—and if she did, he'd just have to change her mind.

Okay. He rubbed his temples, then placed his next call. He needed a big old Cadillac convertible and knew exactly where to find the prettiest firethorn metallic '76 El Dorado on the planet.

Woofer picked up on the second ring.

While he caught up with his old friend, Tucker loped upstairs and dug out a suitcase. His tux hung at the back of the closet, freshly dry-cleaned. When his mother had insisted her boys each have their own, he'd argued with her. As usual, she'd been right.

After he and Woofer finished with football, politics, and life in general, Tucker asked, "You still got the red Caddy we restored?"

"Sure do. She's a thing of beauty."

"Think I could borrow it?"

"You here? Why didn't you say so?" Woofer asked. "I figured you were calling from Georgia."

"I am in Georgia. But if all goes well, I'll be in your neck of the woods later today."

"The Caddy's yours, my friend, for as long as you need it. It'll be at the airport waiting for you. I'll text where it's parked and leave the keys on top of the driver's side rear tire. My curiosity's piqued, boy. Can I ask what you've got goin' on?"

"You can." This time around it wasn't nearly as hard to explain.

One more call, and this one was a biggie. If he ran into a problem here, he'd have to rethink things.

It went smooth as silk. A single call to one of Wylder Rides' celebrity clients netted him a private jet. It would be in Savannah in a couple of hours, fueled and ready to go. Sweet!

He'd run scenario after scenario through his mind, trying to decide how to handle the actual proposal. After learning the jet would be stocked with chilled champagne and caviar, it was a no-brainer. He'd pop the all-important question midair, somewhere between Georgia and Nevada.

This felt beyond right.

Why had he waited so long?

Now came the hardest part of the plan.

He checked the clock. Daisy and her mama would be at Doc's for her check-up right about now. If he hurried, he could be there before they left.

In his prized Mustang, Tucker waited at the end of Doc

Hawkins's walk. The early winter's day was bright, crisp, and clean. Pretty darned perfect.

Time would tell whether or not it remained that way—time and Elisa. She held the key to everything. But he'd done what he could; his plan was in place.

The heavy wooden door opened, and Elisa stepped out, blond hair spilling over her shoulders. Dressed in tan leggings with high leather boots, a white sweater, and a scarf the color of her pants, she stole his breath.

When she saw him, she smiled and waved. Daisy broke free to run to him.

He shot out of the car and caught her when she made a flying leap toward him.

"Hey, squirt. How are you doing?"

"I'm good. Look." She held up a red lollipop. "Brinna gave me this 'cause I'm a big girl."

"You sure are." His gaze traveled to Elisa. "You look wonderful."

"Why, thank you." A hint of pink bloomed on her cheeks.

"What did Doc say?"

She grinned from ear to ear. "Daisy's one hundred percent." Her hand moved to her daughter's hair and swept slowly over it. "My baby's even better than when she was brand new."

"Excellent! Then I guess you can have your surprise, Daisy."

"My 'prise?"

"Yep, you earned it because you did everything the doctor told you to do," Tucker said.

"I did! I get a 'prise, Mommy."

"I heard that."

Holding Daisy, he leaned into his car and came out with a soft yellow teddy bear, a small vase between its paws holding a single yellow daisy.

"A daisy. Like you sended me in the hospital. Just like my name!"

"Just like," Tucker said.

"Look, Mommy! A teddy bear, too."

"It's wonderful, sweetheart. Did you thank Tucker?"

The teddy bear clutched in one hand, the little girl threw her other arm around Tucker's neck. "Thank you, Tut. Will you be my daddy now? My real one instead of my honor one."

He buried his face in her hair. "I love you, Daisy Elizabeth."

"I love you, too, Tut. Be my daddy. Please."

He didn't dare look at Elisa. She'd read too much there, and he wasn't ready to play his trump card yet.

Elisa cleared her throat. "Honey, I think—"

"She's good, Lissie. How about you move her car seat to my Mustang? We'll take a ride."

"For ice cream?" Daisy laid her free hand on his cheek.

"Umm, probably not."

Her lower lip popped out.

He tipped his head. "Not gonna work today, baby. Too much to do."

"Can I play a game?"

"Sure." He slipped the phone from his pocket and handed it to her, ignoring Elisa's eye roll. Reaching out, he took the seat from her and set it in the Mustang.

Phone in one hand, her teddy bear and flower in the other, Daisy let Tucker lift her into the seat and snap all the buckles.

"Want me to set Teddy beside you?"

"His name's Pookie."

"Pookie?" he asked.

"Uh-huh."

"Okay. I'll set Pookie here where you can see him."

When she didn't answer, he saw she was already engrossed in his phone.

"Remember, no calling that boyfriend of yours."

"I don't gots a boyfriend, Tut!"

"Oh, that's what you say."

"Mommy, tell Tut I don't gots a boyfriend."

"Daisy doesn't *have* a boyfriend." Elisa corrected her daughter's English. "And she can't have one until she turns thirty. Maybe thirty-one."

Tucker shot Elisa a thumbs-up. "With you on that."

"Where are we going?" Elisa asked as she buckled up.

He simply grinned.

"Tuck!"

"You'll see."

"Will I like this surprise?"

"I liked mine, Mommy. Pookie was my 'prise."

Tucker's heart hammered in his chest. "I sincerely hope you do, Lissie."

Elisa frowned. "Why so serious all of a sudden?"

Rather than answer, he reached out and enfolded her hand.

They drove to Desdemona's. Like the rest of the town, her house was bedecked with Christmas lights and decorations.

She waited on the porch, dressed in a fuchsia silk jumpsuit and mile-high stilettos. A silver collar shone at her neck and long pendant earrings swung from her lobes.

When she spotted them, she started down the sidewalk.

Tucker turned off the ignition and swiveled toward the child in the backseat. "What are you playing?"

"I'm poppin' 'loons."

"Balloons?"

"Yeah, see?" She held up the phone and pretty colored balloons floated across the screen.

"Nice. How would you like to have a pajama party with Desdemona tonight?" Tucker asked.

A small sound escaped Elisa. Surprise? Outrage? Happiness? A little of each?

By now, Desdemona stood beside the car, a big smile on her face.

Daisy waved at her, and she knelt and waved back. She didn't open the door, though.

The make or break moment. The plan either came together here or the wheels fell off it. "Here's the deal, Lissie. A suitcase, with everything you'll need for tonight and tomorrow, is in my trunk. Desdemona's handling the bookstore tomorrow, and she's excited about having Daisy to herself tonight."

"She's the grandmother Daisy's never had," Elisa said. When he moved to put an arm around her, she held up a wait-just-a-sec finger. "That doesn't mean I'm ready to leave her here."

"Why, Mommy? I wanna stay with Desdi."

Elisa sent Tucker a now-you've-done-it look.

He reached out, took a curl between his fingers and played with it. "You worry about her. I do, too. If it helps any, Doc's having dinner with them tonight and is staying for the pajama party—for a sleepover. Daisy will be in good hands."

"I can't just—"

"Sure you can," Tucker insisted.

"Everybody will know I'm with you," Elisa argued. "They'll think we're..."

"Yes, they will, and they'll be right."

CHAPTER 29

TWENTY MILES DOWN THE ROAD, ELISA SIPPED THE NOW cooling coffee Tucker had picked up for her. Quiet music filled the car, thanks to Molly who'd downloaded some romantic songs to his phone.

His sister-in-law had done her part and more. Now he had to do his.

"You won't tell me where we're going, will you?"

Tucker shook his head. "Not yet."

"Are we almost there?"

"Now you sound like a kid."

She grinned. "I don't ever want to grow up. That's my goal in life."

He squeezed her hand. "It's a darned good goal. One I can get behind."

"You'll have to work some to hit it, Tuck. You're far too serious."

He gave her a slow and lazy smile. "You might be surprised."

Half an hour later, he turned left.

"Isn't this the way to the airport?" she asked.

"Yep."

"But—"

He held up a finger. "No more questions. Sit back and relax."

"I can't."

"Oh yeah? Now who needs to lighten up?"

She stuck her tongue out at him.

Rather than go to long-term parking or the unloading zone, Tucker drove straight into the area reserved for private planes.

Elisa glanced around. "Do you know where you're going?"

"Yes, ma'am, I do."

He pulled into a parking space, pocketed the keys, and opened her door. From the small trunk, he took a duffel and two suitcases.

She eyed the luggage. "How long did you say we're staying?"

"We can be home tomorrow afternoon. If you ask nice, though, we can stay another night."

"I don't know about that. I have a lot going on. This is a busy time at the bookstore, and Daisy—"

"We'll see how you feel about it later."

He turned and walked onto the tarmac, where a sleek white private jet waited. Elisa hurried after him.

"Tuck?"

"Our chariot."

"This is our ride?"

"Yep." He took in her incredulous expression and laughed. "I called in a favor from a former client. Pretty nice, huh?"

"Nice? Nice is a hot bath after a long day. Nice is an expertly made cappuccino. This—" She waved a hand as the door opened and stairs lowered. "This is so far beyond *nice* that I don't have a word for it in my vocabulary."

A uniformed steward hustled down the stairs and reached for their bags.

As he handed the last suitcase over, Tucker said, "Take very good care of this one. It's irreplaceable."

"Yes, sir. Plan on doing some gambling while you're in Vegas?"

"You don't know the half of it," Tucker said with a smile. "I'm taking the biggest gamble of my life."

Elisa elbowed him. "Vegas? We left Daisy with Desdemona to go to Vegas?"

"We did." Tucker draped an arm over Elisa's shoulders and walked beside her up the stairs and into the jet's elegant black-and-white interior.

"Oh my gosh!" She stood inside the door, wide-eyed.

A white leather sofa and chairs were grouped around an ebony coffee table. Fresh Christmas-themed floral arrangements added their sweet scent to that of the leather. A large screen covered one interior wall.

"This isn't quite the way I usually travel," she said. "I'm always in economy class with my knees practically touching my chin. Can I just say *wow*?"

Tucker chuckled. "You can. Pretty impressive, isn't it?"

"Yes, it is."

They were barely in the air when their steward appeared with champagne and hors d'oeuvres. The timing was off. Tucker fumbled a couple of times, trying to find an opening for his proposal, but he couldn't quite make it work.

This was a heck of a lot harder than he'd thought it would be.

"What's wrong, Tuck? You look nervous."

"Nope. Everything's just right."

When they landed in Vegas, Elisa said, "We're here already?"

"We are."

"The flight wasn't nearly long enough. I've never, ever been treated to such decadence—and I loved it." She leaned in and kissed him, long and thoroughly. "Thank you, Tucker."

"Believe me, sugar, it was my pleasure."

Pulling out his phone, Tucker checked his text messages before showing one to the limo driver who'd met them at the plane. He drove them to the vintage Cadillac, which had a huge Christmas wreath attached to its grille.

The key was exactly where Woofer said it would be, and Tucker popped the big old Caddy's trunk.

"This is our car?"

"Oh yeah." As the driver stowed their luggage, Tucker ran a hand over the hood. "Isn't she a beauty?"

Elisa laughed. "Most men only get that glint in their eyes when they're looking at a woman they lust over…or love."

"Then you must see it in mine every time I look at you."

"Tucker—"

He held up a hand. "Sorry. Too serious. Gotta find that kid in me, right?"

He helped her in and waited till she hooked her seatbelt.

"You don't always have to be a child. Sometimes a grown man is exactly what I want."

"Oh boy. See, you're gonna have to hold that thought."

"Or?"

"Or we won't get to the important part of this trip," Tucker warned.

She frowned. "You didn't bring me here on business, did you?"

"There's a little business involved, yeah, but I'm hoping

it won't take long. Let's wait till we get to the hotel to talk about it."

———————————

They stood outside the door to their room.

"The honeymoon suite? Don't you think this is overdoing it a bit, Tuck? I mean, nobody here cares. The people who do already know we've run away for a night of—" Elisa waved her hand in the air.

"You can't say it, can you?"

"What?"

"That we've run away for a night of mind-blowing, nonstop sex."

She opened her mouth, then closed it without saying anything.

He ushered her inside. Taking her hand, he said, "How about we change that to making love?" He dropped to one knee, a small velvet box in his hand.

"Tucker—"

"Hush. Listen to me. You and I have already been through more ups and downs than most married couples ever see. We've run those rapids and beat them. The way I see it, we've got this made."

Trailing his thumb over the back of her hand, he said, "Let me start the way I should have the last time. With you is my favorite place to be, Elisa. I love you with all my heart, with all that I am. I love you for who you are and for who I am when I'm with you. You've filled the cracks in my broken heart and made me want to live again. With you and Daisy, I've finally found home." Tucker flipped open the box, revealing a diamond solitaire ring. "Come on, Lissie, marry me. I love you…and will forever."

"I have a lot of baggage, Tuck. I'm divorced and have a child—one who might still need a lot of extra care."

Tucker nodded. "Yeah, you do have a little girl. Daisy Elizabeth is a big part of who you are and one of the many things I love about you. You're an incredible woman, Lissie, and a fantastic mother. I understand you're a package deal, and I wouldn't have it any other way. A smart, courageous, sexy wife with a beautiful, brilliant daughter."

She stayed quiet until his heart couldn't take it anymore. "Put me out of my misery, Lissie. Tell me you'll marry me."

"Yes, yes, yes!" She threw herself at him, nearly knocking him off balance. "I love you, Tuck!"

Laughing, he stood, swept her up, and kissed her. "Thank you, sugar. I promise to do everything in my power to make you happy. I want to get married now. Right here in Vegas. Today."

Shocked, she glanced down at her sweater and leggings. "Now? I'm not dressed for a wedding."

Opening a suitcase, he pulled out one of Molly's signature blue garment bags. "I haven't seen this yet, because Molly picked it out for you. She packed a few other things, too." He unzipped the second suitcase and turned it so she could see.

"You brought all this?" She fingered the negligees, the underwear, a fun dress and shoes as well as a more formal outfit, plus make-up, bubble bath, and scented lotion. All the necessities. "Pinch me, Tuck. I have to be dreaming."

"Huh-uh. No way I'm marring even an inch of that beautiful body."

"Who'll marry us?"

"Think I'll keep that a secret for right now. You're okay with all this?"

She grinned. "I can't believe it, but I am."

"Take whatever time you need. Get all fixed up and into that gown, then we'll go see the man and say our vows."

"Boy, when you decide to color outside those lines, you do it up right. Obviously, there are sides to you I've yet to discover."

"I intend to give you the rest of my life to find them all. I love you, Elisa Eklund Danvers."

That did it, the reminder he loved her despite her father. She blinked, but couldn't quite stop the tears. "I love you, too, Tucker Kennedy Wylder, and I'll take every one of those days and promise you all of mine in return."

He drew her into his arms and kissed her.

"If you want more after we return home, Lissie, the traditional wedding with our families and friends, we can do it again. I won't deny you that."

She laid a hand on the side of his face. "Tucker, I have the man I love beside me as my groom. The rest is window-dressing."

"Thank you. I called my parents to tell them that I love you and intended to marry you today."

She went mushy inside.

"You didn't get that chance. Your mom and—" He expelled enough air to fill twenty balloons. "And your father."

"Your mom and dad are okay with it?"

"They're more than okay, Elisa. They said they already knew we were in love and wondered what was taking us so long. How about your parents, though?"

"I'll let Mom know the next time she calls. Same with the lieutenant colonel. Of course, Daisy might have three brothers and sisters by the time any of that happens." Her forehead creased in thought. "You do want more children, don't you?"

"I want a houseful, sticky fingerprints and all. I can't imagine my life without Brant, Gaven, and Lainey. I'd like to give Daisy a big family." He nuzzled her ear. "Maybe we could start on that tonight."

Every nerve in her body stood up and took notice.

Feeling as giddy as a teenager on her first date, Elisa checked the full-length bathroom mirror one last time. Then she opened the door and stepped out.

Tucker smiled slowly. "Are you kidding me?"

She arched her brows. "Molly hit the nail on the head, didn't she?"

The strapless, floor-length tulle gown had a wide silk ribbon sash at the waist and fit as though it had been tailored for her. The pièce de résistance? White daisy appliqués that danced over the full skirt.

"I can't believe she had this." She reached out to him. "Before we go, you need to take a picture of my ring."

She held out her hand, and he snapped a shot of it.

"Now one of us together. You in your tux and me in this beautiful dress."

He pulled her close, snapped the selfie, then texted the pictures to Desdemona to share with Daisy, along with a heartfelt message: Tell Daisy that Mommy and Daddy love her.

Elisa thumbed away a tear.

As they drove down the Strip, she smiled and held Tucker's hand, waving at the Santas on every street corner. More than one person stopped to stare at the bright red Caddy convertible with its top down. The car was incredible, and it was oh so clearly a Wylder Rides restoration. The attention to detail was impeccable.

More important to Elisa, though, was the man beside her. Her groom. In a tuxedo, Tucker Wylder looked more handsome than any movie star who'd ever walked the red carpet, and he'd thought of everything. The dress, the ring, the car, the plane. He'd even had a fabulous bouquet waiting for her at the hotel's front desk when they went back downstairs.

As with his cars, he'd paid attention to the tiniest detail.

Tucker pulled up to the drive-through wedding chapel, and Elvis stuck his head out the window, a Santa hat perched crookedly on his raven-black hair.

Elisa laughed out loud. "This is so crazy and so absolutely perfect!"

She pulled Tucker to her and kissed him till she was breathless.

"Well, steam up my aviator sunglasses. Maybe it's time for Elvis to leave the building so you lovebirds can have a few minutes alone."

"Not on your life," Tucker said. "I want to lock this down before she changes her mind." He glanced at Elisa. "Ready?"

"I've never wanted anything more."

"Then let's do it."

Incredulous, she looked again at Elvis and shook her head. "Never in a million years would I have believed you'd come up with something like this."

He winked at her. "Have I mentioned how much I love you?"

She smiled, slow and sexy. "You have, and I love you right back, Tucker Wylder."

Her hand in his, he said, "You'll never have to go it alone again. No matter what life throws at us, no matter what happens, I've got you, babe."

Can't get enough Lynnette Austin?
Keep reading for an excerpt from
The Best Laid Wedding Plans

*Their day is going
to be magical,
no matter
what happens...*

Magnolia Brides

The BEST LAID
WEDDING PLANS

LYNNETTE AUSTIN

CHAPTER 1

"TO HAVE AND TO HOLD, FROM THIS DAY FORWARD..."
Jenni Beth Beaumont whispered the age-old vows.

Tiny white lights transformed Savannah's Chateau
Rouge's gardens into a magical fairyland. The heavily
beaded bridal gown shimmered in their reflected light.

Unfortunately, Jenni Beth was not wearing the gown.

But oh, how she wanted this. Not the wedding itself. No.
She wanted to be the driving force behind making a bride's
wedding day the most special of her life. Instead of organizing events here at Chateau Rouge, she wanted her own
wedding planner business.

Tonight's bride fairly radiated. The groom, Jenni Beth's
second cousin, looked so handsome in his dress uniform.
He'd just last week come off a tour of duty in the Middle
East.

Pain, instant and excruciating, washed over her, left her
light-headed. Her brother Wes had been even more handsome in his dress uniform the day he'd graduated from
Officer Candidate School, then again the day he'd deployed
in his camos. The day she'd kissed him good-bye. The last
time she'd seen him alive. Her throat constricted.

She exhaled, forced herself to shake it off. Not tonight.
Tonight was a celebration of love. The beginning of a new
family. Of dreams come true.

While the bride and groom funneled their guests
through the receiving line, Jenni Beth bolted to a separate

section of the garden to make sure the cake, the bubbly, and the band were in place. She did a last-minute check on table settings, place cards, candles—the list was never ending.

The music started, the bridal party wended their way to the area, and the celebration began.

As the evening wore on, Jenni Beth relaxed.

A familiar voice whispered in her ear. "Dance with me."

Cole Bryson. She hadn't seen his name on the guest list.

Shivers raced down her spine, and her heart stuttered. It had been too long, not long enough. "No."

She wouldn't turn around, wouldn't meet those mesmerizing eyes.

His hands settled on her bare arms, and she nearly jumped. As the work-roughened hands moved over her skin, her stomach started a little dance of its own.

"I'm working, Cole."

"Nothin' needs doin' right now. Sean and Sarah are deliriously happy, and everything's runnin' smoothly. Come on, sugar. You don't want to cause a scene."

Knowing she shouldn't, she turned to face him. Mistake. She had always found him irresistible, and that hadn't changed. He'd perfected that slow Southern drawl, had the sound of a true gentleman. But the twinkle in his eyes gave him away. Revealed the bad boy tucked not far below the surface.

Right now, dressed in a dark suit and tie, the man looked like every woman's dream. He appeared smooth and debonair, but beneath lay the wild.

He took her hand, and, God forgive her, she followed him, weak-kneed, onto the portable dance floor, telling herself she didn't want to, that she only did it to keep peace. Knowing she lied.

A full moon shone overhead and candlelight flickered. When he drew her into his arms and pulled her close, she sighed. One hand held hers, the other settled south of her waist.

"You smell good, Jenni Beth. You always do."

His voice, low and husky, sent goose bumps racing up and down her arms. Despite herself, she rested her head against his chest, seduced by the strong, steady beat of his heart, the illusion that he could make everything and anything all right.

One song drifted into another and she stayed in his arms, her mind drifting to what could have been. What should have been. She'd loved this man—or had it simply been a bad case of puppy love?

Whatever. She was over him.

And yet one glance at that face had her insides turning to jelly. She was deceiving herself. Sometimes, late at night, her thoughts still turned to him. The man was drop-dead handsome. All that gorgeous dark, wavy hair, those sexy hazel eyes, and that mouth—capable of making her lose her mind. Her survival instincts.

His feet? Well, they were made for walking, and she'd better darned well remember that.

Still, one night, a dance or two. What could it hurt?

"Your hair looks like molten gold in the moonlight, Jenni Beth." He brushed a hand over it. "Sure wish you'd let me loosen some of these pins and set it free."

Her own hand moved up to the chignon she'd arranged earlier that afternoon, bringing her back to reality. "Sorry, Cole. I'm working, and it's time for me to clock back in."

Before she could change her mind, she stepped out of his arms, felt the slight chill in the air.

She forced herself to stand still, to show no reaction while his eyes traveled the length of her, taking in the slim black sheath, the black pumps, and the understated jewelry. Her work uniform.

Despite herself, she ran her own mental inventory. At six foot, Cole's eight-inch advantage made her feel petite. And every bit of him was muscle. When he held her, she felt protected.

Until he walked away.

And tonight? She needed to be the one to do the walking. For oh, so many reasons.

This would be her last wedding at Chateau Rouge. Earlier today, she and her roommate had packed both her car and a tiny U-Haul to the gills, the day bittersweet. She'd miss Molly, her life here in the city.

She'd be risking everything. No choice. Her parents needed her. And this was her shot at her dream. The old go big or go home. She almost laughed. In her case, she had to go home to go big.

Or she'd go home to fall flat on her face.

Either way, by this time tomorrow, her time in Savannah would be history.

"Good-bye, Cole."

"Good-bye?" He grasped her hand as she took a step away.

"I still have a lot to do here tonight."

"How about later? I don't mind waitin.'" He threw her one of those bad-boy looks, the one that made her want to fling herself at him. Made her want to beg for one more minute in his arms, one more kiss.

Stupid, stupid, stupid! She looked away, pretended to check on the wedding crowd.

"That's not a good idea. And after tonight?" Aiming for indifference, she shrugged. "I'm moving home tomorrow, Cole. Back to Magnolia House. So it's not likely we'll be running into each other. You'll be here in Savannah, I'll be in Misty Bottoms."

He frowned. "Thought you liked it here."

"I do."

"But you're goin' home."

"I am."

He leaned toward her.

Her breath caught, but when his lips brushed her forehead, feather light, she let herself relax. Too soon.

With a nearly imperceptible shift, his lips dropped to hers. She fought not to go under as the heat seared her. Battle lost, her hands moved to his shoulders, his hair, and she clung to him.

But sanity returned when his lips slid from hers to taste her neck.

"No, Cole."

He lifted his head, his whiskey-brown eyes heavy-lidded and passion-filled. Wavy brown hair, streaked by the sun, touched his jacket collar in the back.

He winked. "We might be seein' each other sooner than you think, sugar."

With those enigmatic words, he drifted away from the party, into the darkness.

CHAPTER 2

JENNI BETH WOKE BEFORE DAWN.

Nerves ate at her and left her feeling jittery.

She'd been back in Misty Bottoms, back under her parents' roof for a week now. Between her mother and Charlotte, the family's housekeeper since before Jenni Beth had been born, they'd fixed every single one of her favorite foods, and she hadn't figured out how to tell them to stop without hurting their feelings. So she downed pecan pie, corn pudding, fried chicken and catfish, collard greens, and flaky biscuits spread with homemade peach jam. Then she went to her room and did more sit-ups.

The first couple days, her mother clung to her and dragged out old photo albums. Played old favorite music. But she seldom said Wes's name. "Your brother." "My son." But his name? She avoided it.

Dad canceled his golf games, lunches with friends.

They needed her far more than she'd realized. It shamed her she hadn't come sooner.

By the third day, she'd felt smothered. Claustrophobic. Something had to change, or she'd go nuts.

Over breakfast, she showed them her plans for the house. They'd discussed it at length over the phone, but this was the first she'd sat down with them, showed them her actual drawings.

As gently as she could, she explained she needed time to

work, and they both needed to go back to what they'd been doing before she returned.

And this venture of hers? It would either turn out to be the smartest move she'd ever made or the dumbest in history. Today, the die would be tossed.

As the sky turned pink outside her window, she covered her face with a pillow and mentally role-played this morning's scheduled meeting. So much depended on it.

After showering and dressing, she wandered downstairs in search of coffee. Charlotte, bless her heart, already had a pot brewed. Restless, Jenni Beth drank her first cup and started on her second.

"Why are you pacin' like that, honey? You're wearin' out the floorboards." Charlotte didn't mince words.

"Sorry."

On her fourth pass, Charlotte kicked her out of the kitchen. "If you're not gonna eat, you might as well get out of here and let me work."

Half an hour later, Jenni Beth sat in Dee-Ann's Diner at one of the cute little red-and-white-check-covered tables, annoying Dee-Ann.

"Here." The feisty owner tossed a copy of The Bottoms' Daily on her table as she passed, a plate of pancakes in hand. "Maybe it'll take your mind off whatever's makin' you so prickly."

Offended, Jenni Beth sat up straighter. "I'm not prickly."

"Yeah, you are," Jimmy Don said from three tables over.

"Oh, for heaven's sake." Instead of reading the paper, she stared out the diner's window. Main Street, even on this gorgeous day, looked a tad shabby, the quaint brick sidewalk buckled in spots.

Not Dee-Ann's, though. A cheerful red-and-white awning wished passersby a good day. Ferns and baskets of both red and white petunias lined the front of the building.

At this time of day, the place was nearly deserted. Too late for breakfast, too early for lunch. Her eye caught the Confederate flag in the corner, the tin sign on the back wall that read "American by birth, Southern by choice."

Some nights, when she'd been in Savannah, she'd missed this town to the point of hurting. All she had to do, though, was close her eyes to mentally walk down the uneven brick streets of Misty Bottoms. See Wallet Owens, cranky and eccentric, hunting in the trash bins for aluminum cans, the bougainvillea spilling over the brick wall by the newspaper office. Smell Kitty's hummingbird cake straight out of the oven at her bakery, the gardenias blooming in the town park, the scent of fresh-brewed coffee in the diner. Hear the train depot's noon whistle.

Luanna Connors, order pad at the ready, stopped at her table, pulling her back to the moment. Luanna and Jenni Beth had gone through school together, but when Jenni Beth left for college, Luanna had stayed behind—three months pregnant with Les Connors's baby. Seven years later, she was slinging hash in Dee-Ann's, then going home to Les and three little kids. Through the grapevine Jenni Beth had heard that Les lost another job last week. She'd have to remember to leave a hefty tip, even if it would make her wallet cry.

All things considered, maybe her life wasn't so bad.

"When'd y'all get back into town?" Luanna asked.

"Last week."

"Stayin' long?"

"I've moved back. Permanently." Jenni Beth didn't want to say more. Not yet.

"Really? I heard you had a real good job in Savannah."

"I did. But Mama and Daddy need me here."

"Yeah, they're havin' a rough time, aren't they?"

She nodded at the understatement, felt that quick little jab to her heart.

"What can I get for y'all today?" Her old classmate pulled a pencil stub from behind one ear, loosening a strand of maroon hair from her ponytail.

"Just a big old glass of sweet tea."

"Comin' up."

She picked up the paper and immediately wished she hadn't.

Its headline, "Long-time Misty Bottoms Business Closes Its Doors," spelled disaster for her.

Perched on the worn vinyl chair, Jenni Beth stirred the sweet tea Luanna delivered. She'd worked so hard, had stayed up till the wee hours every night this past week preparing for today's meeting. Everything rode on it. And now this.

Perspiration crept down her back, as much a result of this news as the changing weather. Spring was giving way to summer, the Georgia temperature and humidity rising to meet it. Even this early in the day, the closeness threatened to make a person's clothes cling, despite the overhead ceiling fans that stirred the air. They'd run nonstop from now till late autumn in a futile attempt to cool Dee-Ann's customers.

Jenni Beth gripped the paper and straightened her shoulders. Time to suck it up and remember her heritage. A woman born and raised in the South did not cry uncle. Ever. And by all that was holy, she'd uphold that tradition.

About the Author

Lynnette Austin loves long rides with the top down and the music cranked up, standing by the Gulf of Mexico when a storm is brewing, and sitting in her local coffee shop reading, writing, and enjoying a cappuccino. She grew up in Pennsylvania, accepted her first teaching job in New York, then moved to Wyoming. Now she splits her time between the beaches of Florida and the Blue Ridge Mountains of Northern Georgia. She's been a finalist in the Romance Writers of America's Golden Heart Contest, PASIC's Book of Your Heart Contest, and Georgia Romance Writers' Maggie Contest. Having grown up in a small town, that's where her heart takes her—to those quirky small towns where everybody knows everybody…and all their business, for better or worse. Visit Lynnette at authorlynnetteaustin. com.

Also by Lynnette Austin

Magnolia Brides
The Best Laid Wedding Plans
Every Bride Has Her Day
Picture Perfect Wedding

Must Love Babies
Must Love Babies
I've Got You, Babe